The Nest of the Sparrowhawk

The Nest of the Sparrowhawk

Baroness Emmuska Orczy

MINT EDITIONS

The Nest of the Sparrowhawk was first published in 1909.

This edition published by Mint Editions 2021.

ISBN 9781513272214 | E-ISBN 9781513277219

Published by Mint Editions®

 MINT
EDITIONS

minteditionbooks.com

Publishing Director: Jennifer Newens
Design & Production: Rachel Lopez Metzger
Project Manager: Micaela Clark
Typesetting: Westchester Publishing Services

Contents

PART IV

PART I

I

The House of a Kentish Squire

Master Hymn-of-Praise Busy folded his hands before him ere he spoke:

"Nay! but I tell thee, woman, that the Lord hath no love for such frivolities! and alack! but 'tis a sign of the times that an English Squire should favor such evil ways."

"Evil ways? The Lord love you, Master Hymn-of-Praise, and pray do you call half an hour at the skittle alley 'evil ways'?"

"Aye, evil it is to indulge our sinful bodies in such recreation as doth not tend to the glorification of the Lord and the sanctification of our immortal souls."

He who sermonized thus unctuously and with eyes fixed with stern disapproval on the buxom wench before him, was a man who had passed the meridian of life not altogether—it may be surmised—without having indulged in some recreations which had not always the sanctification of his own immortal soul for their primary object. The bulk of his figure testified that he was not averse to good cheer, and there was a certain hidden twinkle underlying the severe expression of his eyes as they rested on the pretty face and round figure of Mistress Charity that did not necessarily tend to the glorification of the Lord.

Apparently, however, the admonitions of Master Hymn-of-Praise made but a scanty impression on the young girl's mind, for she regarded him with a mixture of amusement and contempt as she shrugged her plump shoulders and said with sudden irrelevance:

"Have you had your dinner yet, Master Busy?"

"'Tis sinful to address a single Christian person as if he or she were several," retorted the man sharply. "But I'll tell thee in confidence, mistress, that I have not partaken of a single drop more comforting than cold water the whole of to-day. Mistress de Chavasse mixed the sack-posset with her own hands this morning, and locked it in the cellar, of which she hath rigorously held the key. Ten minutes ago when she placed the bowl on this table, she called my attention to the fact that the delectable beverage came to within three inches of the brim. Meseems I shall have to seek for a less suspicious, more

Christian-spirited household, whereon to bestow in the near future my faithful services."

Hardly had Master Hymn-of-Praise finished speaking when he turned very sharply round and looked with renewed sternness—wholly untempered by a twinkle this time—in the direction whence he thought a suppressed giggle had just come to his ears. But what he saw must surely have completely reassured him; there was no suggestion of unseemly ribaldry about the young lad who had been busy laying out the table with spoons and mugs, and was at this moment vigorously—somewhat ostentatiously, perhaps—polishing a carved oak chair, bending to his task in a manner which fully accounted for the high color in his cheeks.

He had long, lanky hair of a pale straw-color, a thin face and high cheek-bones, and was dressed—as was also Master Hymn-of-Praise Busy—in a dark purple doublet and knee breeches, all looking very much the worse for wear; the brown tags and buttons with which these garments had originally been roughly adorned were conspicuous in a great many places by their absence, whilst all those that remained were mere skeletons of their former selves.

The plain collars and cuffs which relieved the dull color of the men's doublets were of singularly coarse linen not beyond reproach as to cleanliness, and altogether innocent of starch; whilst the thick brown worsted stockings displayed many a hole through which the flesh peeped, and the shoes of roughly tanned leather were down at heel and worn through at the toes.

Undoubtedly even in these days of more than primitive simplicity and of sober habiliments Master Hymn-of-Praise Busy, butler at Acol Court in the county of Kent, and his henchman, Master Courage Toogood, would have been conspicuous for the shabbiness and poverty of the livery which they wore.

The hour was three in the afternoon. Outside a glorious July sun spread radiance and glow over an old-fashioned garden, over tall yew hedges, and fantastic forms of green birds and heads of beasts carefully cut and trimmed, over clumps of late roses and rough tangles of marguerites and potentillas, of stiff zinnias and rich-hued snapdragons.

Through the open window came the sound of wood knocking against wood, of exclamations of annoyance or triumph as the game proceeded, and every now and then a ripple of prolonged laughter, girlish, fresh, pure as the fragrant air, clear as the last notes of the cuckoo before he speaks his final farewell to summer.

Every time that echo of youth and gayety penetrated into the oak-raftered dining-room, Master Hymn-of-Praise Busy pursed his thick lips in disapproval, whilst the younger man, had he dared, would no doubt have gone to the window, and leaning out as far as safety would permit, have tried to catch a glimpse of the skittle alley and of a light-colored kirtle gleaming among the trees. But as it was he caught the older man's stern eyes fixed reprovingly upon him, he desisted from his work of dusting and polishing, and, looking up to the heavy oak-beam above him, he said with becoming fervor:

"Lord! how beautifully thou dost speak, Master Busy!"

"Get on with thy work, Master Courage," retorted the other relentlessly, "and mix not thine unruly talk with the wise sayings of thy betters."

"My work is done, Master."

"Go fetch the pasties then, the quality will be in directly," rejoined the other peremptorily, throwing a scrutinizing look at the table, whereon a somewhat meager collation of cherries, raspberries and gooseberries and a more generous bowl of sack-posset had been arranged by Mistress Charity and Master Courage under his own supervision.

"Doubtless, doubtless," here interposed the young maid somewhat hurriedly, desirous perhaps of distracting the grave butler's attention from the mischievous oglings of the lad as he went out of the room, "as you remark—hem—as thou remarkest, this place of service is none to the liking of such as. . . thee. . ."

She threw him a coy glance from beneath well-grown lashes, which caused the saintly man to pass his tongue over his lips, an action which of a surety had not the desire for spiritual glory for its mainspring. With dainty hands Mistress Charity busied herself with the delicacies upon the table. She adjusted a gooseberry which seemed inclined to tumble, heaped up the currants into more graceful pyramids. Womanlike, whilst her eyes apparently followed the motions of her hands they nevertheless took stock of Master Hymn-of-Praise's attitude with regard to herself.

She knew that in defiance of my Lord Protector and all his Puritans she was looking her best this afternoon: though her kirtle was as threadbare as Master Courage's breeches it was nevertheless just short enough to display to great advantage her neatly turned ankle and well-arched foot on which the thick stockings—well-darned—and shabby shoes sat not at all amiss.

Her kerchief was neatly folded, white and slightly starched, her cuffs immaculately and primly turned back just above her round elbow and shapely arm.

On the whole Mistress Charity was pleased with her own appearance. Sir Marmaduke de Chavasse and the mistress were seeing company this afternoon, and the neighboring Kentish squires who had come to play skittles and to drink sack-posset might easily find a less welcome sight than that of the serving maid at Acol Court.

"As for myself," now resumed Mistress Charity, after a slight pause, during which she had felt Master Busy's admiring gaze fixed persistently upon her, "as for myself, I'll seek service with a lady less like to find such constant fault with a hard-working maid."

Master Courage had just returned carrying a large dish heaped up with delicious looking pasties fresh from the oven, brown and crisp with butter, and ornamented with sprigs of burrage which made them appear exceedingly tempting.

Charity took the dish from the lad and heavy as it was, she carried it to the table and placed it right in the very center of it. She rearranged the sprigs of burrage, made a fresh disposition of the baskets of fruit, whilst both the men watched her open-mouthed, agape at so much loveliness and grace.

"And," she added significantly, looking with ill-concealed covetousness at the succulent pasties, "where there's at least one dog or cat about the place."

"I know not, mistress," said Hymn-of-Praise, "that thou wast over-fond of domestic pets. . . 'Tis sinful to. . ."

"La! Master Busy, you. . . hem. . . thou mistakest my meaning. I have no love for such creatures—but without so much as a kitten about the house, prithee how am I to account to my mistress for the pasties and. . . and comfits. . . not to speak of breakages."

"There is always Master Courage," suggested Hymn-of-Praise, with a movement of the left eyelid which in the case of any one less saintly might have been described as a sly wink.

"That there is not," interrupted the lad decisively; "my stomach rebels against comfits, and sack-posset could never be laid to my door."

"I give thee assurance, Master Busy," concluded the young girl, "that the county of Kent no longer suits my constitution. 'Tis London for me, and thither will I go next year."

"'Tis a den of wickedness," commented Busy sententiously, "in spite of my Lord Protector, who of a truth doth turn his back on the Saints and hath even allowed the great George Fox and some of the Friends to languish in prison, whilst profligacy holds undisputed sway. Master Courage, meseems those mugs need washing a second time," he added, with sudden irrelevance. "Take them to the kitchen, and do not let me set eyes on thee until they shine like pieces of new silver."

Master Courage would have either resisted the order altogether, or at any rate argued the point of the cleanliness of the mugs, had he dared; but the saintly man possessed on occasions a heavy hand, and he also wore boots which had very hard toes, and the lad realized from the peremptory look in the butler's eyes that this was an occasion when both hand and boot would serve to emphasize Master Busy's orders with unpleasant force if he himself were at all slow to obey.

He tried to catch Charity's eye, but was made aware once more of the eternal truth that women are perverse and fickle creatures, for she would not look at him, and seemed absorbed in the rearrangement of her kerchief.

With a deep sigh which should have spoken volumes to her adamantine heart, Courage gathered all the mugs together by their handles, and reluctantly marched out of the room once more.

Hymn-of-Praise Busy waited a moment or two until the clattering of the pewter died away in the distance, then he edged a little closer to the table whereat Mistress Charity seemed still very busy with the fruit, and said haltingly:

"Didst thou really wish to go, mistress. . . to leave thy fond, adoring Hymn-of-Praise. . . to go, mistress? . . . and to break my heart?"

Charity's dainty head—with its tiny velvet cap edged with lawn which hardly concealed sufficiently the wealth of her unruly brown hair—sank meditatively upon her left shoulder.

"Lord, Master Busy," she said demurely, "how was a poor maid to know that you meant it earnestly?"

"Meant it earnestly?"

"Yes. . . a new kirtle. . . a gold ring. . . flowers. . . and sack-posset and pasties to all the guests," she explained. "Is that what you mean. . . hem. . . what *thou*, meanest, Master Busy?"

"Of a surety, mistress. . . and if thou wouldst allow me to. . . to. . ."

"To what, Master Busy?"

"To salute thee," said the saintly man, with a becoming blush, "as the Lord doth allow his creatures to salute one another. . . with a chaste kiss, mistress."

Then as she seemed to demur, he added by way of persuasion:

"I am not altogether a poor man, mistress; and there is that in my coffer upstairs put by, as would please thee in the future."

"Nay! I was not thinking of the money, Master Busy," said this daughter of Eve, coyly, as she held a rosy cheek out in the direction of the righteous man.

'Tis the duty even of a veracious chronicler to draw a discreet veil over certain scenes full of blissful moments for those whom he portrays.

There are no data extant as to what occurred during the next few seconds in the old oak-beamed dining-room of Acol Court in the Island of Thanet. Certain it is that when next we get a peep at Master Hymn-of-Praise Busy and Mistress Charity Haggett, they are standing side by side, he looking somewhat shame-faced in the midst of his obvious joy, and she supremely unconcerned, once more absorbed in the apparently never-ending adornment of the refreshment table.

"Thou'lt have no cause to regret this, mistress," said Busy complacently, "we will be married this very autumn, and I have it in my mind—an it please the Lord—to go up to London and take secret service under my Lord Protector himself."

"Secret service, Master Busy. . . hem. . . I mean Hymn-of-Praise, dear. . . secret service? . . . What may that be?"

"'Tis a noble business, Charity," he replied, "and one highly commended by the Lord: the business of tracking the wicked to their lair, of discovering evil where 'tis hidden in dark places, conspiracies against my Lord Protector, adherence to the cause of the banished tyrants and. . . and. . . so forth."

"Sounds like spying to me," she remarked curtly.

"Spying? . . . Spying, didst thou say?" he exclaimed indignantly. "Fie on thee, Charity, for the thought! Secret service under my Lord Protector 'tis called, and a highly lucrative business too, and one for which I have remarkable aptitude."

"Indeed?"

"Aye! See the manner in which I find things out, mistress. This house now. . . thou wouldst think 'tis but an ordinary house. . . eh?"

His manner changed; the saintliness vanished from his attitude; the expression of his face became sly and knowing. He came nearer to Charity, took hold of her wrist, whilst he raised one finger to his lips.

"Thou wouldst think 'tis an ordinary house. . . wouldst thou not?" he

BARONESS EMMUSKA ORCZY

repeated, sinking his voice to a whisper, murmuring right into her ear so that his breath blew her hair about, causing it to tickle her cheek.

She shuddered with apprehension. His manner was so mysterious.

"Yes. . . yes. . ." she murmured, terrified.

"But I tell thee that there's something going on," he added significantly.

"La, Master Busy. . . you. . . you terrify me!" she said, on the verge of tears. "What could there be going on?"

Master Busy raised both his hands and with the right began counting off the fingers of the left.

"Firstly," he began solemnly, "there's an heiress! secondly our master—poor as a church mouse—thirdly a young scholar—secretary, they call him, though he writes no letters, and is all day absorbed in his studies. . . Well, mistress," he concluded, turning a triumphant gaze on her, "tell me, prithee, what happens?"

"What happens, Master Hymn-of-Praise? . . . I do not understand. What does happen?"

"I'll tell thee," he replied sententiously, "when I have found out; but mark my words, mistress, there's something going on in this house. . . Hush! not a word to that young jackanapes," he added as a distant clatter of pewter mugs announced the approach of Master Courage. "Watch with me, mistress, thou'lt perceive something. And when I have found out, 'twill be the beginning of our fortunes."

Once more he placed a warning finger on his lips; once more he gave Mistress Charity a knowing wink, and her wrist an admonitory pressure, then he resumed his staid and severe manner, his saintly mien and somewhat nasal tones, as from the gay outside world beyond the window-embrasure the sound of many voices, the ripple of young laughter, the clink of heeled boots on the stone-flagged path, proclaimed the arrival of the quality.

II

On a July Afternoon

In the meanwhile in a remote corner of the park the quality was assembled round the skittle-alley.

Imagine Sir Marmaduke de Chavasse standing there, as stiff a Roundhead as ever upheld my Lord Protector and his Puritanic government in this remote corner of the county of Kent: dour in manner, harsh-featured and hollow-eyed, dressed in dark doublet and breeches wholly void of tags, ribands or buttons. His closely shorn head is flat at the back, square in front, his clean-shaven lips though somewhat thick are always held tightly pressed together. Not far from him sits on a rough wooden seat, Mistress Amelia Editha de Chavasse, widow of Sir Marmaduke's elder brother, a good-looking woman still, save for the look of discontent, almost of suppressed rebellion, apparent in the perpetual dark frown between the straight brows, in the downward curve of the well-chiseled mouth, and in the lowering look which seems to dwell for ever in the handsome dark eyes.

Dame Harrison, too, was there: the large and portly dowager, florid of face, dictatorial in manner, dressed in the supremely unbecoming style prevalent at the moment, when everything that was beautiful in art as well as in nature was condemned as sinful and ungodly; she wore the dark kirtle and plain, ungainly bodice with its hard white kerchief folded over her ample bosom; her hair was parted down the middle and brushed smoothly and flatly to her ears, where but a few curls were allowed to escape with well-regulated primness from beneath the horn-comb, and the whole appearance of her looked almost grotesque, surmounted as it was by the modish high-peaked beaver hat, a marvel of hideousness and discomfort, since the small brim afforded no protection against the sun, and the tall crown was a ready prey to the buffetings of the wind.

Mistress Fairsoul Pyncheon too, was there, the wife of the Squire of Ashe; thin and small, a contrast to Dame Harrison in her mild and somewhat fussy manner; her plain petticoat, too, was embellished with paniers, and in spite of the heat of the day she wore a tippet edged with fur: both of which frivolous adornments had obviously stirred up the wrath of her more Puritanical neighbor.

Then there were the men: busy at this moment with hurling wooden balls along the alley, at the further end of which a hollow-eyed scraggy youth, in shirt and rough linen trousers, was employed in propping up again the fallen nine-pins. Squire John Boatfield had ridden over from Eastry, Sir Timothy Harrison had come in his aunt's coach, and young Squire Pyncheon with his doting mother.

And in the midst of all these sober folk, of young men in severe garments, of portly dames and frowning squires, a girlish figure, young, alert, vigorous, wearing with the charm of her own youth and freshness the unbecoming attire, which disfigured her elders yet seemed to set off her own graceful form, her dainty bosom and pretty arms. Her kirtle, too, was plain, and dull in color, of a soft dovelike gray, without adornment of any kind, but round her shoulders her kerchief was daintily turned, edged with delicate lace, and showing through its filmy folds peeps of her own creamy skin.

'Twas years later that Sir Peter Lely painted Lady Sue when she was a great lady and the friend of the Queen: she was beautiful then, in the full splendor of her maturer charms, but never so beautiful as she was on that hot July afternoon in the year of our Lord 1657, when, heated with the ardor of the game, pleased undoubtedly with the adulation which surrounded her on every side, she laughed and chatted with the men, teased the women, her cheeks aglow, her eyes bright, her brown hair—persistently unruly—flying in thick curls over her neck and shoulders.

"A remarkable talent, good Sir Marmaduke," Dame Harrison was saying to her host, as she cast a complacent eye on her nephew, who had just succeeded in overthrowing three nine-pins at one stroke: "Sir Timothy hath every aptitude for outdoor pursuits, and though my Lord Protector deems all such recreations sinful, yet do I think they tend to the development of muscular energy, which later on may be placed at the service of the Commonwealth."

Sir Timothy Harrison at this juncture had the misfortune of expending his muscular energy in hitting Squire Boatfield violently on the shin with an ill-aimed ball.

"Damn!" exclaimed the latter, heedless of the strict fines imposed by my Lord Protector on unseemly language. "I. . . verily beg the ladies' pardon. . . but. . . this young jackanapes nearly broke my shin-bone."

There certainly had been an exclamation of horror on the part of the ladies at Squire Boatfield's forcible expression of annoyance, Dame Harrison taking no pains to conceal her disapproval.

"Horrid, coarse creature, this neighbor of yours, good Sir Marmaduke," she said with her usual air of decision. "Meseems he is not fit company for your ward."

"Dear Squire Boatfield," sighed Mistress Pyncheon, who was evidently disposed to be more lenient, "how good-humoredly he bears it! Clumsy people should not be trusted in a skittle alley," she added in a mild way, which seemed to be peculiarly exasperating to Dame Harrison's irascible temper.

"I pray you, Sir Timothy," here interposed Lady Sue, trying to repress the laughter which would rise to her lips, "forgive poor Squire John. You scarce can expect him to moderate his language under such provocation."

"Oh! his insults leave me completely indifferent," said the young man with easy unconcern, "his calling me a jackanapes doth not of necessity make me one."

"No!" retorted Squire Boatfield, who was still nursing his shin-bone, "maybe not, Sir Timothy, but it shows how observant I am."

"Oliver, pick up Lady Sue's handkerchief," came in mild accents from Mistress Pyncheon.

"Quite unnecessary, good mistress," rejoined Dame Harrison decisively, "Sir Timothy has already seen it."

And while the two young men made a quick and not altogether successful dive for her ladyship's handkerchief, colliding vigorously with one another in their endeavor to perform this act of gallantry single-handed, Lady Sue gazed down on them, with good-humored contempt, laughter and mischief dancing in her eyes. She knew that she was good to look at, that she was rich, and that she had the pick of the county, aye, of the South of England, did she desire to wed. Perhaps she thought of this, even whilst she laughed at the antics of her bevy of courtiers, all anxious to win her good graces.

Yet even as she laughed, her face suddenly clouded over, a strange, wistful look came into her eyes, and her laughter was lost in a quick, short sigh.

A young man had just crossed the tiny rustic bridge which spanned the ha-ha dividing the flower-garden from the uncultivated park. He walked rapidly through the trees, towards the skittle alley, and as he came nearer, the merry lightheartedness seemed suddenly to vanish from Lady Sue's manner: the ridiculousness of the two young men at her feet, glaring furiously at one another whilst fighting for her handkerchief, seemed now to irritate her; she snatched the bit of delicate linen from their hands, and turned somewhat petulantly away.

"Shall we continue the game?" she said curtly.

The young man, all the while that he approached, had not taken his eyes off Lady Sue. Twice he had stumbled against rough bits of root or branch which he had not perceived in the grass through which he walked. He had seen her laughing gaily, whilst Squire Boatfield used profane language, and smile with contemptuous merriment at the two young men at her feet; he had also seen the change in her manner, the sudden wistful look, the quick sigh, the irritability and the petulance.

But his own grave face expressed neither disapproval at the one mood nor astonishment at the other. He walked somewhat like a somnambulist, with eyes fixed—almost expressionless in the intensity of their gaze.

He was very plainly, even poorly clad, and looked a dark figure even amongst these soberly appareled gentry. The grass beneath his feet had deadened the sound of his footsteps but Sir Marmaduke had apparently perceived him, for he beckoned to him to approach.

"What is it, Lambert?" he asked kindly.

"Your letter to Master Skyffington, Sir Marmaduke," replied the young man, "will you be pleased to sign it?"

"Will it not keep?" said Sir Marmaduke.

"Yes, an you wish it, Sir. I fear I have intruded. I did not know you were busy."

The young man had a harsh voice, and a strange brusqueness of manner which somehow suggested rebellion against the existing conditions of life. He no longer looked at Lady Sue now, but straight at Sir Marmaduke, speaking the brief apology between his teeth, without opening his mouth, as if the words hurt him when they passed his lips.

"You had best speak to Master Skyffington himself about the business," rejoined Sir Marmaduke, not heeding the mumbled apology, "he will be here anon."

He turned abruptly away, and the young man once more left to himself, silently and mechanically moved again in the direction of the house.

"You will join us in a bowl of sack-posset, Master Lambert," said Mistress de Chavasse, striving to be amiable.

"You are very kind," he said none too genially, "in about half-an-hour if you will allow me. There is another letter yet to write."

No one had taken much notice of him. Even in these days when kingship and House of Lords were abolished, the sense of social inequality remained keen. To this coterie of avowed Republicans, young Richard Lambert—secretary or what-not to Sir Marmaduke, a paid dependent at any rate—was not worth more than a curt nod of the head, a condescending acknowledgment of his existence at best.

But Lady Sue had not even bestowed the nod. She had not actually taken notice of his presence when he came; the wistful look had vanished as soon as the young man's harsh voice had broken on her ear: she did not look on him now that he went.

She was busy with her game. Nathless her guardian's secretary was of no more importance in the rich heiress's sight than that mute row of nine-pins at the end of the alley, nor was there, mayhap, in her mind much social distinction between the hollow-eyed lad who set them up stolidly from time to time, and the silent young student who wrote those letters which Sir Marmaduke had not known how to spell.

III

The Exile

B ut despite outward indifference, with the brief appearance of the soberly-garbed young student upon the scene and his abrupt and silent departure, all the zest seemed to have gone out of Lady Sue's mood.

The ingenuous flatteries of her little court irritated her now: she no longer felt either amused or pleased by the extravagant compliments lavished upon her beauty and skill by portly Squire John, by Sir Timothy Harrison or the more diffident young Squire Pyncheon.

"Of a truth, I sometimes wish, Lady Sue, that I could find out if you have any faults," remarked Squire Boatfield unctuously.

"Nay, Squire," she retorted sharply, "pray try to praise me to my female friends."

In vain did Mistress Pyncheon admonish her son to be more bold in his wooing.

"You behave like a fool, Oliver," she said meekly.

"But, Mother. . ."

"Go, make yourself pleasing to her ladyship."

"But, Mother. . ."

"I pray you, my son," she retorted with unusual acerbity, "do you want a million or do you not?"

"But, Mother. . ."

"Then go at once and get it, ere that fool Sir Timothy or the odious Boatfield capture it under your very nose."

"But, Mother. . ."

"Go! say something smart to her at once. . . talk about your gray mare. . . she is over fond of horses. . ."

Then as the young Squire, awkward and clumsy in his manner, more accustomed to the company of his own servants than to that of highborn ladies, made sundry unfortunate attempts to enchain the attention of the heiress, his worthy mother turned with meek benignity to Sir Marmaduke.

"A veritable infatuation, good Sir Marmaduke," she said with a sigh, "quite against my interests, you know. I had no thought to see the dear lad married so soon, nor to give up my home at the Dene yet, in favor of a new mistress. Not but that Oliver is not a good son to his mother—such a good lad!—and such a good husband he would be to any girl who. . ."

"A strange youth that secretary of yours, Sir Marmaduke," here interposed Dame Harrison in her loud, dictatorial voice, breaking in on Mistress Pyncheon's dithyrambs, "modest he appears to be, and silent too: a paragon meseems!"

She spoke with obvious sarcasm, casting covert glances at Lady Sue to see if she heard.

Sir Marmaduke shrugged his shoulders.

"Lambert is very industrious," he said curtly.

"I thought secretaries never did anything but suck the ends of their pens," suggested Mistress Pyncheon mildly.

"Sometimes they make love to their employer's daughter," retorted Dame Harrison spitefully, for Lady Sue was undoubtedly lending an ear to the conversation now that it had the young secretary for object. She was not watching Squire Boatfield who was wielding the balls just then with remarkable prowess, and at this last remark from the portly old dame, she turned sharply round and said with a strange little air of haughtiness which somehow became her very well:

"But then you see, mistress, Master Lambert's employer doth not possess a daughter of his own—only a ward. . . mayhap that is the reason why his secretary performs his duties so well in other ways."

Her cheeks were glowing as she said this, and she looked quite defiant, as if challenging these disagreeable mothers and aunts of fortune-hunting youths to cast unpleasant aspersions on a friend whom she had taken under her special protection.

Sir Marmaduke looked at her keenly; a deep frown settled between his eyes at sight of her enthusiasm. His face suddenly looked older, and seemed more dour, more repellent than before.

"Sue hath such a romantic temperament," he said dryly, speaking between his teeth and as if with an effort. "Lambert's humble origin has fired her imagination. He has no parents and his elder brother is the blacksmith down at Acol; his aunt, who seems to have had charge of the boys ever since they were children, is just a common old woman who lives in the village—a strict adherent, so I am told, of this new sect, whom Justice Bennet of Derby hath so justly nicknamed 'Quakers.' They talk strangely, these people, and believe in a mighty queer fashion.

I know not if Lambert be of their creed, for he does not use the 'thee' and 'thou' when speaking as do all Quakers, so I am told; but his empty pockets, a smattering of learning which he has picked up the Lord knows where, and a plethora of unspoken grievances, have all proved a sure passport to Lady Sue's sympathy."

"Nay, but your village of Acol seems full of queer folk, good Sir Marmaduke," said Mistress Pyncheon. "I have heard talk among my servants of a mysterious prince hailed from France, who has lately made one of your cottages his home."

"Oh! ah! yes!" quoth Sir Marmaduke lightly, "the interesting exile from the Court of King Louis. I did not know that his fame had reached you, mistress."

"A French prince?—in this village?" exclaimed Dame Harrison sharply, "and pray, good Sir Marmaduke, where did you go a-fishing to get such a bite?"

"Nay!" replied Sir Marmaduke with a short laugh, "I had naught to do with his coming; he wandered to Acol from Dover about six months ago it seems, and found refuge in the Lamberts' cottage, where he has remained ever since. A queer fellow I believe. I have only seen him once or twice in my fields. . . in the evening, usually. . ."

Perhaps there was just a curious note of irritability in Sir Marmaduke's voice as he spoke of this mysterious inhabitant of the quiet village of Acol; certain it is that the two matchmaking old dames seemed smitten at one and the same time with a sense of grave danger to their schemes.

An exile from France, a prince who hides his identity and his person in a remote Kentish village, and a girl with a highly imaginative temperament like Lady Sue! here was surely a more definite, a more important rival to the pretensions of homely country youths like Sir Timothy Harrison or Squire Pyncheon, than even the student of humble origin whose brother was a blacksmith, whose aunt was a Quakeress, and who wandered about the park of Acol with hollow eyes fixed longingly on the much-courted heiress.

Dame Harrison and Mistress Pyncheon both instinctively turned a scrutinizing gaze on her ladyship. Neither of them was perhaps ordinarily very observant, but self-interest had made them keen, and it would have been impossible not to note the strange atmosphere which seemed suddenly to pervade the entire personality of the young girl.

There was nothing in her face now expressive of whole-hearted partisanship for an absent friend, such as she had displayed when she felt that young Lambert was being unjustly sneered at; rather was it a kind of entranced and arrested thought, as if her mind, having come in contact with one all-absorbing idea, had ceased to function in any other direction save that one.

Her cheeks no longer glowed, they seemed pale and transparent like those of an ascetic; her lips were slightly parted, her eyes appeared unconscious of everything round her, and gazing at something enchanting beyond that bank of clouds which glimmered, snow-white, through the trees.

"But what in the name of common sense is a French prince doing in Acol village?" exclaimed Dame Harrison in her most strident voice, which had the effect of drawing every one's attention to herself and to Sir Marmaduke, whom she was thus addressing.

The men ceased playing and gathered nearer. The spell was broken. That strange and mysterious look vanished from Lady Sue's face; she turned away from the speakers and idly plucked a few bunches of acorn from an overhanging oak.

"Of a truth," replied Sir Marmaduke, whose eyes were still steadily fixed on his ward, "I know as little about the fellow, ma'am, as you do yourself. He was exiled from France by King Louis for political reasons, so he explained to the old woman Lambert, with whom he is still lodging. I understand that he hardly ever sleeps at the cottage, that his appearances there are short and fitful and that his ways are passing mysterious. . . And that is all I know," he added in conclusion, with a careless shrug of the shoulders.

"Quite a romance!" remarked Mistress Pyncheon dryly.

"You should speak to him, good Sir Marmaduke," said Dame Harrison decisively, "you are a magistrate. 'Tis your duty to know more of this fellow and his antecedents."

"Scarcely that, ma'am," rejoined Sir Marmaduke, "you understand. . . I have a young ward living for the nonce in my house. . . she is very rich, and, I fear me, of a very romantic disposition. . . I shall try to get the man removed from hence, but until that is accomplished, I prefer to know nothing about him. . ."

"How wise of you, good Sir Marmaduke!" quoth Mistress Pyncheon with a sigh of content.

A sentiment obviously echoed in the hearts of a good many people there present.

"One knows these foreign adventurers," concluded Sir Marmaduke

BARONESS EMMUSKA ORCZY

with pleasant irony, "with their princely crowns and forlorn causes... half a million of English money would no doubt regild the former and bolster up the latter."

He rose from his seat as he spoke, boldly encountering even as he did so, a pair of wrathful and contemptuous girlish eyes fixed steadily upon him.

"Shall we go within?" he said, addressing his guests, and returning his young ward's gaze haughtily, even commandingly; "a cup of sack-posset will be welcome after the fatigue of the game. Will you honor my poor house, mistress? and you, too, ma'am? Gentlemen, you must fight among yourselves for the privilege of escorting Lady Sue to the house, and if she prove somewhat disdainful this beautiful summer's afternoon, I pray you remember that faint heart never won fair lady, and that the citadel is not worth storming an it is not obdurate."

The suggestion of sack-posset proved vastly to the liking of the merry company. Mistress de Chavasse who had been singularly silent all the afternoon, walked quickly in advance of her brother-in-law's guests, no doubt in order to cast a scrutinizing eye over the arrangements of the table, which she had entrusted to the servants.

Sir Marmaduke followed at a short distance, escorting the older women, making somewhat obvious efforts to control his own irritability, and to impart some sort of geniality to the proceedings.

Then in a noisy group in the rear came the three men still fighting for the good graces of Lady Sue, whilst she, silent, absorbed, walked leisurely along, paying no heed to the wrangling of her courtiers, her fingers tearing up with nervous impatience the delicate cups of the acorns, which she then threw from her with childish petulance.

And her eyes still sought the distance beyond the boundaries of Sir Marmaduke's private grounds, there where cornfields and sky and sea were merged by the summer haze into a glowing line of emerald and purple and gold.

IV

GRINDING POVERTY

It was about an hour later. Sir Marmaduke's guests had departed, Dame Harrison in her rickety coach, Mistress Pyncheon in her chaise, whilst Squire Boatfield was riding his well-known ancient cob.

Everyone had drunk sack-posset, had eaten turkey pasties, and enjoyed the luscious fruit: the men had striven to be agreeable to the heiress, the old ladies to be encouraging to their protégés. Sir Marmaduke had tried to be equally amiable to all, whilst favoring none. He was an unpopular man in East Kent and he knew it, doing nothing to counterbalance the unpleasing impression caused invariably by his surly manner, and his sarcastic, often violent, temper.

Mistress Amelia Editha de Chavasse was now alone with her brother-in-law in the great bare hall of the Court, Lady Sue having retired to her room under pretext of the vapors, and young Lambert been finally dismissed from work for the day.

"You are passing kind to the youth, Marmaduke," said Mistress de Chavasse meditatively when the young man's darkly-clad figure had disappeared up the stairs.

She was sitting in a high-backed chair, her head resting against the carved woodwork. The folds of her simple gown hung primly round her well-shaped figure. Undoubtedly she was still a very good-looking woman, though past the hey-day of her youth and beauty. The half-light caused by the depth of the window embrasure, and the smallness of the glass panes through which the summer sun hardly succeeded in gaining admittance, added a certain softness to her chiseled features, and to the usually hard expression of her large dark eyes.

She was gazing out of the tall window, wherein the several broken panes were roughly patched with scraps of paper, out into the garden and the distance beyond, where the sea could be always guessed at, even when not seen. Sir Marmaduke had his back to the light: he was sitting astride a low chair, his high-booted foot tapping the ground impatiently, his fingers drumming a devil's tattoo against the back of the chair.

"Lambert would starve if I did not provide for him," he said with a sneer. "Adam, his brother, could do naught for him: he is poor as a church-mouse, poorer even than I—but nathless," he added with a violent oath, "it strikes everyone as madness that I should keep a secretary when I scarce can pay the wages of a serving maid."

"'Twere better you paid your servants' wages, Marmaduke," she retorted harshly, "they were insolent to me just now. Why do you not pay the girl's arrears to-day?"

"Why do I not climb up to the moon, my dear Editha, and bring down a few stars with me in my descent," he replied with a shrug of his broad shoulders. "I have come to my last shilling."

"The Earl of Northallerton cannot live for ever."

"He hath vowed, I believe, that he would do it, if only to spite me. And by the time that he come to die this accursed Commonwealth will have abolished all titles and confiscated every estate."

"Hush, Marmaduke," she said, casting a quick, furtive look all round her, "there may be spies about."

"Nay, I care not," he rejoined roughly, jumping to his feet and kicking the chair aside so that it struck with a loud crash against the flagged floor. "'Tis but little good a man gets for cleaving loyally to the Commonwealth. The sequestrated estates of the Royalists would have been distributed among the adherents of republicanism, and not held to bolster up a military dictatorship. Bah!" he continued, allowing his temper to overmaster him, speaking in harsh tones and with many a violent oath, "it had been wiser to embrace the Royal cause. The Lord Protector is sick, so 'tis said. His son Richard hath no backbone, and the present tyranny is worse than the last. I cannot collect my rents; I have been given neither reward nor compensation for the help I gave in '46. So much for their boasted gratitude and their many promises! My Lord Protector feasts the Dutch ambassadors with music and with wine, my Lords Ireton and Fairfax and Hutchinson and the accursed lot of canting Puritans flaunt it in silks and satins, whilst I go about in a ragged doublet and with holes in my shoes."

"There's Lady Sue," murmured Mistress de Chavasse soothingly.

"Pshaw! the guardianship of a girl who comes of age in three months!"

"You can get another by that time."

"Not I. I am not a sycophant hanging round White Hall! 'Twas sheer good luck and no merit of mine that got me the guardianship of Sue. Lord Middlesborough, her kinsman, wanted it; the Courts would have given her to him, but old Noll thought him too much of a 'gentleman,' whilst I—an out-at-elbows country squire, was more to my Lord Protector's liking. 'Tis the only thing he ever did for me."

There was intense bitterness and a harsh vein of sarcasm running through Sir Marmaduke's talk. It was the speech of a disappointed man, who had hoped, and striven, and fought once; had raised longing hands towards brilliant things and sighed after glory, or riches, or fame, but whose restless spirit had since been tamed, crushed under the heavy weight of unsatisfied ambition.

Poverty—grinding, unceasing, uninteresting poverty, had been Sir Marmaduke's relentless tormentor ever since he had reached man's estate. His father, Sir Jeremy de Chavasse, had been poor before him. The younger son of that Earl of Northallerton who cut such a brilliant figure at the Court of Queen Elizabeth, Jeremy had married Mistress Spanton of Acol Court, who had brought him a few acres of land heavily burdened with mortgage as her dowry. They were a simple-minded, unostentatious couple who pinched and scraped and starved that their two sons might keep up the appearances of gentlemen at the Court of King Charles.

But both the young men seemed to have inherited from their brilliant grandfather luxurious tastes and a love of gambling and of show—but neither his wealth nor yet his personal charm of manner. The eldest, Rowland, however, soon disappeared from the arena of life. He married when scarce twenty years of age a girl who had been a play-actress. This marriage nearly broke his doting mother's heart, and his own, too, for the matter of that, for the union was a most unhappy one. Rowland de Chavasse died very soon after, unreconciled to his father and mother, who refused to see him or his family, even on his deathbed.

Jeremy de Chavasse's few hopes now centered on his younger son, Marmaduke. In order to enable the young man to remain in London, to mix freely and to hold his own in that set into which family traditions had originally gained him admittance, the fond mother and indulgent father denied themselves the very necessities of life.

Marmaduke took everything that was given him, whilst chafing at the paucity of his allowance. Determined to cut a figure at Court, he spent two years and most of his mother's dowry in a vain attempt to capture the heart of one or the other of the rich heiresses who graced the entourage of Charles I.

But Nature who had given Marmaduke boundless ambition, had failed to bestow on him those attributes which would have helped him on towards its satisfaction. He was neither sufficiently prepossessing to please an heiress, nor sufficiently witty and brilliant to catch the royal eye or the favor of his uncle, the present Earl of Northallerton. His efforts in the direction of advantageous matrimony had earned for him at Court the nickname of "The Sparrowhawk." But even these efforts had soon to be relinquished for want of the wherewithal.

The doting mother no longer could supply him with a sufficiency of money to vie with the rich gallants at the Court, and the savings which Sir Jeremy had been patiently accumulating with a view to freeing the Acol estates from mortgage went instead to rescue young Marmaduke from a debtor's prison.

Poor Sir Jeremy did not long survive his disappointment. Marmaduke returned to Acol Court only to find his mother a broken invalid, and his father dead.

Since then it had been a perpetual struggle against poverty and debt, a bitter revolt against Fate, a burning desire to satisfy ambition which had received so serious a check.

When the great conflict broke out between King and Parliament, he threw himself into it, without zest and without conviction, embracing the cause of the malcontents with a total lack of enthusiasm, merely out of disappointment—out of hatred for the brilliant Court and circle in which he had once hoped to become a prominent figure.

He fought under Ireton, was commended as a fairly good soldier, though too rebellious to be very reliable, too self-willed to be wholly trusted.

Even in these days of brilliant reputations quickly made, he remained obscure and practically unnoticed. Advancement never came his way and whilst younger men succeeded in attracting the observant eye of old Noll, he was superseded at every turn, passed over—anon forgotten.

When my Lord Protector's entourage was formed, the Household organized, no one thought of the Sparrowhawk for any post that would have satisfied his desires. Once more he cursed his own poverty. Money—the want of it—he felt was at the root of all his disappointments. A burning desire to obtain it at any cost, even that of honor, filled his entire being, his mind, his soul, his thoughts, every nerve in his body. Money, and social prestige! To be somebody at Court or elsewhere, politically, commercially,—he cared not. To handle money and to command attention!

He became wary, less reckless, striving to obtain by diplomatic means that which he had once hoped to snatch by sheer force of personality. The Court of Chancery having instituted itself sole guardian and administrator of the revenues and fortunes of minors whose fathers had fought on the Royalist side, and were either dead or in exile, and arrogating unto itself the power to place such minors under the tutelage of persons whose loyalty to the Commonwealth was undoubted, Sir Marmaduke bethought himself of applying for one of these official guardianships which were known to be very lucrative and moreover, practically sinecures.

Fate for once favored him; a half-contemptuous desire to do something for this out-at-elbows Kentish squire who had certainly been a loyal adherent of the Commonwealth, caused my Lord Protector to favor his application. The rich daughter of the Marquis of Dover was placed under the guardianship of Sir Marmaduke de Chavasse with an allowance of £4,000 a year for her maintenance, until she came of age. A handsome fortune and stroke of good luck for a wise and prudent man:—a drop in an ocean of debts, difficulties and expensive tastes, in the case of Sir Marmaduke.

A prolonged visit to London with a view either of gaining a foothold in the new Court, or of drawing the attention of the malcontents, of Monk and his party, or even of the Royalists, to himself, resulted in further debts, in more mortgages, more bitter disappointments.

The man himself did not please. His personality was unsympathetic; Lady Sue's money which he now lavished right and left, bought neither friendship nor confidence. He joined all the secret clubs which in defiance of Cromwell's rigid laws against betting and gambling, were the resort of all the smart gentlemen in the town. Ill-luck at hazard and dice pursued him: he was a bad loser, quarrelsome and surly. His ambition had not taught him the salutary lesson of how to make friends in order to attain his desires.

His second return to the ancestral home was scarcely less disastrous than the first; a mortgage on his revenues as guardian of Lady Sue Aldmarshe just saved him this time from the pursuit of his creditors, and this mortgage he had only obtained through false statements as to his ward's age.

As he told his sister-in-law a moment ago, he was at his last gasp. He had perhaps just begun to realize that he would never succeed through the force of his own individuality. Therefore, money had become a still more imperative necessity to him. He was past forty now. Disappointed ambition and an ever rebellious spirit had left severe imprints on his face: his figure was growing heavy, his prominent lips, unadorned by a mustache, had an unpleasant downward droop, and lately he had even noticed that the hair on the top of his head was not so thick as of yore.

The situation was indeed getting desperate, since Lady Sue would be of age in three months, when all revenues for her maintenance would cease.

"Methinks her million will go to one of those young jackanapes who hang about her," sighed Mistress de Chavasse, with almost as much bitterness as Sir Marmaduke had shown.

Her fortunes were in a sense bound up with those of her brother-in-law. He had been most unaccountably kind to her of late, a kindness which his many detractors attributed either to an infatuation for his brother's widow, or to a desire to further irritate his uncle the Earl of Northallerton, who—a rigid Puritan himself—hated the play-actress and her connection with his own family.

"Can naught be done, Marmaduke?" she asked after a slight pause, during which she had watched anxiously the restless figure of her brother-in-law as he paced up and down the narrow hall.

"Can you suggest anything, my dear Editha?" he retorted roughly.

"Pshaw!" she exclaimed with some impatience, "you are not so old, but you could have made yourself agreeable to the wench."

"You think that she would have fallen in love with her middle-aged guardian?" he exclaimed with a harsh, sarcastic laugh. "That girl? . . . with her head full of romantic nonsense. . . and I. . . in ragged doublet, with a bald head, and an evil temper. . . Bah!!! . . . But," he added, with an unpleasant sneer, "'tis unselfish and disinterested on your part, my dear Editha, even to suggest it. Sue does not like you. Her being mistress here would not be conducive to your comfort."

"Nay! 'tis no use going on in this manner any longer, Marmaduke," she said dejectedly. "Pleasant times will not come my way so long as you have not a shilling to give me for a new gown, and cannot afford to keep up my house in London."

She fully expected another retort from him—brutal and unbridled as was his wont when money affairs were being discussed. He was not accustomed to curb his violence in her presence. She had been his helpmeet in many unavowable extravagances, in the days when he was still striving after a brilliant position in town. There had been certain rumors anent a gambling den, whereat Mistress de Chavasse had been the presiding spirit and which had come under the watchful eye of my Lord Protector's spies.

Now she had perforce to share her brother-in-law's poverty. At any rate he provided a roof over her head. On the advent of Lady Sue Aldmarshe into his bachelor establishment he called on his sister-in-law for the part of duenna.

At one time the fair Editha had exercised her undoubted charms over Marmaduke's violent nature, but latterly she had become a mere butt for his outbursts of rage. But now to her astonishment, and in response to her petulant reproach, his fury seemed to fall away from him. He threw his head back and broke out into uncontrolled, half-sarcastic, almost defiant laughter.

"How blind you are, my dear Editha," he said with a shrug of his broad shoulders. "Nay! an I mistake not, in that case there will be some strange surprises for you within the next three months. I pray you try and curb your impatience until then, and to bear with the insolence of a serving wench, 'Twill serve you well, mine oath on that!" he added significantly.

Then without vouchsafing further explanations of his enigmatic utterances, he turned on his heel—still laughing apparently at some pleasing thought—and walked upstairs, leaving her to meditate.

V

The Legal Aspect

Mistress de Chavasse sat musing, in that high-backed chair, for some considerable time. Anon Sir Marmaduke once more traversed the hall, taking no heed of her as he went out into the garden. She watched his broad figure moving along the path and then crossing the rustic bridge until it disappeared among the trees of the park.

There was something about his attitude of awhile ago which puzzled her. And with puzzlement came an inexplicable fear: she had known Marmaduke in all his moods, but never in such an one as he had displayed before her just now. There had been a note almost of triumph in the laughter with which he had greeted her last reproach. The cry of the sparrowhawk when it seizes its prey.

Triumph in Sir Marmaduke filled her with dread. No one knew better than she did the hopeless condition of his financial status. Debt—prison perhaps—was waiting for him at every turn. Yet he seemed triumphant! She knew him to have reached those confines of irritability and rebellion against poverty which would cause him to shrink from nothing for the sake of gaining money. Yet he seemed triumphant!

Instinctively she shuddered as she thought of Sue. She had no cause to like the girl, yet would she not wish to see her come to harm.

She did not dare avow even to herself the conviction which she had, that if Sir Marmaduke could gain anything by the young girl's death, he would not hesitate to. . . Nay! she would not even frame that thought. Marmaduke had been kind to her; she could but hope that temptation such as that, would never come his way.

Hymn-of-Praise Busy broke in on her meditations. His nasal tones—which had a singular knack of irritating her as a rule—struck quite pleasingly on her ear, as a welcome interruption to the conflict of her thoughts.

"Master Skyffington, ma'am," he said in his usual drawly voice, "he is on his way to Dover, and desired his respects, an you wish to see him."

"Yes! yes! I'll see Master Skyffington," she said with alacrity, rising from her chair, "go apprise Sir Marmaduke, and ask Master Skyffington to come within."

She was all agitation now, eager, excited, and herself went forward to meet the quaint, little wizened figure which appeared in the doorway.

Master Skyffington, attorney-at-law, was small and thin—looked doubly so, in fact, in the black clothes which he wore. His eyes were blue and watery, his manner peculiarly diffident. He seemed to present a perpetual apology to the world for his own existence therein.

Even now as Mistress de Chavasse seemed really overjoyed to see him, he backed his meager person out of the doorway as she approached, whereupon she—impatiently—clutched his arm and dragged him forward into the hall.

"Sit down there, master," she said, speaking with obvious agitation, and almost pushing the poor little man off his feet whilst dragging him to a chair. "Sir Marmaduke will see you anon, but 'twas a kind thought to come and bring me news."

"Hem! . . . hem! . . ." stammered Master Skyffington, "I. . . that is. . . hem. . . I left Canterbury this morning and was on my way to Dover. . . hem. . . this lies on my way, ma'am. . . and. . ."

"Yes! yes!" she said impatiently, "but you have some news, of course?"

"News! . . . news!" he muttered apologetically, and clutching at his collar, which seemed to be choking him, "what news—er—I pray you, ma'am?"

"That clew?" she insisted.

"It was very slight," he stammered.

"And it led to naught?"

"Alas!"

Her eagerness vanished. She sank back into her chair and moaned.

"My last hope!" she said dully.

"Nay! nay!" rejoined Master Skyffington quite cheerfully, his courage seemingly having risen with her despair. "We must not be despondent. The noble Earl of Northallerton hath interested himself of late in the search and. . ."

But she shrugged her shoulders, whilst a short, bitter laugh escaped her lips:

"At last?" she said with biting sarcasm. "After twelve years!"

"Nay! but remember, ma'am, that his lordship now is very ill. . . and nigh on seventy years old. . . Failing your late husband, Master Rowland—whom the Lord hath in His keeping—your eldest son is. . . hem. . . that is. . . by law, ma'am, . . . and with all respect due to Sir Marmaduke. . . your eldest son is heir to the Earldom."

"And though his lordship hates me, he still prefers that my son should succeed to his title, rather than Sir Marmaduke whom he abhors."

But that suggestion was altogether too much for poor Master Skyffington's sense of what was due to so noble a family, and to its exalted head.

"That is. . . er. . ." he muttered in supreme discomfort, swallowing great gulps which rose to his throat at this rash and disrespectful speech from the ex-actress. "Family feuds. . . hem. . . er. . . very distressing of a truth. . . and. . . that is. . ."

"I fear me his lordship will be disappointed," she rejoined, quite heedless of the little attorney's perturbation, "and that under these circumstances Sir Marmaduke will surely succeed."

"I was about to remark," he rejoined, "that now, with my lord's help— his wealth and influence. . . now, that is, . . . that he has interested himself in the matter. . . hem. . . we might make fresh inquiries. . . that is. . . er. . ."

"It will be useless, master. I have done all that is humanly possible. I loved my boys dearly—and it was because of my love for them that I placed them under my mother's care. . . I loved them, you understand, but I was living in a gay world in London. . . my husband was dead. . . I could do naught for their comfort. . . I thought it would be best for them. . ."

It was her turn now to speak humbly, almost apologetically, whilst her eyes sought those of the simple little attorney, trying to read approval in his glance, or at any rate an absence of reproof. He was shaking his head, sighing with visible embarrassment the while. In his innermost soul, he could find no excuse for the frivolous mother, anxious to avoid the responsibilities which the Lord Himself had put upon her: anxious to be rid of her children in order that she might pursue with greater freedom and ease that life of enjoyment and thoughtlessness which she craved.

"My mother was a strange woman," continued Mistress de Chavasse earnestly and placing her small white hand on the black sleeve of the attorney, "she cared little enough for me, and not at all for London and for society. She did not understand the many duties that devolve on a woman of fashion. . . And I was that in those days! . . . twenty years ago!"

"Ah! Truly! truly!" sighed Master Skyffington.

"Mayhap she acted according to her own lights. . . After some years she became a convert to that strange new faith. . . of the people who call themselves 'Friends' . . . who salute no one with the hat, and who talk so strangely, saying: 'thee' and 'thou' even when addressing their betters. One George Fox had a great hold on her. He was quite a youth then, but she thought him a saint. 'Tis he, methinks, poisoned her mind against me, and caused her to curse me on her deathbed."

She gave a little shudder—of superstition, perhaps. The maternal curse—she felt—was mayhap bearing fruit after all. Master Skyffington's watery eyes expressed gentle sympathy. His calling had taught him many of the hidden secrets of human nature and of Life: he guessed that the time—if not already here—was nigh at hand, when this unfortunate woman would realize the emptiness of her life, and would begin to reap the bitter harvest of the barren seeds which she had sown.

"Aye! I lay it all at the door of these 'Friends' who turned a mother's heart against her own daughter," continued Mistress de Chavasse vehemently. "She never told me that she was sick, sent me neither letter nor message; only after her death a curt note came to me, writ in her hand, entrusted to one of her own co-worshipers, a canting, mouthing creature, who grinned whilst I read the heartless message. My mother had sent her grandchildren away, so she told me in the letter, when she felt that the Lord was calling her to Him. She had placed my boys—my boys, master!—in the care of a trusted 'friend' who would bring them up in the fear of God, away from the influence of their mother. My boys, master, remember! . . . they were to be brought up in ignorance of their name—of the very existence of their mother. The 'friend,' doubtless a fellow Quaker—had agreed to this on my mother's deathbed."

"Hm! 'tis passing strange, and passing sad," said the attorney, with real sympathy now, for there was a pathetic note of acute sorrow in Mistress de Chavasse's voice, "but at the time. . . hem. . . and with money and influence. . . hem. . . much might have been done."

"Ah! believe me, master, I did what I could. I was in London then. . . I flew to Canterbury where my mother lived. . . I found her dead. . . and the boys gone. . . none of the neighbors could tell me whither. . . All they knew was that a woman had been living with my mother of late and had gone away, taking the boys with her. . . My boys, master, and no one could tell me whither they had gone! I spent what money I had, and Sir Marmaduke nobly bore his share in the cost of a ceaseless search, as the Earl of Northallerton would do nothing then to help me."

"Passing strange. . . passing sad," murmured Master Skyffington, shaking his head, "but methinks I recollect. . . hem. . . some six years

BARONESS EMMUSKA ORCZY

ago. . . a quest which led to a clew. . . er. . . that is. . . two young gentlemen. . ."

"Impostors, master," she rejoined, "aye! I have heard of many such since then. At first I used to believe their stories. . ."

"At first?" he exclaimed in amazement, "but surely. . . hem. . . the faces. . . your own sons, ma'am. . ."

"Ah! the faces!" she said, whilst a blush of embarrassment, even of shame, now suffused her pale cheeks. "I mean. . . you understand. . . I. . . I had not seen my boys since they were babes in arms. . . they were ten years old when they were taken away. . . but. . . but it is nigh on twenty-two years since I have set eyes on their faces. I would not know them, if they passed me by."

Tears choked her voice. Shame had added its bitter sting to the agony of her sorrow. Of a truth it was a terrible epilogue of misery, following on a life-story of frivolity and of heartlessness which Mistress de Chavasse had almost unconsciously related to the poor ignorant country attorney. Desirous at all costs of retaining her freedom, she had parted from her children with a light heart, glad enough that their grandmother was willing to relieve her of all responsibility. Time slipped by whilst she enjoyed herself, danced and flirted, gambled and played her part in that world of sport and Fashion wherein a mother's heart was an unnecessary commodity. Ten years are a long while in the life of an old woman who lives in a remote country town, and sees Death approaching with slow yet certain stride; but that same decade is but as a fleeting hour to the woman who is young and who lives for the moment.

The boys had been forgotten long ere they disappeared! Forgotten? perhaps not!—but their memory put away in a hidden cell of the mind where other inconvenient thoughts were stored: only to be released and gazed upon when other more agreeable ones had ceased to fill the brain.

She felt humbled before this simple-minded man, whom she knew she had shocked by the recital of her callousness. With innate gentleness of disposition he tried to hide his feelings and to set aside the subject for the moment.

"Sir Marmaduke was very disinterested, when he aided you in the quest," he said meekly, glad to be able to praise one whom he felt it his duty to respect, "for under present circumstances. . . hem! . . ."

"I will raise no difficulties in Sir Marmaduke's way," she rejoined, "there is no doubt in my mind that my boys are dead, else I had had news of them ere this."

He looked at her keenly—as keenly as he dared with his mild, blue eyes. It was hard to keep in sympathy with her. Her moods seemed to change as she spoke of her boys and then of Sir Marmaduke. Her last remark seemed to argue that her callousness with regard to her sons had not entirely yielded to softer emotions yet.

"In case of my Lord Northallerton's death," she continued lightly, "I shall not put in a claim on behalf of any son of mine."

"Whereupon—hem Sir Marmaduke as next-of-kin, would have the enjoyment of the revenues—and mayhap would have influence enough then to make good his claim to the title before the House of Lords. . ."

He checked himself: looked furtively round and added:

"Provided it please God and my Lord Protector that the House of Lords come back to Westminster by that time."

"I thank you, master," said Mistress de Chavasse, rising from her chair, intimating that this interview was now over, "you have told me all that I wish to know. Let me assure you, that I will not prove ungrateful. Your services will be amply repaid by whomever succeeds to the title and revenues of Northallerton. Did you wish to see Sir Marmaduke?"

"I thank you, mistress, not to-day," replied Master Skyffington somewhat dryly. The lady's promises had not roused his enthusiasm. He would have preferred to see more definite reward for his labors, for he had worked faithfully and was substantially out of pocket in this quest after the two missing young men.

But he was imbued with that deep respect for the family he had served all his life, which no conflict between privilege and people would ever eradicate, and though Mistress de Chavasse's origin was of the humblest, she was nevertheless herself now within the magic circle into which Master Skyffington never gazed save with the deepest reverence.

He thought it quite natural that she should dismiss him with a curt and condescending nod, and when she had swept majestically out of the room, he made his way humbly across the hall, then by the garden door out towards the tumble-down barn where he had tethered his old mare.

Master Courage helped him to mount, and he rode away in the direction of the Dover Road, his head bent, his thoughts dwelling in puzzlement and wonder on the strange doings of those whom he still reverently called his betters.

VI

UNDER THE SHADOW OF THE ELMS

Her head full of romantic nonsense! Well! perhaps that was the true keynote of Sue's character; perhaps, too, it was that same romantic temperament which gave such peculiar charm to her personality. It was not mere beauty—of which she had a plentiful share—nor yet altogether her wealth which attracted so many courtiers to her feet. Men who knew her in those days at Acol and subsequently at Court said that Lady Sue was magnetic.

She compelled attention, she commanded admiration, through that very romanticism of hers which caused her eyes to glow at the recital of valor, or sorrow, or talent, which caused her to see beauty of thought and mind and character there where it lay most deeply hidden, there—sometimes—where it scarce existed.

The dark figure of her guardian's secretary had attracted her attention from the moment when she first saw him moving silently about the house and park: the first words she spoke to him were words of sympathy. His life-story—brief and simple as it had been—had interested her. He seemed so different from these young and old country squires who frequented Acol Court. He neither wooed nor flattered her, yet seemed to find great joy in her company. His voice at times was harsh, his manner abrupt and even rebellious, but at others it fell to infinite gentleness when he talked to her of Nature and the stars, both of which he had studied deeply.

He never spoke of religion. That subject which was on everybody's tongue, together with the free use of the most sacred names, he rigorously avoided, also politics, and my Lord Protector's government, his dictatorship and ever-growing tyranny: but he knew the name of every flower that grew in meadow or woodland, the note of every bird as it trilled its song.

There is no doubt that but for the advent of that mysterious personality into Acol village, the deep friendship which had grown in Sue's heart for Richard Lambert would have warmed into a more passionate attachment.

But she was too young to reflect, too impulsive to analyze her feelings. The mystery which surrounded the foreigner who lodged at the Quakeress's cottage had made strong appeal to her idealism.

His first introduction to her notice, in the woods beyond the park gate on that cold January evening, with the moon gleaming weirdly through the branches of the elms, his solitary figure leaning against a tree, had fired her imagination and set it wildly galloping after mad fantasies.

He had scarcely spoken on that first occasion, but his silence was strangely impressive. She made up her mind that he was singularly handsome, although she could not judge of that very clearly for he wore a heavy mustache, and a shade over one eye; but he was tall, above the average, and carried the elaborate habiliments which the Cavaliers still affected, with consummate grace and ease. She thought, too, that the thick perruque became him very well, and his muffled voice, when he spoke, sounded singularly sweet.

Since then she had seen him constantly. At rare intervals at first, for maidenly dignity forbade that she should seem eager to meet him. He was ignorant of whom she was—oh! of that she felt quite quite sure: she always wore a dark tippet round her shoulders, and a hood to cover her head. He seemed pleased to see her, just to hear her voice. Obviously he was lonely and in deep trouble.

Then one night—it was the first balmy evening after the winter frosts—the moon was singularly bright, and the hood had fallen back from her head, just as her face was tilted upwards and her eyes glowing with enthusiasm. Then she knew that he had learnt to love her, not through any words which he spoke, for he was silent; his face was in shadow, and he did not even touch her; therefore it was not through any of her natural senses that she guessed his love. Yet she knew it, and her young heart was overfilled with happiness.

That evening when they parted he knelt at her feet and kissed the hem of her kirtle. After which, when she was back again in her own little room at Acol Court, she cried for very joy.

They did not meet very often. Once a week at most. He had vaguely promised to tell her, some day, of his great work for the regeneration of France, which he was carrying out in loneliness and exile here in England, a work far greater and more comprehensive than that which had secured for England religious and political liberty; this work it was which made him a wanderer on the face of the earth and caused his frequent and lengthy absences from the cottage in which he lodged.

She was quite content for the moment with these vague promises:

in her heart she was evolving enchanting plans for the future, when she would be his helpmate in this great and mysterious work.

In the meanwhile she was satisfied to live in the present, to console and comfort the noble exile, to lavish on him the treasures of her young and innocent love, to endow him in her imagination with all those mental and physical attributes which her romantic nature admired most.

The spring had come, clothing the weird branches of the elms with a tender garb of green, the anemones in the woods yielded to the bluebells and these to carpets of primroses and violets. The forests of Thanet echoed with songs of linnets and white-throats. She was happy and she was in love.

With the lengthened days came some petty sorrows. He was obviously worried, sometimes even impatient. Their meetings became fewer and shorter, for the evening hours were brief. She found it difficult to wander out so late across the park, unperceived, and he would never meet her by day-light.

This no doubt had caused him to fret. He loved her and desired her all his own. Yet 'twere useless of a surety to ask Sir Marmaduke's consent to her marriage with her French prince. He would never give it, and until she came of age he had absolute power over her choice of a husband.

She had explained this to him and he had sighed and murmured angry words, then pressed her with increased passion to his heart.

To-night as she walked through the park, she was conscious—for the first time perhaps—of a certain alloy mixed with her gladness. Yet she loved him—oh, yes! just, just as much as ever. The halo of romance with which she had framed in his mystic personality was in no way dimmed, but in a sense she almost feared him, for at times his muffled voice sounded singularly vehement, and his words betrayed the uncontrolled violence of his nature.

She had hoped to bring him some reassuring news anent Sir Marmaduke de Chavasse's intentions with regard to herself, but the conversation round the skittle-alley, her guardian's cruel allusions to "the foreign adventurer," had shown her how futile were such hopes.

Yet, there were only three months longer of this weary waiting. Surely he could curb his impatience until she was of age and mistress of her own hand! Surely he trusted her!

She sighed as this thought crossed her mind, and nearly fell up against a dark figure which detached itself from among the trees.

"Master Lambert!" she said, uttering a little cry of surprise, pressing her hand against her heart which was palpitating with emotion. "I had no thought of meeting you here."

"And I still less of seeing your ladyship," he rejoined coldly.

"How cross you are," she retorted with childish petulance, "what have I done that you should be so unkind?"

"Unkind?"

"Aye! I had meant to speak to you of this ere now—but you always avoid me. . . you scarce will look at me. . . and. . . and I wished to ask you if I had offended you?"

They were standing on a soft carpet of moss, overhead the gentle summer breeze stirred the great branches of the elms, causing the crisp leaves to mutter a long-drawn hush-sh-sh in the stillness of the night. From far away came the appealing call of a blackbird chased by some marauding owl, while on the ground close by, the creaking of tiny branches betrayed the quick scurrying of a squirrel. From the remote and infinite distance came the subdued roar of the sea.

The peace of the woodland, the sighing of the trees, the dark evening sky above, filled his heart with an aching longing for her.

"Offended me?" he murmured, passing his hand across his forehead, for his temples throbbed and his eyes were burning. "Nay! why should you think so?"

"You are so cold, so distant now," she said gently. "We were such good friends when first I came here. Thanet is a strange country to me. It seems weird and unkind—the woods are dark and lonely, that persistent sound of the sea fills me with a strange kind of dread. . . My home was among the Surrey hills you know. . . It is far from here. . . I cannot afford to lose a friend. . ."

She sighed, a quaint, wistful little sigh, curiously out of place, he thought, in this exquisite mouth framed only for smiles.

"I have so few real friends," she added in a whisper, so low that he thought she had not spoken, and that the elms had sighed that pathetic phrase into his ear.

"Believe me, Lady Sue, I am neither cold nor distant," he said, almost smiling now, for the situation appeared strange indeed, that this beautiful young girl, rich, courted, surrounded by an army of sycophants, should be appealing to a poor dependent for friendship. "I am only a little dazed. . . as any man would be who had been dreaming. . . and saw that dream vanish away. . ."

"Dreaming?"

"Yes!—we all dream sometimes you know. . . and a penniless man like myself, without prospects or friends is, methinks, more prone to it than most."

"We all have dreams sometimes," she said, speaking very low, whilst her eyes sought to pierce the darkness beyond the trees. "I too. . ."

She paused abruptly, and was quite still for a moment, almost holding her breath, he thought, as if she were listening. But not a sound came to disturb the silence of the woods. Blackbird and owl had ceased their fight for life, the squirrel had gone to rest: the evening air was filled only by the great murmur of the distant sea.

"Tell me your dream," she said abruptly.

"Alas! it is too foolish! . . . too mad! . . . too impossible. . ."

"But you said once that you would be my friend and would try to cheer my loneliness."

"So I will, with all my heart, an you will permit."

"Yet is there no friendship without confidence," she retorted. "Tell me your dream."

"What were the use? You would only laugh. . . and justly too."

"I should never laugh at that which made you sad," she said gently.

"Sad?" he rejoined with a short laugh, which had something of his usual bitterness in it. "Sad? Mayhap! Yet I hardly know. Think you that the poor peasant lad would be sad because he had dreamed that the fairy princess whom he had seen from afar in her radiance, was sweet and gracious to him one midsummer's day? It was only a dream, remember: when he woke she had vanished. . . gone out of his sight. . . hidden from him by a barrier of gold. . . In front of this barrier stood his pride. . . which perforce would have to be trampled down and crushed ere he could reach the princess."

She did not reply, only bent her sweet head, lest he should perceive the tears which had gathered in her eyes. All round them the wood seemed to have grown darker and more dense, whilst from afar the weird voice of that distant sea murmured of infinity and of the relentlessness of Fate.

They could not see one another very clearly, yet she knew that he was gazing at her with an intensity of love and longing in his heart which caused her own to ache with sympathy; and he knew that she was crying, that there was something in that seemingly brilliant and happy young life, which caused the exquisite head to droop as if under a load of sorrow.

A broken sigh escaped her lips, or was it the sighing of the wind in the elms?

He was smitten with remorse to think that he should have helped to make her cry.

"Sue—my little, beautiful Sue," he murmured, himself astonished at his own temerity in thus daring to address her. It was her grief which had brought her down to his level: the instinct of chivalry, of protection, of friendship which had raised him up to hers.

"Will you ever forgive me?" he said, "I had no right to speak to you as I have done. . . And yet. . ."

He paused and she repeated his last two words—gently, encouragingly.

"And yet. . . good master?"

"Yet at times, when I see the crowd of young, empty-headed fortune-seeking jackanapes, who dare to aspire to your ladyship's hand. . . I have asked myself whether perchance I had the right to remain silent, whilst they poured their farrago of nonsense into your ear. I love you, Sue!"

"No! no! good master!" she exclaimed hurriedly, while a nameless, inexplicable fear seemed suddenly to be holding her in its grip, as he uttered those few very simple words which told the old, old tale.

But those words once uttered, Richard felt that he could not now draw back. The jealously-guarded secret had escaped his lips, passion refused to be held longer in check. A torrent of emotion overmastered him. He forgot where he was, the darkness of the night, the lateness of the hour, the melancholy murmur of the wind in the trees, he forgot that she was rich and he a poor dependent, he only remembered that she was exquisitely fair and that he—poor fool!—was mad enough to worship her.

It was very dark now, for a bank of clouds hid the glory of the evening sky, and he could see only the mere outline of the woman whom he so passionately loved, the small head with the fluttering curls fanned by the wind, the graceful shoulders and arms folded primly across her bosom.

He put out his hand and found hers. Oh! the delight of raising it to his lips.

"By the heaven above us, Sue, by all my hopes of salvation I swear to you that my love is pure and selfless," he murmured tenderly, all the while that her fragrant little hand was pressed against his lips. "But for your fortune, I had come to you long ago and said to you 'Let me work for you!—My love will help me to carve a fortune for you, which it shall be my pride to place at your feet.'—Every nameless child, so 'tis said, may be a king's son. . . and I, who have no name that I can of verity call mine own—no father—no kith or kindred—I would conquer a kingdom, Sue, if you but loved me too."

His voice broke in a sob. Ashamed of his outburst he tried to hide his confusion from her, by sinking on one knee on that soft carpet of moss. From the little village of Acol beyond the wood, came the sound of the church bell striking the hour of nine. Sue was silent and absorbed, intensely sorrowful to see the grief of her friend. He was quite lost in the shadows at her feet now, but she could hear the stern efforts which he made to resume control over himself and his voice.

"Richard. . . good Richard," she said soothingly, "believe me, I am very, very sorry for this. . . I. . . I vow I did not know. . . I had no thought—how could I have? that you cared for me like. . . like this. . . You believe me, good master, do you not?" she entreated. "Say that you believe me, when I say that I would not willingly have caused you such grief."

"I believe that you are the most sweet and pure woman in all the world," he murmured fervently, "and that you are as far beyond my reach as are the stars."

"Nay, nay, good master, you must not talk like that. . . Truly, truly I am only a weak and foolish girl, and quite unworthy of your deep devotion. . . and you must try. . . indeed, indeed you must. . . to forget what happened under these trees to-night."

"Of that I pray you have no fear," he replied more calmly, as he rose and once more stood before her—a dark figure in the midst of the dark wood—immovable, almost impassive, with head bent and arms folded across his chest. "Nathless 'tis foolish for a nameless peasant even to talk of his honor, yet 'tis mine honor, Lady Sue, which will ever help me to remember that a mountain of gold and vast estates stand between me and the realization of my dream."

"No, no," she rejoined earnestly, "it is not that only. You are my friend, good Richard, and I do not wish to see you eating out your heart in vain and foolish regrets. What you. . . what you wish could never—never be. Good master, if you were rich to-morrow and I penniless, I could never be your wife."

"You mean that you could never love me?" he asked.

She was silent. A fierce wave of jealousy—mad, insane, elemental jealousy seemed suddenly to sweep over him.

"You love someone else?" he demanded brusquely.

"What right have you to ask?"

"The right of a man who would gladly die to see you happy."

He spoke harshly, almost brutally. Jealousy had killed all humility in him. Love—proud, passionate and defiant—stood up for its just claims, for its existence, its right to dominate, its desire to conquer.

But even as he thus stood before her, almost frightening her now by the violence of his speech, by the latent passion in him, which no longer would bear to be held in check, the bank of clouds which up to now had obscured the brilliance of the summer sky, finally swept away eastwards, revealing the luminous firmament and the pale crescent moon which now glimmered coldly through the branches of the trees.

A muffled sound as of someone treading cautiously the thick bed of moss, and the creaking of tiny twigs caused Richard Lambert to look up momentarily from the form of the girl whom he so dearly loved, and to peer beyond her into the weirdly illumined density of the wood.

Not twenty yards from where they were, a low wall divided the park itself from the wood beyond, which extended down to Acol village. At an angle of the wall there was an iron gate, also the tumble-down pavilion, ivy-grown and desolate, with stone steps leading up to it, through the cracks of which weeds and moss sprouted up apace.

A man had just emerged from out the thicket and was standing now to the farther side of the gate looking straight at Lambert and at Sue, who stood in the full light of the moon. A broad-brimmed hat, such as cavaliers affected, cast a dark shadow over his face.

It was a mere outline only vaguely defined against the background of trees, but in that outline Lambert had already recognized the mysterious stranger who lodged in his brother's cottage down in Acol.

The fixed intensity of the young man's gaze caused Sue to turn and to look in the same direction. She saw the stranger, who encountering two pairs of eyes fixed on him, raised his hat with a graceful flourish of the arm: then, with a short ironical laugh, went his way, and was once more lost in the gloom.

The girl instinctively made a movement as if to follow him, whilst a quickly smothered cry—half of joy and half of fear—escaped her lips. She checked the movement as well as the cry, but not before Richard Lambert had perceived both.

With the perception came the awful, overwhelming certitude.

"That adventurer!" he exclaimed involuntarily. "Oh my God!"

But she looked him full in the face, and threw back her head with a gesture of pride and of wrath.

"Master Lambert," she said haughtily, "methinks 'twere needless to remind you that—since I inadvertently revealed my most cherished secret to you—it were unworthy a man of honor to betray it to any one."

"My lady. . . Sue," he said, feeling half-dazed, bruised and crushed by the terrible moral blow, which he had just received, "I. . . I do not quite understand. Will you deign to explain?"

"There is naught to explain," she retorted coldly. "Prince Amédé d'Orléans loves me and I have plighted my troth to him."

"Nay! I entreat your ladyship," he said, feeling—knowing the while, how useless it was to make an appeal against the infatuation of a hot-headed and impulsive girl, yet speaking with the courage which ofttimes is born of despair, "I beg of you, on my knees to listen. This foreign adventurer. . ."

"Silence!" she retorted proudly, and drawing back from him, for of a truth he had sunk on his knees before her, "an you desire to be my friend, you must not breathe one word of slander against the man I love. . ."

Then, as he said nothing, realizing, indeed, how futile would be any effort or word from him, she said, with growing enthusiasm, whilst her glowing eyes fixed themselves upon the gloom which had enveloped the mysterious apparition of her lover:

"Prince Amédé d'Orléans is the grandest, most selfless patriot this world hath ever known. For the sake of France, of tyrannized, oppressed France, which he adores, he has sacrificed everything! his position, his home, his wealth and vast estates: he is own kinsman to King Louis, yet he is exiled from his country whilst a price is set upon his head, because he cannot be mute whilst he sees tyranny and oppression grind down the people of France. He could return to Paris to-day a rich and free man, a prince among his kindred,—if he would but sacrifice that for which he fights so bravely: the liberty of France!"

"Sue! my adored lady," he entreated, "in the name of Heaven listen to me. . . You do believe, do you not, that I am your friend? . . . I would give my life for you. . . I swear to you that you have been deceived and tricked by this adventurer, who, preying upon your romantic imagination. . ."

"Silence, master, an you value my friendship!" she commanded. "I will not listen to another word. Nay! you should be thankful that I deal not more harshly with you—that I make allowances for your miserable jealousy. . . Oh! why did you make me say that," she added with one of those swift changes of mood, which were so characteristic of her, and with sudden contrition, for an involuntary moan had escaped his lips. "In the name of Heaven, go—go now I entreat. . . leave me to myself. . . lest anger betray me into saying cruel things. . . I am safe—quite safe. . . I entreat you to let me return to the house alone."

Her voice sounded more and more broken as she spoke: sobs were evidently rising in her throat. He pulled himself together, feeling that it were unmanly to worry her now, when emotion was so obviously overmastering her.

"Forgive me, sweet lady," he said quite gently, as he rose from his knees. "I said more than I had any right to say. I entreat you to forgive the poor, presuming peasant who hath dared to raise his eyes to the fairy princess of his dreams. I pray you to try and forget all that hath happened to-night beneath the shadows of these elms—and only to remember one thing: that my life—my lonely, humble, unimportant life—is yours. . . to serve or help you, to worship or comfort you if need be. . . and that there could be no greater happiness for me than to give it for your sweet sake."

He bowed very low, until his hand could reach the hem of her kirtle, which he then raised to his lips. She was infinitely sorry for him; all her anger against him had vanished.

He was very reluctant to go, for this portion of the park was some distance from the house. But she had commanded and he quite understood that she wished to be alone: love such as that which he felt for his sweet lady is ever watchful, yet ever discreet. Was it not natural that she did not care to look on him after he had angered her so?

She seemed impatient too, and although her feelings towards him had softened, she repeated somewhat nervously: "I pray you go! Good master, I would be alone."

Lambert hesitated a while longer, he looked all round him as if suspicious of any marauders that might be lurking about. The hour was not very late, and had she not commanded him to go?

Nor would he seem to pry on her movements. Having once made up his mind to obey, he did so without reserve. Having kissed the hem of her kirtle he turned towards the house.

BARONESS EMMUSKA ORCZY

He meant to keep on the tiny footpath, which she would be bound to traverse after him, when she returned. He felt sure that something would warn him if she really needed his help.

The park and woodland were still: only the mournful hooting of an owl, the sad sighing of the wind in the old elms broke the peaceful silence of this summer's night.

VII

THE STRANGER WITHIN THE GATES

Sue waited—expectant and still—until the last sound of the young man's footsteps had died away in the direction of the house.

Then with quick impulsive movements she ran to the gate; her hands sought impatiently in the dark for the primitive catch which held it to. A large and rusty bolt! she pulled at it—clumsily, for her hands were trembling. At last the gate flew open; she was out in the woods, peering into the moonlit thicket, listening for that most welcome sound, the footsteps of the man she loved.

"My prince!" she exclaimed, for already he was beside her—apparently he had lain in wait for her, and now held her in his arms.

"My beautiful and gracious lady," he murmured in that curiously muffled voice of his, which seemed to endow his strange personality with additional mystery.

"You heard? . . . you saw just now? . . ." she asked timidly, fearful of encountering his jealous wrath, that vehement temper of his which she had learned to dread.

Strangely enough he replied quite gently: "Yes. . . I saw. . . the young man loves you, my beautiful Suzanne! . . . and he will hate me now. . ."

He had always called her Suzanne—and her name thus spoken by him, and with that quaint foreign intonation of his had always sounded infinitely sweet.

"But I love you with all my heart," she said earnestly, tenderly, her whole soul—young, ardent, full of romance, going out to him with all the strength of its purity and passion. "What matter if all the world were against you?"

As a rule when they met thus on the confines of the wood, they would stand together by the gate, forming plans, talking of the future and of their love. Then after a while they would stroll into the park, he escorting her, as far as he might approach the house without being seen.

She had no thought that Richard Lambert would be on the watch. Nay! so wholly absorbed was she in her love for this man, once she was in his presence, that already—womanlike—she had forgotten the young student's impassioned avowal, his jealousy, his very existence.

And she loved these evening strolls in the great, peaceful park, at evening, when the birds were silent in their nests, and the great shadows of ivy-covered elms enveloped her and her romance. From afar a tiny light gleamed here and there in some of the windows of Acol Court.

She had hated the grim, bare house at first, so isolated in the midst of the forests of Thanet, so like the eyrie of a bird of prey.

But now she loved the whole place; the bit of ill-kept tangled garden, with its untidy lawn and weed-covered beds, in which a few standard rose-trees strove to find a permanent home; she loved the dark and mysterious park, the rusty gate, that wood with its rich carpet which varied as each season came around.

To-night her lover was more gentle than had been his wont of late. They walked cautiously through the park, for the moon was brilliant and outlined every object with startling vividness. The trees here were sparser. Close by was the sunk fence and the tiny rustic bridge—only a plank or two—which spanned it.

Some thirty yards ahead of them they could see the dark figure of Richard Lambert walking towards the house.

"One more stroll beneath the trees, *ma mie*," he said lightly, "you'll not wish to encounter your ardent suitor again."

She loved him in this brighter mood, when he had thrown from him that mantle of jealousy and mistrust which of late had sat on him so ill.

He seemed to have set himself the task of pleasing her to-night—of making her forget, mayhap, the wooing of the several suitors who had hung round her to-day. He talked to her—always in that mysterious, muffled voice, with the quaint rolling of the r's and the foreign intonation of the vowels—he talked to her of King Louis and his tyranny over the people of France: of his own political aims to which he had already sacrificed fortune, position, home. Of his own brilliant past at the most luxurious court the world had ever known. He fired her enthusiasm, delighted her imagination, enchained her soul to his: she was literally swept off the prosy face of this earth and whirled into a realm of romance, enchanting, intoxicating, mystic—almost divine.

She forgot fleeting time, and did not even hear the church bell over at Acol village striking the hour of ten.

He had to bring her back to earth, and to guide her reluctant footsteps again towards the house. But she was too happy to part from him so easily. She forced him to escort her over the little bridge, under the pretense of terror at the lateness of the hour. She vowed that he could not be perceived from the house, since all the lights were out, and everyone indeed must be abed. Her guardian's windows, moreover, gave on the other side of the house; and he of a surety would not be moon or star gazing at this hour of the night.

Her mood was somewhat reckless. The talk with which he had filled her ears had gone to her brain like wine. She felt intoxicated with the atmosphere of mystery, of selfless patriotism, of great and fallen fortunes, with which he knew so well how to surround himself. Mayhap, that in her innermost heart now there was a scarce conscious desire to precipitate a crisis, to challenge discovery, to step boldly before her guardian, avowing her love, demanding the right to satisfy it.

She refused to bid him adieu save at the garden door. Three steps led up straight into the dining-room from the flagged pathway which skirted the house. She ran up these steps, silently and swiftly as a little mouse, and then turned her proud and happy face to him.

"Good-night, sweet prince," she whispered, extending her delicate hand to him.

She stood in the full light of the moon dominating him from the top of the steps, an exquisite vision of youth and beauty and romance.

He took off his broad-brimmed hat, but his face was still in shadow, for the heavy perruque fell in thick dark curls covering both his cheeks. He bent very low and kissed the tips of her fingers.

"When shall we meet again, my prince?" she asked.

"This day week, an it please you, my queen," he murmured.

And then he turned to go. She meant to stand there and watch him cross the tangled lawn, and the little bridge, and to see him lose himself amidst the great shadows of the park.

But he had scarce gone a couple of steps when a voice, issuing from the doorway close behind her, caused her to turn in quick alarm.

"Sue! in the name of Heaven! what doth your ladyship here and at this hour?"

The crisis which the young girl had almost challenged, had indeed arrived. Mistress de Chavasse—carrying a lighted and guttering candle, was standing close behind her. At the sound of her voice and Sue's little cry of astonishment rather than fear, Prince Amédé d'Orléans too, had paused, with a muttered curse on his lips, his foot angrily tapping the flagstones.

But it were unworthy a gallant gentleman of the most chivalrous Court in the world to beat a retreat when his mistress was in danger of an unpleasant quarter of an hour.

Sue was more than a little inclined to be defiant.

"Mistress de Chavasse," she said quietly, "will you be good enough to explain by what right you have spied on me to-night? Hath my guardian perchance set you to dog my footsteps?"

"There was no thought in my mind of spying on your ladyship," rejoined Mistress de Chavasse coldly. "I was troubled in my sleep and came downstairs because I heard a noise, and feared those midnight marauders of which we have heard so much of late. I myself had locked this door, and was surprised to find it unlatched. I opened it and saw you standing there."

"Then we'll all to bed, fair mistress," rejoined Sue gayly. She was too happy, too sure of herself and of her lover to view this sudden discovery of her secret with either annoyance or alarm. She would be free in three months, and he would be faithful to her. Love proverbially laughs at bars and bolts, and even if her stern guardian, apprised of her evening wanderings, prevented her from seeing her prince for the next three months, pshaw! a hundred days at most, and nothing could keep her from his side.

"Good-night, fair prince," she repeated tenderly, extending her hand towards her lover once more, while throwing a look of proud defiance to Mistress de Chavasse. He could not help but return to the foot of the steps; any pusillanimity on his part at this juncture, any reluctance to meet Editha face to face or to bear the brunt of her reproaches and of her sneers, might jeopardize the romance of his personality in the eyes of Sue. Therefore he boldly took her hand and kissed it with mute fervor.

She gave a happy little laugh and added pertly:

"Good-night, mistress. . . I'll leave you to make your own adieux to Monseigneur le Prince d'Orléans. I'll warrant that you and he—despite the lateness of the hour—will have much to say to one another."

And without waiting to watch the issue of her suggestion, her eyes dancing with mischief, she turned and ran singing and laughing into the house.

VIII

Prince Amédé D'Orléans

At first it seemed as if the stranger meant to beat a precipitate and none too dignified retreat now that the adoring eyes of Lady Sue were no longer upon him. But Mistress de Chavasse had no intention of allowing him to extricate himself quite so easily from an unpleasant position.

"One moment, master," she said loudly and peremptorily. "Prince or whatever you may wish to call yourself. . . ere you show me a clean pair of heels, I pray you to explain your presence here on Sir Marmaduke's doorstep at ten o'clock at night, and in company with his ward."

For a moment—a second or two only—the stranger appeared to hesitate. He paused with one foot still on the lowest of the stone steps, the other on the flagged path, his head bent, his hand upraised in the act of re-adjusting his broad-brimmed hat.

Then a sudden thought seemed to strike him, he threw back his head, gave a short laugh as if he were pleased with this new thought, then turned, meeting Mistress de Chavasse's stern gaze squarely and fully. He threw his hat down upon the steps and crossed his arms over his chest.

"One moment, mistress?" he said with an ironical bow. "I do not need one moment. I have already explained."

"Explained? how?" she retorted, "nay! I'll not be trifled with, master, and methinks you will find that Sir Marmaduke de Chavasse will expect some explanation—which will prove unpleasant to yourself—for your unwarrantable impudence in daring to approach his ward."

He put up his hand in gentle deprecation.

"Impudence? Oh, mistress?" he said reproachfully.

"Let me assure you, master," she continued with relentless severity, "that you were wise an you returned straightway to your lodgings now. . . packed your worldly goods and betook yourself and them to anywhere you please."

"Ah!" he sighed gently, "that is impossible."

"You would dare? . . ." she retorted.

"I would dare remain there, where my humble presence is most desired—beside the gracious lady who honors me with her love."

"You are insolent, master. . . and Sir Marmaduke. . ."

"Oh!" he rejoined lightly, "Sir Marmaduke doth not object."

"There, I fear me, you are in error, master! and in his name I now forbid you ever to attempt to speak to Lady Susannah Aldmarshe again."

This command, accompanied by a look of withering scorn, seemed to afford the stranger vast entertainment. He made the wrathful lady a low, ironical bow, and clapped his hands together laughing and exclaiming:

"Brava! brava! of a truth but this is excellent! Pray, mistress, will you deign to tell me if in this your bidding you have asked Sir Marmaduke for his opinion?"

"I need not to ask him. I ask you to go."

"Go? Whither?" he asked blandly.

"Out of my sight and off these grounds at once, ere I rouse the servants and have you whipped off like a dog!" she said, angered beyond measure at his audacity, his irony, his manner, suggestive of insolent triumph. His muffled voice with its curious foreign accent irritated her, as did the shadow of his perruque over his brow, and the black silk shade which he wore over one eye.

Even now in response to her violent outburst he broke into renewed laughter.

"Better and better! Ah, mistress," he said with a shake of the head, "of a truth you are more blind than I thought."

"You are more insolent, master, than I had thought possible."

"Yet meseems, fair lady, that in the lonely and mysterious stranger you might have remembered your humble and devoted servant," he said, drawing his figure up towards her.

"You! an old friend!" she said contemptuously. "I have ne'er set eyes on you in my life before."

"To think that the moon should be so treacherous," he rejoined imperturbably. "Will you not look a little closer, fair mistress, the shadows are somewhat dark, mayhap."

She felt his one eye fixed upon her with cold intentness, a strange feeling of superstitious dread suddenly crept over her from head to foot. Like a bird fascinated by a snake she came a little nearer, down the steps, towards him, her eyes, too, riveted on his face, that curious face of his, surrounded by the heavy perruque hiding ears and cheeks, the mouth overshadowed by the dark mustache, one eye concealed beneath the black silk shade.

He seemed amused at her terror and as she came nearer to him, he too, advanced a little until their eyes met—his, mocking, amused, restless; hers, intent and searching.

Thus they gazed at one another for a few seconds, whilst silence reigned around and the moon peered down cold and chaste from above, illumining the old house, the neglected garden, the vast park with its innumerable dark secrets and the mysteries which it hid.

She was the first to step back, to recoil before the ironical intensity of that fixed gaze. She felt as if she were in a dream, as if a nightmare assailed her, which in her wakeful hours would be dissipated by reason, by common sense, by sound and sober fact.

She even passed her hand across her eyes as if to sweep away from before her vision, a certain image which fancy had conjured up.

His laugh—strident and mocking—roused her from this dreamlike state.

"I. . . I. . . do not understand," she murmured.

"Yet it is so simple," he replied, "did you not ask me awhile ago if nothing could be done?"

"Who. . . who are you?" she whispered, and then repeated once again: "Who are you?"

"I am His Royal Highness, Prince Amédé d'Orléans," said Sir Marmaduke de Chavasse lightly, "the kinsman of His Majesty, King Louis of France, the mysterious foreigner who works for the religious and political freedom of his country, and on whose head *le roi soleil* hath set a price. . . and who, moreover, hath enflamed the romantic imagination of a beautiful young girl, thus winning her ardent love in the present and in the near future together with her vast fortune and estates."

He made a movement as if to remove his perruque but she stopped him with a gesture. She had understood. And in the brilliant moonlight a complete revelation of his personality might prove dangerous. Lady Sue herself might still—for aught they knew—be standing in the dark room behind—unseen yet on the watch.

He seemed vastly amused at her terror, and boldly took the hand with which she had arrested his act of total revelation.

"Nay! do you recognize your humble servant at last, fair Editha?" he queried. "On my honor, madam, Lady Sue is deeply enamored of me. What think you of my chances now?"

"You? You?" she repeated at intervals, mechanically, dazed still, lost in a whirl of conflicting emotions wherein fear, amazement, and a certain vein of superstitious horror fought a hard battle in her dizzy brain.

"The risks," she murmured more coherently.

"Bah!"

"If she discover you, before. . . before. . ."

"Before she is legally my wife? Pshaw! . . . Then of a truth my scheme will come to naught. . . But will you not own, Editha, that 'tis worth the risk?"

"Afterwards?" she asked, "afterwards?"

"Afterwards, mistress," he rejoined enigmatically, "afterwards sits on the knees of the gods."

And with a flourish of his broad-brimmed hat he turned on his heel and anon was lost in the shadows of the tall yew hedge.

How long she stood there watching that spot whereon he had been standing, she could not say. Presently she shivered; the night had turned cold. She heard the cry of some small bird attacked by a midnight prowler; was it the sparrow-hawk after its prey?

From the other side of the house came the sound of slow and firm footsteps, then the opening and shutting of a door.

Sir Marmaduke de Chavasse had played his part for to-night: silently as he had gone, so he returned to his room, whilst in another corner of the sparrow-hawk's nest a young girl slept, dreaming dreams of patriots and heroes, of causes nobly won, of poverty and obscurity gloriously endured.

Mistress de Chavasse with a sigh half of regret, half of indifference, finally turned her back on the moonlit garden and went within.

IX

Secret Service

Master Hymn-of-Praise Busy was excessively perturbed. Matters at the Court were taking a curious turn. That something of unusual moment had happened within the last few days he was thoroughly convinced, and still having it in his mind that he was especially qualified for the lucrative appointments in my Lord Protector's secret service—he thought this an excellent opportunity for perfecting himself in the art of investigation, shrewdly conducted, which he understood to be most essential for the due fulfillment of such appointments.

Thus we see him some few days later on a late afternoon, with back bent nearly double, eyes fixed steadily on the ground and his face a perfect mirror of thoughtful concentration within, slowly walking along the tiny footpath which wound in and out the groups of majestic elms in the park.

Musing and meditating, at times uttering strange and enigmatical exclamations, he reached the confines of the private grounds, the spot where the surrounding wall gave place to a low iron gate, where the disused pavilion stood out gray and forlorn-looking in the midst of the soft green of the trees, and where through the woods beyond the gate, could just be perceived the tiny light which issued from the blacksmith's cottage, the most outlying one in the village of Acol.

Master Hymn-of-Praise leaned thoughtfully against the ivy-covered wall. His eyes, roaming, searching, restless, pried all around him.

"Footprints!" he mused, "footprints which of a surety must mean that human foot hath lately trod this moss. Footprints moreover, which lead up the steps to the door of that pavilion, wherein to my certain knowledge, no one hath had access of late."

Something, of course, was going on at Acol Court, that strange and inexplicable something which he had tried to convey by covert suggestion to Mistress Charity's female—therefore inferior—brain.

Sir Marmaduke's temper was more sour and ill even than of yore, and there was still an unpleasant sensation in the lumbar regions of Master Busy's spine, whenever he sat down, which recalled a somewhat vigorous outburst of his master's ill-humor.

Mistress de Chavasse went about the house like a country wench frightened by a ghost, and Mistress Charity averred that she seldom went to bed now before midnight. Certain it is that Master Busy himself had met the lady wandering about the house candle in hand at an hour when all respectable folk should be abed, and when she almost fell up against Hymn-of-Praise in the dark she gave a frightened scream as if she had suddenly come face to face with the devil.

Then there was her young ladyship.

She was neither ill-tempered nor yet under the ban of fear, but Master Busy vowed unto himself that she was suffering from ill-concealed melancholy, from some hidden secret or wild romance. She seldom laughed, she had spoken with discourtesy and impatience to Squire Pyncheon, who rode over the other day on purpose to bring her a bunch of sweet marjoram which grew in great profusion in his mother's garden: she markedly avoided the company of her guardian, and wandered about the park alone, at all hours of the day—a proceeding which in a young lady of her rank was quite unseemly.

All these facts neatly docketed in Master Busy's orderly brain, disturbed him not a little. He had not yet made up his mind as to the nature of the mystery which was surrounding the Court and its inmates, but vaguely he thought of abductions and elopements, which the presence of the richest heiress in the South of England in the house of the poorest squire in the whole country, more than foreshadowed.

This lonely, somewhat eerie corner of the park appeared to be the center around which all the mysterious happenings revolved, and Master Hymn-of-Praise had found his way hither on this fine July afternoon, because he had distinct hopes of finding out something definite, certain facts which he then could place before Squire Boatfield who was major-general of the district, and who would then, doubtless, commend him for his ability and shrewdness in forestalling what might prove to be a terrible crime.

The days were getting shorter now; it was little more than eight o'clock and already the shades of evening were drawing closely in: the last rays of the setting sun had long disappeared in a glowing haze of gold, and the fantastic branches of the old elms, intertwined with the parasitic ivy looked grim and threatening, silhouetted against the lurid after glow. Master Busy liked neither the solitude, nor yet the silence of the woods; he had just caught sight of a bat circling over the dilapidated roof of the pavilion, and he hated bats. Though he belonged to a community which denied the angels and ignored the saints, he had a firm belief in the existence of a tangible devil, and somehow he could not dissociate his ideas of hell and of evil spirits from those which related to the mysterious flutterings of bats.

Moreover he thought that his duties in connection with the science of secret investigation, had been sufficiently fulfilled for the day, and he prepared to wend his way back to the house, when the sound of voices, once more aroused his somnolent attention.

"Someone," he murmured within himself, "the heiress and the abductor mayhap."

This might prove the opportunity of his life, the chance which would place him within the immediate notice of the major-general, perhaps of His Highness the Protector himself. He felt that to vacate his post of observation at this moment would be unworthy the moral discipline which an incipient servant of the Commonwealth should impose upon himself.

Striving to smother a sense of terror, or to disguise it even to himself under the mask of officiousness, he looked about for a hiding-place—a post of observation as he called it.

A tree with invitingly forked branches seemed to be peculiarly adapted to his needs. Hymn-of-Praise was neither very young nor very agile, but dreams of coming notoriety lent nimbleness to his limbs.

By the time that the voices drew nearer, the sober butler of Acol Court was installed astride an elm bough, hidden by the dense foliage and by the leaf-laden strands of ivy, enfolded by the fast gathering shadows of evening, supremely uncomfortable physically, none too secure on his perch, yet proud and satisfied in the consciousness of fulfilled duty.

The next moment he caught sight of Mistress Charity—Mistress Charity so please you, who had plighted her troth to him, walking arm in arm with Master Courage Toogood, as impudent, insolent and debauched a young jackanapes as ever defaced the forests of Thanet.

"Mistress, fair mistress," he was sighing, and murmuring in her ear, "the most beautiful and gracious thing on God's earth, when I hold you pressed thus against my beating heart. . ."

Apparently his feelings were too deep to be expressed in the words of his own vocabulary, for he paused a while, sighed audibly, and then asked anxiously:

"You do hear my heart beating, mistress, do you not?"

She blushed, for she was naught but a female baggage, and though Master Busy's impassioned protestations of less than half an hour ago, must be still ringing in her ears, she declared emphatically that she could hear the throbbing of that young vermin's heart.

Master Busy up aloft was quite sure that what she heard was a few sheep and cattle of Sir Marmaduke's who were out to grass in a field close by, and had been scared into a canter.

What went on for the next moment or two the saintly man on the elm tree branch could not rightly perceive, but the next words from Mistress Charity's lips sent a thrill of indignation through his heart.

"Oh! Master Courage," she said with a little cry, "you must not squeeze me so! I vow you have taken the breath out of my body! The Lord love you, child! think you I can stay here all this while and listen to your nonsense?"

"Just one minute longer, fair mistress," entreated the young reprobate, "the moon is not yet up, the birds have gone to their nests for sleep, will ye not tarry a while here with me? That old fool Busy will never know!"

It is a fact that at this juncture the saintly man well-nigh fell off his perch, and when Master Courage, amidst many coy shrieks from the fickle female, managed to drag her down beside him, upon the carpet of moss immediately beneath the very tree whereon Hymn-of-Praise was holding watch, the unfortunate man had need of all his strength of mind and of purpose not to jump down with both feet upon the lying face of that young limb of Satan.

But he felt that the discovery of his somewhat undignified position by these two evil-doers would not at this moment be quite opportune, so he endeavored to maintain his equilibrium at the cost of supreme discomfort, and the loud cracking of the branch on which he was perched.

Mistress Charity gave a cry of terror.

"What was that?"

"Nothing, nothing, mistress, I swear," rejoined Courage reassuringly, "there are always noises in old elm trees, the ivy hangs heavy and. . ."

"I have heard it said of late that the pavilion is haunted," she murmured under her breath.

"No! not haunted, mistress! I vow 'tis but the crackling of loose branches, and there is that which I would whisper in your ear. . ."

But before Master Courage had the time to indulge in this, the desire of his heart, something fell upon the top of his lean head which certainly never grew on the elm tree overhead. Having struck his lanky hair the object fell straight into his lap.

It was a button. An ordinary, brown, innocent enough looking button. But still a button. Master Courage took it in his hand and examined it carefully, turning it over once or twice. The little thing certainly wore a familiar air. Master Courage of a truth had seen such an one before.

"That thing never grew up there, master," said Mistress Charity in an agitated whisper.

"No!" he rejoined emphatically, "nor yet doth a button form part of the habiliments of a ghost."

But not a sound came from above: and though Courage and Charity peered upwards with ever-increasing anxiety, the fast gathering darkness effectually hid the mystery which lurked within that elm.

"I vow that there's something up there, mistress," said the youth with sudden determination.

"Could it be bats, master?" she queried with a shudder.

"Nay! but bats do not wear buttons," he replied sententiously. "Yet of a surety, I mean to make an investigation of the affair as that old fool Hymn-of-Praise would say."

Whereupon, heedless of Mistress Charity's ever-growing agitation, he ran towards the boundary wall of the park, and vaulted the low gate with an agile jump even as she uttered a pathetic appeal to him not to leave her alone in the dark.

Fear had rooted the girl to the spot. She dared not move away, fearful lest her running might entice that mysterious owner of the brown button to hurry in her track. Yet she would have loved to follow Master Courage, and to put at least a gate and wall between herself and those terrible elms.

She was just contemplating a comprehensive and vigorous attack of hysterics when she heard Master Courage's voice from the other side of the gate.

"Hist! Hist, mistress! Quick!"

She gathered up what shreds of valor she possessed and ran blindly in the direction whence came the welcome voice.

"I pray you take this," said the youth, who was holding a wooden bucket out over the gate, "whilst I climb back to you."

"But what is it, master?" she asked, as—obeying him mechanically—she took the bucket from him. It was heavy, for it was filled almost to the brim with a liquid which seemed very evil-smelling.

The next moment Master Courage was standing beside her. He took the bucket from her and then walked as rapidly as he could with it back towards the elm tree.

"It will help me to dislodge the bats, mistress," he said enigmatically, speaking over his shoulder as he walked.

She followed him—excited but timorous—until together they once more reached the spot, where Master Courage's amorous declarations had been so rudely interrupted. He put the bucket down beside him, and rubbed his hands together whilst uttering certain sounds which betrayed his glee.

Then only did she notice that he was carrying under one arm a long curious-looking instrument—round and made of tin, with a handle at one end.

She looked curiously into the bucket and at the instrument.

"'Tis the tar-water used for syringing the cattle," she whispered, "ye must not touch it, master. Where did you find it?"

"Just by the wall," he rejoined. "I knew it was kept there. They wash the sheep with it to destroy the vermin in them. This is the squirt for it," he added calmly, placing the end of the instrument in the liquid, "and I will mayhap destroy the vermin which is lodged in that elm tree."

A cry of terror issuing from above froze the very blood in Mistress Charity's veins.

"Stop! stop! you young limb of Satan!" came from Master Busy's nearly choking throat.

"It's evildoers or evil spirits, master," cried Mistress Charity in an agony of fear.

"Whatever it be, mistress, this should destroy it!" said Master Courage philosophically, as turning the syringe upwards he squirted the whole of its contents straight into the fork of the ivy-covered branches.

There was a cry of rage, followed by a cry of terror, then Master Hymn-of-Praise Busy with a terrific clatter of breaking boughs, fell in a heap upon the soft carpet of moss.

Master Courage be it said to the eternal shame of venturesome youth, took incontinently to his heels, leaving Mistress Charity to bear the brunt of the irate saintly man's wrath.

Master Busy, we must admit had but little saintliness left in him now. Let us assume that—as he explained afterwards—he was not immediately aware of Mistress Charity's presence, and that his own sense of propriety and of decorum had been drowned in a cataract of tar water. Certain it is that a volley of oaths, which would have surprised Sir Marmaduke himself, escaped his lips.

Had he not every excuse? He was dripping from head to foot, spluttering, blinded, choked and bruised.

He shook himself like a wet spaniel. Then hearing the sound of a smothered exclamation which did not seem altogether unlike a giggle, he turned round savagely and perceived the dim outline of Mistress Charity's dainty figure.

"The Lord love thee, Master Hymn-of-Praise," she began, somewhat nervously, "but you have made yourself look a sight."

"And by G—d I'll make that young jackanapes look a sight ere I take my hand off him," he retorted savagely.

"But what were you. . . hem! what wert thou doing up in the elm tree, friend Hymn-of-Praise?" she asked demurely.

"Thee me no thou!" he said with enigmatic pompousness, followed by a distinctly vicious snarl, "Master Busy will be my name in future for a saucy wench like thee."

He turned towards the house. Mistress Charity following meekly—somewhat subdued, for Master Busy was her affianced husband, and she had no mind to mar her future, through any of young Courage's dare-devil escapades.

"Thou wouldst wish to know what I was doing up in that forked tree?" he asked her with calm dignity after a while, when the hedges of the flower garden came in sight. "I was making a home for thee, according to the commands of the Lord."

"Not in the elm trees of a surety, Master Busy?"

"I was making a home for thee," he repeated without heeding her flippant observation, "by rendering myself illustrious. I told thee, wench, did I not? that something was happening within the precincts of Acol Court, and that it is my duty to lie in wait and to watch. The heiress is about to be abducted, and it is my task to frustrate the evil designs of the mysterious criminal."

She looked at him in speechless amazement. He certainly looked strangely weird in the semi-darkness with his lanky hair plastered against his cheeks, his collar half torn from round his neck, the dripping, oily substance flowing in rivulets from his garments down upon the ground.

The girl had no longer any desire to laugh, and when Master Busy strode majestically across the rustic bridge, then over the garden

BARONESS EMMUSKA ORCZY

paths to the kitchen quarter of the house, she followed him without a word, awed by his extraordinary utterances, vaguely feeling that in his dripping garments he somehow reminded her of Jonah and the whale.

X

Avowed Enmity

The pavilion had been built some fifty years ago, by one of the Spantons of Acol who had a taste for fanciful architecture.

It had been proudly held by several deceased representatives of the family to be the reproduction of a Greek temple. It certainly had columns supporting the portico, and steps leading thence to the ground. It was also circular in shape and was innocent of windows, deriving its sole light from the door, when it was open.

The late Sir Jeremy, I believe, had been very fond of the place. Being of a somewhat morose and taciturn disposition, he liked the seclusion of this lonely corner of the park. He had a chair or two put into the pavilion and 'twas said that he indulged there in the smoking of that fragrant weed which of late had been more generously imported into this country.

After Sir Jeremy's death, the pavilion fell into disuse. Sir Marmaduke openly expressed his dislike of the forlorn hole, as he was wont to call it. He caused the door to be locked, and since then no one had entered the little building. The key, it was presumed, had been lost; the lock certainly looked rusty. The roof, too, soon fell into disrepair, and no doubt within, the place soon became the prey of damp and mildew, the nest of homing birds, or the lair of timid beasts. Very soon the proud copy of an archaic temple took on that miserable and forlorn look peculiar to uninhabited spots.

From an air of abandonment to that of eeriness was but a step, and now the building towered in splendid isolation, in this remote corner of the park, at the confines of the wood, with a reputation for being the abode of ghosts, of bats and witches, and other evil things.

When Master Busy sought for tracks of imaginary criminals bent on abducting the heiress he naturally drifted to this lonely spot; when Master Courage was bent on whispering sweet nothings into the ear of the other man's betrothed, he enticed her to that corner of the park where he was least like to meet the heavy-booted saint.

Thus it was that these three met on the one spot where as a rule at a late hour of the evening Prince Amédé d'Orléans was wont to commence his wanderings, sure of being undisturbed, and with the final disappearance of Master Busy and Mistress Charity the place was once more deserted.

The bats once more found delight in this loneliness and from all around came that subdued murmur, that creaking of twigs, that silence so full of subtle sounds, which betrays the presence of animal life on the prowl.

Anon there came the harsh noise of a key grating in a rusty lock. The door of the pavilion was cautiously opened from within and the mysterious French prince, bewigged, booted and hatted, emerged into the open. The night had drawn a singularly dark mantle over the woods. Banks of cloud obscured the sky; the tall elm trees with their ivy-covered branches, and their impenetrable shadows beneath, formed a dense wall which the sight of human creatures was not keen enough to pierce. Sir Marmaduke de Chavasse, in spite of this darkness, which he hailed gleefully, peered cautiously and intently round as he descended the steps.

He had not met Lady Sue in the capacity of her romantic lover since that evening a week ago, when his secret had been discovered by Mistress de Chavasse. The last vision he had had of the young girl was one redolent of joy and love and trust, sufficient to reassure him that all was well with her, in regard to his schemes; but on that same evening a week ago he had gazed upon another little scene, which had not filled him with either joy or security.

He had seen Lady Sue standing beside a young man whose personality—to say the least—was well-nigh as romantic as that of the exiled scion of the house of Orléans. He had seen rather than heard a young and passionate nature pouring into girlish ears the avowal of an unselfish and ardent love which had the infinite merit of being real and true.

However well he himself might play his part of selfless hero and of vehement lover, there always lurked the danger that the falseness of his protestations would suddenly ring a warning note to the subtle sense of the confiding girl. Were it not for the intense romanticism of her disposition, which beautified and exalted everything with which it came in contact, she would of a surety have detected the lie ere this. He had acted his dual rôle with consummate skill, the contrast between the surly Puritanical guardian, with his round cropped head and shaven face, and the elegantly dressed cavalier, with a heavy mustache, an enormous perruque and a shade over one eye, was so complete that even Mistress de Chavasse—alert, suspicious, wholly unromantic, had been momentarily deceived, and would have remained so but for his voluntary revelation of himself.

But the watchful and disappointed young lover was the real danger: a danger complicated by the fact that the Prince Amédé d'Orléans actually dwelt in the cottage owned by Lambert's brother, the blacksmith. The mysterious prince had perforce to dwell somewhere; else, whenever spied by a laborer or wench from the village, he would have excited still further comment, and his movements mayhap would have been more persistently dogged.

For this reason Sir Marmaduke had originally chosen Adam Lambert's cottage to be his headquarters; it stood on the very outskirts of the village and as he had only the wood to traverse between it and the pavilion where he effected his change of personality, he ran thus but few risks of meeting prying eyes. Moreover, Adam Lambert, the blacksmith, and the old woman who kept house for him, both belonged to the new religious sect which Judge Bennett had so pertinently dubbed the Quakers, and they kept themselves very much aloof from gossip and the rest of the village.

True, Richard Lambert oft visited his brother and the old woman, but did so always in the daytime when Prince Amédé d'Orléans carefully kept out of the way. Sir Marmaduke de Chavasse had all the true instincts of the beast or bird of prey. He prowled about in the dark, and laid his snares for the seizure of his victim under cover of the night.

This evening certain new schemes had found birth in his active mind; he was impatient that the victim tarried, when his brain was alive with thoughts of how to effect a more speedy capture. He leaned against the wall, close by the gate as was his wont when awaiting Sue, smiling grimly to himself at thought of the many little subterfuges she would employ to steal out of the house, without encountering—as she thought—her watchful guardian.

A voice close behind him—speaking none too kindly—broke in on his meditations, causing him to start—almost to crouch like a frightened cat.

The next moment he had recognized the gruff and nasal tones of Adam Lambert. Apparently the blacksmith had just come from the wood through the gate, and had almost stumbled in the dark against the rigid figure of his mysterious lodger.

"Friend, what dost thou here?" he asked peremptorily. But already Sir Marmaduke had recovered from that sudden sense of fear which had caused him to start in alarm.

"I would ask the same question of you, my friend," he retorted airily, speaking in the muffled voice and with the markedly foreign accent which he had assumed for the rôle of the Prince, "might I inquire what you are doing here?"

"I have to see a sick mare down Minster way," replied Lambert curtly, "this is a short cut thither, and Sir Marmaduke hath granted me leave. But he liketh not strangers loitering in his park."

"Then, friend," rejoined the other lightly, "when Sir Marmaduke doth object to my strolling in his garden, he will doubtless apprise me of the fact, without interference from you."

Adam Lambert, after his uncivil greeting of his lodger, had already turned his back on him, loath to have further speech with a man whom he hated and despised.

Like the majority of country folk these days, the blacksmith had a wholesale contempt for every foreigner, and more particularly for those who hailed from France: that country—in the estimation of all Puritans, Dissenters and Republicans—being the happy abode of every kind of immorality and debauchery.

Prince Amédé d'Orléans—as he styled himself—with his fantastic clothes, his airs and graces and long, curly hair was an object of special aversion to the Quaker, even though the money which the despised foreigner paid for his lodgings was passing welcome these hard times.

Adam resolutely avoided speech with the Prince, whenever possible, but the latter's provocative and sarcastic speech roused his dormant hatred; like a dog who has been worried, he now turned abruptly round and faced Sir Marmaduke, stepping close up to him, his eyes glaring with vindictive rage, a savage snarl rising in his throat.

"Take notice, friend," he said hoarsely, "that I'll not bear thine impudence. Thou mayest go and bully the old woman at the cottage when I am absent—Oh! I've heard thee!" he added with unbridled savagery, "ordering her about as if she were thy serving wench. . . but let me tell thee that she is no servant of thine, nor I. . . so have done, my fine prince. . . dost understand?"

"Prithee, friend, do not excite yourself," said Sir Marmaduke blandly, drawing back against the wall as far as he could to avoid close proximity with his antagonist. "I have never wished to imply that Mistress

Lambert was aught but my most obliging, most amiable landlady—nor have I, to my certain knowledge, overstepped the privileges of a lodger. I trust that your worthy aunt hath no cause for complaint. Mistress Lambert is your aunt?" he added superciliously, "is she not?"

"That is nothing to thee," muttered the other, "if she be my aunt or no, as far as I can see."

"Surely not. I asked in a spirit of polite inquiry."

But apparently this subject was one which had more than any other the power to rouse the blacksmith's savage temper. He fought with it for a moment or two, for anger is the Lord's, and strict Quaker discipline forbade such unseemly wrangling. But Adam was a man of violent temperament which his strict religious training had not altogether succeeded in holding in check: the sneers of the foreign prince, his calm, supercilious attitude, broke the curb which religion had set upon his passion.

"Aye! thou art mighty polite to me, my fine gentleman," he said vehemently. "Thou knowest what I think of thy lazy foreign ways. . . why dost thou not do a bit of honest work, instead of hanging round her ladyship's skirts? . . . If I were to say a word to Sir Marmaduke, 'twould be mightily unpleasant for thee, an I mistake not. Oh! I know what thou'rt after, with thy fine ways, and thy romantic, lying talk of liberty and patriotism! . . . the heiress, eh, friend? That is thy design. . . I am not blind, I tell thee. . . I have seen thee and her. . ."

Sir Marmaduke laughed lightly, shrugging his shoulders in token of indifference.

"Quite so, quite so, good master," he said suavely, "do ye not waste your breath in speaking thus loudly. I understand that your sentiments towards me do not partake of that Christian charity of which ye and yours do prate at times so loudly. But I'll not detain you. Doubtless worthy Mistress Lambert will be awaiting you, or is it the sick mare down Minster way that hath first claim on your amiability? I'll not detain you."

He turned as if to go, but Adam's hard grip was on his shoulder in an instant.

"Nay! thou'lt not detain me—'tis I am detaining thee!" said the blacksmith hoarsely, "for I desired to tell thee that thy ugly French face is abhorrent to me. . . I do not hold with princes. . . For a prince is none better than another man nay, he is worse an he loafs and steals after heiresses and their gold. . . and will not do a bit of honest work. . .

Work makes the man. . . Work and prayer. . . not your titles and fine estates. This is a republic now. . . understand? . . . no king, no House of Lords—please the Lord neither clergymen nor noblemen soon. . . I work with my hands. . . and am not ashamed. The Lord Saviour was a carpenter and not a prince. . . My brother is a student and a gentleman—as good as any prince—understand? Ten thousand times as good as thee."

He relaxed his grip which had been hard as steel on Sir Marmaduke's shoulder. It was evident that he had been nursing hatred and loathing against his lodger for some time, and that to-night the floodgates of his pent-up wrath had been burst asunder through the mysterious prince's taunts, and insinuations anent the cloud and secrecy which hung round the Lamberts' parentage.

Though his shoulder was painful and bruised under the pressure of the blacksmith's rough fingers, Sir Marmaduke did not wince. He looked his avowed enemy boldly in the face, with no small measure of contempt for the violence displayed.

His own enmity towards those who thwarted him was much more subtle, silent and cautious. He would never storm and rage, show his enmity openly and caution his antagonist through an outburst of rage. Adam Lambert still glaring into his lodger's eye, encountered nothing therein but irony and indulgent contempt.

Religion forbade him to swear. Yet was he sorely tempted, and we may presume that he cursed inwardly, for his enemy refused to be drawn into wordy warfare, and he himself had exhausted his vocabulary of sneering abuse, even as he had exhausted his breath.

Perhaps in his innermost heart he was ashamed of his outburst. After all, he had taken this man's money, and had broken bread with him. His hand dropped to his side, and his head fell forward on his breast even as with a pleasant laugh the prince carelessly turned away, and with an affected gesture brushed his silken doublet, there where the blacksmith's hard grip had marred the smoothness of the delicate fabric.

Had Adam Lambert possessed that subtle sixth sense, which hears and sees that which goes on in the mind of others, he had perceived a thought in his lodger's brain cells which might have caused him to still further regret his avowal of open enmity.

For as the blacksmith finally turned away and walked off through the park, skirting the boundary wall, Sir Marmaduke looked over his shoulder at the ungainly figure which was soon lost in the gloom, and muttered a round oath between his teeth.

"An exceedingly unpleasant person," he vowed within himself, "you will have to be removed, good master, an you get too troublesome."

XI

SURRENDER

But this interview with the inimical Quaker had more than strengthened Sir Marmaduke's design to carry his bold scheme more rapidly to its successful issue.

The game which he had played with grave risks for over three months now had begun to be dangerous. The mysterious patriot from France could not afford to see prying enemies at his heels.

Anon when the graceful outline of Lady Sue's figure emerged from out the surrounding gloom, Sir Marmaduke went forward to meet her, and clasped her to him in a passionate embrace.

"My gracious lady. . . my beautiful Sue. . ." he murmured whilst he covered her hands, her brow, her hair with ardent kisses, "you have come so late—and I have been so weary of waiting. . . waiting for you."

He led her through the gardens to where one gigantic elm, grander than its fellows, had thrown out huge gnarled roots which protruded from out the ground. One of these, moss-covered, green and soft, formed a perfect resting place. He drew her down, begging her to sit. She obeyed, scared somewhat as was her wont when she found him so unfettered and violent.

He stretched himself at full length at her feet, extravagant now in his acts and gestures like a man who no longer can hold turbulent passion in check. He kissed the edge of her kirtle, then her cloak and the tips of her little shoes:

"It was cruel to keep me waiting. . . gracious lady—it was cruel," he murmured in the intervals between these ardent caresses.

"I am so sorry, Amédé," she repeated, grieving to see him so sorrowful, not a little frightened at his vehemence,—trying to withdraw her hands from his grasp. "I was detained. . ."

"Detained," he rejoined harshly, "detained by someone else. . . someone who had a greater claim on your time than the poor exile. . ."

"Nay! 'tis unkind thus to grieve me," she said with tender reproach as she felt the hot tears gather in her eyes. "You know—as I do—that I am not my own mistress yet."

"Yes! yes! forgive me—my gracious, sweet, sweet lady. . . I am mad when you are not nigh me. . . You do not know—how could you? . . . what torments I endure, when I think of you so beautiful, so exquisite, so adorable, surrounded by other men who admire you. . . desire you, mayhap. . . Oh! my God! . . ."

"But you need have no fear," she protested gently, "you know that I gave my whole heart willingly to you. . . my prince. . ."

"Nay, but you cannot know," he persisted violently, "sweet, gentle creature that you are, you cannot guess the agonies which a strong man endures when he is gnawed by ruthless insane jealousy. . ."

She gave a cry of pain.

"Amédé!" for she felt hurt, deeply wounded by his mistrust of her, when she had so wholly, so fully trusted him.

"I know. . . I know," he said with quick transition of tone, fearful that he had offended her, striving to master his impatience, to find words which best pleased her young, romantic temperament, "Nay! but you must think me mad. . . Mayhap you despise me," he added with a gentle note of sadness. "Oh, God! . . . mayhap you will turn from me now. . ."

"No! no!"

"Yet do I worship you. . . my saint. . . my divinity. . . my Suzanne. . . You are more beautiful, more adorable than any woman in the world. . . and I am so unworthy."

"You unworthy!" she retorted, laughing gayly through her tears. "You, my prince, my king! . . ."

"Say that once more, my Suzanne," he murmured with infinite gentleness, "oh! the exquisite sweetness of your voice, which is like dream-music in mine ears. . . Oh! to hold you in my arms thus, for ever. . . until death, sweeter than life. . . came to me in one long passionate kiss."

She allowed him to put his arms round her now, glad that the darkness hid the blush on her cheeks; thus she loved him, thus she had first learned to love him, ardent, oh, yes! but so gentle, so meek, yet so great and exalted in his selfless patriotism.

"'Tis not of death you should speak, sweet prince," she said, ineffably happy now that she felt him more subdued, more trusting and fond, "rather should you speak of life. . . with me, your own Suzanne. . . of happiness in the future, when you and I, hand in hand, will work together for that great cause you hold so dear. . . the freedom and liberties of France."

"Ah, yes!" he sighed in utter dejection, "when that happy time comes. . . but. . ."

"You do not trust me?" she asked reproachfully.

"With all my heart, my Suzanne," he replied, "but you are so beautiful, so rich. . . and other men. . ."

"There are no other men for me," she retorted simply. "I love you."

"Will you prove it to me?"

"How can I?"

"Be mine. . . mine absolutely," he urged eagerly with passion just sufficiently subdued to make her pulses throb. "Be my wife. . . my princess. . . let me feel that no one could come between us. . ."

"But my guardian would never consent," she protested.

"Surely your love for me can dispense with Sir Marmaduke's consent. . ."

"A secret marriage?" she asked, terrified at this strange vista which his fiery imagination was conjuring up before her.

"You refuse? . . ." he asked hoarsely.

"No! no! . . . but. . ."

"Then you do not love me, Suzanne."

The coolness in his tone struck a sudden chill to her heart. She felt the clasp of his arms round her relax, she felt rather than saw that he withdrew markedly from her.

"Ah! forgive me! forgive me!" she murmured, stretching her little hands out to him in a pathetic and childlike appeal. "I have never deceived anyone in my life before. . . How could I live a lie? . . . married to you, yet seemingly a girl. . . Whilst in three months. . ."

She paused in her eagerness, for he had jumped to his feet and was now standing before her, a rigid, statuesque figure, with head bent and arms hanging inert by his side.

"You do not love me, Suzanne," he said with an infinity of sadness, which went straight to her own loving heart, "else you would not dream of thus condemning me to three months of exquisite torture. . . I have had my answer. . . Farewell, my gracious lady. . . not mine, alas! but another man's. . . and may Heaven grant that he love you well. . . not as I do, for that were impossible. . ."

His voice had died away in a whisper, which obviously was half-choked with tears. She, too, had risen while he spoke, all her hesitation gone, her heart full of reproaches against herself, and of love for him.

"What do you mean?" she asked trembling.

"That I must go," he replied simply, "since you do not love me. . ."

Oh! how thankful she was that this merciful darkness enwrapped her so tenderly. She was so young, so innocent and pure, that she felt half ashamed of the expression of her own great love which went out to him in a veritable wave of passion, when she began to fear that she was about to lose him.

"No, no," she cried vehemently, "you shall not go. . . you shall not."

Her hands sought his in the gloom, and found them, clung to them with ever-growing ardor; she came quite close to him trying to peer into his face and to let him read in hers all the pathetic story of her own deep love for him.

"I love you," she murmured through her tears. And again she repeated: "I love you. See," she added with sudden determination, "I will do e'en as you wish. . . I will follow you to the uttermost ends of the earth. . . I. . . I will marry you. . . secretly. . . an you wish."

Welcome darkness that hid her blushes! . . . she was so young—so ignorant of life and of the world—yet she felt that by her words, her promise, her renunciation of her will, she was surrendering something to this man, which she could never, never regain.

Did the first thought of fear, or misgiving cross her mind at this moment? It were impossible to say. The darkness which to her was so welcome was—had she but guessed it—infinitely cruel too, for it hid the look of triumph, of rapacity, of satisfied ambition which at her selfless surrender had involuntarily crept into Marmaduke's eyes.

XII

A WOMAN'S HEART

It is difficult, perhaps, to analyze rightly the feelings and sensations of a young girl, when she is literally being swept off her feet in a whirlpool of passion and romance.

Some few years later when Lady Sue wrote those charming memoirs which are such an interesting record of her early life, she tried to note with faithful accuracy what was the exact state of her mind when three months after her first meeting with Prince Amédé d'Orléans, she plighted her troth to him and promised to marry him in secret and in defiance of her guardian's more than probable opposition.

Her sentiments with regard to her mysterious lover were somewhat complex, and undoubtedly she was too young, too inexperienced then to differentiate between enthusiastic interest in a romantic personality, and real, lasting, passionate love for a man, as apart from any halo of romance which might be attached to him.

When she was a few years older she averred that she could never have really loved her prince, because she always feared him. Hers, therefore, was not the perfect love that casteth out fear. She was afraid of him in his ardent moods, almost as much as when he allowed his unbridled temper free rein. Whenever she walked through the dark bosquets of the park, on her way to a meeting with her lover, she was invariably conscious of a certain trepidation of all her nerves, a wonderment as to what he would say when she saw him, how he would act; whether chide, or rave, or merely reproach.

It was the gentle and pathetic terror of a child before a stern yet much-loved parent. Yet she never mistrusted him. . . perhaps because she had never really seen him—only in outline, half wrapped in shadows, or merely silhouetted against a weirdly lighted background. His appearance had no tangible reality for her. She was in love with an ideal, not with a man. . . he was merely the mouthpiece of an individuality which was of her own creation.

Added to all this there was the sense of isolation. She had lost her mother when she was a baby; her father fell at Naseby. She herself had been an only child, left helplessly stranded when the civil war dispersed her relations and friends, some into exile, others in splendid revolt within the fastnesses of their own homes, impoverished by pillage and sequestration, rebellious, surrounded by spies, watching that opportunity for retaliation which was so slow in coming.

Tossed hither and thither by Fate in spite of—or perhaps because of—her great wealth, she had found a refuge, though not a home, at Acol Court; she had been of course too young at the time to understand rightly the great conflict between the King's party and the Puritans, but had naturally embraced the cause—for which her father's life had been sacrificed—blindly, like a child of instinct, not like a woman of thought.

Her guardian and Mistress de Chavasse stood for that faction of Roundheads at which her father and all her relatives had sneered even while they were being conquered and oppressed by them. She disliked them both from the first; and chafed at the parsimonious habits of the house, which stood in such glaring contrast to the easy lavishness of her own luxurious home.

Fortunately for her, her guardian avoided rather than sought her company. She met him at meals and scarcely more often than that, and though she often heard his voice about the house, usually raised in anger or impatience, he was invariably silent and taciturn when she was present.

The presence of Richard Lambert, his humble devotion, his whole-hearted sympathy and the occasional moments of conversation which she had with him were the only bright moments in her dull life at the Court: and there is small doubt but that the friendship and trust which characterized her feelings towards him would soon have ripened into more passionate love, but for the advent into her life of the mysterious hero, who by his personality, his strange, secretive ways, his talk of patriotism and liberty, at once took complete possession of her girlish imagination.

She was perhaps just too young when she met Lambert; she had not yet reached that dangerous threshold when girlhood looks from out obscure ignorance into the glaring knowledge of womanhood. She was a child when Lambert showed his love for her by a thousand little simple acts of devotion and by the mute adoration expressed in his eyes. Lambert drew her towards the threshold by his passionate love, and held her back within the refuge of innocent girlhood by the sincerity and exaltation of his worship.

With the first word of vehement, unreasoning passion, the mysterious prince dragged the girl over that threshold into womanhood. He gave her no time to think, no time to analyze her feelings; he rushed her into a torrent of ardor and of excitement in which she never could pause in order to draw breath.

To-night she had promised to marry him secretly—to surrender herself body and soul to this man whom she hardly knew, whom she had never really seen; she felt neither joy nor remorse, only a strange sense of agitation, an unnatural and morbid impatience to see the end of the next few days of suspense.

For the first time since she had come to Acol, and encountered the kindly sympathy of Richard Lambert, she felt bitterly angered against him when, having parted from the prince at the door of the pavilion, she turned, to walk back towards the house and came face to face with the young man.

A narrow path led through the trees, from the ha-ha to the gate, and Richard Lambert was apparently walking along aimlessly, in the direction of the pavilion.

"I came hoping to meet your ladyship and to escort you home. The night seems very dark," he explained simply in answer to a sudden, haughty stiffening of her young figure, which he could not help but notice.

"I was taking a stroll in the park," she rejoined coldly, "the evening is sweet and balmy but. . . I have no need of escort, Master Lambert. . . I thank you. . . It is late and I would wish to go indoors alone."

"It is indeed late, gracious lady," he said gently, "and the park is lonely at night. . . will you not allow me to walk beside you as far as the house?"

But somehow his insistence, his very gentleness struck a jarring note, for which she herself could not have accounted. Was it the contrast between two men, which unaccountably sent a thrill of disappointment, almost of apprehension, through her heart?

She was angry with Lambert, bitterly angry because he was kind and gentle and long-suffering, whilst the other was violent, even brutal at times.

"I must repeat, master, that I have no need of your escort," she said haughtily, "I have no fear of marauders, nor yet of prowling beasts. And for the future I should be grateful to you," she added, conscious of her own cruelty, determined nevertheless to be remorselessly cruel, "if you were to cease that system which you have adopted of late—that of spying on my movements."

"Spying?"

The word had struck him in the face like a blow. And she, womanlike, with that strange, impulsive temperament of hers, was not at all sorry that she had hurt him. Yet surely he had done her no wrong, save by being so different from the other man, and by seeming to belittle that other in her sight, against her will and his own.

"I am grieved, believe me," she said coldly, "if I seem unkind. . . but you must see for yourself, good master, that we cannot go on as we are doing now. . . Whenever I go out, you follow me. . . when I return I find you waiting for me. . . I have endeavored to think kindly of your actions, but if you value my friendship, as you say you do, you will let me go my way in peace."

"Nay! I humbly beg your ladyship's gracious forgiveness," he said; "if I have transgressed, it is because I am blind to all save your ladyship's future happiness, and at times the thought of that adventurer is more than I can bear."

"You do yourself no good, Master Lambert, by talking thus to me of the man I love and honor beyond all things in this world. You are blind and see not things as they are: blind to the merits of one who is as infinitely above you as the stars. But nathless I waste my breath again. . . I have no power to convince you of the grievous error which you commit. But if you cared for me, as you say you do. . ."

"If I cared!" he murmured, with a pathetic emphasis on that little word "if."

"As a friend I mean," she rejoined still cold, still cruel, still womanlike in that strange, inexplicable desire to wound the man who loved her. "If you care for me as a friend, you will not throw yourself any more in the way of my happiness. Now you may escort me home, an you wish. This is the last time that I shall speak to you as a friend, in response to your petty attacks on the man whom I love. Henceforth you must chose 'twixt his friendship and my enmity!"

And without vouchsafing him another word or look, she gathered her cloak more closely about her, and walked rapidly away along the narrow path.

He followed with head bent, meditating, wondering! Wondering!

XIII

An Idea

The triumph was complete. But of a truth the game was waxing dangerous.

Lady Sue Aldmarshe had promised to marry her prince. She would keep her word, of that Sir Marmaduke was firmly convinced. But there would of necessity be two or three days delay and every hour added to the terrors, the certainty of discovery.

There was a watch-dog at Sue's heels, stern, alert, unyielding. Richard Lambert was probing the secret of the mysterious prince, with the unerring eye of the disappointed lover.

The meeting to-night had been terribly dangerous. Sir Marmaduke knew that Lambert was lurking somewhere in the park.

At present even the remotest inkling of the truth must still be far from the young man's mind. The whole scheme was so strange, so daring, so foreign to the simple ideas of the Quaker-bred lad, that its very boldness had defied suspicion. But the slightest mischance now, a meeting at the door of the pavilion, an altercation—face to face, eye to eye—and Richard Lambert would be on the alert. His hatred would not be so blind, nor yet so clumsy, as that of his brother, the blacksmith. There is no spy so keen in all the world as a jealous lover.

This had been the prince's first meeting with Sue, since that memorable day when the secret of their clandestine love became known to Lambert. Sir Marmaduke knew well that it had been fraught with danger; that every future meeting would wax more and more perilous still, and that the secret marriage itself, however carefully and secretively planned, would hardly escape the prying eyes of the young man.

The unmasking of Prince Amédé d'Orléans before Sue had become legally his wife was a possibility which Sir Marmaduke dared not even think of, lest the very thought should drive him mad. Once she was his wife! . . . well, let her look to herself. . . The marriage tie would be a binding one, he would see to that, and her fortune should be his, even though he had won her by a lie.

He had staked his very existence on the success of his scheme. Lady Sue's fortune was the one aim of his life, for it he had worked and striven, and lied: he would not even contemplate a future without it, now that his plans had brought him so near the goal.

He had one faithful ally, though not a powerful one, in Editha, who, lured by some vague promises of his, desperate too, as regarded her own future, had chosen to throw in her lot whole-heartedly with his.

He was closeted with her on the following day, in the tiny withdrawing-room which leads out of the hall at Acol Court. When he had stolen into the house in the small hours of the morning he had seen Richard Lambert leaning out of one of the windows which gave upon the park.

It seemed as if the young man must have seen him when he skirted the house, for though there was no moonlight, the summer's night was singularly clear. That Lambert had been on the watch—spying, as Sir Marmaduke said with a bitter oath of rage—was beyond a doubt.

Editha too was uneasy; she thought that Lambert had purposely avoided her the whole morning.

"I lingered in the garden for as long as I could," she said to her brother-in-law, watching with keen anxiety his restless movements to and fro in the narrow room, "I thought Lambert would keep within doors if he saw me about. He did not actually see you, Marmaduke, did he?" she queried with ever-growing disquietude.

"No. Not face to face," he replied curtly. "I contrived to avoid him in the park, and kept well within the shadows, when I saw him spying through the window.

"Curse him!" he added with savage fury, "curse him, for a meddlesome, spying cur!"

"The whole thing is becoming vastly dangerous," she sighed.

"Yet it must last for another few weeks at least. . ."

"I know. . . and Lambert is a desperate enemy: he dogs Sue's footsteps, he will come upon you one day when you are alone, or with her. . . he will provoke a quarrel. . ."

"I know—I know. . ." he retorted impatiently, "'tis no use recapitulating the many evil contingencies that might occur. . . I know that Lambert is dangerous. . . damn him! . . . Would to God I could be rid of him. . . somehow."

"You can dismiss him," she suggested, "pay him his wages and send him about his business."

"What were the use? He would remain in the village—in his brother's cottage mayhap. . . with more time on his hands for his spying work. . .

He would dog the wench's steps more jealously than eve. . . No! no!" he added, whilst he cast a quick, furtive look at her—a look which somehow caused her to shiver with apprehension more deadly than heretofore.

"That's not what I want," he said significantly.

"What's to be done?" she murmured, "what's to be done?"

"I must think," he rejoined harshly. "But we must get that love-sick youth out of the way. . . him and his airs of Providence in disguise. . . Something must be done to part him from the wench effectually and completely. . . something that would force him to quit this neighborhood. . . forever, if possible."

She did not reply immediately, but fixed her large, dark eyes upon him, silently for a while, then she murmured:

"If I only knew!"

"Knew what?"

"If I could trust you, Marmaduke!"

He laughed, a harsh, cruel laugh which grated upon her ear.

"We know too much of one another, my dear Editha, not to trust each other."

"My whole future depends on you. I am penniless. If you marry Sue. . ."

"I can provide for you," he interrupted roughly. "What can I do now? My penury is worse than yours. So, my dear, if you have a plan to propound for the furtherance of my schemes, I pray you do not let your fear of the future prevent you from lending me a helping hand."

"A thought crossed my mind," she said eagerly, "the thought of something which would effectually force Richard Lambert to quit this neighborhood for ever."

"What were that?"

"Disgrace."

"Disgrace?" he exclaimed. "Aye! you are right. Something mean. . . paltry. . . despicable. . . something that would make her gracious ladyship turn away from him in disgust. . . and would force him to go away from here. . . for ever."

He looked at her closely, scrutinizing her face, trying to read her thoughts.

"A thought crossed your mind," he demanded peremptorily. "What is it?"

"The house in London," she murmured.

"You are not afraid?"

"Oh!" she said with a careless shrug of the shoulders.

"The Protector's spies are keen," he urged, eager to test her courage, her desire to help him.

"They'll scarce remember me after two years."

"Hm! Their memory is keen. . . and the new laws doubly severe."

"We'll be cautious."

"How can you let your usual clients know? They are dispersed."

"Oh, no! My Lord Walterton is as keen as ever and Sir James Overbury would brave the devil for a night at hazard. A message to them and we'll have a crowd every night."

"'Tis well thought on, Editha," he said approvingly. "But we must not delay. Will you go to London to-morrow?"

"An you approve."

"Aye! you can take the Dover coach and be in town by nightfall. Then write your letters to my Lord Walterton and Sir James Overbury. Get a serving wench from Alverstone's in the Strand, and ask the gentlemen to bring their own men, for the sake of greater safety. They'll not refuse."

"Refuse?" she said with a light laugh, "oh, no!"

"To-day being Tuesday, you should have your first evening entertainment on Friday. Everything could be ready by then."

"Oh, yes!"

"Very well then, on Friday, I, too, will arrive in London, my dear Editha, escorted by my secretary, Master Richard Lambert, and together we will call and pay our respects at your charming house in Bath Street."

"I will do my share. You must do yours, Marmaduke. Endicott will help you: he is keen and clever. And if Lambert but takes a card in his hand. . ."

"Nay! he will take the cards, mine oath on that! Do you but arrange it all with Endicott."

"And, Marmaduke, I entreat you," she urged now with sudden earnestness, "I entreat you to beware of my Lord Protector's spies. Think of the consequences for me!"

"Aye!" he said roughly, laughing that wicked, cruel laugh of his, which damped her eagerness, and struck chill terror into her heart, "aye! the whipping-post for you, fair Editha, for keeping a gaming-house. What? Of a truth I need not urge you to be cautious."

Probably at this moment she would have given worlds—had she

possessed them—if she could but have dissociated herself from her brother-in-law's future altogether. Though she was an empty-headed, brainless kind of woman, she was not by nature a wicked one. Necessity had driven her into linking her fortunes with those of Sir Marmaduke. And he had been kind to her, when she was in deep distress: but for him she would probably have starved, for her beauty had gone and her career as an actress had been, for some inexplicable reason, quite suddenly cut short, whilst a police raid on the gaming-house over which she presided had very nearly landed her in a convict's cell.

She had escaped severe punishment then, chiefly because Cromwell's laws against gambling were not so rigorous at the time as they had since become, also because she was able to plead ignorance of them, and because of the status of first offense.

Therefore she knew quite well what she risked through the scheme which she had so boldly propounded to Sir Marmaduke. Dire disgrace and infamy, if my Lord Protector's spies once more came upon the gamesters in her house—unawares.

Utter social ruin and worse! Yet she risked it all, in order to help him. She did not love him, nor had she any hopes that he would of his own free will do more than give her a bare pittance for her needs once he had secured Lady Sue's fortune; but she was shrewd enough to reckon that the more completely she was mixed up in his nefarious projects, the more absolutely forced would he be to accede to her demands later on. The word blackmail had not been invented in those days, but the deed itself existed and what Editha had in her mind when she risked ostracism for Sir Marmaduke's sake was something very akin to it.

But he, in the meanwhile, had thrown off his dejection. He was full of eagerness, of anticipated triumph now.

The rough idea which was to help him in his schemes had originated in Editha's brain, but already he had elaborated it; had seen in the plan a means not only of attaining his own ends with regard to Sue, but also of wreaking a pleasing vengeance on the man who was trying to frustrate him.

"I pray you, be of good cheer, fair Editha," he said quite gaily. "Your plan is good and sound, and meseems as if the wench's fortune were already within my grasp."

"Within our grasp, you mean, Marmaduke," she said significantly.

"Our grasp of course, gracious lady," he said with a marked sneer, which she affected to ignore. "What is mine is yours. Am I not tied to the strings of your kirtle by lasting bonds of infinite gratitude?"

"I will start to-morrow then. By chaise to Dover and thence by coach," she said coldly, taking no heed of his irony. "'Twere best you did not assume your romantic rôle again until after your own voyage to London. You can give me some money I presume. I can do nothing with an empty purse."

"You shall have the whole contents of mine, gracious Editha," he said blandly, "some ten pounds in all, until the happy day when I can place half a million at your feet."

PART II

XIV

THE HOUSE IN LONDON

It stood about midway down an unusually narrow by-street off the Strand.

A tumble-down archway, leaning to one side like a lame hen, gave access to a dark passage, dank with moisture, whereon the door of the house gave some eighteen feet up on the left.

The unpaved street, undrained and unutterably filthy, was ankle-deep in mud, even at the close of this hot August day. Down one side a long blank wall, stone-built and green with mildew, presented an unbroken frontage: on the other the row of houses with doors perpetually barred, and windows whereon dust and grit had formed effectual curtains against prying eyes, added to the sense of loneliness, of insecurity, of unknown dangers lurking behind that crippled archway, or beneath the shadows of the projecting eaves, whence the perpetual drip-drip of soot water came as a note of melancholy desolation.

From all the houses the plaster was peeling off in many places, a prey to the inclemencies of London winters; all presented gray facades, with an air of eeriness about their few windows, flush with the outside wall—at one time painted white, no doubt, but now of uniform dinginess with the rest of the plaster work.

There was a grim hint about the whole street of secret meetings, and of unavowable deeds done under cover of isolation and of darkness, whilst the great crooked mouth of the archway disclosing the blackness and gloom of the passage beyond, suggested the lair of human wild beasts who only went about in the night.

As a rule but few passers-by availed themselves of this short and narrow cut down to the river-side. Nathless, the unarmed citizen was scared by these dank and dreary shadows, whilst the city watchman, mindful of his own safety, was wont to pass the mean street by.

Only my Lord Protector's new police-patrol fresh to its onerous task, solemnly marched down it once in twenty-four hours, keeping shoulder to shoulder, looking neither to right nor left, thankful when either issue was once more within sight.

But in this same evening in August, 1657, it seemed as if quite a number of people had business in Bath Street off the Strand. At any rate this was specially noticeable after St. Mary's had struck the hour of nine, when several cloaked and hooded figures slipped, one after another, some singly, others in groups of two or three, into the shadow of the narrow lane.

They all walked in silence, and did not greet one another as they passed; some cast from time to time furtive looks behind them; but every one of these evening prowlers seemed to have the same objective, for as soon as they reached the crippled archway, they disappeared within the gloom of its yawning mouth.

Anon when the police-patrol had gone by and was lost in the gloom there where Bath Street debouches on the river bank, two of these heavily cloaked figures walked rapidly down from the Strand, and like the others slipped quickly under the archway, and made straight for the narrow door on the left of the passage.

This door was provided with a heavy bronze knocker, but strangely enough the newcomers did not avail themselves of its use, but rapped on the wooden panels with their knuckles, giving three successive raps at regular intervals.

They were admitted almost immediately, the door seemingly opening of itself, and they quickly stepped across the threshold.

Within the house was just as dark and gloomy as it was without, and as the two visitors entered, a voice came from out the shadows, and said, in a curious monotone and with strange irrelevance:

"The hour is late!"

"And 'twill be later still," replied one of the newcomers.

"Yet the cuckoo hath not called," retorted the voice.

"Nor is the ferret on the prowl," was the enigmatic reply. Whereupon the voice speaking in more natural tones added sententiously:

"Two flights of steps, and 'ware the seventeenth step on the first flight. Door on the left, two raps, then three."

"Thank you, friend," rejoined one of the newcomers, "'tis pleasant to feel that so faithful a watch guards the entrance of this palace of pleasure."

Thereupon the two visitors, who of a truth must have been guided either by instinct or by intimate knowledge of the place, for not a gleam of light illumined the entrance hall, groped their way to a flight of stone stairs which led in a steep curve to the upper floors of the house.

A rickety banister which gave ominously under the slightest pressure helped to guide the visitors in this utter darkness: but obviously the warning uttered by that mysterious challenging voice below was not superfluous, for having carefully counted sixteen steps in an upward direction, the newcomers came to a halt, and feeling their way forward now with uttermost caution, their feet met a yawning hole, which had soon caused a serious accident to a stranger who had ventured thus far in ignorance of pitfalls.

A grim laugh, echoed by a lighter one, showed that the visitors had encountered only what they had expected, and after this brief episode they continued their journey upwards with a firmer sense of security; a smoky oil lamp on the first floor landing guided their footsteps by casting a flickering light on the narrow stairway, whereon slime and filth crept unchecked through the broken crevices between the stones.

But now as they advanced, the silence seemed more broken: a distinct hum as of many voices was soon perceptible, and anon a shrill laugh, followed by another more deep in tone, and echoed by others which presently died away in the distance.

By the time the two men had reached the second floor landing these many noises had become more accentuated, also more distinct; still muffled and subdued as if proceeding from behind heavy doors, but nevertheless obvious as the voices of men and women in lively converse.

The newcomers gave the distinctive raps prescribed by their first mentor, on the thick panels of a solid oak door on their left.

The next moment the door itself was thrown open from within; a flood of light burst forth upon the gloomy landing from the room beyond, the babel of many voices became loud and clear, and as the two men stood for a moment beneath the lintel a veritable chorus of many exclamations greeted them from every side.

"Walterton! begad!"

"And Overbury, too!"

"How late ye come!"

"We thought ye'd fallen a victim to Noll's myrmidons!"

It was of a truth a gay and merry company that stood, and moved, chatted and laughed, within the narrow confines of that small second-floor room in the gloomy house in Bath Street.

The walls themselves were dingy and bare, washed down with some grayish color, which had long since been defaced by the grime and dust of London. Thick curtains of a nondescript hue fell in straight folds before each window, and facing these there was another door—double paneled—which apparently led to an inner room.

But the place itself was brilliantly illuminated with many wax candles set in chandeliers. These stood on the several small tables which were dotted about the room.

These tables—covered with green baize, and a number of chairs of various shapes and doubtful solidity were the only furniture of the room, but in an arched recess in the wall a plaster figure holding a cornucopia, from whence fell in thick profusion the plaster presentments of the fruits of this earth, stood on an elevated pedestal, which had been draped with crimson velvet.

The goddess of Fortune, with a broken nose and a paucity of fingers, dominated the brilliant assembly, from the height of her crimson throne. Her head had been crowned with a tall peaked modish beaver hat, from which a purple feather rakishly swept over the goddess's left ear. An ardent devotee had deposited a copper coin in her extended, thumbless hand, whilst another had fixed a row of candle stumps at her feet.

There was nothing visible in this brilliantly lighted room of the sober modes to which the eye of late had become so accustomed. Silken doublets of bright and even garish colors stood out in bold contrast against the gray monotone of the walls and hangings. Fantastic buttons, tags and laces, gorgeously embroidered cuffs and collars edged with priceless Mechlin or d'Alençon, bunches of ribands at knee and wrists, full periwigs and over-wide boot-hose tops were everywhere to be seen, whilst the clink of swords against the wooden boards and frequent volleys of loudly spoken French oaths, testified to the absence of those Puritanic fashions and customs which had become the general rule even in London.

Some of the company sat in groups round the green-topped tables whereon cards or dice and heaps of gold and smaller coins lay in profusion. Others stood about watching the games or chatting to one another. Mostly men they were, some old, some young—but there were women too, women in showy kirtles, with bare shoulders showing well above the colverteen kerchief and faces wherein every line had been obliterated by plentiful daubs of cosmetics. They moved about the room from table to table, laughing, talking, making comments on the games as these proceeded.

The men apparently were all intent—either as actual participants or merely as spectators—upon a form of amusement which His Highness the Lord Protector had condemned as wanton and contrary to law.

The newcomers soon divested themselves of their immense dark cloaks, and they, too, appeared in showy apparel of silk and satin, with tiny bows of ribands at the ends of the long curls which fell both sides of their faces, and with enormous frills of lace inside the turned-over tops of their boots.

Lord Walterton quite straddled in his gait, so wide were his boot tops, and there was an extraordinary maze of tags and ribands round the edge of Sir James Overbury's breeches.

"Make your game, gentlemen, make your game," said the latter as he advanced further into the room. And his tired, sleepy eyes brightened at sight of the several tables covered with cards and dice, the guttering candles, the mountains of gold and small coin scattered on the green baize tops.

"Par Dieu! but 'tis a sight worth seeing after the ugly sour faces one meets in town these days!" he added, gleefully rubbing his beringed hands one against the other.

"But where is our gracious hostess?" added Lord Walterton, a melancholy-looking young man with pale-colored eyes and lashes, and a narrow chest.

"You are thrice welcome, my lord!" said Editha de Chavasse, whose elegant figure now detached itself from amongst her guests.

She looked very handsome in her silken kirtle of a brilliant greenish hue, lace primer, and high-heeled shoes—relics of her theatrical days; her head was adorned with the bunches of false curls which the modish hairdressers were trying to introduce. The plentiful use of cosmetics had obliterated the ravages of time and imparted a youthful appearance to her face, whilst excitement not unmixed with apprehension lent a bright glitter to her dark eyes.

Lord Walterton and Sir James Overbury lightly touched with their lips the hand which she extended to them. Their bow, too, was slight, though they tossed their curls as they bent their heads in the most approved French fashion. But there was a distinct note of insolence, not altogether unmixed with irony, in the freedom with which they had greeted her.

"I met de Chavasse in town to-day," said Lord Walterton, over his shoulder before he mixed with the crowd.

"Yes! he will be here to-night," she rejoined. Sir James Overbury also made a casual remark, but it was evident that the intention and purpose of these gay gentlemen was not the courteous entertainment of their hostess. Like so many men of all times and all nations in this world, they were ready enough to enjoy what she provided for them—the illicit pastime which they could not get elsewhere—but they despised her for giving it them, and cared naught for the heavy risks she ran in keeping up this house for their pleasure.

XV

A Game of Primero

At a table in the immediate center of the room a rotund gentleman in doublet and breeches of cinnamon brown taffeta and voluminous lace cuffs at the wrists was presiding over a game of Spanish primero.

A simple game enough, not difficult of comprehension, yet vastly exciting, if one may form a judgment of its qualities through watching the faces of the players.

The rotund gentleman dealt a card face downwards to each of his opponents, who then looked at their cards and staked on them, by pushing little piles of gold or silver forward.

Then the dealer turned up his own card, and gave the amount of the respective stakes to those players whose cards were of higher value than his own, whilst sweeping all other moneys to swell his own pile.

A simple means, forsooth, of getting rid of any superfluity of cash.

"Art winning, Endicott?" queried Lord Walterton as, he stood over the other man, looking down on the game.

Endicott shrugged his fat shoulders, and gave an enigmatic chuckle.

"I pay King and Ace only," he called out imperturbably, as he turned up a Queen.

Most of the stakes came to swell his own pile, but he passed a handful of gold to a hollow-eyed youth who sat immediately opposite to him, and who clutched at the money with an eager, trembling grasp.

"You have all the luck to-night, Segrave," he said with an oily smile directed at the winner.

"Make your game, gentlemen," he added almost directly, as he once more began to deal.

"I pay knave upwards!" he declared, turning up the ten of clubs.

"Mine is the ten of hearts," quoth one of the players.

"Ties pay the bank," quoth Endicott imperturbably.

"Mine is a queen," said Segrave in a hollow tone of voice.

Endicott with a comprehensive oath threw the entire pack of cards into a distant corner of the room.

"A fresh pack, mistress!" he shouted peremptorily.

Then as an overdressed, florid woman, with high bullhead fringe and old-fashioned Spanish farthingale, quickly obeyed his behests, he said with a coarse laugh:

"Fresh cards may break Master Segrave's luck and improve yours, Sir Michael."

"Before this round begins," said Sir James Overbury who was standing close behind Lord Walterton, also watching the game, "I will bet you, Walterton, that Segrave wins again."

"Done with you," replied the other, "and I'll back mine own opinion by taking a hand."

The florid woman brought him a chair, and he sat down at the table, as Endicott once more began to deal.

"Five pounds that Segrave wins," said Overbury.

"A queen," said Endicott, turning up his card. "I pay king and ace only."

Everyone had to pay the bank, for all turned up low cards; Segrave alone had not yet turned up his.

"Well! what is your card, Master Segrave?" queried Lord Walterton lightly.

"An ace!" said Segrave simply, displaying the ace of hearts.

"No good betting against the luck," said young Walterton lightly, as he handed five sovereigns over to his friend, "moreover it spoils my system."

"Ye play primero on a system!" quoth Sir Michael Isherwood in deep amazement.

"Yes!" replied the young man. "I have played on it for years. . . and it is infallible, 'pon my honor."

In the meanwhile the doors leading to the second room had been thrown open; serving men and women advanced carrying trays on which were displayed glasses and bottles filled with Rhenish wine and Spanish canary and muscadel, also buttered ale and mead and hypocras for the ladies.

Editha did not occupy herself with serving but the florid woman was most attentive to the guests. She darted in and out between the tables, managing her unwieldy farthingale with amazing skill. She poured out the wines, and offered tarts and dishes of anchovies and of cheese, also strange steaming beverages lately imported into England called coffee and chocolate.

The women liked the latter, and supped it out of mugs, with many little cries of astonishment and appreciation of its sugariness.

BARONESS EMMUSKA ORCZY

The men drank heavily, chiefly of the heady Spanish wines; they ate the anchovies and cheese with their fingers, and continually called for more refreshments.

Play was of necessity interrupted. Groups of people eating and drinking congregated round the tables. The men mostly discussed various phases of the game; there was so little else for idlers to talk about these days. No comedies or other diversions, neither cock-fighting nor bear-baiting, and abuse of my Lord Protector and his rigorous disciplinarian laws had already become stale.

The women talked dress and coiffure, the new puffs, the fanciful pinners.

But at the center table Segrave still sat, refusing all refreshment, waiting with obvious impatience for the ending of this unwelcome interval. When first he found himself isolated in the crowd, he had counted over with febrile eagerness the money which lay in a substantial heap before him.

"Saved!" he muttered between his teeth, speaking to himself like one who is dreaming, "saved! Thank God! . . . Two hundred and fifty pounds. . . only another fifty and I'll never touch these cursed cards again. . . only another fifty. . ."

He buried his face in his hands; the moisture stood out in heavy drops on his forehead. He looked all round him with ever-growing impatience.

"My God! why don't they come back! . . . Another fifty pounds. . . and I can put the money back. . . before it has been missed. . . Oh! why don't they come back!"

Quite a tragedy expressed in those few muttered words, in the trembling hands, the damp forehead. Money taken from an unsuspecting parent, guardian or master, which? What matter? A tragedy of ordinary occurrence even in those days when social inequalities were being abolished by act of Parliament.

In the meanwhile Lord Walterton, halting of speech, insecure of foothold, after his third bumper of heady sack, was explaining to Sir Michael Isherwood the mysteries of his system for playing the noble game of primero.

"It is sure to break the bank in time," he said confidently, "I am for going to Paris where play runs high, and need not be carried on in this hole and corner fashion to suit cursed Puritanical ideas."

"Tell me your secret, Walterton," urged worthy Sir Michael, whose broad Shropshire acres were heavily mortgaged, after the rapine and pillage of civil war.

"Well! I can but tell you part, my friend," rejoined the other, "yet 'tis passing simple. You begin with one golden guinea. . . and lose it. . . then you put up two and lose again. . ."

"Passing simple," assented Sir Michael ironically.

"But after that you put up four guineas."

"And lose it."

"Yea! yea! mayhap you lose it. . . but then you put up eight guineas. . . and win. Whereupon you are just as you were before."

And with a somewhat unsteady hand the young man raised a bumper to his lips, whilst eying Sir Michael with the shifty and inquiring eye peculiar to the intoxicated.

"Meseems that if you but abstain from playing altogether," quoth Sir Michael impatiently, "the result would still be the same. . . And suppose you lose the eight guineas, what then?"

"Oh! 'tis vastly simple—you put up sixteen."

"But if you lose that?"

"Put up thirty-two. . ."

"But if you have not thirty-two guineas to put up?" urged Sir Michael, who was obstinate.

"Nay! then, my friend," said Lord Walterton with a laugh which soon broke into an ominous hiccough, "ye must not in that case play upon my system."

"Well said, my lord," here interposed Endicott, who had most moderately partaken of a cup of hypocras, and whose eye and hand were as steady as heretofore. "Well said, pardi! . . . My old friend the Marquis of Swarthmore used oft to say in the good old days of Goring's Club, that 'twas better to lose on a system, than to play on no system at all."

"A smart cavalier, old Swarthmore," assented Sir Michael gruffly, "and nathless, a true friend to you, Endicott," he added significantly.

"Another deal, Master Endicott," said Segrave, who for the last quarter of an hour had vainly tried to engage the bank-holder's attention.

Nor was Lord Walterton averse to this. The more the wine got into his head, the more unsteady his hand became, the more strong was his desire to woo the goddess whose broken-nosed image seemed to be luring him to fortune.

"You are right, Master Segrave," he said thickly, "we are wasting valuable time. Who knows but what old Noll's police-patrol is lurking in this cutthroat alley? . . . Endicott, take the bank again. . . I'll swear

I'll ruin ye ere the moon—which I do not see—disappears down the horizon. Sir Michael, try my system... Overbury, art a laggard?... Let us laugh and be merry—to-morrow is the Jewish Sabbath—and after that Puritanic Sunday... after which mayhap, we'll all go to hell, driven thither by my Lord Protector. Wench, another bumper... canary, sack or muscadel... no thin Rhenish wine shall e'er defile this throat! Gentlemen, take your places... Mistress Endicott, can none of these wenches discourse sweet music whilst we do homage to the goddess of Fortune?... To the tables... to the tables, gentlemen... here's to King Charles, whom may God protect... and all in defiance of my Lord Protector!"

XVI

A Conflict

In the hubbub which immediately followed Lord Walterton's tirade, Editha de Chavasse beckoned to the florid woman—who seemed to be her henchwoman—and drew her aside to a distant corner of the room, where there were no tables nigh and where the now subdued hum of the voices, mingling with the sound of music on virginal and stringed instruments, made a murmuring noise which effectually drowned the talk between the two women.

"Have you arranged everything, Mistress Endicott?" asked Editha, speaking in a whisper.

"Everything, mistress," replied the other.

"Endicott understands?"

"Perfectly," said the woman, with perceptible hesitation, "but. . ."

"What ails you, mistress?" asked Editha haughtily, noting the hesitation, and frowning with impatience thereat.

"My husband thinks the game too dangerous."

"I was not aware," retorted Mistress de Chavasse dryly, "that I had desired Master Endicott's opinion on the subject."

"Mayhap not," rejoined the other, equally dryly, "but you did desire his help in the matter. . . and he seems unmindful to give it."

"Why?"

"I have explained. . . the game is too dangerous."

"Or the payment insufficient?" sneered Editha. "Which is it?"

"Both, mayhap," assented Mistress Endicott with a careless shrug of her fat shoulders, "the risks are very great. To-night especially. . ."

"Why especially to-night?"

"Because ever since you have been away from it, this house—though we did our best to make it seem deserted—hath been watched—of that I feel very sure. . . My Lord Protector's watchmen have a suspicion of our. . . our evening entertainments. . . and I doubt not but that they desire to see for themselves how our guests enjoy themselves these nights."

"Well?" rejoined Editha lightly. "What of that?"

"As you know, we did not play for nigh on twelve months now. . . Endicott thought it too dangerous. . . and to-night. . ."

She checked herself abruptly, for Editha had turned an angry face and flashing eyes upon her.

"To-night?" said Mistress de Chavasse curtly, but peremptorily, "what of to-night? . . . I sent you orders from Thanet that I wished the house opened to-night. . . Lord Walterton, Sir James Overbury and as many of our usual friends as were in the town, apprised that play would be in full progress. . . Meseems," she added, casting a searching look all round the room, "that we have singularly few players."

"It was difficult," retorted the other with somewhat more diffidence in her tone than had characterized her speech before now. "Young Squire Delamere committed suicide. . . you remember him? . . . and Lord Cooke killed Sir Humphrey Clinton in a duel after that fracas we had here, when the police-patrol well-nigh seized upon your person. . . Squire Delamere's suicide and Sir Humphrey's death caused much unpleasant talk. And old Mistress Delamere, the mother, hath I fear me, still a watchful eye on us. She means to do us lasting mischief. . . It had been wiser to tarry yet awhile. . . Twelve months is not sufficient for throwing the dust of ages over us and our doings. . . That is my husband's opinion and also mine. . . A scandal such as you propose to have to-night, will bring the Protector's spies about our ears. . . his police too, mayhap. . . and then Heaven help us all, mistress. . . for you, in the country, cannot conceive how rigorously are the laws enforced now against gambling, betting, swearing or any other form of innocent amusement. . . Why! two wenches were whipped at the post by the public hangman only last week, because forsooth they were betting on the winner amongst themselves, whilst watching a bout of pell-mell. . . And you know that John Howthill stood in the pillory for two hours and had both his hands bored through with a hot iron for allowing gambling inside his coffeehouse. . . And so, mistress, you will perceive that I am speaking but in your own interests. . ."

Editha, who had listened to the long tirade with marked impatience, here interrupted the voluble lady, with harsh command.

"I crave your pardon, mistress," she said peremptorily. "My interests pre-eminently consist in being obeyed by those whom I pay for doing my behests. Now you and your worthy husband live here rent free and derive a benefit of ten pounds every time our guests assemble. . . Well! in return for that, I make use of you and your names, in case of any unpleasantness with the vigilance patrol. . . or in case of a scandal which might reach my Lord Protector's ears. . . Up to this time your positions here have been a sinecure. . . I even bore the brunt of the last fracas whilst you remained practically scathless. . . But to-night, I own it, there may be some risks. . . but of a truth you have been well paid to take them."

"But if we refuse to take the risks," retorted the other.

"If you refuse, mistress," said Editha with a careless shrug of the shoulders, "you and your worthy lord go back to the gutter where I picked you up. . . and within three months of that time, I should doubtless have the satisfaction of seeing you both at the whipping-post, for of a truth you would be driven to stealing or some other equally unavowable means of livelihood."

"We could send *you* there," said Mistress Endicott, striving to suppress her own rising fury, "if we but said the word."

"Nay! you would not be believed, mistress. . . but even so, I do not perceive how my social ruin would benefit you."

"Since we are doomed anyhow. . . after this night's work," said the woman sullenly.

"Nay! but why should you take so gloomy a view of the situation? . . . My Lord Protector hath forgot our existence by now, believe me. . . and of a surety his patrol hath not yet knocked at our door. . . And methinks, mistress," added Editha significantly, "'tis not in *your* interest to quarrel with me."

"I have no wish to quarrel with you," quoth Mistress Endicott, who apparently had come to the end of her resistance, and no doubt had known all along that her fortunes were too much bound up with those of Mistress de Chavasse to allow of a rupture between them.

"Then everything is vastly satisfactory," said Editha with forced gayety. "I rely on you, mistress, and on Endicott's undoubted talents to bring this last matter to a successful issue to-night. . . Remember, mistress. . . I rely on you."

Perhaps Mistress Endicott would have liked to prolong the argument. As a matter of fact, neither she nor her husband counted the risks of a midnight fracas of great moment to themselves: they had so very little to lose. A precarious existence based on illicit deeds of all sorts had rendered them hard and reckless.

All they wished was to be well paid for the risks they ran; neither of them was wholly unacquainted with the pillory, and it held no great terrors for them. There were so many unavowable pleasures these days, which required a human cloak to cover the identity of the real transgressor, that people like Master and Mistress Endicott prospered vastly.

The case of Mistress de Chavasse's London house wherein the ex-actress had some few years ago established a gaming club, together with its various emoluments attached thereunto, suited the Endicotts' requirements to perfection: but the woman desired an increase of payment for the special risk she would run to-night, and was sorely vexed that she could not succeed in intimidating Editha with threats of vigilance-patrol and whipping-posts.

Mistress de Chavasse knew full well that the Endicotts did not intend to quarrel with her, and having threatened rupture unless her commands were obeyed, she had no wish to argue the matter further with her henchwoman.

At that moment, too, there came the sound of significant and methodical rappings at the door. Editha, who had persistently throughout her discussion with Mistress Endicott, kept one ear open for that sound, heard it even through the buzz of talk. She made a scarcely visible gesture of the hand, bidding the other woman to follow her: that gesture was quickly followed by a look of command.

Mistress Endicott presumably had finally made up her mind to obey. She shrugged her fat shoulders and followed Mistress de Chavasse as far as the center of the room.

"Remember that you are the hostess now," murmured Editha to her, as she herself went to the door and opened it.

With an affected cry of surprise and pleasure she welcomed Sir Marmaduke de Chavasse, who was standing on the threshold, prepared to enter and escorted by his young secretary, Master Richard Lambert.

XVII

Rus in Urbe

One or two of the men looked up as de Chavasse entered, but no one took much notice of him.

Most of those present remembered him from the past few years when still with pockets well filled through having forestalled Lady Sue's maintenance money, he was an habitual frequenter of some of the smart secret clubs in town; but here, just the same as elsewhere, Sir Marmaduke was not a popular man, and many there were who had unpleasant recollections of his surly temper and uncouth ways, whenever fickle Fortune happened not to favor him.

Even now, he looked sullen and disagreeable as, having exchanged a significant glance with his sister-in-law, he gave a comprehensive nod to the assembled guests, which had nothing in it either of cordiality or of good-will. He touched Editha's finger tips with his lips, and then advanced into the room.

Here he was met by Mistress Endicott, who had effectually thrown off the last vestige of annoyance and of rebellion, for she greeted the newcomer with marked good-humor and an encouraging smile.

"It is indeed a pleasure to see that Sir Marmaduke de Chavasse hath not forgot old friends," she said pleasantly.

"It was passing kind, gracious mistress," he responded, forcing himself to speak naturally and in agreeable tones, "to remember an insignificant country bumpkin like myself. . . and you see I have presumed on your lavish hospitality and brought my young friend, Master Richard Lambert, to whom you extended so gracious an invitation."

He turned to Lambert, who a little dazed to find himself in such brilliant company, had somewhat timidly kept close to the heels of his employer. He thought Mistress Endicott vulgar and overdressed the moment he felt bold enough to raise his eyes to hers. But he chided himself immediately for thus daring to criticize his betters.

His horizon so far had been very limited; only quite vaguely had he heard of town and Court life. The little cottage where dwelt the old Quakeress who had brought him and his brother up, and the tumble-down, dilapidated house of Sir Marmaduke de Chavasse were the only habitations in which he was intimate. The neighboring Kentish Squires, Sir Timothy Harrison, Squire Pyncheon and Sir John Boatfield, were the only presentations of "gentlemen" he had ever seen.

Sir Marmaduke de Chavasse had somewhat curtly given him orders the day before, that he was to accompany him to London, whither he himself had to go to consult his lawyer. Lambert had naturally obeyed, without murmur, but with vague trepidations at thought of this, his first journey into the great town.

Sir Marmaduke had been very kind, had given him a new suit of grogram, lined with flowered silk, which Lambert thought the richest garment he had ever seen. He was very loyal in his thoughts to his employer, bearing with the latter's violence and pandering to his fits of ill-humor for the sake of the home which Sir Marmaduke had provided for him.

To Lambert's mind, Sir Marmaduke's kindness to him was wholly gratuitous. His own position as secretary being but a sinecure, the young man readily attributed de Chavasse's interest in himself to innate goodness of heart, and desire to help the poor orphan lad.

This estimate of his employer's character Richard Lambert had not felt any cause to modify. He continued to serve him faithfully, to look after his interests in and around Acol Court to the best of his ability; above all he continued to be whole-heartedly grateful. He was so absolutely conscious of the impassable social barrier which existed between himself and the rich daughter of the great Earl of Dover, that he never for a moment resented Sir Marmaduke's sneers when they were directed against his obvious, growing love for Sue.

Remember that he had no cause to suspect Sir Marmaduke de Chavasse of any nefarious projects or of any evil intentions with regard to himself, when he told him that together they would go this night to the house of an old friend, Mrs. Endicott, where they would derive much pleasure and entertainment.

They had spent the previous night at the Swan Inn in Fleet Street and the day in visiting the beautiful sights of London, which caused the young lad from the country to open wide eyes in astonishment and pleasure.

Sir Marmaduke had been peculiarly gracious, even taking Richard with him to the Frenchman's house in Queen's Head Alley, where that curious beverage called coffee was dispensed and where several clever people met and discussed politics in a manner which was vastly interesting to the young man.

Then when the evening began to draw in, and Lambert thought it high time to go to bed, for 'twas a pity to burn expensive candles longer than was necessary, Sir Marmaduke had astonished his secretary by telling him that he must now clean and tidy himself for they would proceed to the house of a great lady named Mistress Endicott—a friend of the ex-Queen Henrietta Maria and a lady of peculiar virtues and saintliness, who would give them vast and pleasing entertainment.

Lambert was only too ready to obey. Enjoyment came naturally to him beneath his Quaker bringing-up: his youth, good-health and pure, naturally noble intellect, all craved companionship, with its attendant pleasures and joys. He himself could not afterwards have said exactly how he had pictured in his mind the saintly lady—friend of the unhappy Queen—whom he was to meet this night.

Certainly Mistress Endicott, with her red face surmounted by masses of curls that were obviously false, since they did not match the rest of her hair, was not the ideal paragon of all the virtues, and when he was first made to greet her, a strange, unreasoning instinct seemed to draw him away from her, to warn him to fly from this noisy company, from the sight of those many faces, all unnaturally flushed, and from the sounds of those strange oaths which greeted his ears from every side.

A great wave of thankfulness came over him that, his gracious lady— innocent, tender, beautiful Lady Sue, had not come to London with her guardian. Whilst he gazed on the marvels of Westminster Hall and of old Saint Paul's he had longed that she should be near him, so that he might watch the brilliance of her eyes, and the glow of pleasure which, of a surety would have mantled in her cheeks when she was shown the beauties of the great city.

But now he was glad—very glad, that Sir Marmaduke had so sternly ordained that she should remain these few days alone at Acol in charge of Mistress Charity and of Master Busy. At the time he had chafed bitterly at his own enforced silence: he would have given all he possessed in the world for the right to warn Sir Marmaduke de Chavasse that a wolf was prowling in the fold under cover of the night. He had seen Lady Sue's eyes brighten at the dictum that she was to remain behind—they told him in eloquent language the joy she felt to be free for two days that she might meet her prince undisturbed.

But all these thoughts and fears had fled the moment Lambert found himself in the midst of these people, whom he innocently believed to be great ladies and noble gentlemen, friends of his employer

Sir Marmaduke de Chavasse. It seemed to him at once as if there was something here—in this room—which he would not wish Lady Sue to see.

He was clumsy and *gauche* in his movements as he took the hand which Mistress Endicott extended to him, but he tried to imitate the salute which he had seen his employer give on the flat—not very clean—finger-tips of the lady.

She was exceedingly gracious to him, saying with great kindliness and a melancholy sigh:

"Ah! you come from the country, master? . . . So delightful, of a truth. . . Milk for breakfast, eh? . . . You get up at dawn and go to bed at sunset? . . . I know country life well—though alas! duty now keeps me in town. . . But 'tis small wonder that you look so young!"

He tried to talk to her of the country, for here she had touched on a topic which was dear to him. He knew all about the birds and beasts, the forests and the meadows, and being unused to the art of hypocritical interest, he took for real sympathy the lady's vapid exclamations of enthusiasm, with which she broke in now and again upon his flow of eloquence.

Sir Marmaduke de Chavasse, who was watching the young man with febrile keenness, had the satisfaction to note that very soon Richard began to throw off his bucolic timidity, his latent yet distinctly perceptible disapproval of the company into which he had been brought. He sought out his sister-in-law and drew her attention to Lambert in close conversation with Mrs. Endicott.

"Is everything arranged?" he asked under his breath.

"Everything," she replied.

"No trouble with our henchmen?"

"A little. . . but they are submissive now."

"What is the arrangement?"

"Persuade young Lambert to take a hand at primero. . . Endicott will do the rest."

"Who is in the know?" he queried, after a slight pause, during which he watched his unsuspecting victim with a deep frown of impatience and of hate.

"Only the Endicotts," she explained. "But do you think that he will play?" she added, casting an anxious look on her brother-in-law's face.

He nodded affirmatively.

"Yes!" he said curtly. "I can arrange that, as soon as you are ready."

She turned from him and walked to the center table. She watched the game for a while, noting that young Segrave was still the winner, and that Lord Walterton was very flushed and excited.

Then she caught Endicott's eye, and immediately lowered her lashes twice in succession.

"Ventre-saint-gris!" swore Endicott with an unmistakable British accent in the French expletive, "but I'll play no more. . . The bank is broken. . . and I have lost too much money. Mr. Segrave there has nearly cleaned me out and still I cannot break his luck."

He rose abruptly from his chair, even as Mistress de Chavasse quietly walked away from the table.

But Lord Walterton placed a detaining, though very trembling hand, on the cinnamon-colored sleeve.

"Nay! parbleu! ye cannot go like this. . . good Master Endicott. . ." he said, speaking very thickly, "I want another round or two. . .'pon my honor I do. . . I haven't lost nearly all I meant to lose."

"Ye cannot stop play so abruptly, master," said Segrave, whose eyes shone with an unnatural glitter, and whose cheeks were covered with a hectic flush, "ye cannot leave us all in the lurch."

"Nay, I doubt not, my young friend," quoth Endicott gruffly, "that you would wish to play all night. . . You have won all my money and Lord Walterton's, too."

"And most of mine," added Sir Michael Isherwood ruefully.

"Why should not Master Segrave take the bank," here came in shrill accents from Mistress Endicott, who throughout her conversation with Lambert had kept a constant eye on what went on around her husband's table. "He seems the only moneyed man amongst you all," she added with a laugh, which grated most unpleasantly on Richard's ear.

"I will gladly take the bank," said Segrave eagerly.

"Pardi! I care not who hath the bank," quoth Lord Walterton, with the slow emphasis of the inebriated. "My system takes time to work. . . And I stand to lose a good deal unless. . . hic. . . unless I win!"

"You are not where you were, when you began," commented Sir Michael grimly.

"By Gad, no! . . . hic. . . but 'tis no matter. . . Give me time!"

"Methought I saw Sir Marmaduke de Chavasse just now," said Endicott, looking about him. "Ah! and here comes our worthy baronet," he added cheerily as Sir Marmaduke's closely cropped head—very noticeable in the crowd of periwigs—emerged from amidst the group that clustered round Mistress Endicott. "A hand at primero, sir?"

"I thank you, no!" replied Sir Marmaduke, striving to master his habitual ill-humor and to speak pleasantly. "My luck hath long since deserted me, if it e'er visited me at all. A fact of which I grow daily more doubtful."

"But ventre-saint-gris!" exclaimed Lord Walterton, who showed an inclination to become quarrelsome in his cups, "we must have someone to take Endicott's place, I cannot work my system hic. . . if so few play. . ."

"Perhaps your young friend, Sir Marmaduke. . ." suggested Mistress Endicott, waving an embroidered handkerchief in the direction of Richard Lambert.

"No doubt! no doubt!" rejoined Sir Marmaduke, turning with kindly graciousness to his secretary. "Master Lambert, these gentlemen are requiring another hand for their game. . . I pray you join in with them. . ."

"I would do so with pleasure, sir," replied Lambert, still unsuspecting, "but I fear me I am a complete novice at cards. . . What is the game?"

He was vaguely distrustful of cards, for he had oft heard this pastime condemned as ungodly by those with whom he had held converse in his early youth, nevertheless it did not occur to him that there might be anything wrong in a game which was countenanced by Sir Marmaduke de Chavasse, whom he knew to be an avowed Puritan, and by the saintly lady who had been the friend of ex-Queen Henrietta Maria.

"'Tis a simple round game," said Sir Marmaduke lightly, "you would soon learn."

"And. . ." said Lambert diffidently questioning, and eying the gold and silver which lay in profusion on the table, "there is no money at stake. . . of course? . . ."

"Oh! only a little," rejoined Mistress Endicott, "a paltry trifle. . . to add zest to the enjoyment of the game."

"However little it may be, Sir Marmaduke," said Lambert firmly, speaking directly to his employer, "I humbly pray you to excuse me before these gentlemen. . ."

The three players at the table, as well as the two Endicotts, had listened to this colloquy with varying feelings. Segrave was burning with impatience, Lord Walterton was getting more and more fractious, whilst Sir Michael Isherwood viewed the young secretary with marked hauteur. At the last words spoken by Lambert there came from all these gentlemen sundry exclamations, expressive of contempt or annoyance, which caused an ugly frown to appear between de Chavasse's eyes, and a deep blush to rise in the young man's pale cheek.

"What do you mean?" queried Sir Marmaduke harshly.

"There are other gentlemen here," said Lambert, speaking with more firmness and decision now that he encountered inimical glances and felt as if somehow he was on his trial before all these people, "and I am not rich enough to afford the luxury of gambling."

"Nay! if that is your difficulty," rejoined Sir Marmaduke, "I pray you, good master, to command my purse. . . you are under my wing tonight. . . and I will gladly bear the burden of your losses."

"I thank you, Sir Marmaduke," said the young man, with quiet dignity," and I entreat you once again to excuse me. . . I have never staked at cards, either mine own money or that of others. I would prefer not to begin."

"Meseems. . . hic. . . de Chavasse, that this. . . this young friend of yours is a hic. . . damned Puritan. . ." came in ever thickening accents from Lord Walterton.

"I hope, Sir Marmaduke de Chavasse," here interposed Endicott with much pompous dignity, "that your. . . hem. . . your young friend doth not desire to bring insinuations doubts, mayhap, against the honor of my house. . . or of my friends!"

"Nay! nay! good Endicott," said Sir Marmaduke, speaking in tones that were so conciliatory, so unlike his own quarrelsome temper, quick at taking offense, that Richard Lambert could not help wondering what was causing this change, "Master Lambert hath no such intention—'pon my honor. . . He is young. . . and. . . and he misunderstands. . . You see, my good Lambert," he added, once more turning to the young man, and still speaking with unwonted kindness and patience, "you are covering yourself with ridicule and placing me—who am your protector to-night—in a very awkward position. Had I known you were such a gaby I should have left you to go to bed alone."

"Nay! Sir Marmaduke," here came in decisive accents from portly Mistress Endicott, "methinks 'tis you who misunderstand Master Lambert. He is of a surety an honorable gentleman, and hath no desire to insult me, who have ne'er done him wrong, nor yet my friends by refusing a friendly game of cards in my house!"

She spoke very pointedly, causing her speech to seem like a menace, even though the words betokened gentleness and friendship.

Lambert's scruples and his desire to please struggled hopelessly in his mind. Mistress Endicott's eye held him silent even while it urged him to speak. What could he say? Sir Marmaduke, toward whom he felt gratitude and respect, surely would not urge what he thought would be wrong for Lambert.

And if a chaste and pure woman did not disapprove of a game of primero among friends, what right had he to set up his own standard of right or wrong against hers? What right had he to condemn what she approved? To offend his generous employer, and to bring opprobrium and ridicule on himself which would of necessity redound against Sir Marmaduke also?

Vague instinct still entered a feeble protest, but reason and common sense and a certain undetermined feeling of what was due to himself socially—poor country bumpkin!—fought a hard battle too.

"I am right, am I not, good Master Lambert?" came in dulcet tones from the virtuous hostess, "that you would not really refuse a quiet game of cards with my friends, at my entreaty. . . in my house?"

And Lambert, with a self-deprecatory sigh, and a shrug of the shoulders, said quietly:

"I have no option, gracious mistress!"

XVIII

The Trap

Richard Lambert fortunately for his own peace of mind and the retention of his dignity, was able to wave aside the hand full of gold and silver coins which Sir Marmaduke extended towards him.

"I thank you, sir," he said calmly; "I am able to bear the cost of mine own unavoidable weakness. I have money of mine own."

From out his doublet he took a tiny leather wallet containing a few gold coins, his worldly all bequeathed to him the same as to his brother—so the old friend who had brought the lads up had oft explained—by his grandmother. The little satchel never left his person from the moment that the old Quakeress had placed it in his hands. There were but five guineas in all, to which he had added from time to time the few shillings which Sir Marmaduke paid him as salary.

He chided his own weakness inwardly, when he felt the hot tears surging to his eyes at thought of the unworthy use to which his little hoard was about to be put.

But he walked to the table with a bold step; there was nothing now of the country lout about him; on the contrary, he moved with remarkable dignity, and bore himself so well that many a pair of feminine eyes watched him kindly, as he took his seat at the baize-covered table.

"Will one of you gentlemen teach me the game?" he asked simply.

It was remarkable that no one sneered at him again, and in these days of arrogance peculiar to the upper classes this was all the more noticeable, as these secret clubs were thought to be very exclusive, the resort pre-eminently of gentlemen and noblemen who were anti-Puritan, anti-Republican, and very jealous of their ranks and privileges.

Yet when after those few unpleasant moments of hesitation Lambert boldly accepted the situation and with much simple dignity took his seat at the table, everyone immediately accepted him as an equal, nor did anyone question his right to sit there on terms of equality with Lord Walterton or Sir Michael Isherwood.

His own state of mind was very remarkable at the moment.

Of course he disapproved of what he did: he would not have been the Puritanically trained, country-bred lad that he was, if he had accepted with an easy conscience the idea of tossing about money from hand to hand, money that he could in no sense afford to lose, or money that no one was making any honest effort to win.

He knew—somewhat vaguely perhaps, yet with some degree of certainty—that gambling was an illicit pastime, and that therefore he—by sitting at this table with these gentlemen, was deliberately contravening the laws of his country.

Against all that, it is necessary to note that Richard Lambert took two matters very much in earnest: first, his position as a paid dependent; second, his gratitude to Sir Marmaduke de Chavasse.

And both these all-pervading facts combined to force him against his will into this anomalous position of gentlemanly gambler, which suited neither his temperament nor his principles.

With it all Lambert's was one of those dispositions, often peculiar to those who have led an isolated and introspective life, which never do anything half-heartedly; and just as he took his somewhat empty secretarial duties seriously, so did he look on this self-imposed task, against which his better judgment rebelled, with earnestness and determination.

He listened attentively to the preliminary explanations given him sotto voce by Endicott. Segrave in the meanwhile had taken the latter's place at the head of the table. He had put all his money in front of him, some two hundred and sixty pounds all told, for his winnings during the last half hour had not been as steady as heretofore, and he had not yet succeeded altogether in making up that sum of money for which he yearned with all the intensity of a disturbed conscience, eager to redeem one miserable fault by another hardly more avowable.

He shuffled the cards and dealt just as Endicott had done.

"Now will you look at your card, young sir," said Endicott, who stood behind Lambert's chair, whispering directions in his ear. "A splendid card, begad! and one on which you must stake freely. . . Nay! nay! that is not enough," he added, hurriedly restraining the young man's hand, who had timidly pushed a few silver coins forward. "'Tis thus you must do!"

And before Lambert had time to protest the rotund man in the cinnamon doublet and the wide lace cuffs, had emptied the contents of the little leather wallet upon the table.

Five golden guineas rested on Lambert's card. Segrave turned up his own and declared:

"I pay queen and upwards!"

"A two, by gad!" said Lord Walterton, too confused in his feeble head now to display any real fury. "Did anyone ever see such accursed luck?"

"And look at this nine," quoth Sir Michael, who had become very sullen; "not a card to-night!"

"I have a king," said Lambert quietly.

"And as I had the pleasure to remark before, my dear young friend," said Endicott blandly, "'tis a mighty good card to hold. . . And see," he continued, as Segrave without comment added five more golden guineas to Lambert's little hoard, "see how wise it was to stake a goodly sum. . . That is the whole art of the game of primero. . . to know just what to stake on each card in accordance with its value and the law of averages. . . But you will learn in time, young man you will learn. . ."

"The game doth not appear to be vastly complicated," assented Lambert lightly.

"I have played primero on a system for years. . ." quoth Lord Walterton sententiously, "but to-night. . . hic. . . by Gad! . . . I cannot make the system work right. . . hic!"

But already Segrave was dealing again. Lambert staked more coolly now. In his mind he had already set aside the original five guineas which came from his grandmother. With strange ease and through no merit of his own, yet perfectly straightforwardly and honestly, he had become the owner of another five; these he felt more justified in risking on the hazard of the game.

But the goddess of Fortune smiling benignly on this country-bred lad, had in a wayward mood apparently taken him under her special protection. He staked and won again, and then again pleased at his success. . . in spite of himself feeling the subtle poison of excitement creeping into his veins. . . yet remaining perfectly calm outwardly the while.

Segrave, on the other hand, was losing in exact proportion to the newcomer's winnings: already his pile of gold had perceptibly diminished, whilst the hectic flush on his cheeks became more and more accentuated, the glitter in his eyes more unnatural and feverish, his hands as they shuffled and dealt the cards more trembling and febrile.

"'Pon my honor," quoth Sir Marmaduke, throwing a careless glance at the table, "meseems you are in luck, my good Lambert. Doubtless, you are not sorry now that you allowed yourself to be persuaded."

"'Tis not unpleasant to win," rejoined Lambert lightly, "but believe me, sir, the game itself gives me no pleasure."

"I pay knave and upwards," declared Segrave in a dry and hollow voice, and with burning eyes fixed upon his new and formidable opponent.

"My last sovereign, par Dieu!" swore Lord Walterton, throwing the money across to Segrave with an unsteady hand.

"And one of my last," said Sir Michael, as he followed suit.

"And what is your stake, Master Lambert?" queried Segrave.

"Twenty pounds I see," replied the young man, as with a careless hand he counted over the gold which lay pell-mell on his card; "I staked on the king without counting."

Segrave in his turn pushed some gold towards him. The pile in front of him was not half the size it had been before this stranger from the country had sat down to play. He tried to remain master of himself, not to show before these egotistical, careless cavaliers all the agony of mind which he now endured and which had turned to positive physical torture.

The ghost of stolen money, of exposure, of pillory and punishment which had so perceptibly paled as he saw the chance of replacing by his unexpected winnings that which he had purloined, once more rose to confront him. Again he saw before him the irascible employer, pointing with relentless finger at the deficiency in the accounts, again he saw his weeping mother, his stern father,—the disgrace, the irretrievable past.

"You are not leaving off playing, Sir Michael?" he asked anxiously, as the latter having handed him over a golden guinea, rose from the table and without glancing at his late partners in the game, turned his back on them all.

"Par Dieu!" he retorted, speaking roughly, and none too civilly over his shoulder, "my pockets are empty. . . Like Master Lambert here," he added with an unmistakable sneer, "I find no pleasure in *this* sort of game!"

"What do you mean?" queried Segrave hotly.

"Oh, nothing," rejoined the other dryly, "you need not heed my remark. Are you not losing, too?"

"What does he mean?" said Lambert with a puzzled frown, instinctively turning to his employer.

"Naught! naught! my good Lambert," replied Sir Marmaduke, dropping his voice to a whisper. "Sir Michael Isherwood hath lost more than he can afford and is somewhat choleric of temper, that is all."

"And in a little quiet game, my good young friend," added Endicott, also in a whisper, "'tis wisest to take no heed of a loser's vapors."

"I pay ace only!" quoth Segrave triumphantly, who in the meanwhile had continued the game.

Lord Walterton swore a loud and prolonged oath. He had staked five guineas on a king and had lost.

"Ventre-saint-gris, and likewise par le sang-bleu!" he said, "the first time I have had a king! Segrave, ye must leave me these few little yellow toys, else I cannot pay for my lodgings to-night. . . I'll give you a bill. . . but I've had enough of this, by Gad!"

And somewhat sobered, though still unsteady, he rose from the table.

"Surely, my lord, you are not leaving off, too?" asked Segrave.

"Nay! . . . how can I continue?" He turned his breeches pockets ostentatiously inside out. "Behold, friend, these two beautiful and innocent little dears!"

"You can give me more bills. . ." urged Segrave, "and you lose. . . you may not lose after this. . . 'tis lucky to play on credit. . . and. . . and your bills are always met, my lord. . ."

He spoke with feverish volubility, though his throat was parched and every word he uttered caused him pain. But he was determined that the game should proceed.

He had won a little of his own back again the last few rounds. Certainly his luck would turn once more. His luck *must* turn once more, or else. . .

"Nay! nay! I've had enough," said Lord Walterton, nodding a heavy head up and down, "there are too many of my bills about as it is. . . I've had enough."

"Methinks, of a truth," said Lambert decisively, "that the game has indeed lasted long enough. . . And if some other gentleman would but take my place. . ."

He made a movement as if to rise from the table, but was checked by a harsh laugh and a peremptory word from Segrave.

"Impossible," said the latter, "you, Master Lambert, cannot leave off in any case. . . My lord. . . another hand. . ." he urged again.

"Nay! nay! my dear Segrave," replied Lord Walterton, shaking himself like a sleepy dog, "the game hath ceased to have any pleasure for me, as our young friend here hath remarked. . . I wish you good luck. . . and good-night."

Whereupon he turned on his heel and straddled away to another corner of the room, away from the temptation of that green-covered table.

"We two then, Master Lambert," said Segrave with ever-growing excitement, "what say you? Double or quits?"

BARONESS EMMUSKA ORCZY

And he pointed, with that same febrile movement of his, to the heap of gold standing on the table beside Lambert.

"As you please," replied the latter quietly, as he pushed the entire pile forward.

Segrave dealt, then turned up his card.

"Ten!" he said curtly.

"Mine is a knave," rejoined Lambert.

"How do we stand?" queried the other, as with a rapid gesture he passed a trembling hand over his burning forehead.

"Methinks you owe me a hundred pounds," replied Richard, who seemed strangely calm in the very midst of this inexplicable and volcanic turmoil which he felt was seething all round him. He had won a hundred pounds—a fortune in those days for a country lad like himself; but for the moment the thought of what that hundred pounds would mean to him and to his brother Adam, was lost in the whirl of excitement which had risen to his head like wine.

He had steadily refused the glasses of muscadel or sack which Mistress Endicott had insinuatingly and persistently been offering him, ever since he began to play; yet he felt intoxicated, with strange currents of fire which seemed to run through his veins.

The subtle poison had done its work. Any remorse which he may have felt at first, for thus acting against his own will and better judgment, and for yielding like a weakling to persuasion, which had no moral rectitude for basis, was momentarily smothered by the almost childish delight of winning, of seeing the pile of gold growing in front of him. He had never handled money before; it was like a fascinating yet insidious toy which he could not help but finger.

"Are you not playing rather high, gentlemen?" came in dulcet tones from Mistress Endicott; "I do not allow high play in my house. Master Lambert, I would fain ask you to cease."

"I am more than ready, madam," said Richard with alacrity.

"Nay! but I am not ready," interposed Segrave vehemently. "Nay! nay!" he repeated with feverish insistence, "Master Lambert cannot cease playing now. He is bound in honor to give me a chance for revenge. . . Double or quits, Master Lambert! . . . Double or quits?"

"As you please," quoth Lambert imperturbably.

"Ye cannot cut to each other," here interposed Endicott didactically. "The rules of primero moreover demand that if there are but two players, a third and disinterested party shall deal the cards."

"Then will you cut and deal, Master Endicott," said Segrave impatiently; "I care not so long as I can break Master Lambert's luck and redeem mine own. . . Double or quits, Master Lambert. . . Double or quits. . . I shall either owe you two hundred pounds or not one penny. . . In which case we can make a fresh start. . ."

Lambert eyed him with curiosity, sympathetically too, for the young man was in a state of terrible mental agitation, whilst he himself felt cooler than before.

Endicott dealt each of the two opponents a card face downwards, but even as he did so, the one which he had dealt to Lambert fluttered to the ground.

He stooped and picked it up.

Segrave's eyes at the moment were fixed on his own card, Lambert's on the face of his opponent. No one else in the room was paying any attention to the play of the two young men, for everyone was busy with his own affairs. Play was general, the hour late. The wines had been heady, and all tempers were at fever pitch.

No one, therefore, was watching Endicott's movements at the moment when he ostensibly stooped to pick up the fallen card.

"It is not faced," he said, "what shall we do?"

"Give it to Master Lambert forsooth," quoth Mistress Endicott, "'tis unlucky to re-deal. . . providing," she added artfully, "that Master Segrave hath no objection."

"Nay! nay!" said the latter. "Begad! why should we stop the game for a trifle?"

Then as Lambert took the card from Endicott and casually glanced at it, Segrave declared:

"Queen!"

"King!" retorted Lambert, with the same perfect calm. "King of diamonds. . . that card has been persistently faithful to me to-night."

"The devil himself hath been faithful to you, Master Lambert. . ." said Segrave tonelessly, "you have the hell's own luck. . . What do I pay you now?"

"It was double or quits, Master Segrave," rejoined Lambert, "which brings it up to two hundred pounds. . . You will do me the justice to own that I did not seek this game."

In his heart he had already resolved not to make use of his own winnings. Somehow as in a flash of intuition he perceived the whole tragedy of dishonor and of ruin which seemed to be writ on his opponent's face. He understood that what he had regarded as a toy—welcome no doubt, but treacherous for all that—was a matter of life or death—nay! more mayhap to that pallid youth, with the hectic flush, the unnaturally bright eyes and trembling hands.

There was silence for a while round the green-topped table, whilst thoughts, feelings, presentiments of very varied kinds congregated there. With Endicott and his wife, and also with Sir Marmaduke, it was acute tension, the awful nerve strain of anticipation. The seconds for them seemed an eternity, the obsession of waiting was like lead on their brains.

During that moment of acute suspense Richard Lambert was quietly co-ordinating his thoughts.

With that one mental flash-light which had shown up to him the hitherto unsuspected tragedy, the latent excitement in him had vanished. He saw his own weakness in its true light, despised himself for having yielded, and looked upon the heap of gold before him as so much ill-gotten wealth, which it would be a delight to restore to the hand from whence it came.

He heartily pitied the young man before him, and was forming vague projects of how best to make him understand in private and without humiliation that the money which he had lost would be returned to him in full. Strangely enough he was still holding in his hand that king of diamonds which Endicott had dealt to him.

XIX

Disgrace

Segrave, too, had been silent, of course. In his mind there was neither suspense nor calm. It was utter, dull and blank despair which assailed him, the ruin of his fondest hopes, an awful abyss of disgrace, of punishment, of death at best, which seemed to yawn before him from the other side of the baize-covered table.

Instinct—that ever-present instinct of self-control peculiar to the gently-bred race of mankind—caused him to make frantic efforts to keep himself and his nerves in check. He would—even at this moment of complete ruin—have given the last shreds of his worldly possessions to be able to steady the febrile movements of his hand.

The pack of cards was on the table, just as Endicott had put it down, after dealing, with the exception of the queen of hearts in front of Segrave and the lucky king of diamonds on which Lambert was still mechanically gazing.

He was undoubtedly moved by the desire to hide the trembling of his hands and the gathering tears in his eyes when he began idly to scatter the pack upon the table, spreading out the cards, fingering them one by one, setting his teeth the while lest that latent cry of misery should force its way across his lips.

Suddenly he paused in this idle fingering of the cards. His eyes which already were burning with hot tears, seemed to take on an almost savage glitter. A hoarse cry escaped his parched lips.

"In the name of Heaven, Master Segrave, what ails you?" cried Endicott with well-feigned concern.

Segrave's hand wandered mechanically to his own neck; he tugged at the fastening of his lace collar, as if, in truth, he were choking.

"The king. . . The king of diamonds," he murmured in a hollow voice. "Two. . . two kings of diamonds. . ."

He laughed, a long, harsh laugh, the laugh of a maniac, or of a man possessed, whilst one long thin finger pointed tremblingly to the card still held by Richard Lambert, and then to its counterpart in the midst of the scattered pack.

That laugh seemed to echo all round the room. Dames and cavaliers, players and idlers, looked up to see whence that weird sound had come. Instinctively the crowd drew nigh, dice and cards were pushed aside. Some strange drama was being enacted between two young men, more interesting even than the caprices of Fortune.

But already Endicott and also Sir Marmaduke de Chavasse had followed the beckonings of Segrave's feverish hand.

There could be no mistake in what they saw nor yet in the ominous consequences which it foretold. There was a king of diamonds in the scattered pack of cards upon the table, and yet the card which Lambert held, in consequence of which he had just won two hundred pounds, was also the king of diamonds.

"Two kings of diamonds. . . by all that's damnable!" quoth Lord Walterton, who had been the first to draw nigh.

"But in Heaven's name, what does it all mean?" exclaimed Lambert, gazing at the two cards, hearing the comments round him, yet utterly unable to understand.

Segrave jumped to his feet.

"It means, young man," he exclaimed in a wild state of frenzy, maddened by his losses, his former crime, his present ruin, "it means that you are a damned thief."

And with frantic, excited gesture he gathered up the cards and threw them violently into Richard Lambert's face.

A curious sound went round the room—a gasp, hardly a cry—and all those present held their breath, silent, appalled at the terrible tragedy expressed by these two young men standing face to face on the brink of a deathly and almost blasphemous conflict.

Mistress Endicott was the first to utter a cry.

"Silence! silence!" she shouted shrilly. "Master Segrave, I adjure you to be silent. . . I'll not permit you to insult my guest."

Already Lambert had made a quick movement to throw himself on Segrave. The elemental instinct of self-defense, of avenging a terrible insult by physical violence, rose within him, whispering of strength and power, of the freedom, muscle-giving life of the country as against the enervating, weakening influence of the town.

He knew that in a hand-to-hand struggle with the feverish, emaciated townsman, he, the country-bred lad, the haunter of woods and cliffs, the dweller of the Thanet smithy, would be more than a match for his opponent. But even as his whole body stiffened for a spring, his muscles tightened and his fists clenched, a dozen restraining hands held him back from his purpose, whilst Mistress Endicott's shrill tones seemed to bring him back to the realities of his own peril.

"Mistress Endicott," he said, turning a proud, yet imploring look to the lady whose virtues had been so loudly proclaimed in his ears, "Madam, I appeal to you. . . I implore you to listen. . . a frightful insult which you have witnessed. . . an awful accusation on which I scarce can trust myself to dwell has been hurled at me. . . I entreat you to allow me to challenge these two gentlemen to explain."

And he pointed both to Segrave and to Endicott, The former, after his mad outburst of ungovernable rage, had regained a certain measure of calm. He stood, facing Lambert, with arms folded across his chest, whilst a smile of insulting irony curled his thin lips.

Endicott's eyes seemed to be riveted on Lambert's breast.

At mention of his own name, he suddenly darted forward, and seemed to be plunging his hand—the hand which almost disappeared within the ample folds of the voluminous lace cuff—into the breast pocket of the young man's doublet.

His movements were so quick, so sure and so unexpected that no one—least of all Lambert—could possibly guess what was his purpose.

The next moment—less than a second later—he had again withdrawn his hand, but now everyone could see that he held a few cards in it. These he dropped with an exclamation of loathing and contempt upon the table, whilst those around, instinctively drew back a step or two as if fearful of coming in contact with something impure and terrible.

Endicott's movements, his quick gestures, well aided by the wide lace cuffs which fell over his hand, his exclamation of contempt, had all contributed to make it seem before the spectators as if he had found a few winning cards secreted inside the lining of Richard Lambert's doublet.

"Nay! young sir," he said with an evil sneer, "meseems that explanations had best come from you. Here," he added, pointing significantly at the cards which he had just dropped out of his own hand, "here is a vastly pleasing collection. . . aces and kings. . . passing serviceable in a quiet game of primero among friends."

Lambert had been momentarily dumfounded, for undoubtedly he had not perceived Endicott's treacherous movements, and had absolutely no idea whence had come those awful cards which somehow or other seemed to be convicting him of lying and cheating: so conscious was he of his own innocence, that never for a moment did the slightest fear cross his mind that he could not immediately make clear his own position, and proclaim his own integrity.

"This is an infamous plot," he said calmly, but very firmly. "Sir Marmaduke de Chavasse," he added, turning to face his employer, who still stood motionless and silent in the background, "in the name of Heaven I beg of you to explain to these gentlemen that you have known me from boyhood. Will you speak?" he added insistently, conscious of a strange tightening of his heartstrings as the man on whom he relied, remained impassive and made no movement to come to his help. "Will you tell them, I pray you, sir, that you know me to be a man of honor, incapable of such villainy as they suggest? . . . You know that I did not even wish to play. . ."

"That reluctance of yours, my good Lambert, seems to have been a pretty comedy forsooth," replied Sir Marmaduke lightly, "and you played to some purpose, meseems, when you once began. . . Nay! I pray you," he added with unmitigated harshness, "do not drag me into your quarrels. . . I cannot of a truth champion your virtue."

Lambert's cheeks became deathly pale. The first inkling of the deadly peril of his own situation had suddenly come to him with Sir Marmaduke's callous words. It seemed to him as if the very universe must stand still in the face of such treachery. The man whom he loved with all the fervor of a grateful nature, the man who knew him and whom he had wholly trusted, was proving his most bitter, most damning enemy.

After Sir Marmaduke's speech, his own employer's repudiation, he felt that all his chances of clearing his character before these sneering gentlemen had suddenly vanished.

"This is cruel, and infamous," he protested, conscious innocence within him still striving to fight a hard battle against overwhelming odds. "Gentlemen! . . . as I am a man of honor, I swear that I do not know what all this means!"

"It means, young man, that you are an accursed cheat. . . a thief. . . a liar!" shouted Segrave, whose last vestige of self-control suddenly vanished, whilst mad frenzy once more held him in its grip. "I swear by God that you shall pay me for this!"

He threw himself with all the strength of a raving maniac upon Lambert, who for the moment was taken unawares, and yielded to the suddenness of the onslaught. But it was indeed a conflict 'twixt town and country, the simple life against nightly dissipations, the forests and cliffs of Thanet against the enervating atmosphere of the city.

After that first onrush, Lambert, with marvelous agility and quick knowledge of a hand-to-hand fight, had shaken himself free of his opponent's trembling grasp. It was his turn now to have the upper hand, and in a trice he had, with a vigorous clutch, gripped his opponent by the throat.

In a sense, his calmness had not forsaken him, his mind was as quiet, as clear as heretofore; it was only his muscle—his bodily energy in the face of a violent and undeserved attack—which had ceased to be under his control.

"Man! man!" he murmured, gazing steadily into the eyes of his antagonist, "ye shall swallow those words—or by Heaven I will kill you!"

The tumult which ensued drowned everything save itself. . . everything, even the sound of that slow and measured tramp, tramp, tramp, which was wafted up from the street.

The women shouted, the men swore. Some ran like frightened sheep to the distant corners of the room, fearful lest they be embroiled in this unpleasant fracas. . . others crowded round Segrave and Lambert, trying to pacify them, to drag the strong youth away from his weaker opponent—almost his victim now.

Some were for forcibly separating them, others for allowing them to fight their own battles and loud-voiced arguments, subsidiary quarrels, mingled with the shrill cries of terror and caused a din which grew in deafening intensity, degenerating into a wild orgy as glasses were knocked off the tables, cards strewn about, candles sent flying and spluttering upon the ground.

And still that measured tramp down the street, growing louder, more distinct, a muffled "Halt!" the sound of arms, of men moving about beneath that yawning archway and along the dark and dismal passage with its hermetically closed front door.

XX

My Lord Protector's Patrol

A lone, Sir Marmaduke de Chavasse had taken no part in the confused turmoil which raged around the personalities of Segrave and Richard Lambert. From the moment that he had—with studied callousness—turned his back on his erstwhile protégé he had held aloof from the crowd which had congregated around the two young men.

He saw before him the complete success of his nefarious plan, which had originated in the active brain of Editha, but had been perfected in his own—of heaping dire and lasting disgrace on the man who had become troublesome and interfering of late, who was a serious danger to his more important schemes.

After the fracas of this night Richard Lambert forsooth could never show his face within two hundred miles of London, the ugly story of his having cheated at cards and been publicly branded as a liar and a thief by a party of gentlemen would of a surety penetrate even within the fastnesses of Thanet.

So far everything was for the best, nay, it might be better still, for Segrave enraged and maddened at his losses, might succeed in getting Lambert imprisoned for stealing, and cheating, even at the cost of his own condemnation to a fine for gambling.

The Endicotts had done their part well. The man especially, with his wide cuffs and his quick movements. No one there present could have the slightest doubt but that Lambert was guilty. Satisfied, therefore, that all had gone according to his own wishes, Sir Marmaduke withdrew from further conflict or argument with the unfortunate young man, whom he had so deliberately and so hopelessly ruined.

And because he thus kept aloof, his ears were not so completely filled with the din, nor his mind so wholly engrossed by the hand-to-hand struggle between the two young men, that he did not perceive that other sound, which, in spite of barred windows and drawn curtains, came up from the street below.

At first he had only listened carelessly to the measured tramp. But the cry of "Halt!" issuing from immediately beneath the windows caused his cheeks to blanch and his muscles to stiffen with a sudden sense of fear.

He cast a rapid glance all around. Segrave and Lambert—both flushed and panting—were forcibly held apart. Sir Marmaduke noted with a grim smile that the latter was obviously the center of a hostile group, whilst Segrave was surrounded by a knot of sympathizers who were striving outwardly to pacify him, whilst in reality urging him on through their unbridled vituperations directed against the other man.

The noise of arguments, of shrill voices, of admonitions and violent abuse had in no sense abated.

Over the sea of excited faces Sir Marmaduke caught the wide-open, terrified eyes of Editha de Chavasse.

She too, had heard.

He beckoned to her across the room with a slight gesture of the hand, and she obeyed the silent call as quickly as she dared, working her way round to him, without arousing the attention of the crowd.

"Do not lose your head," he whispered as soon as she was near him and seeing the wild terror expressed in every line of her face. "Slip into the next room. . . and leave the door ajar. . . Do this as quietly as may be. . . now. . . at once. . . then wait there until I come."

Again she obeyed him silently and swiftly, for she knew what that cry of "Halt!" meant, uttered at the door of her house. She had heard it, even as Sir Marmaduke had done, and after it the peremptory knocks, the loud call, the word of command, followed by the sound of an awed and supplicating voice, entering a feeble protest.

She knew what all that meant, and she was afraid.

As soon as Sir Marmaduke saw that she had done just as he had ordered, he deliberately joined the noisy groups which were congregated around Segrave and Lambert.

He pushed his way forward and anon stood face to face with the young man on whom he had just wreaked such an irreparable wrong. Not a thought of compunction or remorse rose in his mind as he looked down at the handsome flushed face—quite calm and set outwardly in spite of the terrible agony raging within heart and mind.

"Lambert!" he said gruffly, "listen to me. . . Your conduct hath been most unseemly. . . Mistress Endicott has for my sake, already shown you much kindness and forbearance. . . Had she acted as she had the right to do, she would have had you kicked out of the house by her servants. . . In your own interests now I should advise you to follow me quietly out of the house. . ."

But this suggestion raised a hot protest on the part of all the spectators.

"He shall not go!" declared Segrave violently.

"Not without leaving behind him what he has deliberately stolen," commented Endicott, raising his oily voice above the din.

Lambert had waited patiently, whilst his employer spoke. The last remnant of that original sense of deference and of gratitude caused him to hold himself in check lest he should strike that treacherous coward in the face. Sir Marmaduke's callousness in the face of his peril and unmerited disgrace, had struck Lambert with an overwhelming feeling of disappointment and loneliness. But his cruel insults now quashed despair and roused dormant indignation to fever pitch. One look at Sir Marmaduke's sneering face had told him not only that he could expect no help from the man who—by all the laws of honor—should have stood by him in his helplessness, but that he was the fount and source, the instigator of the terrible wrong and injustice which was about to land an innocent man in the veriest abyss of humiliation and irretrievable disgrace.

"And so this was your doing, Sir Marmaduke de Chavasse," he said, looking his triumphant enemy boldly in the face, even whilst compelling silent attention from those who were heaping opprobrious epithets upon him. "You enticed me here. . . You persuaded me to play, . . . Then you tried to rob me of mine honor, of my good name, the only valuable assets which I possess. . . Hell and all its devils alone know why you did this thing, but I swear before God that your hideous crime shall not remain unpunished. . ."

"Silence!" commanded Sir Marmaduke, who was the first to perceive the strange, almost supernatural, effect produced on all those present, by the young man's earnestness, his impressive calm. Segrave himself stood silent and abashed, whilst everyone listened, unconsciously awed by that unmistakable note of righteousness which somehow rang through Lambert's voice.

"Nay! but I'll not be silent," quoth Richard unperturbed. "I have been condemned. . . and I have the right to speak. . . You have disgraced me. . . and I have the right to defend mine honor. . . by protesting mine innocence. . . And now I will leave this house," he added loudly and firmly, "for it is accursed and infamous. . . but God is my witness that I leave it without a stain upon my soul. . ."

He pointed to the fateful table whereon a pile of gold lay scattered in an untidy heap, with the tiny leather wallet containing his five guineas conspicuously in its midst.

"There lies the money," he said, speaking directly to Segrave, "take it, sir, for I had never the intention to touch a penny of it. . . This I swear by all that I hold most sacred. . . Take it without fear or remorse—even though you thought such evil things of me. . . and let him who still thinks me a thief, repeat it now to my face—an he dare!"

Even as the last of his loudly uttered words resounded through the room, there was a loud knock at the door, and a peremptory voice commanded:

"Open! in the name of His Highness, the Lord Protector of England!"

In the dead silence that followed, the buzz of a fly, the spluttering of wax candles, could be distinctly heard.

In a moment with the sound of that peremptory call outside, tumultuous passions seemed to sink to rest, every cheek paled, and masculine hands instinctively sought the handles of swords whilst lace handkerchiefs were hastily pressed to trembling lips, in order to smother the cry of terror which had risen to feminine throats.

"Open! in the name of His Highness, the Lord Protector of England."

Mistress Endicott was the color of wax, her husband was gripping her wrist with a clutch of steel, trying, through the administration of physical pain, to keep alive her presence of mind.

And for the third time came the loud summons:

"Open! in the name of His Highness the Lord, Protector of England!"

Still that deathly silence in the room, broken only now by the firm step of Endicott, who went to open the door.

Resistance had been worse than useless. The door would have yielded at the first blow. There was a wailing, smothered cry from a dozen terrified throats, and a general rush for the inner room. But this door now was bolted and barred, Sir Marmaduke—unperceived—had slipped quickly within, even whilst everyone held his breath in the first moment of paralyzed terror.

Had there been time, there would doubtless have ensued a violent attack against that locked door, but already a man in leather doublet and wearing a steel cap and collar had peremptorily pushed Endicott aside, who was making a futile effort to bar the way, after he had opened the door.

This man now advanced into the center of the room, whilst a couple of soldierly-looking, stalwart fellows remained at attention on the threshold.

"Let no one attempt to leave this room," he commanded. "Here, Bradden," he added, turning back to his men, "take Pyott with you and search that second room there. . . then seize all those cards and dice and also that money."

It was not likely that these hot-headed cavaliers would submit thus quietly to an arbitrary act of confiscation and of arrest. Hardly were the last words out of the man's mouth than a dozen blades flashed out of their scabbards.

The women screamed, and like so many frightened hens, ran into the corner of the room furthest out of reach of my Lord Protector's police-patrol, the men immediately forming a bulwark in front of them.

The whole thing was not very heroic perhaps. A few idlers caught in an illicit act and under threat of arrest. The consequences—of a truth— would not be vastly severe for the frequenters of this secret club; fines mayhap, which most of those present could ill afford to pay, and at worst a night's detention in one of those horrible wooden constructions which had lately been erected on the river bank for the express purpose of causing sundry lordly offenders to pass an uncomfortable night.

These were days of forcible levelings: and my lord who had contravened old Noll's laws against swearing and gambling, fared not one whit better than the tramp who had purloined a leg of mutton from an eating-house.

Nay! in a measure my lord fared a good deal worse, for he looked upon his own detention through the regicide usurper's orders, as an indignity to himself; hence the reason why in this same house wherein a few idle scions of noble houses indulged in their favorite pastime, when orders rang out in the name of His Highness, swords jumped out of their sheaths, and resistance was offered out of all proportion to the threat.

The man who seemed to be the captain of the patrol smiled somewhat grimly when he saw himself confronted by this phalanx of gentlemanly weapons. He was a tall, burly fellow, broad of shoulder and well-looking in his uniform of red with yellow facings; his round bullet-shaped head, covered by the round steel cap, was suggestive of obstinacy, even of determination.

He eyed the flushed and excited throng with some amusement not wholly unmixed with contempt. Oh! he knew some of the faces well enough by sight—for he had originally served in the train-bands of London, and had oft seen my Lord Walterton, for instance, conspicuous at every entertainment—now pronounced illicit by His Highness, and Sir Anthony Bridport, a constant frequenter at Exeter House, and young Lord Naythmire the son of the Judge. He also had certainly seen young Segrave before this, whose father had been a member of the Long Parliament; the only face that was totally strange to him was that of the youngster in the dark suit of grogram, who stood somewhat aloof from the irate crowd, and seemed to be viewing the scene with astonishment rather than with alarm.

Lord Walterton, flushed with wine, more than with anger, constituted himself the spokesman of the party:

"Who are you?" he asked somewhat unsteadily, "and what do you want?"

"My name is Gunning," replied the man curtly, "captain commanding His Highness' police. What I want is that you gentlemen offer no resistance, but come with me quietly to answer on the morrow before Judge Parry, a charge of contravening the laws against betting and gambling."

A ribald and prolonged laugh greeted this brief announcement, and some twenty pairs of gentlemanly shoulders were shrugged in token of derision.

"Hark at the man!" quoth Sir James Overbury lightly, "methinks, gentlemen, that our wisest course would be to put up our swords and to throw the fellows downstairs, what say you?"

"Aye! aye!" came in cheerful accents from the defiant little group.

"Out with you fellow, we've no time to waste in bandying words with ye. . ." said Walterton, with the tone of one accustomed to see the churl ever cringe before the lord, "and let one of thy myrmidons touch a thing in this room if he dare!"

The young cavalier was standing somewhat in advance of his friends, having stepped forward in order to emphasize the peremptoriness of his words. The women were still in the background well protected by a phalanx of resolute defenders who, encouraged by the captain's silence and Walterton's haughty attitude, were prepared to force the patrol of police to beat a hasty retreat.

Endicott and his wife had seemed to think it prudent to keep well out of sight: the former having yielded to Gunning's advance had discreetly retired amongst the petticoats.

No one, least of all Walterton, who remained the acknowledged leader of the little party of gamesters, had any idea of the numerical strength of the patrol whose interference with gentlemanly pastimes was unwarrantable and passing insolent. In the gloom on the landing beyond, a knot of men could only be vaguely discerned. Captain Gunning and his lieutenant, Bradden, had alone advanced into the room.

But now apparently Gunning gave some sign, which Bradden then interpreted to the men outside. The sign itself must have been very slight for none of the cavaliers perceived it—certainly no actual word of command had been spoken, but the next moment—within thirty seconds of Walterton's defiant speech, the room itself, the doorway and apparently the landing and staircase too, were filled with men, each one attired in scarlet and yellow, all wearing leather doublets and steel caps, and all armed with musketoons which they were even now pointing straight at the serried ranks of the surprised and wholly unprepared gamesters.

"I would fain not give an order to fire," said Captain Gunning curtly, "and if you, gentlemen, will follow me quietly, there need be no bloodshed."

It may be somewhat unromantic but it is certainly prudent, to listen at times to the dictates of common sense, and one of wisdom's most cogent axioms is undoubtedly that it is useless to stand up before a volley of musketry at a range of less than twelve feet, unless a heroic death is in contemplation.

It was certainly very humiliating to be ordered about by a close-cropped Puritan, who spoke in nasal tones, and whose father probably had mended boots or killed pigs in his day, but the persuasion of twenty-four musketoons, whose muzzles pointed collectively in one direction, was bound—in the name of common sense—to prevail ultimately.

Of a truth, none of these gentlemen—who were now content to oppose a comprehensive vocabulary of English and French oaths to the brand-new weapons of my Lord Protector's police—were cowards in any sense of the word. Less than a decade ago they had proved their mettle not only sword in hand, but in the face of the many privations, sorrows and humiliations consequent on the failure of their cause and the defeat, and martyrdom of their king. There was, therefore, nothing mean or pusillanimous in their attitude when having exhausted their vocabulary of oaths and still seeing before them the muzzles of four-and-twenty musketoons pointed straight at them, they one after another dropped their sword points and turned to read in each other's faces uniform desire to surrender to *force majeure*.

The Captain watched them—impassive and silent—until the moment when he too, could discern in the sullen looks cast at him by some twenty pairs of eyes, that these elegant gentlemen had conquered their impulse to hot-headed resistance.

But the four-and-twenty musketoons were still leveled, nor did the round-headed Captain give the order to lower the firearms.

"I can release most of you, gentlemen, on parole," he said, "an you'll surrender your swords to me, you may go home this night, under promise to attend the Court to-morrow morning."

Bradden in the meanwhile had gone to the inner door and finding it locked had ordered his companion to break it open. It yielded to the first blow dealt with a vigorous shoulder. The lieutenant went into the room, but finding it empty, he returned and soon was busy in collecting the various "*pièces de convictions*," which would go to substantiate the charges of gambling and betting against these noble gentlemen. No resistance now was offered, and after a slight moment of hesitation and a brief consultation 'twixt the more prominent cavaliers there present, Lord Walterton stepped forward and having unbuckled his sword, threw it with no small measure of arrogance and disdain at the feet of Captain Gunning.

His example was followed by all his friends, Gunning with arms folded across his chest, watching the proceeding in silence. When Endicott stood before him, however, he said curtly:

"Not you, I think. Meseems I know you too well, fine sir, to release you on parole. Bradden," he added, turning to his lieutenant, "have this man duly guarded and conveyed to Queen's Head Alley to-night."

Then as Endicott tried to protest, and Gunning gave a sharp order for his immediate removal, Segrave pushed his way forward; he wore no sword, and like Lambert, had stood aloof throughout this brief scene of turbulent yet futile resistance, sullen, silent, and burning with a desire for revenge against the man who had turned the current of his luck, and brought him back to that abyss of despair, whence he now knew there could be no release.

"Captain," he said firmly, "though I wear no sword I am at one with all these gentlemen, and I accept my release on parole. To-morrow I will answer for my offense of playing cards, which apparently, is an illicit pastime. I am one of the pigeons who have been plucked in this house."

"By that gentleman?" queried Gunning with a grim smile and nodding over his shoulder in the direction where Endicott was being led away by a couple of armed men.

"No! not by him!" replied Segrave boldly.

With a somewhat theatrical gesture he pointed to Lambert, who, more of a spectator than a participant in the scene, had been standing mutely by outside the defiant group, absorbed in his own misery, wondering what effect the present unforeseen juncture would have on his future chances of rehabilitating himself.

He was also vaguely wondering what had become of Sir Marmaduke and Mistress de Chavasse.

But now Segrave's voice was raised, and once more Lambert found himself the cynosure of a number of hostile glances.

"There stands the man who has robbed us all," said Segrave wildly, "and now he has heaped disgrace upon us, upon me and mine. . . Curse him! . . . curse him, I say!" he continued, whilst all the pent-up fury, forcibly kept in check all this while by the advent of the police, now once more found vent in loud vituperation and almost maniacal expressions of rage. "Liar. . . cheat! . . . Look at him, Captain! there stands the man who must bear the full brunt of the punishment, for he is the decoy, he is the thief! . . . The pillory for him. . . the pillory. . . the lash. . . the brand! . . . Curse him! . . . Curse him! . . . the thief! . . ."

He was surrounded and forcibly silenced. The foam had risen to his lips, impotent fury and agonized despair had momentarily clouded his brain. Lambert tried to speak, but the Captain, unwilling to prolong a conflict over which he was powerless to arbitrate, gave a sign to Bradden and anon the two young men were led away in the wake of Endicott.

The others on giving their word that they would appear before the Court on the morrow, and answer to the charge preferred against them, were presently allowed to walk out of the room in single file between a double row of soldiers whose musketoons were still unpleasantly conspicuous.

Thus they passed out one by one, across the passage and down the dark staircase. The door below they found was also guarded; as well as the passage and the archway giving on the street.

Here they were permitted to collect or disperse at will. The ladies, however, had not been allowed to participate in the order for release. Gunning knew most of them by sight,—they were worthy neither of consideration nor respect,—paid satellites of Mistress Endicott's, employed to keep up the good spirits of that lady's clientèle.

The soldiers drove them all together before them, in a compact, shrinking and screaming group. Then the word of command was given.

The soldiers stood at attention, turned and finally marched out of the room with their prisoners, Gunning being the last to leave.

He locked the door behind him and in the wake of his men presently wended his way down the tortuous staircase.

Once more the measured tramp was heard reverberating through the house, the cry of "Attention!" of "Quick march!" echoed beneath the passage and the tumble-down archway, and anon the last of these ominous sounds died away down the dismal street in the direction of the river.

And in one of the attics at the top of the now silent and lonely house in Bath Street—lately the scene of so much gayety and joy, of such turmoil of passions and intensity of despair—two figures, a man and a woman, crouched together in a dark corner, listening for the last dying echo of that measured tramp.

PART III

XXI

In the Meanwhile

The news of the police raid on a secret gambling club in London, together with the fracas which it entailed, had of necessity reached even as far as sea-girt Thanet. Squire Boatfield had been the first to hear of it; he spread the news as fast as he could, for he was overfond of gossip, and Dame Harrison over at St. Lawrence had lent him able assistance.

Sir Marmaduke had, of course, the fullest details concerning the affair, for he himself owned to having been present in the very house where the disturbance had occurred. He was not averse to his neighbors knowing that he was a frequenter of those exclusive and smart gambling clubs, which were avowedly the resort of the most elegant cavaliers of the day, and his account of some of the events of that memorable night had been as entertaining as it was highly-colored.

He avowed, however, that, disgusted at Richard Lambert's shameful conduct, he had quitted the place early, some little while before my Lord Protector's police had made a descent upon the gamblers. As for Mistress de Chavasse, her name was never mentioned in connection with the affair. She had been in London at the time certainly, staying with a friend, who was helping her in the choice of a new gown for the coming autumn.

She returned to Acol Court with her brother-in-law, apparently as horrified as he was at the disgrace which she vowed Richard Lambert had heaped upon them all.

The story of the young man being caught in the very act of cheating at cards lost nothing in the telling. He had been convicted before Judge Parry of obtaining money by lying and other illicit means, had been condemned to fine and imprisonment and as he refused to pay the former—most obstinately declaring that he was penniless—he was made to stand for two hours in the pillory, and was finally dragged through the streets in a rickety cart in full sight of a jeering crowd, sitting with his back to the nag in company of the public hangman, and attired in shameful and humiliating clothes.

What happened to him after undergoing this wonderfully lenient sentence—for many there were who thought he should have been publicly whipped and branded as a cheat—nobody knew or cared.

They kept him in prison for over ten weeks, it seems, but Sir Marmaduke did not know what had become of him since then.

The other gentlemen got off fairly lightly with fines and brief periods of imprisonment. Young Segrave, so 'twas said, had been shipped to New England by his father, but Master and Mistress Endicott had gone beyond the seas at the expense of the State, and not for their own pleasure or advancement. It appears that my Lord Protector's vigilance patrol had kept a very sharp eye on these two people, who had more than once had to answer for illicit acts before the Courts. They tried in a most shameful manner it appears, to implicate Sir Marmaduke and Mistress de Chavasse in their disgrace, but as the former very pertinently remarked, "How could he, a simple Kentish squire have aught to do with a smart London club? and people of such evil repute as the Endicotts could of a truth never be believed."

All these rumors and accounts had, of course, also reached Sue's ears. At first she took up an attitude of aggressive incredulity when her former friend was accused: nothing but the plain facts as set forth in the *Public Advertiser* of August the 5th would convince her that Richard Lambert could be so base and mean as Sir Marmaduke had averred.

Even then, in her innermost heart, a vague and indefinable instinct called out to her in Lambert's name, not to believe all that was said of him. She could not think of him as lying, and cheating at a game of cards, when common sense itself told her that he was not sufficiently conversant with its rules to turn them to his own advantage. Her hot-headed partisanship of him gave way of necessity as the weeks sped by, to a more passive disapproval of his condemnation, and this in its turn to a kindly charity for what she thought must have been his ignorance rather than his sin.

What worried her most was that he was not nigh her, now that her sentimental romance was reaching its super-acute crisis. During her guardian's temporary absence from Acol she had made earnest and resolute efforts to see her mysterious lover. She thought that he must know that Sir Marmaduke and Mistress de Chavasse were away and that she herself was free momentarily from watchful eyes.

Yet though with pathetic persistence she haunted the park and the woodlands around the Court, she never even once caught sight of the broad-brimmed hat and drooping plume of her romantic prince. It seemed as if the earth had swallowed him up.

Upset and vaguely terrified, she had on one occasion thrown prudence to the winds and sought out the old Quakeress and Adam Lambert with whom he lodged. But the old Quakeress was very deaf, and explanations with her were laborious and unsatisfactory, whilst Adam seemed to entertain a sullen and irresponsible dislike for the foreigner.

All she gathered from these two was that there was nothing unusual in this sudden disappearance of their lodger. He came and went most erratically, went no one knew whither, returned at most unexpected moments, never slept more than an hour or two in his bed which he quitted at amazingly early hours, strolling out of the cottage when all decent folk were just beginning their night's rest, and wandering off unseen, unheard, only to return as he had gone.

He paid his money for his room regularly, however, and this was vastly acceptable these hard times.

But to Sue it was passing strange that her prince should be out of her reach, just when Sir Marmaduke's and Mistress de Chavasse's absence had made their meetings more easy and pleasant.

Yet with it all, she was equally conscious of an unaccountable feeling of relief, and every evening, when at about eight o'clock she returned homewards after having vainly awaited the prince, there was nothing of the sadness and disappointment in her heart which a maiden should feel when she has failed to see her lover.

She was just as much in love with him as ever!—oh! of that she felt quite sure! she still thrilled at thought of his heroic martyrdom for the cause which he had at heart, she still was conscious of a wonderful feeling of elation when she was with him, and of pride when she saw this remarkable hero, this selfless patriot at her feet, and heard his impassioned declarations of love, even when these were alloyed with frantic outbursts of jealousy. She still yearned for him when she did not see him, even though she dreaded his ill-humor when he was nigh.

She had promised to be his wife, soon and in secret, for he had vowed that she did not love him if she condemned him to three long months of infinite torture from jealousy and suspense.

This promise she had given him freely and whole-heartedly more than a fortnight ago. Since that memorable evening when she had thus plighted her troth to him, when she had without a shadow of fear or a tremor of compunction entrusted her entire future, her heart and soul to his keeping, since then she had not seen him.

Sir Marmaduke had gone to London, also Mistress de Chavasse, and she had not even caught sight of the weird silhouette of her French prince. Lambert, too, had gone, put out of her way temporarily—or mayhap, forever—through the irresistible force of a terrible disgrace. There was no one to spy on her movements, no one to dog her footsteps, yet she had not seen him.

When her guardian returned, he seemed so engrossed with Lambert's misdeeds that he gave little thought to his ward. He and Mistress de Chavasse were closeted together for hours in the small withdrawing-room, whilst she was left to roam about the house and grounds unchallenged.

Then at last one evening—it was late August then—when despair had begun to grip her heart, and she herself had become the prey of vague fears, of terrors for his welfare, his life mayhap, on which he had oft told her that the vengeful King of France had set a price—one evening he came to greet her walking through the woods, treading the soft carpet of moss with a light elastic step.

Oh! that had been a rapturous evening! one which she oft strove to recall, now that sadness had once more overwhelmed her. He had been all tenderness, all love, all passion! He vowed that he adored her as an idolater would worship his divinity. Jealous? oh, yes! madly, insanely jealous! for she was fair above all women and sweet and pure and tempting to all men like some ripe and juicy fruit ready to fall into a yearning hand.

But his jealousy took on a note of melancholy and of humility. He worshiped her so and wished to feel her all his own. She listened entranced, forgetting her terrors, her disappointments, the vague ennui which had assailed her of late. She yielded herself to the delights of his caresses, to the joy of this hour of solitude and rapture. The night was close and stormy; from afar, muffled peals of thunder echoed through the gigantic elms, whilst vivid flashes of lightning weirdly lit up at times the mysterious figure of this romantic lover, with his face forever in shadow, one eye forever hidden behind a black band, his voice forever muffled.

But it was a tempestuous wooing, a renewal of that happy evening in the spring—oh! so long ago it seemed now!—when first he had poured in her ear the wild torrents of his love. The girl—so young, so inexperienced, so romantic—was literally swept off her feet; she listened to his wild words, yielded her lips to his kiss, and whilst she half feared the impetuosity of his mood, she delighted in the very terrors it evoked.

A secret marriage? Why, of course! since he suffered so terribly through not feeling her all his own. Soon!—at once!—at Dover before the clergyman at All Souls, with whom he—her prince—had already spoken.

Yes! it would have to be at Dover, for the neighboring villages might prove too dangerous. Sir Marmaduke might hear of it, mayhap. It would rest with her to free herself for one day.

Then came that delicious period of scheming, of stage-managing everything for the all-important day. He would arrange about a chaise, and she should walk up to the Canterbury Road to meet it. He would await her in the church at Dover, for 'twas best that they should not be seen together until after the happy knot was tied, when he declared that he would be ready to defy the universe.

It had been a long interview, despite the tempest that raged above and around them. The great branches of the elms groaned and cracked under fury of the wind, the thunder pealed overhead and then died away with slow majesty out towards the sea. From afar could be heard the angry billows dashing themselves against the cliffs.

They had to seek shelter under the colonnaded porch of the summerhouse, and Sue had much ado to keep the heavy drops of rain from reaching her shoes and the bottom of her kirtle.

But she was attune with the storm, she loved to hear the weird sh-sh-sh of the leaves, the monotonous drip of the rain on the roof of the summer house, and in the intervals of intense blackness to catch sight of her lover's face, pale of hue, with one large eye glancing cyclops-like into hers, as a vivid flash of lightning momentarily tore the darkness asunder and revealed him still crouching at her feet.

Intense lassitude followed the wild mental turmoil of that night. She had arranged to meet him again two days hence in order to repeat to him what she had heard the while of Sir Marmaduke's movements, and when she was like to be free to go to Dover. During those intervening two days she tried hard to probe her own thoughts; her mind, her feelings: but what she found buried in the innermost recesses of her heart frightened her so, that she gave up thinking.

She lay awake most of the night, telling herself how much she loved her prince; she spent half a day in the perusal of a strange book called *The Tragedie of Romeo and Juliet* by one William Shakespeare who had lived not so long ago: and found herself pondering as to whether her own sentiments with regard to her prince were akin to those so exquisitely expressed by those two young people who had died because they loved one another so dearly.

Then she heard that towards the end of the week Sir Marmaduke and Mistress de Chavasse would be journeying together to Canterbury in order to confer with Master Skyffington the lawyer, anent her own fortune, which was to be handed to her in its entirety in less than three months, when she would be of age.

XXII

Breaking the News

Sir Marmaduke talked openly of this plan of going to Canterbury with Editha de Chavasse, mentioning the following Friday as the most likely date for his voyage.

Full of joy she brought the welcome news to her lover that same evening; nor had she cause to regret then her ready acquiescence to his wishes. He was full of tenderness then, of gentle discretion in his caresses, showing the utmost respect to his future princess. He talked less of his passion and more of his plans, in which now she would have her full share. He confided some of his schemes to her: they were somewhat vague and not easy to understand, but the manner in which he put them before her, made them seem wonderfully noble and selfless.

In a measure this evening—so calm and peaceful in contrast to the turbulence of the other night—marked one of the great crises in the history of her love. Even when she heard that Fate itself was conspiring to help on the clandestine marriage by causing Sir Marmaduke and Mistress de Chavasse to absent themselves at a most opportune moment, she had resolved to break the news to her lover of her own immense wealth.

Of this he was still in total ignorance. One or two innocent remarks which he had let fall at different times convinced her of that. Nor was this ignorance of his to be wondered at: he saw no one in or about the village except the old Quakeress and Adam Lambert with whom he lodged. The woman was deaf and uncommunicative, whilst there seemed to be some sort of tacit enmity against the foreigner, latent in the mind of the blacksmith. It was, therefore, quite natural that he should suppose her no whit less poor than Sir Marmaduke de Chavasse or the other neighboring Kentish squires whose impecuniousness was too blatant a fact to be unknown even to a stranger in the land.

Sue, therefore, was eagerly looking forward to the happy moment when she would explain to her prince that her share in the wonderful enterprise which he always vaguely spoke of as his "great work" would not merely be one of impassiveness. Where he could give the benefit of his personality, his eloquence, his knowledge of men and things, she could add the weight of her wealth.

Of course she was very, very young, but already from him she had realized that it is impossible even to regenerate mankind and give it political and religious freedom without the help of money.

Prince Amédé d'Orléans himself was passing rich: the fact that he chose to hide in a lonely English village and to live as a poor man would live, was only a part of his schemes. For the moment, too, owing to that ever-present vengefulness of the King of France, his estates and revenues were under sequestration. All this Sue understood full well, and it added quite considerably to her joy to think that soon she could relieve the patriot and hero from penury, and that the news that she could do so would be a glad surprise for him.

Nor must Lady Sue Aldmarshe on this account be condemned for an ignorant or a vain fool. Though she was close on twenty-one years of age, she had had absolutely no experience of the world or of mankind: all she knew of either had been conceived in the imaginings of her own romantic brain.

Her entire childhood, her youth and maidenhood had gone by in silent and fanciful dreamings, whilst one of the greatest conflicts the world had ever known was raging between men of the same kith and the same blood. The education of women—even of those of rank and wealth—was avowedly upon a very simple plan. Most of the noble ladies of that time knew not how to spell—most of them were content to let the world go by them, without giving it thought or care, others had accomplished prodigies of valor, of heroism, aye! and of determination to help their brothers, husbands, fathers during the worst periods of the civil war.

But Sue had been too young when these same prodigies were being accomplished, and her father died before she had reached the age when she could take an active part in the great questions of the day. A mother she had never known, she had no brothers and sisters. A brief time under the care of an old aunt and a duenna in a remote Surrey village, and her stay at Pegwell Court under Sir Marmaduke's guardianship, was all that she had ever seen of life.

Prince Amédé d'Orléans was the embodiment of all her dreams—or nearly so! The real hero of her dreams had been handsomer, and also more gentle and more trusting, but on the whole, he had not been one whit more romantic in his personality and his doings.

The manner in which he received the news that unbeknown to him, he had been wooing one of the richest brides in the land, was characteristic of him. He seemed boundlessly disappointed.

It was a beautiful clear night and she could see his face quite distinctly, and could note how its former happy expression was marred suddenly by a look of sorrow. He owned to being disappointed. He had loved the idea, so he explained, of taking her to him, just as she was, beautiful beyond compare, but penniless—having only her exquisite self to give.

Oh! the joy after that of coaxing him back to smiles! the pride of proving herself his Egeria for the nonce, teaching him how to look upon wealth merely as a means for attaining his great ends, for continuing his great work.

It had been perhaps the happiest evening in her short life of love.

For that day at Dover now only seemed a dream. The hurried tramp to the main road in a torrent of pouring rain: the long drive in the stuffy chaise, the arrival just in time for the brief—very brief—ceremony in the dark church, with the clergyman in a plain black gown muttering unintelligible words, and the local verger and the church cleaner acting as the witnesses to her marriage.

Her marriage!

How differently had she conceived that great, that wonderful day, the turning point of a maiden's life. Music, flowers, beautiful gowns and sweet scents filling the air! the sunlight peeping gold, red, purple or blue through the glass windows of some exquisite cathedral! The bridegroom arrayed in white, full of joy and pride, she the bride with a veil of filmy lace falling over her face to hide the happy blushes!

It was a beautiful dream, and the reality was so very, very different.

A dark little country church, with the plaster peeling off the walls! the drone of a bewhiskered, bald-headed parson being the sole music which greeted her ears. The rain beating against the broken window-panes, through which icy cold draughts of damp air reached her shoulders and caused her to shiver beneath her kerchief. She wore her pretty dove-colored gown, but it was not new nor had she a veil over her face, only a straw hat such as countrywomen wore, for though she was an heiress and passing rich, her guardian did but ill provide her with smart clothing.

And the bridegroom?

He had been waiting for her inside the church, and seemed impatient when she arrived. No one had helped her to alight from the rickety chaise, and she had to run in the pouring rain, through the miserable and deserted churchyard.

His face seemed to scowl as she finally stood up beside him, in front of that black-gowned man, who was to tie between them the sacred and irrevocable knot of matrimony. His hand had perceptibly trembled when he slipped the ring on her finger, whilst she felt that her own was irresponsive and icy cold.

She tried to speak the fateful "I will!" buoyantly and firmly, but somehow—owing to the cold, mayhap—the two little words almost died down in her throat.

Aye! it had all been very gloomy, and inexpressibly sad. The ceremony—the dear, sweet, sacred ceremony which was to give her wholly to him, him unreservedly to her—was mumbled and hurried through in less than ten minutes.

Her bridegroom said not a word. Together they went into the tiny vestry and she was told to sign her name in a big book, which the bald-headed parson held open before her.

The prince also signed his name, and then kissed her on the forehead.

The clergyman also shook hands and it was all over.

She understood that she had been married by a special license, and that she was now legally and irretrievably the wife of Amédé Henri, Prince d'Orléans, de Bourgogne and several other places and dependencies abroad.

She also understood from what the bald-headed clergyman had spoken when he stood before them in the church and read the marriage service that she as the wife owed obedience to her husband in all things, for she had solemnly sworn so to do. She herself, body and soul and mind, her goods and chattels, her wealth and all belongings were from henceforth the property of her husband.

Yes, she had sworn to all that, willingly, and there was no going back on that, now or ever!

But, oh! how she wished it had been different!

Afterwards, when in the privacy of her own little room at Acol Court, she thought over the whole of that long and dismal day, she oft found herself wondering what it was through it all that had seemed so terrifying to her, so strange, so unreal.

Something had struck her as weird: something which she could not then define; but she was quite sure that it was not merely the unusual chilliness of that rainy summer's day, which had caused her to tremble so, when—in the vestry—her husband had taken her hand and kissed her.

She had then looked into his face, which—though the vestry was but ill lighted by a tiny very dusty window—she had never seen quite so clearly before, and then it was that that amazing sense of something awful and unreal had descended upon her like a clammy shroud.

He had very swiftly averted his own gaze from her, but she had seen something in his face which she did not understand, over which she had pondered ever since without coming to any solution of this terrible riddle.

She had pondered over it during that interminable journey back from Dover to Acol. Her husband had not even suggested accompanying her on her homeward way, nor did she ask him to do so. She did not even think it strange that he gave her no explanation of the reason why he should not return to his lodgings at Acol. She felt like a somnambulist, and wondered how soon she would wake and find herself in her small and uncomfortable bed at the Court.

The next day that feeling of unreality was still there; that sensation of mystery, of something supernatural which persistently haunted her.

One thing was quite sure; that all joy had gone out of her life. It was possible that love was still there—she did not know—she was too young to understand the complex sensations which suddenly had made a woman of her. . . but it was a joyless love now: and all that she knew of a certainty about her own feelings at the present was that she hoped she would never have to gaze into her lover's face again. . . and. . . Heaven help her! . . . that he might never touch her again with his lips.

Obedient to his behests—hurriedly spoken as she stepped into the chaise at Dover after the marriage ceremony—she had wandered out every evening beyond the ha-ha into the park, on the chance of meeting him.

The evenings now were soft and balmy after the rain: the air carried a pungent smell of dahlias and of oak-leaved geraniums to her nostrils, which helped her to throw off that miserable feeling of mental lassitude which had weighed her down ever since that fateful day at Dover. She walked slowly along, treading the young tendrils of the moss, watching with wistful eyes the fleecy clouds, as they appeared through the branches of the elms, scurrying swiftly out towards the sea. . . out towards freedom.

But evening after evening passed away, and she saw no sign of him. She felt the futility, the humiliating uselessness of these nightly peregrinations in search of a man who seemed to have a hundred more desirable occupations than that of meeting his wife. But she had not the power to drift out towards freedom now. She obeyed mechanically because she must. She had sworn to obey and he had bidden her come and wait for him.

August yielded to September, the oak-leaved geraniums withered whilst from tangled bosquets the melancholy eyes of the Michaelmas daisies peeped out questioningly upon the coming autumn.

Then one evening his voice suddenly sounded close to her ear, causing her to utter a quickly-smothered cry. It had been the one dull day throughout this past glorious month, the night was dark and a warm drizzle had soaked through to her shoulders and wetted the bottom of her kirtle so that it hung heavy and dank round her ankles. He had come to her as usual from out the gloom, just as she was about to cross the little bridge which spanned the sunk fence.

She realized then, with one of those sudden quivers of her sensibilities, to which, alas! she had become so accustomed of late, that he had always met her thus in the gloom—always chosen nights when she could scarce see him distinctly, and this recollection still further enhanced that eerie feeling of terror which had assailed her since that fateful moment in the vestry.

But she tried to be natural and even gay with him, though at the first words of tender reproach with which she gently chided him for his prolonged absence, he broke into one of those passionate accesses of fury which had always frightened her, but now left her strangely cold and unresponsive.

Was the subtle change in him as well as in her? She could not say. Certain it is that, though his hands had sought hers in the darkness, and pressed them vehemently, when first they met he had not attempted to kiss her.

For this she was immeasurably grateful.

He was obviously constrained, and so was she, and when she opposed a cold silence to his outburst of passion, he immediately, and seemingly without any effort, changed his tone and talked more reasonably, even glibly of his work, which he said was awaiting him now in France.

Everything was ready there, he explained, for the great political propaganda which he had planned and which could be commenced immediately.

All that was needed now was the money. In what manner it would be needed and for what definite purpose he did not condescend to explain, nor did she care to ask. But she told him that she would be sole mistress of her fortune on the 2d of November, the date of her twenty-first birthday.

After that he spoke no more of money, but promised to meet her at regular intervals during the six weeks which would intervene until the great day when she would be free to proclaim her marriage and place herself unreservedly in the hands of her husband.

XXIII

The Absent Friend

The prince kept his word, and she was fairly free to see him at least once a week, somewhere within the leafy thicknesses of the park or in the woods, usually at the hour when dusk finally yields to the overwhelming embrace of night.

Sir Marmaduke was away. In London or Canterbury, she could not say, but she had scarcely seen him since that terrible time, when he came back from town having left Richard Lambert languishing in disgrace and in prison.

Oh! how she missed the silent and thoughtful friend who in those days of pride and of joy had angered her so, because he seemed to stand for conscience and for prudence, when she only thought of happiness and of love.

There was an almost humiliating isolation about her now. Nobody seemed to care whither she went, nor when she came home. Mistress de Chavasse talked from time to time about Sue's infatuation for the mysterious foreign adventurer, but always as if this were a thing of the past, and from which Sue herself had long since recovered.

Thus there was no one to say her nay, when she went out into the garden after evening repast, and stayed there until the shades of night had long since wrapped the old trees in gloom.

And strangely enough this sense of freedom struck her with a chill sense of loneliness. She would have loved to suddenly catch sight of Lambert's watchful figure, and to hear his somewhat harsh voice, warning her against the foreigner.

This had been wont to irritate her twelve weeks ago. How mysteriously everything had altered round her!

And yearning for her friend, she wondered what had become of him. The last she had heard was toward the middle of October when Sir Marmaduke, home from one of his frequent journeyings, one day said that Lambert had been released after ten weeks spent in prison, but that he could not say whither he had gone since then.

All Sue's questionings anent the young man only brought forth violent vituperations from Sir Marmaduke, and cold words of condemnation from Mistress de Chavasse; therefore, she soon desisted, storing up in her heart pathetic memories of the one true friend she had in the world.

She saw without much excitement, and certainly without tremor, the rapid advance of that date early in November when she would perforce have to leave Acol Court in order to follow her husband whithersoever he chose to command her.

The last time that they had met there had been a good deal of talk between them, about her fortune and its future disposal. He declared himself ready to administer it all himself, as he professed a distrust of those who had watched over it so far—Master Skyffington, the lawyer, and Sir Marmaduke de Chavasse, both under the control of the Court of Chancery.

She explained to him that the bulk of her wealth consisted of obligations and shares in the Levant and Russian Companies, her mother having been the only daughter and heiress of Peter Ford the great Levantine and Oriental merchant; her marriage with the proud Earl of Dover having caused no small measure of comment in Court circles in those days.

There were also deeds of property owned in Holland, grants of monopolies for trading given by Ivan the Terrible to her grandfather, and receipts for moneys deposited in the great banks of Amsterdam and Vienna. Master Skyffington had charge of all those papers now: they represented nearly five hundred thousand pounds of money and she told her husband that they would all be placed in her own keeping, the day she was of age.

He appeared to lend an inattentive ear to all these explanations, which she gave in those timid tones, which had lately become habitual to her, but once—when she made a slip, and talked about a share which she possessed in the Russian Company being worth £50,000, he corrected her and said it was a good deal more, and gave her some explanations as to the real distribution of her capital, which astonished her by their lucidity and left her vaguely wondering how it happened that he knew. She had finally to promise to come to him at the cottage in Acol on the 2d of November—her twenty-first birthday—directly after her interview with the lawyer and with her guardian, and having obtained possession of all the share papers, the obligations, the grants of monopolies and the receipts from the Amsterdam and Vienna banks, to forthwith bring them over to the cottage and place them unreservedly in her husband's hands.

And she would in her simplicity and ignorance gladly have given every scrap of paper—now in Master Skyffington's charge—in exchange for a return of those happy illusions which had surrounded the early history of her love with a halo of romance. She would have given this mysterious prince, now her husband, all the money that he wanted for this wonderful "great work" of his, if he would but give her back some of that enthusiastic belief in him which had so mysteriously been killed within her, that fateful moment in the vestry at Dover.

XXIV

November the 2D

A dreary day, with a leaden sky overhead and the monotonous patter of incessant rain against the window panes.

Sir Marmaduke de Chavasse had just come downstairs, and opening the door which lead from the hall to the small withdrawing-room on the right, he saw Mistress de Chavasse, half-sitting, half-crouching in one of the stiff-backed chairs, which she had drawn close to the fire.

There was a cheerful blaze on the hearth, and the room itself—being small—always looked cozier than any other at Acol Court.

Nevertheless, Editha's face was pallid and drawn, and she stared into the fire with eyes which seemed aglow with anxiety and even with fear. Her cloak was tied loosely about her shoulders, and at sight of Sir Marmaduke she started, then rising hurriedly, she put her hood over her head, and went towards the door.

"Ah! my dear Editha!" quoth her brother-in-law, lightly greeting her, "up betimes like the lark I see. . . Are you going without?" he added as she made a rapid movement to brush past him and once more made for the door.

"Yes!" she replied dully, "I must fain move about. . . tire myself out if I can. . . I am consumed with anxiety."

"Indeed?" he retorted blandly, "why should you be anxious? Everything is going splendidly. . . and to-night at the latest a fortune of nigh on £500,000 will be placed in my hands by a fond and adoring woman."

He caught the glitter in her eyes, that suggestion of power and of unspoken threats which she had adopted since the episode in the Bath Street house. For an instant an ugly frown further disfigured his sour face: but this frown was only momentary, it soon gave way to a suave smile. He took her hand and lightly touched it with his lips.

"After which, my dear Editha," he said, "I shall be able to fulfill those obligations, which my heart originally dictated."

She seemed satisfied at this assurance, for she now spoke in less aggressive tones:

"Are you so sure of the girl, Marmaduke?" she asked.

"Absolutely," he replied, his thoughts reverting to a day spent at Dover nearly three months ago, when a knot was tied of which fair Editha was not aware, but which rendered Sir Marmaduke de Chavasse very sure of a fortune.

"Yet you have oft told me that Sue's love for her mysterious prince had vastly cooled of late!" urged Editha still anxiously.

"Why yes! forsooth!" he retorted grimly, "Sue's sentimental fancy for the romantic exile hath gone the way of all such unreasoning attachments; but she has ventured too far to draw back. . . And she will not draw back," he concluded significantly.

"Have a care, Marmaduke! . . . the girl is more willful than ye wot of. . . You may strain at a cord until it snap."

"Pshaw!" he said, with a shrug of his wide shoulders, "you are suffering from vapors, my dear Editha. . . or you would grant me more knowledge of how to conduct mine own affairs. . . Do you remember, perchance, that the bulk of Sue's fortune will be handed over to her this day?"

"Aye! I remember!"

"Begad, then to-night I'll have that bulk out of her hands. You may take an oath on that!" he declared savagely.

"And afterwards?" she asked simply.

"Afterwards?"

"Yes. . . afterwards? . . . when Sue has discovered how she has been tricked? . . . Are you not afraid of what she might do? . . . Even though her money may pass into your hands. . . even though you may inveigle her into a clandestine marriage. . . she is still the daughter of the late Earl of Dover. . . she has landed estates, wealth, rich and powerful relations. . . There must be an 'afterwards,' remember! . . ."

His ironical laugh grated on her nerves, as he replied lightly:

"Pshaw! my dear Editha! of a truth you are not your own calm self to-day, else you had understood that forsooth! in the love affairs of Prince Amédé d'Orléans and Lady Susannah Aldmarshe there must and can be no 'afterwards.'"

"I don't understand you."

"Yet, 'tis simple enough. Sue is my wife."

"Your wife! . . ." she exclaimed.

"Hush! An you want to scream, I pray you question me not, for what I say is bound to startle you. Sue is my wife. I married her, having obtained a special license to do so in the name of Prince Amédé Henri d'Orléans, and all the rest of the romantic paraphernalia. She is my wife, and therefore, her money and fortune are mine, every penny of it, without question or demur."

"She will appeal to the Court to have the marriage annulled. . . she'll rouse public indignation against you to such a pitch that you'll not be able to look one of your kith and kin in the face. . . The whole shameful story of the mysterious French prince. . . your tricks to win the hand of your ward by lying, cheating and willful deceit will resound from one end of the country to the other. . . What is the use of a mint of money if you have to herd with outcasts, and not an honest man will shake you by the hand?"

"None, my dear Editha, none," he replied quietly, "and 'tis of still less use for you to rack your nerves in order to place before me a gruesome picture of the miserable social pariah which I should become, if the story of my impersonation of a romantic exile for the purpose of capturing the hand of my ward came to the ears of those in authority."

"Whither it doubtless would come!" she affirmed hotly.

"Whither it doubtless would come," he assented, "and therefore, my dear Editha, once the money is safely in my hands I will leave her Royal Highness the Princesse d'Orléans in full possession, not only of her landed estates but of the freedom conferred on her by widowhood, for Prince Amédé, her husband, will vanish like the beautiful dream which he always was."

"But how? . . . how?" she reiterated, puzzled, anxious, scenting some nefarious scheme more unavowable even than the last.

"Ah! time will show! . . . But he will vanish, my dear Editha, take my word on it. Shall we say that he will fly up into the clouds and her Highness the Princess will know him no more?"

"Then why have married her?" she exclaimed: some womanly instinct within her crying out against this outrage. "'Twas cruel and unnecessary."

He shrugged his shoulders.

"Cruel perhaps! . . . But surely no more than necessary. I doubt if she would have entrusted her fortune to anyone but her husband."

"Had she ceased to trust her romantic prince then?"

"Perhaps. At any rate, I chose to make sure of the prize. . . I have worked hard to get it and would not fail for lack of a simple ceremony. . . moreover. . ."

"Moreover?"

"Moreover, my dear Editha, there is always the possibility. . . remote, no doubt. . . but nevertheless tangible. . . that at some time or other. . .

soon or late—who knows?—the little deception practiced on Lady Sue may come to the light of day. . . In that case, even if the marriage be annulled on the ground of fraud. . . which methinks is more than doubtful. . . no one could deny my right as the heiress's. . . hem. . . shall we say?—temporary husband—to dispose of her wealth as I thought fit. If I am to become a pariah and an outcast, as you so eloquently suggested just now. . . I much prefer being a rich one. . . With half a million in the pocket of my doublet the whole world is open to me."

There was so much cool calculation, such callous contempt for the feelings and thoughts of the unfortunate girl whom he had so terribly wronged, in this exposé of the situation, that Mistress de Chavasse herself was conscious of a sense of repulsion from the man whom she had aided hitherto.

She believed that she held him sufficiently in her power, through her knowledge of his schemes and through the help which she was rendering him, to extract a promise from him that he would share his ill-gotten spoils in equal portions with her. At one time after the fracas in Bath Street, he had even given her a vague promise of marriage; therefore, he had kept secret from her the relation of that day spent at Dover. Now she felt that even if he were free, she would never consent to link her future irretrievably with his.

But her share of the money she meant to have. She was tired of poverty, tired of planning and scheming, of debt and humiliation. She was tired of her life of dependence at Acol Court, and felt a sufficiency of youth and buoyancy in herself yet, to enjoy a final decade of luxury and amusement in London.

Therefore, she closed her ears to every call of conscience, she shut her heart against the lonely young girl who so sadly needed the counsels and protection of a good woman, and she was quite ready to lend a helping hand to Sir Marmaduke, at least until a goodly share of Lady Sue's fortune was safely within her grasp.

One point occurred to her now, which caused her to ask anxiously:

"Have you not made your reckonings without Richard Lambert, Marmaduke? He is back in these parts, you know?"

"Ah!" he exclaimed, with a quick scowl of impatience. "He has returned?"

"Yes! Charity was my informant. He looks very ill, so the wench says: he has been down with fever, it appears, all the while that he was in prison, and was only discharged because they feared that he would die.

He contrived to work or beg his way back here, and now he is staying in the village. . . I thought you would have heard."

"No! I never speak to the old woman. . . and Adam Lambert avoids me as he would the plague. . . I see as little of them as I can. . . I had to be prudent these last, final days."

"Heaven grant he may do nothing fatal to-day!" she murmured.

"Nay! my dear Editha," he retorted with a harsh laugh, "'tis scarcely Heaven's business to look after our schemes. But Lambert can do us very little harm now! For his own sake, he will keep out of Sue's way."

"At what hour does Master Skyffington arrive?"

"In half an hour."

Then as he saw that she was putting into effect her former resolve of going out, despite the rain, and was once more readjusting her hood for that purpose, he opened the door for her, and whispered as he followed her out:

"An you will allow me, my dear Editha, I'll accompany you on your walk. . . we might push on down the Canterbury Road, and perchance meet Master Skyffington. . . I understand that Sue has been asking for me, and I would prefer to meet her as seldom as possible just now. . . This is my last day," he concluded with a laugh, "and I must be doubly careful."

XXV

An Interlude

Master Hymn-of-Praise Busy was vastly perturbed. Try how he might, he had been unable to make any discovery with regard to the mysterious events, which he felt sure were occurring all round him, a discovery which—had he but made it—would have enabled him to apply with more chance of success, for one of the posts in my Lord Protector's secret service, and moreover, would have covered his name with glory.

This last contingency was always uppermost in his mind. Not from any feeling of personal pride, for of a truth vanity is a mortal sin, but because Mistress Charity had of late cast uncommonly kind eyes on that cringing worm, Master Courage Toogood, and the latter, emboldened by the minx's favors, had been more than usually insolent to his betters.

To have the right to administer serious physical punishment to the youth, and moral reproof to the wench, was part of Master Busy's comprehensive scheme for his own advancement and the confusion of all the miscreants who dwelt in Acol Court. For this he had glued both eye and ear to draughty keyholes, had lain for hours under cover of prickly thistles in the sunk fence which surrounded the flower garden. For this he now emerged, on that morning of November 2, accompanied by a terrific clatter and a volley of soot from out the depth of the monumental chimney in the hall of Acol Court.

As soon as he had recovered sufficient breath, and shaken off some of the soot from his hair and face, he looked solemnly about him, and was confronted by two pairs of eyes round with astonishment and two mouths agape with surprise and with fear.

Mistress Charity and Master Courage Toogood—interrupted in the midst of their animated conversation—were now speechless with terror, at sight of this black apparition, which, literally, had descended on them from the skies.

"Lud love ye, Master Busy!" exclaimed Mistress Charity, who was the first to recognize in the sooty wraith the manly form of her betrothed, "where have ye come from, pray?"

"Have you been scouring the chimney, good master?" queried Master

Courage, with some diffidence, for the saintly man looked somewhat out of humor.

"No!" replied Hymn-of-Praise solemnly, "I have not. But I tell ye both that my hour hath come. I knew that something was happening in this house, and I climbed up that chimney in order to find out what it was."

Pardonable curiosity caused Mistress Charity to venture a little nearer to the soot-covered figure of her adorer.

"And did you hear anything, Master Busy?" she asked eagerly. "I did see Sir Marmaduke and the mistress in close conversation here this morning."

"So they thought," said Master Hymn-of-Praise with weird significance.

"Well? . . . And what happened, good master?"

"Thou beest in too mighty an hurry, mistress," he retorted with quiet dignity. "I am under no obligation to report matters to thee."

"Oh! but Master Busy," she rejoined coyly, "methought I was to be your. . . hem. . . thy partner in life. . . and so. . ."

"My partner? My partner, didst thou say, sweet Charity? . . . Nay, then, an thou'lt permit me to salute thee with a kiss, I'll tell thee all I know."

And in asking for that chaste salute we may assume that Master Hymn-of-Praise was actuated with at least an equal desire to please Mistress Charity, to gratify his own wishes, and to effectually annoy Master Courage.

But Mistress Charity was actuated by curiosity alone, and without thought of her betrothed's grimy appearance, she presented her cheek to him for the kiss.

The result caused Master Courage an uncontrollable fit of hilarity.

"Oh, mistress," he said, pointing to the black imprint left on her face by her lover's kiss, "you should gaze into a mirror now."

But already Mistress Charity had guessed what had occurred, her good humor vanished, and she began scouring her cheek with her pinner.

"I'll never forgive you, master," she said crossly. "You had no right to. . . hem. . . with your face in that condition. . . And you have not yet told us what happened."

"What happened?"

"Aye! you promised to tell me if I allowed you to kiss me. 'Tis done. . ."

"I well nigh broke my back," said Master Busy sententiously. "I hurt my knee. . . that is what happened. . . I am well-nigh choked with soot. . . Ugh! . . . that is what happened."

"Lud love you, Master Busy," she retorted with a saucy toss of her head, "I trust your life's partner will not need to hide herself in chimneys."

"Listen, wench, and I'll tell thee. No kind of servant of my Lord Protector's should ever be called upon to hide in chimneys. They are not comfortable and they are not clean."

"Bless the man!" she cried angrily, "are you ever going to tell us what did happen whilst you were there?"

"I was about to come to that point," he said imperturbably, "hadst thou not interrupted me. What with holding on so as not to fall, and the soot falling in my ears. . ."

"Aye! aye! . . ."

"I heard nothing," he concluded solemnly. "Master Courage," he added with becoming severity, seeing that the youth was on the verge of making a ribald remark, which of necessity had to be checked betimes, "come into my room with me and help me to clean the traces of my difficult task from off my person. Come!"

And with ominous significance, he approached the young scoffer, his hand on an exact level with the latter's ear, his right foot raised to indicate a possible means of enforcing obedience to his commands.

On the whole, Master Courage thought it wise to repress both his hilarity and his pertinent remarks, and to follow the pompous, if begrimed, butler to the latter's room upstairs.

XXVI

The Outcast

I t took Mistress Charity some little time to recover her breath.

She had thrown herself into a chair, with her pinner over her face, in an uncontrollable fit of laughter.

When this outburst of hilarity had subsided, she sat up, and looked round her with eyes still streaming with merry tears.

But the laughter suddenly died on her lips and the merriment out of her eyes. A dull, tired voice had just said feebly:

"Is Sir Marmaduke de Chavasse within?"

Charity jumped up from the chair and stared stupidly at the speaker.

"The Lord love you, Master Richard Lambert," she murmured. "I thought you were your ghost!"

"Forgive me, mistress, if I have frightened you," he said. "It is mine own self, I give you assurance of that, and I, fain would have speech with Sir Marmaduke."

Mistress Charity was visibly embarrassed. She began mechanically to rub the black stain on her cheek.

"Sir Marmaduke is without just at present, Master Lambert," she stammered shyly, ". . . and. . ."

"Yes? . . . and? . . ." he asked, "what is it, wench? . . . speak out? . . ."

"Sir Marmaduke gave orders, Master Lambert," she began with obvious reluctance, "that. . ."

She paused, and he concluded the sentence for her:

"That I was not to be allowed inside his house. . . Was that it?"

"Alas! yes, good master."

"Never mind, girl," he rejoined as he deliberately crossed the hall and sat down in the chair which she had just vacated. "You have done your duty: but you could not help admitting me, could you? since I walked in of mine own accord. . . and now that I am here I will remain until I have seen Sir Marmaduke. . ."

"Well! of a truth, good master," she said with a smile, for 'twas but natural that her feminine sympathies should be on the side of a young and good-looking man, somewhat in her own sphere of life, as against the ill-humored, parsimonious master whom she served, "an you sit there so determinedly, I cannot prevent you, can I? . . ."

Then as she perceived the look of misery on the young man's face, his pale cheeks, his otherwise vigorous frame obviously attenuated by fear, the motherly instinct present in every good woman's heart caused her to go up to him and to address him timidly, offering such humble solace as her simple heart could dictate:

"Lud preserve you, good master, I pray you do not take on so. . . You know Master Courage and I, now, never believed all those stories about ye. Of a truth Master Busy, he had his own views, but then. . . you see, good master, he and I do not always agree, even though I own that he is vastly clever with his discoveries and his clews; but Master Courage now. . . Master Courage is a wonderful lad. . . and he thinks that you are a persecuted hero! . . . and I am bound to say that I, too, hold that view. . ."

"Thank you! . . . thank you, kind mistress," said Lambert, smiling despite his dejection, at the girl's impulsive efforts at consolation.

His head had sunk down on his breast, and he sat there in the high-backed chair, one hand resting on each leather-covered arm, his pale face showing almost ghostlike against the dark background, and with the faint November light illumining the dark-circled eyes, the bloodless lips, and deeply frowning brow.

Mistress Charity gazed down on him with mute and kindly compassion.

Then suddenly a slight rustling noise as of a kirtle sweeping the polished oak of the stairs caused the girl to look up, then to pause a brief while, as if what she had now seen had brought forth a new train of thought; finally, she tiptoed silently out through the door of the dining-hall.

"Charity! Mistress Charity, I want you! . . ." called Lady Sue from above.

We must presume, however, that the wench had closed the heavy door behind her, for certainly she did not come in answer to the call. On the other hand, Richard Lambert had heard it; he sprang to his feet and saw Sue descending the stairs.

She saw him, too, and it seemed as if at sight of him she had turned and meant to fly. But a word from him detained her.

"Sue!"

Only once had he thus called her by her name before, that long ago night in the woods, but now the cry came from out his heart, brought forth by his misery and his sorrow, his sense of terrible injustice and of an irretrievable wrong.

It never occurred to her to resent the familiarity. At sound of her name thus spoken by him she had looked down from the stairs and seen his pallid face turned up to her in such heartrending appeal for sympathy, that all her womanly instincts of tenderness and pity were aroused, all her old feeling of trustful friendship for him.

She, too, felt much of that loneliness which his yearning eyes expressed so pathetically; she, too, was conscious of grave injustice and of an irretrievable wrong, and her heart went out to him immediately in kindness and in love.

"Don't go, for pity's sake," he added entreatingly, for he thought that she meant to turn away from him; "surely you will not begrudge me a few words of kindness. I have gone through a great deal since I saw you. . ."

She descended a few steps, her delicate hand still resting on the banisters, her silken kirtle making a soft swishing noise against the polished oak of the stairs. It was a solace to him, even to watch her now. The sight of his adored mistress was balm to his aching eyes. Yet he was quick to note—with that sharp intuition peculiar to Love—that her dear face had lost much of its brightness, of its youth, of its joy of living. She was as exquisite to look on as ever, but she seemed older, more gentle, and, alas! a trifle sad.

"I heard you had been ill," she said softly, "I was very sorry, believe me, but. . . Oh! do you not think," she added with sudden inexplicable pathos, whilst she felt hot tears rising to her eyes and causing her voice to quiver, "do you not think that an interview between us now can only be painful to us both?"

He mistook the intention of her words, as was only natural, and whilst she mistrusted her own feelings for him, fearing to betray that yearning for his friendship and his consolation, which had so suddenly overwhelmed her at sight of him, he thought that she feared the interview because of her condemnation of him.

"Then you believed me guilty?" he said sadly. "They told you this hideous tale of me, and you believed them, without giving the absent one, who alas! could not speak in his own defense, the benefit of the doubt."

For one of those subtle reasons of which women alone possess the secret, and which will forever remain inexplicable to the more logical sex, she steeled her heart against him, even when her entire sensibilities went out to him in passionate sympathy.

"I could not help but believe, good master," she said a little coldly. "Sir Marmaduke de Chavasse, who, with all his faults of temper, is a man of honor, confirmed that horrible story which appeared in the newspaper and of which everyone in Thanet hath been talking these weeks past."

"And am *I* not a man of honor?" he retorted hotly. "Because I am poor and must work in order to live, am *I* to be condemned unheard? Is a whole life's record of self-education and honest labor to be thus obliterated by the word of my most bitter enemy?"

"Your bitter enemy? . . ." she asked. "Sir Marmaduke? . . ."

"Aye! Sir Marmaduke de Chavasse. It seems passing strange, does it not?" he rejoined bitterly. "Yet somehow in my heart, I feel that Sir Marmaduke hates me, with a violent and passionate hatred. Nay! I know it, though I can explain neither its cause nor its ultimate aim. . ."

He drew nearer to the stairs whereon she still stood, her graceful figure slightly leaning towards him; he now stood close to her, his head just below the level of her own; his hand had he dared to raise it, could have rested on hers.

"Sue! my beautiful and worshiped lady," he cried impassionedly, "I entreat you to look into my eyes! . . . Can you see in them the reflex of those shameful deeds which have been imputed to me? Do I look like a liar and a cheat? In the name of pity and of justice, for the sweet sake of our first days of friendship, I beg of you not to condemn me unheard."

He lowered his head, and rested his aching brow against her cool, white hand. She did not withdraw it, for a great joy had suddenly filled her heart, mingling with its sadness, a sense of security and of bitter, yet real, happiness pervaded her whole being: a happiness which she could not—wished not—to explain, but which prompted her to stoop yet further towards him, and to touch his hair with her lips.

Hot tears which he tried vainly to repress fell upon her fingers. He had felt the kiss descending on him almost like a benediction. The exquisite fragrance of her person filled his soul with a great delight which was almost pain. Never had he loved her so ardently, so passionately, as at this moment, when he felt that she too loved him, and yet was lost to him irrevocably.

"Nay! but I will hear you, good master," she murmured with infinite gentleness, "for the sake of that friendship, and because now that I have seen you again I no longer believe any evil of you."

"God bless my dear lady," he replied fervently. "Heaven is my witness that I am innocent of those abominable crimes imputed to me. Sir Marmaduke took me to that house of evil, and a cruel plot was there concocted to make me appear before all men as a liar and a cheat, and to disgrace me before the world and before you. That the object of this plot was to part me from you," added Richard Lambert more calmly and firmly, "I am absolutely confident; what its deeper motive was I dare not even think. It was known that I. . . loved you, Sue. . . that I would give my life to save you from trouble. . . I was your slave, your watch-dog. . . I was forcibly removed, torn from you, my name disgraced, my health broken down. . . But my life was not for them. . . it belongs to my lady alone. . . Heaven would not allow it to be sacrificed to their villainous schemes. I fought against sickness and death with all the energy of despair. . . It was a hand-to-hand fight, for discouragement, and anon despair, ranged themselves among my foes. . . And now I have come back," he said with proud energy, "broken mayhap, yet still standing. . . a snapped oak yet full of vigor, yet. . . I have come back, and with God's help will be even with them yet."

He had straightened his young figure, and his strong, somewhat harsh voice echoed through the oak-paneled hall. He cared not if all the world heard him, if his enemies lurked about striving to spy upon him. His profession of love and of service to his lady was the sole remaining pride of his life, and now that he knew that she believed and trusted him, he longed for every man to hear what he had to say.

"Nay! what you say, kind Richard, fills me with dread," said Sue after a little pause. "I am glad. . . glad that you have come back. . . For some weeks, nay, months past, I have had the presentiment of some coming evil. . . I have. . . I have felt lonely and. . ."

"Not unhappy?" he asked with his usual earnestness. "I would not have my lady unhappy for all the treasures of this world."

"No!" she replied meditatively, striving to be conscious of her own feelings, "I do not think that I am unhappy. . . only anxious. . . and. . . a little lonely: that is all. . . Sir Marmaduke is oft away: when he is at home, I scarce ever see him, and he but rarely speaks to me. . . and methinks there is but scant sympathy 'twixt Mistress de Chavasse and me, though she is kind at times in her way."

Then she turned her eyes, bright with unshed tears, down again to him.

"But all seems right again!" she said with a sweet, sad smile, "now that you have come back, my dear. . . dear friend!"

"God bless you for these words!"

"I grieved terribly when I heard. . . about you. . . at first. . ." she said almost gaily now, "yet somehow I could not believe it all. . . and now. . ."

"Yes? . . . and now?" he asked.

"Now I believe in you," she replied simply. "I believe that you care for me, and that you are my friend."

"Your friend, indeed, for I would give my life for you."

Once more he stooped, but now he kissed her hand. He was her friend, and had the right to do this. He had gradually mastered his emotion, his sense of wrong, and with that exquisite selflessness which real love alone can kindle in a human heart, he had succeeded in putting aside all thought of his own great misery, his helplessness and the hopelessness of his position, and remembered only that she looked fragile, a little older, sadder, and had need of his help.

"And now, sweet lady," he said, forcing himself to speak calmly of that which always set his heart and senses into a turmoil of passionate jealousy, "will you tell me something about him."

"Him?"

"The prince. . ." he suggested.

But she shook her head resolutely.

"No, kind Richard," she said gently, "I will not speak to you of the prince. I know that you do not think well of him. . . I wish to look upon you as my friend, and I could not do that if you spoke ill of him, because. . ."

She paused, for what she now had to tell him was very hard to say, and she knew what a terrible blow she would be dealing to his heart, from the wild beating of her own.

"Yes?" he asked. "Because? . . ."

"Because he is my husband," she whispered.

Her head fell forward on her breast. She would not trust herself to look at him now, for she knew that the sight of his grief was more than she could bear. She was conscious that at her words he had drawn his hand away from hers, but he spoke no word, nor did the faintest exclamation escape his lips.

Thus they remained for a few moments longer side by side: she slightly above him, with head bent, with hot tears falling slowly from her downcast eyes, her heart well-nigh breaking with the consciousness of the irreparable; he somewhat below, silent too, and rigid, all passion, all emotion, love even, numbed momentarily by the violence, the suddenness of this terrible blow.

Then without a word, without a sigh or look, he turned, and she heard his footsteps echoing across the hall, then dying away on the threshold of the door beyond. Anon the door itself closed to with a dull bang which seemed to find an echo in her heart like the tolling of a passing bell.

Then only did she raise her head, and look about her. The hall was deserted and seemed infinitely lonely, silent, and grim. The young girl-wife, who had just found a friend only to lose him again, called out in mute appeal to this old house, the oak-covered walls, the very stones themselves, for sympathy.

She was so infinitely, so immeasurably lonely, with that awful, irretrievable day at Dover behind her, with all its dreariness, its silent solemnity, its weird finish in the vestry, the ring upon her finger, her troth plighted to a man whom she feared and no longer loved.

Oh! the pity of it all! the broken young life! the vanished dreams!

Sue bent her head down upon her hands, her lips touched her own fingers there where her friend's had rested in gratitude and love, and she cried, cried like a broken-hearted woman, cried for her lost illusions, and the end of her brief romance!

XXVII

LADY SUE'S FORTUNE

L ess than an hour later four people were assembled in the small withdrawing-room of Acol Court.

Master Skyffington sat behind a central table, a little pompous of manner, clad in sober black with well-starched linen cuffs and collar, his scanty hair closely cropped, his thin hands fingering with assurance and perfect calm the various documents laid out before him. Near him Sir Marmaduke de Chavasse, sitting with his back to the dim November light, which vainly strove to penetrate the tiny glass panes of the casement windows.

In a more remote corner of the room sat Editha de Chavasse, vainly trying to conceal the agitation which her trembling hands, her quivering face and restless eyes persistently betrayed. And beside the central table, near Master Skyffington and facing Sir Marmaduke, was Lady Susannah Aldmarshe, only daughter and heiress of the late Earl of Dover, this day aged twenty-one years, and about to receive from the hands of her legal guardians the vast fortune which her father had bequeathed to her, and which was to become absolutely hers this day to dispose of as she list.

"And now, my dear child," said Master Skyffington with due solemnity, when he had disposed a number of documents and papers in methodical order upon the table, "let me briefly explain to you the object. . . hem. . . of this momentous meeting here to-day."

"I am all attention, master," said Sue vaguely, and her eyes wide-open, obviously absent, she gazed fixedly on the silhouette of Sir Marmaduke, grimly outlined against the grayish window-panes.

"I must tell you, my dear child," resumed Master Skyffington after a slight pause, during which he had studied with vague puzzledom the inscrutable face of the young girl, "I must tell you that your late father, the noble Earl of Dover, had married the heiress of Peter Ford, the wealthiest merchant this country hath ever known. She was your own lamented mother, and the whole of her fortune, passing through her husband's hands, hath now devolved upon you. My much-esteemed patron—I may venture to say friend—Sir Marmaduke de Chavasse, having been appointed your legal guardian by the Court of Chancery, and I myself being thereupon named the repository of your securities, these have been administered by me up to now. . . You are listening to me, are you not, my dear young lady?"

The question was indeed necessary, for even to Master Skyffington's unobservant mind it was apparent that Sue's eyes had a look of aloofness in them, of detachment from her surroundings, which was altogether inexplicable to the worthy attorney's practical sense of the due fitness of things.

At his query she made a sudden effort to bring her thoughts back from the past to the present, to drag her heart and her aching brain away from that half-hour spent in the hall, from that conversation with her friend, from the recollection of that terribly cruel blow which she had been forced to deal to the man who loved her best in all the world.

"Yes, yes, kind master," she said, "I am listening."

And she fixed her eyes resolutely on the attorney's solemn face, forcing her mind to grasp what he was about to say.

"By the terms of your noble father's will," continued Master Skyffington, as soon as he had satisfied himself that he at last held the heiress's attention, "the securities, receipts and all other moneys are to be given over absolutely and unconditionally into your own hands on your twenty-first birthday."

"Which is to-day," said Sue simply.

"Which is to-day," assented the lawyer. "The securities, receipts and other bonds, grants of monopolies and so forth lie before you on this table. . . They represent in value over half a million of English money. . . A very large sum indeed for so young a girl to have full control of. . . Nevertheless, it is yours absolutely and unconditionally, according to the wishes of your late noble father. . . and Sir Marmaduke de Chavasse, your late guardian, and I myself, have met you here this day for the express purpose of handing these securities, grants and receipts over to you, and to obtain in exchange your own properly attested signature in full discharge of any further obligation on our part."

Master Skyffington was earnestly gazing into the young girl's face, whilst he thus literally dangled before her the golden treasures of wealth, which were about to become absolutely her own. He thought, not unnaturally, that a girl of her tender years, brought up in the loneliness and seclusion of a not too luxurious home, would feel in a measure dazzled and certainly overjoyed at the brilliant prospect which such independent and enormous wealth opened out before her.

But the amiable attorney was vastly disappointed to see neither pleasure, nor even interest, expressed in Lady Sue's face, which on this joyous and momentous occasion looked unnaturally calm and pallid. Even now when he paused expectant and eager, waiting for some comment or exclamation of approval or joy from her, she was silent for a while, and then said in a stolidly inquiring tone:

"Then after to-day. . . I shall have full control of my money?"

"Absolute control, my dear young lady," he rejoined, feeling strangely perturbed at this absence of emotion.

"And no one. . . after to-day. . . will have the right to inquire as to the use I make of these securities, grants or whatever you, Master Skyffington, have called them?" she continued with the same placidity.

"No one, of a surety, my dear Sue," here interposed Sir Marmaduke, speaking in his usual harsh and dictatorial way, "but this is a strange and somewhat peremptory question for a young maid to put at this juncture. Master Skyffington and I myself had hoped that you would listen to counsels of prudence, and would allow him, who hath already administered your fortune in a vastly able manner, to continue so to do, for a while at any rate."

"That question we can discuss later on, Sir Marmaduke," said Sue now, with sudden hauteur. "Shall we proceed with our business, master?" she added, turning deliberately to the lawyer, ignoring with calm disdain the very presence of her late guardian.

The studied contempt of his ward's manner, however, seemed not to disturb the serenity of Sir Marmaduke to any appreciable extent. Casting a quick, inquisitorial glance at Sue, he shrugged his shoulders in token of indifference and said no more.

"Certainly, certainly," responded Master Skyffington, somewhat embarrassed, "my dear young lady. . . hem. . . as. . . er. . . as you wish. . . but. . ."

Then he turned deliberately to Sir Marmaduke, once more bringing him into the proceedings, and tacitly condemning her ladyship's extraordinary attitude towards his distinguished patron.

"Having now explained to Lady Sue Aldmarshe the terms of her noble father's will," he said, "methinks that she is ready to receive the moneys from our hands, good Sir Marmaduke, and thereupon to give us the proper receipt prescribed by law, for the same. . ."

He checked himself for a moment, and then made a respectful, if pointed, suggestion:

"Mistress de Chavasse?" he said inquiringly.

"Mistress de Chavasse is a member of the family," replied Sir Marmaduke, "the business can be transacted in her presence."

"Nothing therefore remains to be said, my dear young lady," rejoined Master Skyffington, once more speaking directly to Sue and placing his lean hands with fingers outstretched, over the bundles of papers lying before him. "Here are your securities, your grants, moneys and receipts, worth £500,000 of the present currency of this realm. . . These I, in mine own name and that of my honored friend and patron, Sir Marmaduke de Chavasse, do hereby hand over to you. You will, I pray, verify and sign the receipt in proper and due form."

He began sorting and overlooking the papers, muttering half audibly the while, as he transferred each bundle from his own side of the table to that beside which Lady Sue was sitting:

"The deeds of property in Holland. . . hem. . . Receipt of moneys deposited at the bank of Amsterdam. . . The same from the Bank of Vienna. . . Grant of monopoly for the hemp trade in Russia. . . hem. . ."

Thus he mumbled for some time, as these papers, representing a fortune, passed out of his keeping into those of a young maid but recently out of her teens. Sue watched him silently and placidly, just as she had done throughout this momentous interview, which was, of a truth, the starting point of her independent life.

Her face expressed neither joy nor excitement of any kind. She knew that all the wealth which now lay before her, would only pass briefly through her hands. She knew that the prince—her husband—was waiting for it even now. Doubtless, he was counting the hours when his young wife's vast fortune would come to him as the realization of all his dreams.

In spite of her present disbelief in his love, in spite of the bitter knowledge that her own had waned, Sue had no misgivings as yet as to the honor, the truth, the loyalty of the man whose name she now bore. Her illusions were gone, her romance had become dull reality, but to one thought she clung with all the tenacity of despair, and that was to the illusion that Prince Amédé d'Orléans was the selfless patriot, the regenerator of downtrodden France, which he represented himself to be.

Because of that belief she welcomed the wealth, which she would this day be able to place in his hands. Her own girlish dreams had vanished, but her temperament was far too romantic and too poetic not to recreate illusions, even when the old ones had been so ruthlessly shattered.

But this recreation would occur anon—not just now, not at the very moment when her heart ached with an intolerable pain at thought of the sorrow which she had caused to her one friend. Presently, no doubt, when she met her husband, when his usual grandiloquent phrases had once more succeeded in arousing her enthusiasm for the cause which he pleaded, she would once more feel serene and happy at thought of the help which she, with her great wealth, would be giving him; for the nonce the whole transaction grated on her sense of romance; money passing from hand to hand, a man waiting somewhere in the dark to receive wealth from a woman's hand.

Master Skyffington desired her to look over the papers, ere she signed the formal receipt for them, but she waved them gently aside:

"Quite unnecessary, kind master," she said decisively, "since I receive them at your hands."

She bent over the document which the lawyer now placed before her, and took the pen from him.

"Where shall I sign?" she asked.

Sir Marmaduke and Editha de Chavasse watched her keenly, as with a bold stroke of the pen she wrote her name across the receipt.

"Now the papers, please, master," said Lady Sue peremptorily.

But the prudent lawyer had still a word of protest to enter here.

"My dear young lady," he said tentatively, awed in spite of himself by the self-possessed behavior of a maid whom up to now he had regarded as a mere child, "let me, as a man of vast experience in such matters, repeat to you the well-meant advice which Sir Marmaduke. . ."

But she checked him decisively, though kindly.

"You said, Master Skyffington, did you not," she said, "that after to-day no one had the slightest control over my actions or over my fortune?"

"That is so, certainly," he rejoined, "but. . ."

"Well, then, kind master, I pray you," she said authoritatively, "to hand me over all those securities, grants and moneys, for which I have just signed a receipt."

There was naught to do for a punctilious lawyer, as was Master Skyffington, but to obey forthwith. This he did, without another word, collecting the various bundles of paper and placing them one by one in the brown leather wallet which he had brought for the purpose. Sue

BARONESS EMMUSKA ORCZY

watched him quietly, and when the last of the important documents had been deposited in the wallet, she held out her hand for it.

With a grave bow, and an unconsciously pompous gesture, Master Skyffington, attorney-at-law, handed over that wallet which now contained a fortune to Lady Susannah Aldmarshe.

She took it, and graciously bowed her head to him in acknowledgment. Then, after a slight, distinctly haughty nod to Sir Marmaduke and to Editha, she turned and walked silently out of the room.

XXVIII

Husband and Wife

Mistress Martha Lambert was a dignified old woman, on whose wrinkled face stern virtues, sedulously practiced, had left their lasting imprint. Among these virtues which she had thus somewhat ruthlessly exercised throughout her long life, cleanliness and orderliness stood out pre-eminently. They undoubtedly had brought some of the deepest furrows round her eyes and mouth, as indeed they had done round those of Adam Lambert, who having lived with her all his life, had had to suffer from her passion of scrubbing and tidying more than anyone else.

But her cottage was resplendent: her chief virtues being apparent in every nook and corner of the orderly little rooms which formed her home and that of the two lads whom a dying friend had entrusted to her care.

The parlor below, with its highly polished bits of furniture, its spotless wooden floor and whitewashed walls, was a miracle of cleanliness. The table in the center was laid with a snowy white cloth, on it the pewter candlesticks shone like antique silver. Two straight-backed mahogany chairs were drawn cozily near to the hearth, wherein burned a bright fire made up of ash logs. There was a quaint circular mirror in a gilt frame over the hearth, a relic of former, somewhat more prosperous times.

In one of the chairs lolled the mysterious lodger, whom a strange Fate in a perverse mood seemed to have wafted to this isolated little cottage on the outskirts of the loneliest village in Thanet.

Prince Amédé d'Orléans was puffing at that strange weed which of late had taken such marked hold of most men, tending to idleness in them, for it caused them to sit staring at the smoke which they drew from pipes made of clay; surely the Lord had never intended such strange doings, and Mistress Martha would willingly have protested against the unpleasant odor thus created by her lodger when he was puffing away, only that she stood somewhat in awe of his ill-humor and of his violent language, especially when Adam himself was from home.

On these occasions—such, for instance, as the present one—she had, perforce, to be content with additional efforts at cleanliness, and, as she was convinced that so much smoke must be conducive to soot and dirt, she plied her dusting-cloth with redoubled vigor and energy. Whilst the prince lolled and pulled at his clay pipe, she busied herself all round the tiny room, polishing the backs of the old elm chairs, and the brass handles of the chest of drawers.

"How much longer are you going to fuss about, my good woman?" quoth Prince Amédé d'Orléans impatiently after a while. "This shuffling round me irritates my nerves."

Mistress Martha, however, suffered from deafness. She could see from the quick, angry turn of the head that her lodger was addressing her, but did not catch his words. She drew a little nearer, bending her ear to him.

"Eh? . . . what?" she queried in that high-pitched voice peculiar to the deaf. "I am somewhat hard of hearing just now. I did not hear thee."

But he pushed her roughly aside with a jerk of his elbow.

"Go away!" he said impatiently. "Do not worry me!"

"Ah! the little pigs?" she rejoined blithely. "I thank thee. . . they be doing nicely, thank the Lord. . . six of them and. . . eh? what? . . . I'm a bit hard of hearing these times."

He had some difficulty in keeping up even a semblance of calm. The placidity of the old Quakeress irritated him beyond endurance. He dreaded the return of Adam Lambert from his work, and worse still, he feared the arrival of Richard. Fortunately he had gathered from Martha that the young man had come home early in the day in a state of high nervous tension, bordering on acute fever. He had neither eaten nor drunk, but after tidying his clothes and reassuring her as to his future movements, he had sallied out into the woods and had not returned since then.

Sir Marmaduke had quickly arrived at the conclusion that Richard Lambert had seen and spoken to Lady Sue and had learned from her that she was now irrevocably married to him, whom she always called her prince. Doubtless, the young man was frenzied with grief, and in his weak state of health after the terrible happenings of the past few weeks, would mayhap, either go raving mad, or end his miserable existence over the cliffs. Either eventuality would suit Sir Marmaduke admirably, and he sighed with satisfaction at the thought that the knot between the heiress and himself was indeed tied sufficiently firm now to ensure her obedience to his will.

There was to be one more scene in the brief and cruel drama which he had devised for the hoodwinking and final spoliation of a young and inexperienced girl. She had earlier in the day been placed in possession of all the negotiable part of her fortune. This, though by no means representing the whole of her wealth, which also lay in landed estates, was nevertheless of such magnitude that the thought of its possession caused every fiber in Sir Marmaduke's body to thrill with the delight of expectancy.

One more brief scene in the drama: the handing over of that vast fortune, by the young girl-wife—blindly and obediently—to the man whom she believed to be her husband. Once that scene enacted, the curtain would fall on the love episode 'twixt a romantic and ignorant maid and the most daring scoundrel that had ever committed crime to obtain a fortune.

In anticipation of that last and magnificent *dénouement*, Sir Marmaduke had once more donned the disguise of the exiled Orléans prince: the elaborate clothes, the thick perruque, the black silk shade over the left eye, which gave him such a sinister expression.

Now he was literally devoured with the burning desire to see Sue arriving with that wallet in her hand, which contained securities and grants to the value of £500,000. A brief interlude with her, a few words of perfunctory affection, a few assurances of good faith, and he—as her princely husband—would vanish from her ken forever.

He meant to go abroad immediately—this very night, if possible. Prudence and caution could easily be thrown to the winds, once the negotiable securities were actually in his hands. What he could convert into money, he would do immediately, going to Amsterdam first, to withdraw the sum standing at the bank there on deposit, and for which anon, he would possess the receipt; after that the sale of the grant of monopolies should be easy of accomplishment. Sir Marmaduke had boundless faith in his own ability to carry through his own business. He might stand to lose some of the money perhaps; prudence and caution might necessitate the relinquishing of certain advantages, but even then he would be rich and passing rich, and he knew that he ran but little risk of detection. The girl was young, inexperienced and singularly friendless: Sir Marmaduke felt convinced that none of the foreign transactions could ever be directly traced to himself.

He would be prudent and Europe was wide, and he meant to leave English grants and securities severely alone.

He had mused and pondered on his plans all day. The evening found him half-exhausted with nerve-strain, febrile and almost sick with the agony of waiting.

BARONESS EMMUSKA ORCZY

He had calculated that Sue would be free towards seven o'clock, as he had given Editha strict injunctions to keep discreetly out of the way, whilst at a previous meeting in the park, it had been arranged that the young girl should come to the cottage with the money, on the evening of her twenty-first birthday and there hand her fortune over to her rightful lord.

Now Sir Marmaduke cursed himself and his folly for having made this arrangement. He had not known—when he made it—that Richard would be back at Acol then. Adam the smith, never came home before eight o'clock and the old Quakeress herself would not have been much in the way.

Even now she had shuffled back into her kitchen, leaving her ill-humored lodger to puff away at the malodorous weed as he chose. But Richard might return at any moment, and then. . .

Sir Marmaduke had never thought of that possible contingency. If Richard Lambert came face to face with him, he would of a surety pierce the disguise of the prince, and recognize the man who had so deeply wronged poor, unsuspecting Lady Sue. If only a kindly Fate had kept the young man away another twenty-four hours! or better still, if it led the despairing lover's footsteps to the extremest edge of the cliffs!

Sir Marmaduke now paced the narrow room up and down in an agony of impatience. Nine o'clock had struck long ago, but Sue had not yet come. The wildest imaginings run riot in the schemer's brain: every hour, nay! every minute spent within was fraught with danger. He sought his broad-brimmed hat, determined now to meet Sue in the park, to sally forth at risk of missing her, at risk of her arriving here at the cottage when he was absent, and of her meeting Richard Lambert perhaps, before the irrevocable deed of gift had been accomplished.

But the suspense was intolerable.

With a violent oath Sir Marmaduke pressed the hat over his head, and strode to the door.

His hand was on the latch, when he heard a faint sound from without: a girl's footsteps, timorous yet swift, along the narrow flagged path which led down the tiny garden gate.

The next moment he had thrown open the door and Sue stood before him.

Anyone but a bold and unscrupulous schemer would have been struck by the pathos of the solitary figure which now appeared in the tiny doorway. The penetrating November drizzle had soaked through the dark cloak and hood which now hung heavy and dank round the young girl's shoulders. Framed by the hood, her face appeared preternaturally pale, her lips were quivering and her eyes, large and dilated, had almost a hunted look in them.

Oh! the pity and sadness of it all! For in her small and trembling hands she was clutching with pathetic tenacity a small, brown wallet which contained a fortune worthy of a princess.

She looked eagerly into her husband's face, dreading the scowl, the outburst of anger or jealousy mayhap with which of late, alas! he had so oft greeted her arrival. But as was his wont, he stood with his back to the lighted room, and she could not read the expression of that one cyclops-like eye, which to-night appeared more sinister than ever beneath the thick perruque and broad-brimmed hat.

"I am sorry to be so late," she said timidly, "the evening repast at the Court was interminable and Mistress de Chavasse full of gossip."

"Yes, yes, I know," he replied, "am I not used to seeing that your social duties oft make you forget your husband?"

"You are unjust, Amédé," she rejoined.

She entered the little parlor and stood beside the table, making no movement to divest herself of her dripping cloak, or to sit down, nor indeed did her husband show the slightest inclination to ask her to do either. He had closed the door behind her, and followed her to the center of the room. Was it by accident or design that as he reached the table he threw his broad-brimmed hat, down with such an unnecessary flourish of the arm that he knocked over one of the heavy pewter candlesticks, so that it rolled down upon the floor, causing the tallow candle to sputter and die out with a weird and hissing sound?

Only one dim yellow light now illumined the room, it shone full into the pallid face of the young wife standing some three paces from the table, whilst Prince Amédé d'Orléans' face between her and the light, was once more in deep shadow.

"You are unjust," she repeated firmly. "Have I not run the gravest possible risks for your sake, and those without murmur or complaint, for the past six months? Did I not compromise my reputation for you by meeting you alone. . . of nights? . . ."

"I was laboring under the idea, my wench, that you were doing all that because you cared for me," he retorted with almost brutal curtness, "and because you had the desire to become the Princess d'Orléans; that desire is now gratified and. . ."

He had not really meant to be unkind. There was of a truth no object to be gained by being brutal to her now. But that wallet, which she held so tightly clutched, acted as an irritant to his nerves. Never of very equable temperament and holding all women in lofty scorn, he chafed against all parleyings with his wife, now that the goal of his ambition was so close at hand.

She winced at the insult, and the tears which she fain would have hidden from him, rose involuntarily to her eyes.

"Ah!" she sighed, "if you only knew how little I care for that title of princess! . . . Did you perchance think that I cared? . . . Nay! how gladly would I give up all thought of ever bearing that proud appellation, in exchange for a few more happy illusions such as I possessed three months ago."

"Illusions are all very well for a school-girl, my dear Suzanne," he remarked with a cool shrug of his massive shoulders. "Reality should be more attractive to you now. . ."

He looked her up and down, realizing perhaps for the first time that she was exquisitely beautiful; beautiful always, but more so now in the pathos of her helplessness. Somewhat perfunctorily, because in his ignorance of women he thought that it would please her, and also because vaguely something human and elemental had suddenly roused his pulses, he relinquished his nonchalant attitude, and came a step nearer to her.

"You are very beautiful, my Suzanne," he said half-ironically, and with marked emphasis on the possessive.

Again he drew nearer, not choosing to note the instinctive stiffening of her figure, the shrinking look in her eyes. He caught her arm and drew her to him, laughing a low mocking laugh as he did so, for she had turned her face away from him.

"Come," he said lightly, "will you not kiss me, my beautiful Suzanne? . . . my wife, my princess."

She was silent, impassive, indifferent so he thought, although the arm which he held trembled within his grip.

He stretched out his other hand, and taking her chin between his fingers, he forcibly turned her face towards him. Something in her face, in her attitude, now roused a certain rough passion in him. Mayhap the weary wailing during the day, the agonizing impatience, or the golden argosy so near to port, had strung up his nerves to fever pitch.

Irritation against her impassiveness, in such glaring contrast to her glowing ardor of but a few weeks ago, mingled with that essentially male desire to subdue and to conquer that which is inclined to resist, sent the blood coursing wildly through his veins.

"Ah!" he said with a sigh half of desire, half of satisfaction, as he looked into her upturned face, "the chaste blush of the bride is vastly becoming to you, my Suzanne! . . . it acts as fuel to the flames of my love. . . since I can well remember the passionate kisses you gave me so willingly awhile ago."

The thought of that happy past, gave her sudden strength. Catching him unawares she wrenched herself free from his hold.

"This is a mockery, prince," she said with vehemence, and meeting his half-mocking glance with one of scorn. "Do you think that I have been blind these last few weeks? . . . Your love for me hath changed, if indeed it ever existed, whilst I. . ."

"Whilst you, my beautiful Suzanne," he rejoined lightly, "are mine. . . irrevocably, irretrievably mine. . . mine because I love you, and because you are my wife. . . and owe me that obedience which you vowed to Heaven that you would give me. . . That is so, is it not?"

There was a moment's silence in the tiny cottage parlor now, whilst he—gauging the full value of his words, knowing by instinct that he had struck the right cord in that vibrating girlish heart, watched the subtle change in her face from defiance and wrath to submission and appeal.

"Yes, Amédé," she murmured after a while, "I owe you obedience, honor and love, and you need not fear that I will fail in either. But you," she added with pathetic anxiety, "you do care for me still? do you not?"

"Of course I care for you," he remarked, "I worship you. . . There! . . . will that satisfy you? . . . And now?" he added peremptorily, "have you brought the money?"

The short interlude of passion was over. His eye had accidentally rested for one second on the leather wallet, which she still held tightly clutched, and all thoughts of her beauty, of his power or his desires, had flown out to the winds.

"Yes," she replied meekly, "it is all here, in the wallet."

She laid it down upon the table, feeling neither anxiety nor remorse. He was her husband and had a right to her fortune, as he had to her person and to her thoughts and heart an he wished. Nor did she care about the money, as to the value of which she was, of course, ignorant.

Her wealth, up to now, had only had a meaning for her, as part of some noble scheme for the regeneration of mankind. Now she hoped vaguely, as she put that wallet down on the table, then pushed it towards her husband, that she was purchasing her freedom with her wealth.

Certainly she realized that his thoughts had very quickly been diverted from her beauty to the contents of the wallet. The mocking laugh died down on his lips, giving place to a sigh of deep satisfaction.

"You were very prudent, my dear Suzanne, to place this portion of your wealth in my charge," he said as he slipped the bulky papers into the lining of his doublet. "Of course it is all yours, and I—your husband—am but the repository and guardian of your fortune. And now methinks 'twere prudent for you to return to the Court. Sir Marmaduke de Chavasse will be missing you. . ."

It did not seem to strike her as strange that he should dismiss her thus abruptly, and make no attempt to explain what his future plans might be, nor indeed what his intentions were with regard to herself.

The intensity of her disappointment, the utter loneliness and helplessness of her position had caused a veritable numbing of her faculties and of her spirit and for the moment she was perhaps primarily conscious of a sense of relief at her dismissal.

Like her wedding in the dismal little church, this day of her birthday, of her independence, of her handing over her fortune to her husband for the glorious purposes of his selfless schemes had been so very, very different to what she had pictured to herself in her girlish and romantic dreams.

The sordidness of it all had ruthlessly struck her; for the first time in her intercourse with this man, she doubted the genuineness of his motives. With the passing of her fortune from her hands to his, the last vestige of belief in him died down with appalling suddenness.

It could not have been because of the expression in his eyes, as he fingered the wallet, for this she could not see, since his face was still in shadow. It must have been just instinct—that, and the mockery of his attempt to make love to her. Had he ever loved her, he could not have mocked. . . not now, that she was helpless and entirely at his mercy.

Love once felt, is sacred to him who feels: mockery even of the ashes of love is an impossible desecration, one beyond the power of any man. Then, if he had never loved her, why had he pretended? Why have deceived her with a semblance of passion?

And the icy whisper of reason blew into her mental ear, the ugly word: "Money."

He opened the door for her, and without another word, she passed out into the dark night. Only when she reached the tiny gate at the end of the flagged path, did she realize that he was walking with her.

"I can find my way alone through the woods," she said coldly. "I came alone."

"It was earlier then," he rejoined blandly, "and I prefer to see you safely as far as the park."

And they walked on side by side in silence. Overhead the melancholy drip of moisture falling from leaf to leaf, and from leaf to the ground, was the only sound that accompanied their footsteps. Sue shivered beneath her damp cloak; but she walked as far away from him as the width of the woodland path allowed. He seemed absorbed in his own thoughts and not to notice how she shrank from the slightest contact with him.

At the park gate he paused, having opened it for her to pass through.

"I must bid you good-night here, Suzanne," he said lightly, "there may be footpads about and I must place your securities away under lock and key. I may be absent a few days for that purpose. . . London, you know," he added vaguely.

Then as she made no comment:

"I will arrange for our next meeting," he said, "anon, there will be no necessity to keep our marriage a secret, but until I give you permission to speak of it, 'twere better that you remained silent on that score."

She contrived to murmur:

"As you will."

And presently, as he made no movement towards her, she said: "Good-night!"

This time he had not even desired to kiss her.

The next moment she had disappeared in the gloom. She fled as fast as she dared in the inky blackness of this November night. She could have run for miles, or for hours, away! away from all this sordidness, this avarice, this deceit and cruelty! Away! away from him!!

How glad she was that darkness enveloped her, for now she felt horribly ashamed. Instinct, too, is cruel at times! Instinct had been silent so long during the most critical juncture of her own folly. Now it spoke loudly, warningly; now that it was too late.

Ashamed of her own stupidity and blindness! her vanity mayhap had alone led her to believe the passionate protestations of a liar.

A liar! a mean, cowardly schemer, but her husband for all that! She owed him love, honor and obedience; if he commanded, she must obey; if he called she must fain go to him.

Oh! please God! that she had succeeded in purchasing her freedom from him by placing £500,000 in his hands.

Shame! shame that this should be! that she should have mistaken vile schemes for love, that a liar's kisses should have polluted her soul! that she should be the wife, the bondswoman of a cheat!

XXIX

Good-Bye

S ue!"

The cry rang out in the night close to her, and arrested her fleeing footsteps. She was close to the ha-ha, having run on blindly, madly, guided by that unaccountable instinct which makes for the shelter of home.

In a moment she had recognized the voice. In a moment she was beside her friend. Her passionate mood passed away, leaving her calm and almost at peace. Shame still caused her cheeks to burn, but the night was dark and doubtless he would not see.

But she could feel that he was near her, therefore, there was no fear in her. What had guided her footsteps hither she did not know. Of course he had guessed that she had been to meet her husband.

There were no exclamations or protestations between them. She merely said quite simply:

"I am glad that you came to say 'good-bye!'"

The park was open here. The nearest trees were some fifty paces away, and in the ghostly darkness they could just perceive one another's silhouettes. The mist enveloped them as with a shroud, the damp cold air caused them to shiver as under the embrace of death.

"It is good-bye," he rejoined calmly.

"Mayhap that I shall go abroad soon," she said.

"With that man?"

The cry broke out from the bitterness of his heart, but a cold little hand was placed restrainingly on his.

"When I go. . . if I go," she murmured, "I shall do so with my husband. . . You see, my friend, do you not, that there is naught else to say but 'good-bye'?"

"And you will be happy, Sue?" he asked.

"I hope so!" she sighed wistfully.

"You will always remember, will you not, my dear lady, that wherever you may be, there is always someone in remote Thanet, who is ready at any time to give his life for you?"

"Yes! I will remember," she said simply.

"And you must promise me," he insisted, "promise me now, Sue, that if. . . which Heaven forbid. . . you are in any trouble or sorrow, and I can do aught for you, that you will let me know and send for me. . . and I will come."

"Yes, Richard, I promise. . . Good-bye."

And she was gone. The mist, the gloom hid her completely from view. He waited by the little bridge, for the night was still and he would have heard if she called.

He heard her light footsteps on the gravel, then on the flagged walk. Anon came the sound of the opening and shutting of a door. After that, silence: the silence of a winter's night, when not a breath of wind stirs the dead branches of the trees, when woodland and field and park are wrapped in the shroud of the mist.

Richard Lambert turned back towards the village.

Sue—married to another man—had passed out of his life forever.

XXX

All Because of the Tinder-Box

How oft it is in life that Fate, leading a traveler in easy gradients upwards along a road of triumph, suddenly assumes a madcap mood and with wanton hand throws a tiny obstacle in his way; an obstacle at times infinitesimal, scarce visible on that way towards success, yet powerful enough to trip the unwary traveler and bring him down to earth with sudden and woeful vigor.

With Sir Marmaduke so far everything had prospered according to his wish. He had inveigled the heiress into a marriage which bound her to his will, yet left him personally free; she had placed her fortune unreservedly and unconditionally in his hands, and had, so far as he knew, not even suspected the treachery practiced upon her by her guardian.

Not a soul had pierced his disguise, and the identity of Prince Amédé d'Orléans was unknown even to his girl-wife.

With the disappearance of that mysterious personage, Sir Marmaduke having realized Lady Sue's fortune, could resume life as an independent gentleman, with this difference, that henceforth he would be passing rich, able to gratify his ambition, to cut a figure in the world as he chose.

Fortune which had been his idol all his life, now was indeed his slave. He had it, he possessed it. It lay snug and safe in a leather wallet inside the lining of his doublet.

Sue had gone out of his sight, desirous apparently of turning her back on him forever. He was free and rich. The game had been risky, daring beyond belief, yet he had won in the end. He could afford to laugh now at all the dangers, the subterfuges, the machinations which had all gone to the making of that tragic comedy in which he had been the principal actor.

The last scene in the drama had been successfully enacted. The curtain had been finally lowered; and Sir Marmaduke swore that there should be no epilogue to the play.

Then it was that Fate—so well-named the wanton jade—shook herself from out the torpor in which she had wandered for so long beside this Kentish squire. A spirit of mischief seized upon her and whispered that she had held this man quite long enough by the hand and that it would be far more amusing now to see him measure his length on the ground.

And all that Fate did, in order to satisfy this spirit of mischief, was to cause Sir Marmaduke to forget his tinder-box in the front parlor of Mistress Martha Lambert's cottage.

A tinder-box is a small matter! an object of infinitesimal importance when the broad light of day illumines the interior of houses or the bosquets of a park, but it becomes an object of paramount importance, when the night is pitch dark, and when it is necessary to effect an exchange of clothing within the four walls of a pavilion.

Sir Marmaduke had walked to the park gates with his wife, not so much because he was anxious for her safety, but chiefly because he meant to retire within the pavilion, there to cast aside forever the costume and appurtenances of Prince Amédé d'Orléans and to reassume the sable-colored doublet and breeches of the Roundhead squire, which proceeding he had for the past six months invariably accomplished in the lonely little building on the outskirts of his own park.

As soon, therefore, as he realized that Sue had gone, he turned his steps towards the pavilion. The night seemed additionally dark here under the elms, and Sir Marmaduke searched in his pocket for his tinder-box.

It was not there. He had left it at the cottage, and quickly recollected seeing it lying on the table at the very moment that Sue pushed the leather wallet towards him.

He had mounted the few stone steps which led up to the building, but even whilst he groped for the latch with an impatient hand, he realized how impossible it would be for him anon, to change his clothes, in the dark; not only to undress and dress again, but to collect the belongings of the Prince d'Orléans subsequently, for the purpose of destroying them at an early opportunity.

Groping about in inky blackness might mean the forgetting of some article of apparel, which, if found later on, might lead to suspicion or even detection of the fraud. Sir Marmaduke dared not risk it.

Light he needed, and light he ought to have. The tinder-box had become of paramount importance, and it was sheer wantonness on the part of Fate that she should have allowed that little article to rest forgotten on the table in Mistress Lambert's cottage.

Sir Marmaduke remained pondering—in the darkness and the mist—for a while. His own doublet and breeches, shoes and stockings were in the pavilion: would he ever be able to get at them without a light? No, certainly not! nor could he venture to go home to the Court in his present disguise, and leave his usual clothes in this remote building.

Prying, suspicious eyes—such as those of Master Hymn-of-Praise Busy, for instance, might prove exceedingly uncomfortable and even dangerous.

On the other hand, would it not be ten thousand times more dangerous to go back to the cottage now and risk meeting Richard Lambert face to face?

And it was Richard whom Sir Marmaduke feared.

He had, therefore, almost decided to try his luck at dressing in the dark, and was once more fumbling with the latch of the pavilion door, when through the absolute silence of the air, there came to his ear through the mist the sound of a young voice calling the name of "Sue!"

The voice was that of Richard Lambert.

The coast would be clear then. Richard had met Sue in the park: no doubt he would hold her a few moments in conversation. The schemer cared not what the two young people would or would not say to one another; all that interested him now was the fact that Richard was not at the cottage, and that, therefore, it would be safe to run back and fetch the tinder-box.

All this was a part of Fate's mischievous prank. Sir Marmaduke was not afraid of meeting the old Quakeress, nor yet the surly smith; Richard being out of the way, he had no misgivings in his mind when he retraced his steps towards the cottage.

It was close on eight o'clock then, in fact the tiny bell in Acol church struck the hour even as Sir Marmaduke lifted the latch of the little garden gate.

The old woman was in the parlor, busy as usual with her dusting-cloth. Without heeding her, Sir Marmaduke strode up to the table and pushing the crockery, which now littered it, aside, he searched for his tinder-box.

It was not there. With an impatient oath, he turned to Mistress Martha, and roughly demanded if she had seen it.

"Eh? . . . What?" she queried, shuffling a little nearer to him, "I am somewhat hard of hearing. . . as thou knowest. . ."

"Have you seen my tinder-box?" he repeated with ever-growing irritation.

"Ah, yea, the fog!" she said blandly, "'tis damp too, of a truth, and. . ."

"Hold your confounded tongue!" he shouted wrathfully, "and try and hear me. My tinder-box. . ."

"Thy what? I am a bit. . ."

"Curse you for an old fool," swore Sir Marmaduke, who by now was in a towering passion.

With a violent gesture he pushed the old woman aside and turning on her in an uncontrolled access of fury, with both arms upraised, he shouted:

"If you don't hear me now, I'll break every bone in your ugly body. . . Where is my. . ."

It had all happened in a very few seconds: his entrance, his search for the missing box, the growing irritation in him which had caused him to lose control of his temper. And now, even before the threatening words were well out of his mouth, he suddenly felt a vigorous onslaught from the rear, and his own throat clutched by strong and sinewy fingers.

"And I'll break every bone in thy accursed body!" shouted a hoarse voice close to his ear, "if thou darest so much as lay a finger on the old woman."

The struggle was violent and brief. Sir Marmaduke already felt himself overmastered. Adam Lambert had taken him unawares. He was rough and very powerful. Sir Marmaduke was no weakling, yet encumbered by his fantastic clothes he was no match for the smith. Adam turned him about in his nervy hands like a puppet.

Now he was in front and above him, glaring down at the man he hated with eyes which would have searched the very depths of his enemy's soul.

"Thou damned foreigner!" he growled between clenched teeth, "thou vermin! . . . Thou toad! Thou. . . on thy knees! . . . on thy knees, I say. . . beg her pardon for thy foul language. . . now at once. . . dost hear? . . . ere I squeeze the breath out of thee. . ."

Sir Marmaduke felt his knees giving way under him, the smith's grasp on his throat had in no way relaxed. Mistress Martha vainly tried to interpose. She was all for peace, and knew that the Lord liked not a fiery temper. But the look in Adam's face frightened her, and she had always been in terror of the foreigner. Without thought, and imagining that 'twas her presence which irritated the lodger, she beat a hasty retreat to her room upstairs, even as Adam Lambert finally succeeded in forcing Sir Marmaduke down on his knees, not ceasing to repeat the while:

"Her pardon. . . beg her pardon, my fine prince. . . lick the dust in an English cottage, thou foreign devil. . . or, by God, I will kill thee! . . ."

"Let me go!" gasped Sir Marmaduke, whom the icy fear of imminent discovery gripped more effectually even than did the village blacksmith's muscular fingers, "let me go. . . damn you!"

"Not before I have made thee lick the dust," said Adam grimly, bringing one huge palm down on the elaborate perruque, and forcing Sir Marmaduke's head down, down towards the ground, "lick it. . . lick it. . . Prince of Orléans. . ."

He burst out laughing in the midst of his fury, at sight of this disdainful gentleman, with the proud title, about to come in violent contact with a cottage floor. But Sir Marmaduke struggled violently still. He had been wiser no doubt, to take the humiliation quietly, to lick the dust and to pacify the smith: but what man is there who would submit to brute force without using his own to protect himself?

Then Fate at last worked her wanton will.

In the struggle the fantastic perruque and heavy mustache of Prince Amédé d'Orléans remained in the smith's hand whilst it was the round head and clean-shaven face of Sir Marmaduke de Chavasse which came in contact with the floor.

In an instant, stricken at first dumb with surprise and horror, but quickly recovering the power of speech, Adam Lambert murmured:

"You? . . . You? . . . Sir Marmaduke de Chavasse! . . . Oh! my God! . . ."

His grip on his enemy had, of course, relaxed. Sir Marmaduke was able to struggle to his feet. Fate had dealt him a blow as unexpected as it was violent. But he had not been the daring schemer that he was, if throughout the past six months, the possibility of such a moment as this had not lurked at the back of his mind.

The blow, therefore, did not find him quite unprepared. It had been stunning but not absolutely crushing. Even whilst Adam Lambert was staring with almost senseless amazement alternately at him and at the bundle of false hair which he was still clutching, Sir Marmaduke had struggled to his feet.

XXXI

THE ASSIGNATION

H e had recovered his outward composure at any rate, and the next moment was busy re-adjusting his doublet and bands before the mirror over the hearth.

"Yes! my violent friend!" he said coolly, speaking over his shoulder, "of a truth it is mine own self! Your landlord you see, to whom that worthy woman upstairs owes this nice cottage which she has had rent free for over ten years. . . not the foreign vermin, you see," he added with a pleasant laugh, "which maketh your actions of just now, somewhat unpleasant to explain. Is that not so?"

"Nay! but by the Lord!" quoth Adam Lambert, still somewhat dazed, vaguely frightened himself now at the magnitude, the importance of what he had done, "meseems that 'tis thine actions, friend, which will be unpleasant to explain. Thou didst not put on these play-actor's robes for a good purpose, I'll warrant! . . . I cannot guess what is thy game, but methinks her young ladyship would wish to know something of its rules. . . or mayhap, my brother Richard who is no friend of thine, forsooth."

Gradually his voice had become steadier, his manner more assured. A glimmer of light on the Squire's strange doings had begun to penetrate his simple, dull brain. Vaguely he guessed the purport of the disguise and of the lies, and the mention of Lady Sue's name was not an arrow shot thoughtlessly into the air. At the same time he had not perceived the slightest quiver of fear or even of anxiety on Sir Marmaduke's face.

The latter had in the meanwhile put his crumpled toilet in order and now turned with an urbane smile to his glowering antagonist.

"I will not deny, kind master," he said pleasantly, "that you might cause me a vast amount of unpleasantness just now. . . although of a truth, I do not perceive that you would benefit yourself overmuch thereby. On the contrary, you would vastly lose. Your worthy aunt, Mistress Lambert, would lose a pleasant home, and you would never know what you and your brother Richard have vainly striven to find out these past ten years."

"What may that be, pray?" queried the smith sullenly.

"Who you both are," rejoined Sir Marmaduke blandly, as he calmly sat down in one of the stiff-backed elm chairs beside the hearth, "and why worthy Mistress Lambert never speaks to you of your parentage."

"Who we both are?" retorted Lambert with obvious bitterness, "two poor castaways, who, but for the old woman would have been left to starve, and who have tried, therefore, to be a bit grateful to her, and to earn an honest livelihood. That is what we are, Sir Marmaduke de Chavasse; and now prithee tell me, who the devil art thou?"

"You are overfond of swearing, worthy master," quoth Sir Marmaduke lightly, "'tis sinful so I'm told, for one of your creed. But that is no matter to me. You are, believe me, somewhat more interesting than you imagine. Though I doubt if to a Quaker, being heir to title and vast estates hath more than a fleeting interest."

But the smith had shrugged his broad shoulders and uttered an exclamation of contempt.

"Title and vast estates?" he said with an ironical laugh. "Nay! Sir Marmaduke de Chavasse, the bait is passing clumsy. An you wish me to hold my tongue about you and your affairs, you'll have to be vastly sharper than that."

"You mistake me, friend smith, I am not endeavoring to purchase your silence. I hold certain information relating to your parentage. This I would be willing to impart to a friend, yet loath to do so to an enemy. A man doth not like to see his enemy in possession of fifteen thousand pounds a year. Does he?"

And Sir Marmaduke appeared absorbed in the contemplation of his left shoe, whilst Adam Lambert repeated stupidly and vaguely:

"Fifteen thousand pounds a year? I?"

"Even you, my friend."

This was said so simply, and with such conviction-carrying certainty— that in spite of himself Lambert's sulkiness vanished. He drew nearer to Sir Marmaduke, looked down on him silently for a second or two, then muttered through his teeth:

"You have the proofs?"

"They will be at your service, my choleric friend," replied the other suavely, "in exchange for your silence."

Adam Lambert drew a chair close to his whilom enemy, sat down opposite to him, with elbows resting on his knee, his clenched fists supporting his chin, and his eyes—anxious, eager, glowing, fixed resolutely on de Chavasse.

"I'll hold my tongue, never fear," he said curtly. "Show me the proofs."

Sir Marmaduke gave a pleasant little laugh.

"Not so fast, my friend," he said, "I do not carry such important papers about in my breeches' pocket."

And he rose from his chair, picked up the perruque and false mustache which the other man had dropped upon the floor, and adjusting these on his head and face he once more presented the appearance of the exiled Orléans prince.

"But thou'lt show them to me to-night," insisted the smith roughly.

"How can I, mine impatient friend?" quoth de Chavasse lightly, "the hour is late already."

"Nay! what matter the lateness of the hour? I am oft abroad at night, early and late, and thou, methinks, hast oft had the midnight hour for company. When and where wilt meet me?" added Lambert peremptorily, "I must see those proofs to-night, before many hours are over, lest the blood in my veins burn my body to ashes with impatience. When wilt meet me? Eleven? . . . Midnight? . . . or the small hours of the morn?"

He spoke quickly, jerking out his words through closed teeth, his eyes burning with inward fever, his fists closing and unclosing with rapid febrile movements of the fingers.

The pent-up disappointment and rebellion of a whole lifetime against Fate, was expressed in the man's attitude, the agonizing eagerness which indeed seemed to be consuming him.

De Chavasse, on the other hand, had become singularly calm. The black shade as usual hid one of his eyes, masking and distorting the expression of his face; the false mustache, too, concealed the movements of his lips, and the more his opponent's eyes tried to search the schemer's face, the more inscrutable and bland did the latter become.

"Nay, my friend," he said at last, "I do not know that the thought of a midnight excursion with you appeals to my sense of personal security. I. . ."

But with a violent oath, Adam had jumped to his feet, and kicked the chair away from under him so that it fell backwards with a loud clatter.

"Thou'lt meet me to-night," he said loudly and threateningly now, "thou'lt meet me on the path near the cliffs of Epple Bay half an hour before midnight, and if thou hast lied to me, I'll throw thee over and Thanet then will be rid of thee. . . but if thou dost not come, I'll to my brother Richard even before the church clock of Acol hath sounded the hour of midnight."

De Chavasse watched him silently for the space of three seconds, realizing, of course, that he was completely in that man's power, and also that the smith meant every word that he said. The discovery of the monstrous fraud by Richard Lambert within the next few hours was a contingency which he could not even contemplate without shuddering. He certainly would much prefer to give up to this uncouth laborer the proofs of his parentage which eventually might mean an earldom and a fortune to a village blacksmith.

Sir Marmaduke had reflected on all this, of course, before broaching the subject to Adam Lambert at all. Now he was prepared to go through with the scheme to the end if need be. His uncle, the Earl of Northallerton, might live another twenty years, whilst he himself—if pursued for fraud, might have to spend those years in jail.

On the whole it was simpler to purchase the smith's silence. . . this way or another. Sir Marmaduke's reflections at this moment would have delighted those evil spirits who are supposed to revel in the misdoings of mankind.

The thought of the lonely path near the cliffs of Epple Bay tickled his fancy in a manner for which perhaps at this moment he himself could not have accounted. He certainly did not fear Adam Lambert and now said decisively:

"Very well, my friend, an you wish it, I'll come."

"Half an hour before midnight," insisted Lambert, "on the cliffs at Epple Bay."

"Half an hour before midnight: on the cliffs of Epple Bay," assented the other.

He picked up his hat.

"Where art going?" queried the smith suspiciously.

"To change my clothing," replied Sir Marmaduke, who was fingering that fateful tinder-box which alone had brought about the present crisis, "and to fetch those proofs which you are so anxious to see."

"Thou'lt not fail me?"

"Surely not," quoth de Chavasse, as he finally went out of the room.

XXXII

The Path Near the Cliffs

The mist had not lifted. Over the sea it hung heavy and dank like a huge sheet of gray thrown over things secret and unavowable. It was thickest down in the bay lurking in the crevices of the chalk, in the great caverns and mighty architecture carved by the patient toil of the billows in the solid mass of the cliffs.

Up above it was slightly less dense: allowing distinct peeps of the rough carpet of coarse grass, of the downtrodden path winding towards Acol, of the edge of the cliff, abrupt, precipitous, with a drop of some ninety feet into that gray pall of mist to the sands below.

And higher up still, above the mist itself, a deep blue sky dotted with stars, and a full moon, pale and circled with luminous vapors. A gentle breeze had risen about half an hour ago and was blowing the mist hither and thither, striving to disperse it, but not yet succeeding in mastering it, for it only shifted restlessly to and fro, like the giant garments of titanic ghosts, revealing now a distant peep of sea, anon the interior of a colonnaded cavern, abode of mysterious ghouls, or again a nest of gulls in a deep crevice of the chalk: revealing and hiding again:—a shroud dragged listlessly over monstrous dead things.

Sir Marmaduke de Chavasse had some difficulty in keeping to the footpath which leads from the woods of Acol straight toward the cliffs. Unlike Adam Lambert, his eyes were unaccustomed to pierce the moist pall which hid the distance from his view.

Strangely enough he had not cast aside the fantastic accouterments of the French prince, and though these must have been as singularly uncomfortable, as they were inappropriate, for a midnight walk, nevertheless, he still wore the heavy perruque, the dark mustache, broad-brimmed hat, and black shade which were so characteristic of the mysterious personage.

He had heard the church clock at Acol village strike half an hour after eleven and knew that the smith would already be waiting for him.

The acrid smell of seaweed struck forcibly now upon his nostrils. The grass beneath his feet had become more sparse and more coarse. The moisture which clung to his face had a taste of salt in it. Obviously he was quite close to the edge of the cliffs.

The next moment and without any warning a black outline appeared in the moon-illumined density. It was Adam Lambert pacing up and down with the impatience of an imprisoned beast of prey.

A second or two later the febrile hand of the smith had gripped Sir Marmaduke's shoulder.

"You have brought those proofs?" he queried hoarsely.

His face was wet with the mist, and he had apparently oft wiped it with his hand or sleeve, for great streaks of dirt marked his cheeks and forehead, giving him a curious satanic expression, whilst his short lank hair obviously roughed up by impatient fingers, bristled above his square-built head like the coat of a shaggy dog.

In absolute contrast to him, Sir Marmaduke looked wonderfully calm and tidy. In answer to the other man's eager look of inquiry, he made pretense of fumbling in his pockets, as he said quietly:

"Yes! all of them!"

As if idly musing, he continued to walk along the path, whilst the smith first stooped to pick up a small lantern which he had obviously brought with him in order to examine the papers by its light, and then strode in the wake of Sir Marmaduke.

The breeze was getting a bother hold on the mist, and was tossing it about from sea to cliff and upwards with more persistence and more vigor.

The pale, cold moon glistened visibly on the moist atmosphere, and far below and far beyond weird streaks of shimmering silver edged the surface of the sea. The breeze itself had scarcely stirred the water; or,— the soft sound of tiny billows lapping the outstanding boulders was wafted upwards as the tide drew in.

The two men had reached the edge of the cliff. With a slight laugh, indicative of nervousness, Sir Marmaduke had quickly stepped back a pace or two.

"I have brought the proofs," he said, as if wishing to conciliate a dangerous enemy, "we need not stand so near the edge, need we?"

But Adam Lambert shrugged his shoulders in token of contempt at the other's cowardice.

"I'll not harm thee," he said, "an thou hast not lied to me. . ."

He deposited his lantern by the side of a heap of white chalk, which had, no doubt, been collected at some time or other by idle or childish hands, and stood close to the edge of the cliff. Sir Marmaduke now took his stand beside it, one foot placed higher than the other. Close to him Adam in a frenzy of restlessness had thrown himself down on the heap; below them a drop of ninety feet to the seaweed covered beach.

"Let me see the papers," quoth Adam impatiently.

"Gently, gently, kind sir," said de Chavasse lightly. "Did you think that you could dictate your own terms quite so easily?"

"What dost thou mean?" queried the other.

"I mean that I am about to place in your hands the proof that you are heir to a title and fifteen thousand pounds a year, but at the same time I wish to assure myself that you will be pleasant over certain matters which concern me."

"Have I not said that I would hold my tongue."

"Of a truth you did say so my friend, and therefore, I am convinced that you will not refuse to give me a written promise to that effect."

"I cannot write," said Adam moodily.

"Oh! just your signature!" said de Chavasse pleasantly. "You can write your name?"

"Not well."

"The initials A. and L. They would satisfy me,"

"Why dost thou want written promises," objected the smith, looking up with sullen wrath at Sir Marmaduke. "Is not the word of an honest man sufficient for thee?"

"Quite sufficient," rejoined de Chavasse blandly, "those initials are a mere matter of form. You cannot object if your intentions are honest."

"I do not object. Hast brought ink or paper?"

"Yes, and the form to which you only need to affix your initials."

Sir Marmaduke now drew a packet of papers from the inner lining of his doublet.

"These are the proofs of your parentage," he said lightly.

Then he took out another single sheet of paper from his pocket, unfolded it and handed it to Lambert. "Can you read it?" he asked.

He stooped and picked up the lantern, whilst handing the paper to Adam. The smith took the document from him, and Sir Marmaduke held the lantern so that he might read.

Adam Lambert was no scholar. The reading of printed matter was oft a difficulty to him, written characters were a vast deal more trouble, but suspicion lurked in the smith's mind, and though his very sinews ached with the desire to handle the proofs, he would not put his initials to any writing which he did not fully comprehend.

It was all done in a moment. Adam was absorbed in deciphering the contents of the paper. De Chavasse held the lantern up with one hand, but at such an angle that Lambert was obliged to step back in order to get its full light.

Then with the other hand, the right, Sir Marmaduke drew a double-edged Italian knife from his girdle, and with a rapid and vigorous gesture, drove it straight between the smith's shoulder blades.

Adam uttered a groan:

"My God. . . I am. . ."

Then he staggered and fell.

Fell backwards down the edge of the cliff into the mist-enveloped abyss below.

Sir Marmaduke had fallen on one knee and his trembling fingers clutched at the thick short grass, sharp as the blade of a knife, to stop himself from swooning—from falling backwards in the wake of Adam the smith.

A gust of wind wafted the mist upwards, covering him with its humid embrace. But he remained quite still, crouching on his stomach now, his hands clutching the grass for support, whilst great drops of perspiration mingled with the moisture of the mist on his face.

Anon he raised his head a little and turned to look at the edge of the cliff. On hands and knees, like a gigantic reptile, he crawled, then lay flat on the ground, on the extreme edge, his eyes peering down into those depths wherein floating vapors lolled and stirred, with subtle movements like spirits in unrest.

As far as the murderer's eye could reach and could penetrate the density of the fog, white crag succeeded white crag, with innumerable projections which should have helped to toss a falling and inert mass as easily as if it had been an air bubble.

Sir Marmaduke tried to penetrate the secrets which the gray and shifting veil still hid from his view. Beside him lay the Italian knife, its steely surface shimmering in the vaporous light, there where a dull and ruddy stain had not dimmed its brilliant polish. The murderer gazed at his tool and shuddered feebly. But he picked up the knife and mechanically wiped it in the grass, before he restored it to his belt.

Then he gazed downwards again, straining his eyes to pierce the mist, his ears to hear a sound.

But nothing came upwards from that mighty abyss save the now more distinct lapping of the billows round the boulders, for the tide was rapidly setting in.

Down the white sides of the cliff the projections seemed ready to afford a foothold bearing somewhat toward the right, the descent was not so abrupt as it was immediately in front. The chalk of a truth looked slimy and green, and might cause the unwary to trip, but there was that to see down below and that to do, which would make any danger of a fall well worth the risking.

Sir Marmaduke de Chavasse slowly rose to his feet. His knees were still shaking under him, and there was a nervous tremor in his jaw and in his wrists which he tried vainly to conquer.

Nevertheless he managed to readjust his clothes, his perruque, his broad-brimmed hat. The papers he slipped back into his pocket together with the black silk shade and false mustache, then, with the lantern in his left hand he took the first steps towards the perilous descent.

There was something down below that he must see, something that he wished to do.

He walked sidewise at times, bent nearly double, looking like some gigantic and unwieldy crab, as the feeble rays of the mist-hidden moon caught his rounded back in its cloth doublet of a dull reddish hue. At other times he was forced to sit, and to work his way downwards with his hands and heels, tearing his clothes, bruising his elbows and his shoulders against the projections of the titanic masonry. Lumps of chalk detached themselves from beneath and around him and slipped down the precipitous sides in advance of him, with a dull reverberating sound which seemed to rouse the echoes of this silent night.

The descent seemed interminable. His flesh ached, his sinews creaked, his senses reeled with the pain, the mind-agony, the horror of it all.

At last he caught a glimmer of the wet sand, less than ten feet below. He had just landed on a bit of white tableland wantonly carved in the naked cliff. The rough gradients which up to now had guided him in his descent ceased abruptly. Behind him the cliff rose upwards, in front and, to his right, and left a concave wall, straight down to the beach.

Exhausted and half-paralyzed, de Chavasse perforce had to throw himself down these last ten feet, hardly pausing to think whether his head would or would not come in violent contact with one of the chalk boulders which stand out here and there in the flat sandy beach.

He threw down the lantern first, which was extinguished as it fell. Then he took the final jump, and soon lay half-unconscious, numbed and aching in every limb in the wet sand.

Anon he tried to move. His limbs were painful, his shoulders ached, and he had some difficulty in struggling to his feet. An unusually large boulder close by afforded a resting place. He reached it and sat down. His head was still swimming but his limbs were apparently sound. He sat quietly for a while, recouping his strength, gathering his wandering senses. The lantern lay close to his feet, extinguished but not broken.

He groped for his tinder-box, and having found it, proceeded to relight the tiny tallow dip. It was a difficult proceeding for the tinder was damp, and the breeze, though very slight in this hollow portion of the cliffs, nevertheless was an enemy to a trembling little flame.

But Sir Marmaduke noted with satisfaction that his nerves were already under his control. He succeeded in relighting the lantern, which he could not have done if his hands had been as unsteady as they were awhile ago.

He rose once more to his feet, stamped them against the boulders, stretched out his arms, giving his elbows and shoulders full play. Mayhap he had spent a quarter of an hour thus resting since that final jump, mayhap it had been an hour or two; he could not say for time had ceased to be.

But the mist had penetrated to his very bones and he did not remember ever having felt quite so cold.

Now he seized his lantern and began his search, trying to ascertain the exact position of the portion of the cliff's edge where he and Lambert the smith had been standing a while ago.

It was not a difficult matter, nor was the search a long one. Soon he saw a huddled mass lying in the sand.

He went up to it and placed the lantern down upon a boulder.

Horror had entirely left him. The crisis of terror at his own fell deed had been terrible but brief. His was not a nature to shrink from unpleasant sights, nor at such times do men have cause to recoil from contact with the dead.

In the murderer's heart there was no real remorse for the crime which he had committed.

"Bah! why did the fool get in my way?" was the first mental comment which he made when he caught sight of Lambert's body.

Then with a final shrug of the shoulders he dismissed pity, horror or remorse, entirely from his thoughts.

What he now did was to raise the smith's body from the ground and to strip it of its clothing. 'Twas a grim task, on which his chroniclers have never cared to dwell. His purpose was fixed. He had planned and thought it all out minutely, and he was surely not the man to flinch at the execution of a project once he had conceived it.

The death of Adam Lambert should serve a double purpose: the silencing of an avowed enemy and the wiping out of the personality of Prince Amédé d'Orléans.

The latter was as important as the first. It would facilitate the realizing of the fortune and, above all, clear the way for Sir Marmaduke's future life.

Therefore, however gruesome the task, which was necessary in order to attain that great goal, the schemer accomplished it, with set teeth and an unwavering hand.

What he did do on that lonely fog-ridden beach and in the silence of that dank and misty night, was to dress up the body of Adam Lambert, the smith, in the fantastic clothing of Prince Amédé d'Orléans: the red cloth doublet, the lace collars and cuffs, the bunches of ribbon at knee and waist, and the black silk shade over the left eye. All he omitted were the perruque and the false mustache.

Having accomplished this work, he himself donned the clothes of Adam Lambert.

This part of his task being done, he had to rest for a while. 'Tis no easy matter to undress and redress an inert mass.

The smith, dressed in the elaborate accouterments of the mysterious French prince, now lay face upwards on the sand.

The tide was rapidly setting in. In less than half an hour it would reach this portion of the beach.

Sir Marmaduke de Chavasse, however, had not yet accomplished all that he meant to do. He knew that the sea-waves had a habit of returning that which they took away. Therefore, his purpose was not fully accomplished when he had dressed the dead smith in the clothes of the Orléans prince. Else had he wished it, he could have consigned his victim to the tide.

But Adam—dead—had now to play a part in the grim comedy which Sir Marmaduke de Chavasse had designed for his own safety, and the more assured success of all his frauds and plans.

Therefore, after a brief rest, the murderer set to work again. A more grim task yet! one from which of a truth more than one evil-doer would recoil.

Not so this bold schemer, this mad worshiper of money and of self. Everything! anything for the safety of Sir Marmaduke de Chavasse, for the peaceful possession of £500,000.

Everything! Even the desecration of the dead!

The murderer was powerful, and there is a strength which madness gives. Heavy boulders pushed by vigorous arms had to help in the monstrous deed!

Heavy boulders thrown and rolled over the face of the dead, so as to obliterate all identity!

Nay! had a sound now disturbed the silence of this awesome night, surely it had been the laughter of demons aghast at such a deed!

The moon indeed hid her face, retreating once more behind the veils of mist. The breeze itself was lulled and the fog gathered itself together and wrapped the unavowable horrors of the night in a gray and ghoul-like shroud.

Madness lurked in the eyes of the sacrilegious murderer. Madness which helped him not only to carry his grim task to the end, but, having accomplished it, to see that it was well done.

And his hand did not tremble, as he raised the lantern and looked down on *that* which had once been Adam Lambert, the smith.

Nay, had those laughing demons looked on it, they would have veiled their faces in awe!

The gentle wavelets of the torpid tide were creeping round that thing in red doublet and breeches, in high top boots, lace cuffs and collar.

Sir Marmaduke looked down calmly upon his work, and did not even shudder with horror.

Madness had been upon him and had numbed his brain.

But the elemental instinct of self-preservation whispered to him that his work was well done.

When the sea gave up the dead, only the clothes, the doublet, the ribands, the lace, the black shade, mayhap, would reveal his identity, as the mysterious French prince who for a brief while had lodged in a cottage at Acol.

But the face was unrecognizable.

PART IV

XXXIII

THE DAY AFTER

The feeling which prevailed in Thanet with regard to the murder of the mysterious foreigner on the sands of Epple Bay was chiefly one of sullen resentment.

Here was a man who had come from goodness knows where, whose strange wanderings and secret appearances in the neighborhood had oft roused the anger of the village folk, just as his fantastic clothes, his silken doublet and befrilled shirt had excited their scorn; here was a man, I say, who came from nowhere, and now he chose—the yokels of the neighborhood declared it that he chose—to make his exit from the world in as weird a manner as he had effected his entrance into this remote and law-abiding little island.

The farmhands and laborers who dwelt in the cottages dotted about around St. Nicholas-at-Wade, Epple or Acol were really angry with the stranger for allowing himself to be murdered on their shores. Thanet itself had up to now enjoyed a fair reputation for orderliness and temperance, and that one of her inhabitants should have been tempted to do away with that interloping foreigner in such a violent manner was obviously the fault of that foreigner himself.

The watches had found him on the sands at low tide. One of them walking along the brow of the cliff had seen the dark object lying prone amongst the boulders, a black mass in the midst of the whiteness of the chalk.

The whole thing was shocking, no doubt, gruesome in the extreme, but the mystery which surrounded this strange death had roused ire rather than horror.

Of course the news had traveled slowly from cottage to cottage, although Petty Constable Pyot, who resided at St. Nicholas, had immediately apprised Squire Boatfield and Sir Marmaduke de Chavasse of the awesome discovery made by the watches on the sands of Epple Bay.

Squire Boatfield was major-general of the district and rode over from Sarre directly he heard the news. The body in the meanwhile had been placed under the shelter of one of the titanic caves which giant hands have carved in the acclivities of the chalk. Squire Boatfield ordered it to be removed. It was not fitting that birds of prey should be allowed to peck at the dead, nor that some unusually high tide should once more carry him out to sea, ere his murderer had been brought to justice.

Therefore, the foreigner with the high-sounding name was conveyed by the watches at the squire's bidding to the cottage of the Lamberts over at Acol, the only place in Thanet which he had ever called his home.

The old Quakeress, wrathful and sullen, had scarce understood what the whole pother was about. She was hard of hearing, and Petty Constable Pyot was at great pains to explain to her that by the major-general's orders the body of the murdered man should be laid decently under shelter, until such time as proper burial could be arranged for it.

Fortunately before the small cortège bearing the gruesome burden had arrived at the cottage, young Richard Lambert had succeeded in making the old woman understand what was expected of her.

Even then she flatly and obstinately refused to have the stranger brought into her house.

"He was a heathen," she declared emphatically, "his soul hath mayhap gone to hell. His thoughts were evil, and God had him not in His keeping. 'Tis not fit that the mortal hulk of a damned soul should pollute the saintliness of mine own abode."

Pyot thought that the old woman was raving, but Master Lambert very peremptorily forbade him to interfere with her. The young man, though quite calm, looked dangerous—so thought the petty constable—and between them, the old Quakeress and the young student defied the constables and the watches and barred the cottage to the entrance of the dead.

Unfortunately, the smith was from home. Pyot thought that the latter had been more reasonable, that he would have understood the weight of authority, and also of seemliness, which was of equally grave importance.

There was a good deal of parleying before it was finally decided to place the body in the forge, which was a wooden lean-to, resting against the north wall of the cottage. There was no direct access from the cottage to the forge, and old Mistress Lambert seemed satisfied that the foreigner should rest there, at any rate until the smith came home, when, mayhap, he would decide otherwise.

At the instance of the petty constable she even brought out a sheet, which smelt sweetly of lavender, and gave it to the watchmen, so that they might decently cover up the dead; she also gave them three elm chairs on which to lay him down.

Across those three chairs the body now lay, covered over with the lavender-scented sheet, in the corner of the blacksmith's forge, over by the furnace. A watchman stayed beside it, to ward off sacrilege: anyone who desired could come, and could—if his nerves were strong enough— view the body and state if, indeed, it was that of the foreigner who all through last summer had haunted the woods and park of Acol.

Of a truth there was no doubt at all as to the identity of the dead. His fantastic clothes were unmistakable. Many there were who had seen him wandering in the woods of nights, and several could swear to the black silk shade and the broad-brimmed hat which the watchmen had found—high and dry—on a chalk boulder close to where the body lay.

Mistress Lambert had refused to look on the dead. 'Twas, of course, no fit sight for females, and the constable had not insisted thereon: but she knew the black silk shade again, and young Master Lambert had caught sight of the murdered man's legs and feet, and had thereupon recognized the breeches and the quaint boots with their overwide tops filled with frills of lace.

Master Hymn-of-Praise Busy, too, though unwilling to see a corpse, thought it his duty to help the law in investigating this mysterious crime. He had oft seen the foreigner of nights in the park, and never doubted for a moment that the body which lay across the elm chairs in the smith's forge was indeed that of the stranger.

Squire Boatfield was now quite satisfied that the identity of the victim was firmly established, and anon he did his best—being a humane man—to obtain Christian burial for the stranger. After some demur, the parson at Minster declared himself willing to do the pious deed.

Heathen or not, 'twas not for Christian folk to pass judgment on him who no longer now could give an explanation of his own mysterious doings, and had of a truth carried his secrets with him in silence to the grave.

Was it not strange that anyone should have risked the gallows for the sake of putting out of the way a man who of a surety was not worth powder or shot?

And the nerve and strength which the murderer had shown! . . . displacing great boulders with which to batter in his victim's face so that not even his own kith and kin could recognize that now!

XXXIV

Afterwards

Sir Marmaduke de Chavasse cursed the weather and cursed himself for being a fool.

He had started from Acol Court on horseback, riding an old nag, for the roads were heavy with mud, and the short cut through the woods quite impassable.

The icy downpour beat against his face and lashed the poor mare's ears and mane until she tossed her head about blindly and impatiently, scarce heeding where she placed her feet. The rider's cloak was already soaked through, and soon even his shirt clung dank and cold to his aching back; the bridle was slippery with the wet, and his numbed fingers could hardly feel its resistance as the mare went stumbling on her way.

Beside horse and rider, Master Hymn-of-Praise Busy and Master Courage Toogood walked ankle-deep in mud—one on each side of the mare, and lantern in hand, for the shades of evening would have drawn in ere the return journey could be undertaken. The two men had taken off their shoes and stockings and had slung them over their shoulders, for 'twas better to walk barefoot than to feel the icy moisture soaking through leather and worsted.

It was then close on two o'clock of an unusually bleak November afternoon. The winds of Heaven, which of a truth do oft use the isle of Thanet as a meeting place, wherein to discuss the mischief which they severally intend to accomplish in sundry quarters later on, had been exceptionally active this day. The southwesterly hurricane had brought, a deluge of rain with it a couple of hours ago, then—satisfied with this prowess—had handed the downpour over to his brother of the northeast, who breathing on it with his icy breath, had soon converted it into sleet: whereupon he turned his back on the mainland altogether, and wandered out towards the ocean, determined to worry the deep-sea fishermen who were out with their nets: but not before he had deputed his brother of the northeast to marshal his army of snow-laden cloud on the firmament.

This the northeast, was over-ready to do, and in answer to his whim a leaden, inky pall now lay over Thanet, whilst the gale continued its mighty, wanton frolic, lashing the sleet against the tiny window-panes of the cottage, or sending it down the chimneys, upon the burning logs below, causing them to splutter and to hiss ere they changed their glow to black and smoking embers.

'Twere impossible to imagine a more discomforting atmosphere in which to be abroad: yet Sir Marmaduke de Chavasse was trudging through the mire, and getting wet to the skin, even when he might just as well be sitting beside the fire in the withdrawing-room at the Court.

He was on his way to the smith's forge at Acol and had ordered his serving-men to accompany him thither: and of a truth neither of them were loath to go. They cared naught about the weather, and the excitement which centered round the Quakeress's cottage at Acol more than counterbalanced the discomfort of a tramp through the mud.

A rumor had reached the Court that the funeral of the murdered man would, mayhap, take place this day, and Master Busy would not have missed such an event for the world, not though the roads lay thick with snow and the drifts rendered progress impossible to all save to the keenest enthusiast. He for one was glad enough that his master had seemed so unaccountably anxious for the company of his own serving men. Sir Marmaduke had ever been overfond of wandering about the lonely woods of Thanet alone.

But since that gruesome murder on the beach forty-eight hours ago and more, both the quality and the yokels preferred to venture abroad in company.

At the same time neither Master Busy nor young Courage Toogood could imagine why Sir Marmaduke de Chavasse should endure such amazing discomfort in order to attend the funeral of an obscure adventurer, who of a truth was as naught to him.

Nor, if the truth were known, could Sir Marmaduke himself have accounted for his presence here on this lonely road, and on one of the most dismal, bleak and unpleasant afternoons that had ever been experienced in Thanet of late.

He should at this moment have been on the other side of the North Sea. The most elemental prudence should indeed have counseled an immediate journey to Amsterdam and a prompt negotiation of all marketable securities which Lady Sue Aldmarshe had placed in his hands.

Yet twice twenty-four hours had gone by since that awful night, when, having finally relinquished his victim to the embrace of the tide, he had picked his way up the chalk cliffs and through the terror-haunted woods to his own room in Acol Court.

He should have left for abroad the next day, ere the news of the discovery of a mysterious murder had reached the precincts of his own park. But he had remained in England. Something seemed to have rooted him to the spot, something to be holding him back whenever he was ready to flee.

At first it had been a mere desire to know. On the morning following his crime he made a vigorous effort to rally his scattered senses, to walk, to move, and to breathe as if nothing had happened, as if nothing lay out there on the sands of Epple, high and dry now, for the tide would have gone out.

Whether he had slept or not since the moment when he had crept stealthily into his own house, silently as the bird of prey when returning to its nest—he could not have said. Undoubtedly he had stripped off the dead man's clothes, the rough shirt and cord breeches which had belonged to Lambert, the smith. Undoubtedly, too, he had made a bundle of these things, hiding them in a dark recess at the bottom of an old oak cupboard which stood in his room. With these clothes he had placed the leather wallet which contained securities worth half a million of solid money.

All this he had done, preparatory to destroying the clothes by fire, and to converting the securities into money abroad. After that he had thrown himself on the bed, without thought, without sensations save those of bodily ache and of numbing fatigue.

Vaguely, as the morning roused him to consciousness, he realized that he must leave for Dover as soon as may be and cross over to France by the first packet available, or, better still, by boat specially chartered. And yet, when anon he rose and dressed, he felt at once that he would not go just yet; that he could not go until certain queries which had formed in his brain had been answered by events.

How soon would the watches find the body? Having found it, what would they do? Would the body be immediately identified by the clothes upon it? or would doubt on that score arise in the minds of the neighboring folk? Would the disappearance of Adam Lambert be known at once and commented upon in connection with the crime?

Curiosity soon became an obsession; he wandered down into the hall where the serving-wench was plying her duster. He searched her face, wondering if she had heard the news.

The mist of the night had yielded to an icy drizzle, but Sir Marmaduke could not remain within. His footsteps guided him in the direction of Acol, on towards Epple Bay. On the path which leads to the edge of the cliffs he met the watches who were tramping on towards the beach.

The men saluted him and went on their way, but he turned and fled as quickly as he dared.

In the afternoon Master Busy brought the news down from Prospect Inn. The body of the man who had called himself a French prince had been found murdered and shockingly mutilated on the sands at Epple. Sir Marmaduke was vastly interested. He, usually so reserved and ill-humored with his servants, had kept Hymn-of-Praise in close converse for nigh upon an hour, asking many questions about the crime, about the petty constables' action in the matter and the comments made by the village folk.

At the same time he gave strict injunctions to Master Busy not to breathe a word of the gruesome subject to the ladies, nor yet to the serving-wench; 'twas not a matter fit for women's ears.

Sir Marmaduke then bade his butler push on as far as Acol, to glean further information about the mysterious event.

That evening he collected all the clothes which had belonged to Lambert, the smith, and wrapping up the leather wallet with them which contained the securities, he carried this bundle to the lonely pavilion on the outskirts of the park.

He was not yet ready to go abroad.

Master Busy returned from his visit to Acol full of what he had seen. He had been allowed to view the body, and to swear before Squire Boatfield that he recognized the clothes as being those usually worn by the mysterious foreigner who used to haunt the woods and park of Acol all last summer.

Hymn-of-Praise had his full meed of pleasure that evening, and the next day, too, for Sir Marmaduke seemed never tired of hearing him recount all the gossip which obtained at Acol and at St. Nicholas: the surmises as to the motive of the horrible crime, the talk about the stranger and his doings, the resentment caused by his weird demise, and the conjectures as to what could have led a miscreant to do away with so insignificant a personage.

All that day—the second since the crime—Sir Marmaduke still lingered in Thanet. Prudence whispered urgent counsels that he should go, and yet he stayed, watching the progress of events with that same morbid and tenacious curiosity.

And now it was the thought of what folk would say when they heard that Adam Lambert had disappeared, and was, of a truth, not returning home, which kept Sir Marmaduke still lingering in England.

That and the inexplicable enigma which ever confronts the searcher of human motives: the overwhelming desire of the murderer to look once again upon his victim.

Master Busy had on that second morning brought home the news from Acol, that Squire Boatfield had caused a rough deal coffin to be made by the village carpenter at the expense of the county, and that mayhap the stranger would be laid therein this very afternoon and conveyed down to Minster, where he would be accorded Christian burial.

Then Sir Marmaduke realized that it would be impossible for him to leave England until after he had gazed once more on the dead body of the smith.

After that he would go. He would shake the sand of Thanet from his heels forever.

When he had learned all that he wished to know he would be free from the present feeling of terrible obsession which paralyzed his movements to the extent of endangering his own safely.

He was bound to look upon his victim once again: an inexplicable and titanic force compelled him to that. Mayhap, that same force would enable him to keep his nerves under control when, presently, he should be face to face with the dead.

Face to face? . . . Good God! . . .

Yet neither fear nor remorse haunted him. It was only curosity, and, at one thought, a nameless horror! . . . Not at the thought of murder. . . there he had no compunction, but at that of the terrible deed which from instinct of self-protection had perforce to succeed the graver crime.

The weight of those chalk boulders seemed still to weigh against the muscles of his back. He felt that Sisyphus-like he was forever rolling, rolling a gigantic stone which, failing of its purpose—recoiled on him, rolling back down a precipitous incline, and crushing him beneath its weight. . . only to release him again. . . to leave him free to endure the same torture over and over again. . . and yet again. . . forever the same weight. . . forever the self-same, intolerable agony. . .

BARONESS EMMUSKA ORCZY

XXXV

The Smith's Forge

Up to the hour of his departure from Acol Court, Sir Marmaduke had been convinced that neither his sister-in-law nor Lady Sue had heard of the news which had set the whole of Thanet in commotion. Acol Court lies very isolated, well off the main Canterbury Road, and just for two days and a half Master Hymn-of-Praise Busy had contrived to hold his tongue.

Most of the village gossips, too, met at the local public bars, and had had up to now no time to wander as far as the Court, nor any reason to do so, seeing that Master Busy was always to be found at Prospect Inn and always ready to discuss the mystery in all its bearings, with anyone who would share a pint of ale with him.

Sir Marmaduke had taken jealous care only to meet the ladies at meal-time, and under penalty of immediate dismissal had forbidden Hymn-of-Praise to speak to the serving-wench of the all-absorbing topic.

So far Master Busy had obeyed, but at the last moment, just before starting for Acol village, Sir Marmaduke had caught sight of Mistress Charity talking to the stableman in the yard. Something in the wench's eyes told him—with absolute certainty that she had just heard of the murder.

That morbid and tenacious curiosity once more got hold of him. He would have given all he possessed at this moment—the entire fruits of his crime perhaps—to know what that ignorant girl thought of it all, and it caused him acute, almost physical pain, to refrain from questioning her.

There was enough of the sense of self-protection in him, however, to check himself from betraying such extraordinary interest in the matter: but he turned on his heel and went quickly back to the house. He wanted to catch sight of Editha's face, if only for a moment; he wanted to see for himself, then and there, if she had also heard the news.

As he entered the hall, she was coming down the stairs. She had on her cloak and hood as if preparing to go out. Their eyes met and he saw that she knew.

Knew what? He broke into a loud and fierce laugh as he met her wildly questioning gaze. There was a look almost of madness in the hopeless puzzlement of her expression.

Of course Editha must be hopelessly puzzled. The very thought of her vague conjecturings had caused him to laugh as maniacs laugh at times.

The mysterious French prince had been found on the sands murdered and mutilated. . . But then. . .

Still laughing, Sir Marmaduke once more turned, running away from the house now and never pausing until his foot had touched the stirrup and his fingers were entangled in the damp mane of the mare. Even whilst he settled himself into the saddle as comfortably as he could, the grim humor of Editha's bewilderment caused him to laugh, within himself.

The nag stepped slowly along in the mud at first, then broke into a short trot. The two serving-men had started on ahead with their lanterns; they would, of course, be walking all the way.

The icy rain mingled with tiny flakes of snow was insufferably cutting and paralyzing: yet Sir Marmaduke scarcely heeded it, until the mare became unpleasantly uncertain in her gait. Once she stumbled and nearly pitched her rider forward into the mud: whereupon, lashing into her, he paid more heed to her doings.

Once just past the crossroad toward St. Nicholas, he all but turned his horse's head back towards Acol Court. It seemed as if he must find out now at once whether Editha had spoken to Lady Sue and what the young girl had done and said when she heard, in effect, that her husband had been murdered.

Nothing but the fear of missing the last look at the body of Adam Lambert ere the lid of the coffin was nailed down stopped him from returning homewards.

Anon he came upon Busy and Toogood painfully trudging in the mire, and singing lustily to keep themselves cheerful and warm.

Sir Marmaduke drew the mare in, so as to keep pace with his men. On the whole, the road had been more lonely than he liked and he was glad of company.

Outside the Lamberts' cottage a small crowd had collected. From the crest of the hill the tiny bell of Acol church struck the hour of two.

Squire Boatfield had ridden over from Sarre, and Sir Marmaduke—as he dismounted—caught sight of the heels and crupper of the squire's well-known cob. The little crowd had gathered in the immediate neighborhood of the forge, and de Chavasse, from where he now stood, could not see the entrance of the lean-to, only the blank side wall of the shed, and the front of the Lamberts' cottage, the doors and windows of which were hermetically closed.

Up against the angle formed by the wall of the forge and that of the cottage, the enterprising landlord of the local inn had erected a small trestle table, from behind which he was dispensing spiced ale, and bottled Spanish wines.

Squire Boatfield was standing beside that improvised bar, and at sight of Sir Marmaduke he put down the pewter mug which he was in the act of conveying to his lips, and came forward to greet his friend.

"What is the pother about this foreigner, eh, Boatfield?" queried de Chavasse with gruff good-nature as he shook hands with the squire and allowed himself to be led towards that tempting array of bottles and mugs on the trestle table.

The yokels who were assembled at the entrance of the forge turned to gaze with some curiosity at the squire of Acol. De Chavasse was not often seen even in this village: he seldom went beyond the boundary of his own park.

All the men touched their forelocks with deferential respect. Master Jeremy Mounce humbly whispered a query as to what His Honor would condescend to take.

Sir Marmaduke desired a mug of buttered ale or of lamb's wool, which Master Mounce soon held ready for him. He emptied the mug at one draught. The spiced liquor went coursing through his body, and he felt better and more sure of himself. He desired a second mug.

"With more substance in it, Master Landlord," he said pleasantly. "Nay, man! ye are not giving milk to children, but something warm to cheer a man's inside."

"I have a half bottle of brandy here, good Sir Marmaduke," suggested Master Mounce with some diffidence, for brandy was an over-expensive commodity which not many Kentish squires cared to afford.

"Brandy, of course, good master!" quoth de Chavasse lustily, "brandy is the nectar of the gods. Here!" he added, drawing a piece of gold from a tiny pocket concealed in the lining of his doublet, "will this pay for thy half-bottle of nectar."

"Over well, good Sir Marmaduke," said Master Mounce, as he stooped to the ground. From underneath the table he now drew forth a glass and a bottle: the latter he uncorked with slow and deliberate care, and then filled the glass with its contents, whilst Sir Marmaduke watched him with impatient eyes.

"Will you join me, squire?" asked de Chavasse, as he lifted the small tumbler and gazed with marked appreciation at the glistening and transparent liquid.

"Nay, thanks," replied Boatfield with a laugh, "I care naught for these foreign decoctions. Another mug, or even two, of buttered ale, good landlord," he added, turning to Master Mounce.

In the meanwhile petty constable Pyot had stood respectfully at attention ready to relate for the hundredth time, mayhap, all that he knew and all that he meant to know about the mysterious crime.

Sir Marmaduke would of a surety ask many questions, for it was passing strange that he had taken but little outward interest in the matter up to now.

"Well, Pyot," he now said, beckoning to the man to approach, "tell us what you know. By Gad, 'tis not often we indulge in a genuine murder in Thanet! Where was it done? Not on my land, I hope."

"The watches found the body on the beach, your Honor," replied Pyot, "the head was mutilated past all recognition. . . the heavy chalk boulders, your Honor. . . and a determined maniac methinks, sir, who wanted revenge against a personal enemy. . . Else how to account for such a brutal act? . . ."

"I suppose," quoth Sir Marmaduke lightly, as he sipped the brandy, "that the identity of the man has been quite absolutely determined."

"Aye! aye! your Honor," rejoined Pyot gravely, "the opinion of all those who have seen the body is that it is that of a foreigner. . . Prince of Orleans he called himself, who has been lodging these past months at this place here!"

And the petty constable gave a quick nod in the direction of the cottage.

"Ah! I know but little about him," now said Sir Marmaduke, turning to speak to Squire Boatfield, "although he lived here, on what is my own property, and haunted my park, too. . . so I've been told. There was a good deal of talk about him among the wenches in the village."

"Aye! I had heard all about that prince," said Squire Boatfield meditatively, "lodging in this cottage. . . 'twas passing strange."

"He was a curious sort of man, your Honor," here interposed Pyot. "We got what information about him we could, seeing that the smith is from home, and that Mistress Lambert, his aunt, I think, is hard of hearing, and gave us many crooked answers. But she told us that the stranger paid for his lodging regularly, and would arrive at the cottage unawares of an evening and stay part of the night. . . then he would go off again at cock-crow, and depart she knew not whither."

The man paused in his narrative. Something apparently had caused Sir Marmaduke to turn giddy.

He tugged at his neckbands and his hand fell heavily against the trestle-table.

"Nay! 'tis nothing," he said with a harsh laugh as Master Mounce with an exclamation of deep concern ran round to him with a chair, whilst Squire Boatfield quickly put out an arm as if he were afraid that his friend would fall. "'Tis nothing," he repeated, "the tramp in the cold, then this heady draught. . . I am well I assure you."

He drank half a glass of brandy at a draught, and now the hand which replaced the glass upon the table had not the slightest tremor in it.

"'Tis all vastly interesting," he remarked lightly. "Have you seen the body, Boatfield?"

"Aye! aye!" quoth the squire, speaking with obvious reluctance, for he hated this gruesome subject. "'Tis no pleasant sight. And were I in your shoes, de Chavasse, I would not go in there," and he nodded significantly towards the forge.

"Nay! 'tis my duty as a magistrate," said Sir Marmaduke airily.

He had to steady himself against the table again for a moment or two, ere he turned his back on the hospitable board, and started to walk round towards the forge: no doubt the shaking of his knees was attributable to the strong liquor which he had consumed.

The little crowd parted and dispersed at his approach. The lean-to wherein Adam Lambert was wont to do his work consisted of four walls, one of which was that of the cottage, whilst the other immediately facing it, had a wide opening which formed the only entrance to the shed. A man standing in that entrance would have the furnace on his left: and now in addition to that furnace also the three elm chairs, whereon rested a rough deal case, without a lid, but partly covered with a sheet.

To anyone coming from the outside, this angle of the forge would always seem weird and even mysterious even when the furnace was blazing and the sparks flying from the anvil, beneath the smith's powerful blows, or when—as at present—the fires were extinguished and this part of the shed, innocent of windows, was in absolute darkness.

Sir Marmaduke paused a moment under the lintel which dominated the broad entrance. His eyes had some difficulty in penetrating the density which seemed drawn across the place on his left like some ink-smeared and opaque curtain.

The men assembled outside, watched him from a distance with silent respect. In these days the fact of a gentleman drinking more liquor than was good for him was certes not to his discredit.

The fact that Sir Marmaduke seemed to sway visibly on his legs, as he thus stood for a moment outlined against the dark interior beyond, roused no astonishment in the minds of those who saw him.

Presently he turned deliberately to his left and the next moment his figure was merged in the gloom.

Round the angle of the wall Squire Boatfield was still standing, sipping buttered ale.

Less than two minutes later, Sir Marmaduke reappeared in the doorway. His face was a curious color, and there were beads of perspiration on his forehead, and as he came forward he would have fallen, had not one of the men stepped quickly up to him and offered a steadying arm. But there was nothing strange in that.

The sight of that which lay in Adam Lambert's forge had unmanned a good many ere this.

"I am inclined to believe, my good Boatfield," quoth Sir Marmaduke, as he went back to the trestle-table, and poured himself out another half-glass full of brandy, "I am inclined to believe that when you advised me not to go in there, you spoke words of wisdom which I had done well to follow."

XXXVI

The Girl-Wife

B ut the effort of the past few moments had been almost more than Marmaduke de Chavasse could bear.

Anon when the church bell over at Acol began a slow and monotonous toll he felt as if his every nerve must give way: as if he must laugh, laugh loudly and long at the idiocy, the ignorance of all these people who thought that they were confronted by an impenetrable mystery, whereas it was all so simple. . . so very, very simple.

He had a curious feeling as if he must grip every one of these men here by the throat and demand from each one separately an account of what he thought and felt, what he surmised and what he guessed when standing face to face with the weird enigma presented by that mutilated thing in its rough deal case. He would have given worlds to know what his friend Boatfield thought of it all, or what had been the petty constable's conjectures.

A haunting and devilish desire seized him to break open the skulls of all these yokels and to look into their brains. Above all now the silence of the cottage close to him had become unendurable torment. That closed door, the tiny railing which surrounded the bit of front garden, that little gate the latch of which he himself so oft had lifted, all seemed to hold the key to some terrible mystery, the answer to some fearful riddle which he felt would drive him mad if he could not hit upon it now at once.

The brandy had fired his veins: he no longer felt numb with the cold. A passion of rage was seething in him, and he longed to attack with fists and heels those curtained windows which now looked like eyes turned mutely and inquiringly upon him.

But there was enough sanity in him yet to prevent his doing anything rash: an uncontrolled act might cause astonishment, suspicion mayhap, in the minds of those who witnessed it. He made a violent effort to steady himself even now, above all to steady his voice and to veil that excited glitter which he knew must be apparent in his eyes.

"Meseems that 'tis somewhat strange," he said quite calmly, even lightly, to Squire Boatfield who seemed to be preparing to go, "that these people—the Lamberts—who alone knew the. . . the murdered man intimately, should keep so persistently, so determinedly out of the way."

Even while the words escaped his mouth—certes involuntarily—he knew that the most elementary prudence should have dictated silence on this score, and at this juncture. The man was about to be buried, the disappearance of the smith had passed off so far without comment. Peace, the eternal peace of the grave, would soon descend on the weird events which occupied everyone's mind for the present.

What the old Quakeress thought and felt, what Richard—the brother—feared and conjectured was easy for Sir Marmaduke to guess: for him, but for no one else. To these others the silence of the cottage, the absence of the Lamberts from this gathering was simple enough of explanation, seeing that they themselves felt such bitter resentment against the dead man. They quite felt with the old woman's sullenness, her hatred of the foreigner who had disturbed the serenity of her life.

Everyone else was willing to let her be, not to drag her and young Lambert into the unpleasant vortex of these proceedings. Their home was an abode of mourning: it was proper and seemly for them to remain concealed and silent within their cottage; seemly, too, to have curtained their windows and closed their doors.

No one wished to disturb them; no one but Sir Marmaduke, and with him it was once again that morbid access of curiosity, the passionate, intense desire to know and to probe every tiny detail in connection with his own crime.

"The old woman Lambert should be made to identify the body, before it is buried," he now repeated with angry emphasis, seeing that a look of disapproval had crossed Squire Boatfield's pleasant face.

"We are satisfied as to the man's identity," rejoined the squire impatiently, "and the sight is not fit for women's eyes."

"Nay, then she should be shown the clothes and effects. . . And, if I mistake not, there's Richard Lambert, my late secretary, has he laid sworn information about the man?"

"Yes, I believe so," said Boatfield with some hesitation.

"Nay, Boatfield, an you are so reluctant to do your duty in this matter, I'll speak to these people myself. . . You are chief constable of the district. . . indeed, 'tis you should do it. . . and in the meanwhile I pray you, at least to give orders that the coffin be not nailed down."

The kindly squire would have entered a further protest. He did not see the necessity of confronting an old woman with the gruesome sight of a mutilated corpse, nor did he perceive justifiable cause for further formalities of identification.

But Sir Marmaduke having spoken very peremptorily, had already turned on his heel without waiting for his friend's protest, and was striding across the patch of rough stubble, which bordered the railing round the front of the cottage. Squire Boatfield reluctantly followed him. The next moment de Chavasse had lifted the latch of the gate, crossed the short flagged path and now knocked loudly against the front door.

Apparently there was no desire for secrecy or rebellion on the part of the dwellers of the cottage, for hardly had Sir Marmaduke's imperious knock echoed against the timbered walls, than the door was opened from within by Richard Lambert who, seeing the two gentlemen standing on the threshold, stepped back immediately, allowing them to pass.

The old Quakeress and Richard were seemingly not alone. Two ladies sat in those same straight-backed chairs, wherein, some fifty hours ago Adam Lambert and the French prince had agreed upon that fateful meeting on the brow of the cliff.

Sir Marmaduke's restless eyes took in at a glance every detail of that little parlor, which he had known so intimately. The low lintel of the door, which had always forced him to stoop as he entered, the central table with the pewter candlesticks upon it, the elm chairs shining like mirrors in response to the Quakeress' maddening passion for cleanliness.

Everything was just as it had been those few hours ago, when last he had picked up his broad-brimmed hat from the table and walked out of the cottage into the night. Everything was the same as it had been when his young girl-wife pushed a leather wallet across the table to him: the wallet which contained the fortune that he had not yet dared to turn fully to his own account.

Aye! it was all just the same: for even at this moment as he stood there in the room, Sue, pale and still, faced him from across the table. For a moment he was silent, nor did anybody speak. Squire Boatfield felt unaccountably embarrassed, certain that he was intruding, vaguely wondering why the atmosphere in the cottage was so heavy and oppressive.

Behind him, Richard Lambert had quietly closed the front door; the old woman stood in the background; the dusting-cloth which she had been plying so vigorously had dropped out of her hand when the two gentlemen had appeared in her little parlor so unexpectedly.

Sir Marmaduke was the first to break the silence.

"My dear Sue," he said curtly, "this is a strange place indeed wherein to find your ladyship."

He cast a sharp, inquiring glance at her, then at his sister-in-law, who was still sitting by the hearth.

"She insisted on coming," said Mistress de Chavasse with a shrug of the shoulders, "and I had not the power to stop her; I thought it best, therefore, to accompany her."

She was wearing the cloak and hood which Sir Marmaduke had seen round her shoulders when awhile ago he had met her in the hall of the Court. Apparently she had started out with Sue in his immediate wake, and now he had a distinct recollection that while the mare was slowly ambling along, he had looked back once or twice and seen two dark figures walking some fifty yards behind him on the road which he himself had just traversed.

At the moment he had imagined that they were some village folk, wending their way towards Acol: now he was conscious of nerve-racking irritation at the thought that if he had only turned the mare's head back toward the Court—as he had at one time intended to do—he could have averted this present meeting—it almost seemed like a confrontation—here, in this cottage on the self-same spot, where thought of murder had first struck upon his brain.

There was something inexplicable, strangely puzzling now in Sue's attitude.

When de Chavasse had entered, she had risen from her chair and, as if deliberately, had walked over to the spot where she had stood during that momentous interview, when she relinquished her fortune entirely and without protest, into the hands of the man whom she had married, and whom she believed to be her lord.

Her gaze now—calm and fixed, and withal vaguely searching—rested on her guardian's face. The fixity of her look increased his nerve-tension. The others, too, were regarding him with varying feelings which were freely expressed in their eyes. Boatfield seemed upset and somewhat resentful, the old woman sullen, despite the deference in her attitude, Lambert defiant, wrathful, nay! full of an incipient desire to avenge past wrongs.

And dominating all, there was Editha's look of bewilderment, of puzzledom in her face at a mystery whereat her senses were beginning to reel, that mute questioning of the eyes, which speaks of turbulent thoughts within.

Sir Marmaduke uttered an exclamation of impatience.

"You must return to the Court and at once," he said, avoiding Sue's gaze and speaking directly to Editha, "the men are outside, with lanterns. You'll have to walk quickly an you wish to reach home before twilight."

But even while he spoke, Sue—not heeding him—had turned to Squire Boatfield. She went up to him, holding out her hands as if in instinctive childlike appeal for protection, to a kindly man.

"This mystery is horrible!" she murmured.

Boatfield took her small hands in his, patting them gently the while, desiring to soothe and comfort her, for she seemed deeply agitated and there was a wild look of fear from time to time in her pale face.

"Sir Marmaduke is right," said the squire gently, "this is indeed no place for your ladyship. I did not see you arrive or I had at once persuaded you to go."

De Chavasse would again have interposed. He stooped and picked up Sue's cloak which had fallen to the ground, and as he went up to her with the obvious intention of replacing it around her shoulders, she checked him, with a slight motion of her hand.

"I only heard of this terrible crime an hour ago," she said, speaking once more to Boatfield, "and as I methinks, am the only person in the world who can throw light upon this awesome mystery, I thought it my duty to come."

"Of a truth 'twas brave of your ladyship," quoth the squire, feeling a little bewildered at this strange announcement, "but surely. . . you did not know this man?"

"If the rumor which hath reached me be correct," she replied quietly, "then indeed did I know the murdered man intimately. Prince Amédé d'Orléans was my husband."

XXXVII

THE OLD WOMAN

There was silence in the tiny cottage parlor as the young girl made this extraordinary announcement in a firm if toneless voice, without flinching and meeting with a sort of stubborn pride the five pairs of eyes which were now riveted upon her.

From outside came the hum of many voices, dull and subdued, like the buzzing of a swarm of bees, and against the small window panes the incessant patter of icy rain driven and lashed by the gale. Anon the wind moaned in the wide chimney, . . . it seemed like the loud sigh of the Fates, satisfied at the tangle wrought by their relentless fingers in the threads of all these lives.

Sir Marmaduke, after a slight pause, had contrived to utter an oath—indicative of the wrath he, as Lady Sue's guardian, should have felt at her statement. Squire Boatfield frowned at the oath. He had never liked de Chavasse and disapproved more than ever of the man's attitude towards his womenkind now.

The girl was in obvious, terrible distress: what she was feeling at this moment when she was taking those around her into her confidence could be as nothing compared to what she must have endured when she first heard the news that her strange bridegroom had been murdered.

The kindly squire, though admitting the guardian's wrath, thought that its violent expression was certainly ill-timed. He allowed Sue to recover herself, for the more calm was her attitude outwardly, the more terrible must be the effort which she was making at self-control.

Sue's eyes were fixed steadily upon her guardian, and Richard Lambert's upon her. Both these young people who had carved their own Fate in the very rock which now had shattered their lives, seemed to be searching for something vague, unavowed and mysterious which instinct told them was there, but which was so elusive, so intangible that the soul of each recoiled, even whilst it tried to probe.

Entirely against her will Sue—whilst she looked on her guardian—could think of nothing save of that day in Dover, the lonely church, the gloomy vestry, and that weird patter of the rain against the window panes.

She was not ashamed of what she had done, only of what she had felt for him, whom she now believed to be dead; that she gave him her fortune was nothing, she neither regretted nor cared about that. What, in the mind of a young and romantic girl, was the value of a fortune squandered, when that priceless treasure—her first love—had already been thrown away? But now she would no longer judge the dead. The money which he had filched from her, Fate and a murderous hand had quickly taken back from him, crushing beneath those chalk boulders his many desires, his vast ambitions, a worthless life and incomparable greed.

Her love, which he had stolen. . . that he could not give back: not that ardent, whole-souled, enthusiastic love; not the romantic idealism, the hero-worship, that veil of fantasy behind which first love is wont to hide its ephemerality. But she would not now judge the dead. Her romantic love lay buried in the lonely church at Dover, and she was striving not to think even of its grave.

Squire Boatfield's kindly voice recalled her to her immediate surroundings and to the duty—self-imposed—which had brought her thither.

"My dear child," he said, speaking with unwonted solemnity, "if what you have just stated be, alas! the truth, then indeed, you and you only can throw some light on the terrible mystery which has been puzzling us all. . . you may be the means which God hath chosen for bringing an evildoer to justice. . . Will you, therefore, try. . . though it may be very painful to you. . . will you try and tell us everything that is in your mind. . . everything which may draw the finger of God and our poor eyes to the miscreant who hath committed such an awful crime."

"I fear me I have not much to tell," replied Sue simply, "but I feel that it is my duty to suggest to the two magistrates here present what I think was the motive which prompted this horrible crime."

"You can suggest a motive for the crime?" interposed Sir Marmaduke, striving to sneer, although his voice sounded quite toneless, for his throat was parched and his tongue clove to the roof of his mouth, "by Gad! 'twere vastly interesting to hear your ladyship's views."

He tried to speak flippantly, at which Squire Boatfield frowned deprecation. Lambert, without a word, had brought a chair near to Lady Sue, and with a certain gentle authority, he forced her to sit down.

"It was a crime, of that I feel sure," said Sue, "nathless, that can be easily proven. . . when. . . when it has been discovered whether money and securities contained in a wallet of leather have been found among Prince Amédé's effects."

"Money and securities?" exclaimed Sir Marmaduke with a loud oath, which he contrived to bring forth with the violence of genuine wrath, "Money and securities? . . . Forsooth, I trust. . ."

"My money and my securities, sir," she interposed with obvious hauteur, "which I had last night and in this self-same room placed in the hands of Prince Amédé d'Orléans, my husband."

She said this with conscious pride. Whatever change her feelings may have undergone towards the man who had at one time been the embodiment of her most cherished dreams, she would not let her sneering guardian see that she had repented of her choice.

Death had endowed her exiled prince with a dignity which had never been his in life, and the veil of tragedy which now lay over the mysterious stranger and his still more mysterious life, had called forth to its uttermost the young wife's sense of loyalty to him.

"Not your entire fortune, my dear, dear child, I hope. . ." exclaimed Squire Boatfield, more horror-struck this time than he had been when first he had heard of the terrible murder.

"The wallet contained my entire fortune," rejoined Sue calmly, "all that Master Skyffington had placed in my hands on the day that my father willed that it should be given me."

"Such folly is nothing short of criminal," said Sir Marmaduke roughly, "nathless, had not the gentleman been murdered that night he would have shown Thanet and you a clean pair of heels, taking your money with him, of course."

"Aye! aye! but he was murdered," said Squire Boatfield firmly, "the question only is by whom?"

"Some footpad who haunts the cliffs," rejoined de Chavasse lightly, "'tis simple enough."

"Simple, mayhap. . ." mused the squire, "yet. . ."

He paused a moment and once more silence fell on all those assembled in the small cottage parlor. Sir Marmaduke felt as if every vein in his body was gradually being turned to stone.

The sense of expectancy was so overwhelming that it completely paralyzed every other faculty within him, and Editha's searching eyes seemed like a corroding acid touching an aching wound. Yet for the moment there was no danger. He had so surrounded himself and his crimes with mystery that it would take more than a country squire's slowly moving brain to draw aside that weird and ghostlike curtain which hid his evil deeds.

No! there was no danger—as yet!

But he cursed himself for a fool and a coward, not to have gone away—abroad—long ere such a possible confrontation threatened him. He cursed himself for being here at all—and above all for having left the smith's clothes and the leather wallet in that lonely pavilion in the park.

Squire Boatfield's kind eyes now rested on the old woman, who, awed and silent—shut out by her infirmities from this strange drama which was being enacted in her cottage—had stood calm and impassive by, trying to read with that wonderful quickness of intuition which the poverty of one sense gives to the others—what was going on round her, since she could not hear.

Her eyes—pale and dim, heavy-lidded and deeply-lined—rested often on the face of Richard Lambert, who, leaning against the corner of the hearth, had watched the proceedings silently and intently. When the Quakeress's faded gaze met that of the young man, there was a quick and anxious look which passed from her to him: a look of entreaty for comfort, one of fear and of growing horror.

"And so the exiled prince lodged in your cottage, mistress?" said Squire Boatfield, after a while, turning to Mistress Lambert.

The old woman's eyes wandered from Richard to the squire. The look of fear in them vanished, giving place to good-natured placidity. She shuffled forward, in the manner which had so oft irritated her lodger.

"Eh? . . . what?" she queried, approaching the squire, "I am somewhat hard of hearing these times."

"We were speaking of your lodger, mistress," rejoined Boatfield, raising his voice, "harm hath come to him, you know."

"Aye! aye!" she replied blandly, "harm hath come to our lodger. . . Nay! the Lord hath willed it so. . . The stranger was queer in his ways. . . I don't wonder that harm hath come to him. . ."

"You remember him well, mistress?—him and the clothes he used to wear?" asked Squire Boatfield.

"Oh, yes! I remember the clothes," she rejoined. "I saw them again on the dead who now lieth in Adam's forge. . . the same curious clothes of a truth. . . clothes the Lord would condemn as wantonness and vanity. . . I saw them again on the dead man," she reiterated garrulously, "the frills and furbelows. . . things the Lord hateth. . . and which no Christian should place upon his person. . . yet the foreigner wore them. . . he had none other. . . and went out with them on him that night that the Lord sent him down into perdition. . ."

"Did you see him go out that night, mistress?" asked the squire.

"Eh? . . . what? . . ."

"Did he go out alone?"

The dimmed eyes of the old woman roamed restlessly from face to face. It seemed as if that look of horror and of fear once more struggled to appear within the pale orbs. Yet the squire looked on her with kindness, and Lady Sue's tear-veiled eyes expressed boundless sympathy. Richard, on the other hand, did not look at her, his gaze was riveted on Sir Marmaduke de Chavasse with an intensity which caused the latter to meet that look, trying to defy it, and then to flinch before its expression of passionate wrath.

"We wish to know where your nephew Adam is, mistress," now broke in de Chavasse roughly, "the squire and I would wish to ask him a few questions."

Then as the Quakeress did not reply, he added almost savagely:

"Why don't you answer, woman? Are ye still hard of hearing?"

"Your pardon, Sir Marmaduke," interposed Lambert firmly, "my aunt is old and feeble. She hath been much upset and over anxious. . . seeing that my brother Adam is still from home."

Sir Marmaduke broke into a loud and prolonged laugh.

"Ha! ha! ha! good master. . . so I understand. . . your brother is from home. . . whilst the wallet containing her ladyship's fortune has disappeared along with him, eh?"

"What are they saying, lad?" queried the old woman in her trembling voice, "what are they saying? I am fearful lest there's something wrong with Adam. . ."

"Nay, nay, dear. . . there's naught amiss," said Lambert soothingly, "there's naught amiss. . ."

Instinctively now Sue had risen. Sir Marmaduke's cruel laugh had grated horribly on her ear, rousing an echo in her memory which she could not understand but which caused her to encircle the trembling figure of the old Quakeress with young, protecting arms.

"Are Squire Boatfield and I to understand, Lambert," continued Sir Marmaduke, speaking to the young man, "that your brother Adam has unaccountably disappeared since the night on which the foreigner met with his tragic fate? Nay, Boatfield," he added, turning to the squire, as Lambert had remained silent, "methinks you, as chief magistrate, should see your duty clearly. 'Tis a warrant you should sign and quickly, too, ere a scoundrel slip through the noose of justice. I can on the morrow to Dover, there to see the chief constable, but Pyot and his men should not be idle the while."

"What is he saying, my dear?" murmured Mistress Lambert, timorously, as she clung with pathetic fervor to the young girl beside her, "what is the trouble?"

"Where is your nephew Adam?" said de Chavasse roughly.

"I do not know," she retorted with amazing strength of voice, as she gently but firmly disengaged herself from the restraining arms that would have kept her back. "I do not know," she repeated, "what is it to thee, where he is? Art accusing him perchance of doing away with that foreign devil?"

Her voice rose shrill and resonant, echoing in the low-ceilinged room; her pale eyes, dimmed with many tears, with hard work, and harder piety were fixed upon the man who had dared to accuse her lad.

He tried not to flinch before that gaze, to keep up the air of mockery, the sound of a sneer. Outside the murmur of voices had become somewhat louder, the shuffling of bare feet on the flag-stones could now be distinctly heard.

XXXVIII

The Voice of the Dead

The next moment a timid knock against the front door caused everyone to start. A strange eerie feeling descended on the hearts of all, of innocent and of guilty, of accuser and of defender. The knock seemed to have come from spectral hands, for 'twas followed by no further sound.

Then again the knock.

Lambert went to the door and opened it.

"Be the quality here?" queried a timid voice.

"Squire Boatfield is here and Sir Marmaduke de Chavasse," replied Lambert, "what is it, Mat? Come in."

The squire had risen at sound of his name, and now went to the door, glad enough to shake himself free from that awful oppression which hung on the cottage like a weight of evil.

"What is it, Mat?" he asked.

A man in rough shirt and coarse breeches and with high boots reaching up to the thigh was standing humbly in the doorway. He was bareheaded and his lanky hair, wet with rain and glittering with icy moisture, was blown about by the gale. At sight of the squire he touched his forelock.

"The hour is getting late, squire," he said hesitatingly, "we carriers be ready. . . 'Tis an hour or more down to Minster. . . walking with a heavy burden I mean. . . If your Honor would give the order, mayhap we might nail down the coffin lid now and make a start."

Marmaduke de Chavasse, too, had turned towards the doorway. Both men looked out on the little crowd which had congregated beyond the little gate. It was long past three o'clock now, and the heavy snow clouds overhead obscured the scanty winter light, and precipitated the approach of evening. In the gray twilight, a group of men could be seen standing somewhat apart from the others. All were bareheaded, and all wore rough shirts and breeches of coarse worsted, drab or brown in color, toning in with the dull monochrome of the background.

Between them in the muddy road stood the long deal coffin. The sheet which covered it, rendered heavy with persistent wet, flapped dismally against the wooden sides of the box. Overhead a group of rooks were circling whilst uttering their monotonous call.

A few women had joined their men-folk, attracted by the novelty of the proceedings, yielding their momentary comfort to their feeling of curiosity. They had drawn their kirtles over their heads and looked like gigantic oval balls, gray or black, with small mud-stained feet peeping out below.

Sue had thrown an appealing look at Squire Boatfield, when she saw that dismal cortège. Her husband, her prince! the descendant of the Bourbons, the regenerator of France lying there—unrecognizable, horrible and loathsome—in a rough wooden coffin hastily nailed together by a village carpenter.

She did not wish to look on him: and with mute eyes begged the squire to spare her and to spare the old woman, who, through the doorway had caught sight of the drabby little crowd, and of the deal box on the ground.

Lambert, too, at sight of the cortège had gone to the Quakeress, the kind soul who had cared for him and his brother, two nameless lads, without home save the one she had provided for them. He trusted in Squire Boatfield's sense of humanity not to force this septuagenarian to an effort of nerve and will altogether beyond her powers.

Together the two young people were using gentle persuasion to get the old woman to the back room, whence she could not see the dreary scene now or presently, the slow winding of the dismal little procession down the road which leads to Minster, and whence she could not hear that weird flapping of the wet sheet against the side of the coffin, an echo to the slow and muffled tolling of the church bell some little distance away.

But the old woman was obstinate. She struggled against the persuasion of young arms. Things had been said in her cottage just now, which she must hear more distinctly: vague accusations had been framed, a cruel and sneering laugh had echoed through the house from whence one of her lads—Adam—was absent.

"No! no!" she said with quiet firmness, as Lambert urged her to withdraw, "let be, lad. . . let be. . . ye cannot deceive the old woman all of ye. . . The Lord hath put wool in my ears, so I cannot hear. . . but my eyes are good. . . I can see your faces. . . I can read them. . . Speak man!" she said, as she suddenly disengaged herself from Richard's restraining arms and walked deliberately up to Marmaduke de Chavasse, "speak man. . . Didst thou accuse Adam?"

An involuntary "No!" escaped from the squire's kindly heart and lips. But Sir Marmaduke shrugged his shoulders.

The crisis which by his own acts, by his own cowardice, he himself had precipitated, was here now. Fatality had overtaken him. Whether the whole truth would come to light he did not know. Truly at this moment he hardly cared. He did not feel as if he were himself, but another being before whom stood another Sir Marmaduke de Chavasse, on whom he—a specter, a ghoul, a dream figure—was about to pass judgment.

He knew that he need do nothing now, for without his help or any effort on his part, that morbid curiosity which had racked his brain for two days would be fully satisfied. He would know absolutely now, exactly what everyone thought of the mysterious French prince and of his terrible fate on Epple sands.

Thank Satan and all his hordes of devils that heavy chalk boulders had done so complete a work of obliteration.

But whilst he looked down with complete indifference on the old woman, she looked about from one face to the other, trying to read what cruel thoughts of Adam lurked behind those obvious expressions of sympathy.

"So that foreign devil hath done mischief at last," she now said loudly, her tremulous voice gaining in strength as she spoke, "the Lord would not allow him to do it living. . . so the devil hath helped him to it now that he is dead. . . But I tell you that Adam is innocent. . . There was no harm in the lad. . . a little rough at times. . . but no harm. . . he'd no father to bring him up. . . and his mother was a wanton. . . so there was only the foolish old woman to look after the boys. . . but there's no harm in the lad. . . there's no harm!"

Her voice broke down now in a sob, her throat seemed choked, but with an effort which seemed indeed amazing in one of her years, she controlled her tears, and for a moment was silent. The gray twilight crept in through the door of the cottage, where Mat, bareheaded and humble, still waited for the order to go.

Sir Marmaduke would have interrupted the old woman's talk ere this, but his limbs were now completely paralyzed: he might have been made of stone, so rigid did he feel himself to be: a marble image, or else a specter, a shadow-figure that existed yet could not move.

There was such passionate earnestness in the old woman's words that everyone else remained dumb. Richard, whose heart was filled with dread, who had endured agonies of anxiety since the disappearance of his brother, had but one great desire, which was to spare to the kind soul a knowledge which would mean death or worse to her.

As for Editha de Chavasse, she was a mere spectator still: so puzzled, so bewildered that she was quite convinced at this moment, that she must be mad. She could not encounter Marmaduke's eyes, try how she might. The look in his face horrified her less than it mystified her. She alone—save the murderer himself—knew that the man who lay in that deal coffin out there was not the mysterious foreigner who had never existed.

But if not the stranger, then who was it, who was dead? and what had Adam Lambert to do with the whole terrible deed?

Sue once more tried to lead Mistress Lambert gently away, but she pushed the young girl aside quite firmly:

"Ye don't believe me?" she asked, looking from one face to the other, "ye don't believe me, yet I tell ye all that Adam is innocent. . . and that the Lord will not allow the innocent to be unjustly condemned. . . Aye! He will e'en let the dead arise, I say, and proclaim the innocence of my lad!"

Her eyes—with dilated pupils and pale opaque rims—had the look of the seer in them now; she gazed straight out before her into the rain-laden air, and it seemed almost as if in it she could perceive visions of avenging swords, of defending angels and accusing ghouls, that she could hear whisperings of muffled voices and feel beckoning hands guiding her to a world peopled by specters and evil beings that prey upon the dead.

"Let me pass!" she said with amazing vigor, as Squire Boatfield, with kindly concern, tried to bar her exit through the door, "let me pass I say! the dead and I have questions to ask of one another."

"This is madness!" broke in Marmaduke de Chavasse with an effort; "that body is not a fit sight for a woman to look upon."

He would have seized the Quakeress by the arm in order to force her back, but Richard Lambert already stood between her and him.

"Let no one dare to lay a hand on her," he said quietly.

And the old woman escaping from all those who would have restrained her, walked rapidly through the doorway and down the flagged path rendered slippery with the sleet. The gale caught the white wings of her coif, causing them to flutter about her ears, and freezing strands of her gray locks which stood out now all round her head like a grizzled halo.

She could scarcely advance, for the wind drove her kirtle about her lean thighs, and her feet with the heavy tan shoes sank ankle deep in the puddles formed by the water in the interstices of the flagstones. The rain beat against her face, mingling with the tears which now flowed freely down her cheeks. But she did not heed the discomfort nor yet the cold, and she would not be restrained.

The next moment she stood beside the rough wooden coffin and with a steady hand had lifted the wet sheet, which continued to flap with dull, mournful sound round the feet of the dead.

The Quakeress looked down upon the figure stretched out here in death—neither majestic nor peaceful, but horrible and weirdly mysterious. She did not flinch at the sight. Resentment against the foreigner dimmed her sense of horror.

"So my fine prince," she said, whilst awed at the spectacle of this old woman parleying with the dead, carriers and mourners had instinctively moved a few steps away from her, "so thou wouldst harm my boy! . . . Thou always didst hate him. . . thou with thy grand airs, and thy rough ways. . . Had the Lord allowed it, this hand of thine would ere now have been raised against him. . . as it oft was raised against the old woman. . . whose infirmities should have rendered her sacred in thy sight."

She stooped, and deliberately raised the murdered man's hand in hers, and for one moment fixed her gaze upon it. For that one moment she was silent, looking down at the rough fingers, the coarse nails, the blistered palm.

Then still holding the hand in hers, she looked up, then round at every face which was turned fixedly upon her. Thus she encountered the eyes of the men and women, present here only to witness an unwonted spectacle, then those of the kindly squire, of Lady Sue, of Mistress de Chavasse, and of her other lad—Richard—all of whom had instinctively followed her down the short flagged path in the wake of her strange and prophetic pilgrimage.

Lastly her eyes met those of Marmaduke de Chavasse. Then she spoke slowly in a low muffled voice, which gradually grew more loud and more full of passionate strength.

"Aye! the Lord is just," she said, "the Lord is great! It is the dead which shall rise again and proclaim the innocence of the just, and the guilt of the wicked."

She paused a while, and stooped to kiss the marble-like hand which she held tightly grasped in hers.

BARONESS EMMUSKA ORCZY

"Adam!" she murmured, "Adam, my boy! . . . my lad! . . ."

The men and women looked on, stupidly staring, not understanding yet, what new tragedy had suddenly taken the place of the old.

"Aunt, aunt dear," whispered Lambert, who had pushed his way forward, and now put his arm round the old woman, for she had begun to sway, "what is the matter, dear?" he repeated anxiously, "what does it mean?"

And conquering his own sense of horror and repulsion, he tried to disengage the cold and rigid hand of the dead from the trembling grasp of the Quakeress. But she would not relinquish her hold, only she turned and looked steadily at the young lad, whilst her voice rose firm and harsh above the loud patter of the rain and the moaning of the wind through the distant; trees.

"It means, my lad," she said, "it means all of you. . . that what I said was true. . . that Adam is innocent of crime. . . for he lies here dead. . . and the Lord will see that his death shall not remain unavenged."

Once more she kissed the rough hand, beautiful now with that cold beauty which the rigidity of death imparts; then she replaced it reverently, silently, and fell upon her knees in the wet mud, beside the coffin.

XXXIX

The Home-Coming of Adam Lambert

All heads were bent; none of the ignorant folk who stood around would have dared even to look at the old woman kneeling beside that rough deal box which contained the body of her lad. A reverent feeling had killed all curiosity: bewilderment at the extraordinary and wholly unexpected turn of events had been merged in a sense of respectful awe, which rendered every mouth silent, and lowered every lid.

Squire Boatfield, almost paralyzed with astonishment, had murmured half stupidly:

"Adam Lambert. . . dead? . . . I do not understand."

He turned to Marmaduke de Chavasse as if vaguely, instinctively expecting an answer to the terrible puzzle from him.

De Chavasse's feet, over which he himself seemed to have no control, had of a truth led him forward, so that he, too, stood not far from the old woman now. He had watched her—silent and rigid,—conscious only of one thing—a trivial matter certes—of Editha's inquiring eyes fixed steadily upon him.

Everything else had been merged in a kind of a dream. But the mute question in those eyes was what concerned him. It seemed to represent the satisfaction of that morbid curiosity which had been such a terrible obsession during these past nerve-racking days.

Editha, realizing the identity of the dead man, would there and then know the entire truth. But Editha's fate was too closely linked to his own to render her knowledge of that truth dangerous to de Chavasse: therefore, with him it was merely a sense of profound satisfaction that someone would henceforth share his secret with him.

It is quite impossible to analyze the thoughts of the man who thus stood by—a silent and almost impassive spectator—of a scene, wherein his fate, his life, an awful retribution and deadly justice, were all hanging in the balance. He was not mad, nor did he act with either irrelevance or rashness. The sense of self-protection was still keen in him. . . violently keen. . . although undoubtedly he, and he alone, was responsible for the events which culminated in the present crisis.

The whole aspect of affairs had changed from the moment that the real identity of the dead had been established. Everyone here present would regard this new mystery in an altogether different light to that by which they had viewed the former weird problem; but still there need be no danger to the murderer.

Editha would know, of course, but no one else, and it would be vastly curious anon to see what lady Sue would do.

Therefore, Sir Marmaduke was chiefly conscious of Editha's presence, and then only of Sue.

"Some old woman's folly," he now said roughly, in response to Squire Boatfield's mute inquiry, "awhile ago she identified the clothes as having belonged to the foreign prince."

"Aye, the clothes, de Chavasse," murmured the squire meditatively, "the clothes, but not the man. . . and 'twas you yourself who just now. . ."

"Master Lambert should know his own brother," here came in a suppressed murmur from one or two of the men, who respectful before the quality, had now become too excited to keep altogether silent.

"Of course I know my brother," retorted Richard Lambert boldly, "and can but curse mine own cowardice in not defending him ere this."

"What more lies are we to hear?" sneered de Chavasse, "surely, Boatfield, this stupid scene hath lasted long enough."

"Put my knowledge to the test, sir," rejoined Lambert. "My brother's arm was scarred by a deep cut from shoulder to elbow, caused by the fall of a sharp-bladed ax—'twas the right arm. . . will you see, Sir Marmaduke, or will you allow me to lay bare the right arm of this man. . . to see if I had lied? . . ."

Squire Boatfield, conquering his reluctance, had approached nearer to the coffin; he, too, lifted the dead man's arm, as the old woman had done just now, and he gazed down meditatively at the hand, which though shapely, was obviously rough and toil-worn. Then, with a firm and deliberate gesture, he undid the sleeve of the doublet and pushed it back, baring the arm up to the shoulder.

He looked at the lifeless flesh for a moment, there where a deep and long scar stood out plainly between the elbow and shoulder like the veining in a block of marble. Then he pulled the sleeve down again.

"Neither you, nor Mistress Lambert have lied, master," he said simply. "'Tis Adam Lambert who lies here. . . murdered. . . and if that be so," he continued firmly, "then the man who put these clothes upon the body of the smith is his murderer. . . the foreigner who called himself Prince Amédé d'Orléans."

"The husband of Lady Sue Aldmarshe," quoth Sir Marmaduke, breaking into a loud laugh.

The rain had momentarily ceased, although the gale, promising further havoc, still continued that mournful swaying of the dead branches of the trees. But a gentle drip-drip had replaced that incessant patter. The humid atmosphere had long ago penetrated through rough shirts and worsted breeches, causing the spectators of this weird tragedy to shiver with the cold.

The shades of evening had begun to gather in. It were useless now to attempt to reach Minster before nightfall: nor presumably would the old Quakeress thus have parted from the dead body of her lad.

Richard Lambert had begged that the coffin might be taken into the cottage. The old woman's co-religionists would help her to obtain for Adam fitting and Christian burial.

After Sir Marmaduke's sneering taunt no one had spoken. For these yokels and their womenfolk the matter had passed altogether beyond their ken. Bewildered, not understanding, above all more than half fearful, they consulted one another vaguely and mutely with eyes and quaint expressive gestures, wondering what had best be done.

'Twas fortunate that the rain had ceased. One by one the women, still holding their kirtles tightly round their shoulders, began to move away. The deal box seemed to have reached a degree of mystery from which 'twas best to keep at a distance. The men, too—those who had come as spectators—were gradually edging away; some walked off with their womenfolk, others hung back in groups of three or four discussing the most hospitable place to which 'twere best to adjourn.

All wore a strangely shamed expression of timidity—almost of self-deprecation, as if apologetic for their presence here when the quality had matters of such grave import to discuss. No one had really understood Sir Marmaduke's sneering taunt, only they felt instinctively that there were some secrets which it had been disrespectful even to attempt to guess.

Those who had been prepared to carry the coffin to Minster were the last to hang back. Squire Boatfield was obviously giving some directions to their foreman, Mat, who tugged at his forelock at intervals, indicating that he was prepared to obey. The others stood aside waiting for instructions.

　　　　　　　　　　　　　　　　　　BARONESS EMMUSKA ORCZY

Thus the deal box remained on the ground, exactly opposite the tiny wooden gate, strangely isolated and neglected-looking after the dispersal of the interested crowd which had surrounded it awhile ago. It seemed as if with the establishment of the real identity of the dead the intensity of the excitement had vanished. The mysterious foreigner had a small court round him; Adam Lambert, only his brother and the old Quakeress.

They remained beside the coffin, she kneeling with her head buried in her wrinkled hands, he standing silent and passionately wrathful both against one man and against destiny. He had almost screamed with horror when de Chavasse thus brutally uttered Lady Sue's name: he had seen the young girl almost sway on her feet, as she smothered the cry of agony and horror which at her guardian's callous taunt had risen to her lips.

He had seen and in his heart worshiped her for the heroic effort which she made to remain outwardly calm, not to betray before a crowd the agonizing horror, the awful fear and the burning shame which of a truth would have crushed most women of her tender years. And because he saw that she did not wish to betray one single thought or emotion, he did not approach, nor attempt to show the overwhelming sympathy which he felt.

He knew that any word from him to her would only call forth more malicious sneers from that strange man, who seemed to be pursuing Lady Sue and also himself—Lambert—with a tenacious and incomprehensible hatred.

Richard remained, therefore, beside his dead brother's coffin, supporting and anon gently raising the old woman from the ground.

Mat—the foreman—had joined his comrades and after a word of explanation, they once more gathered round the wooden box. Stooping to their task, their sinews cracking under the effort, the perspiration streaming from their foreheads, they raised the mortal remains of Adam Lambert from the ground and hoisted the burden upon their shoulders.

Then they turned into the tiny gate and slowly walked with it along the little flagged path to the cottage. The men had to stoop as they crossed the threshold, and the heavy box swayed above their powerful shoulders.

The Quakeress and Richard followed, going within in the wake of the six men. The parlor was then empty, and thus it was that Adam Lambert finally came home.

The others—Squire Boatfield and Mistress de Chavasse, Lady Sue and Sir Marmaduke—had stood aside in the small fore-court, to enable the small cortège to pass. Directly Richard Lambert and the old woman disappeared within the gloom of the cottage interior, these four people—each individually the prey of harrowing thoughts—once more turned their steps towards the open road.

There was nothing more to be done here at this cottage, where the veil of mystery which had fallen over the gruesome murder had been so unexpectedly lifted by a septuagenarian's hand.

XL

EDITHA'S RETURN

S quire Boatfield was vastly perturbed. Never had his position as magistrate seemed so onerous to him, nor his duties as major-general quite so arduous. A vague and haunting fear had seized him, a fear that—if he did do his duty, if he did continue his investigations of the mysterious crime—he would learn something vastly horrible and awesome, something he had best never know.

He tried to take indifferent leave of the ladies, yet he quite dreaded to meet Lady Sue's eyes. If all the misery, the terror which she must feel, were expressed in them, then indeed, would her young face be a heart-breaking sight for any man to see.

He kissed the hand of Editha de Chavasse, and bowed in mute and deferential sympathy to the young girl-wife, who of a truth had this day quaffed at one draught the brimful cup of sorrow and of shame.

An inexplicable instinct restrained him from taking de Chavasse's hand; he was quite glad indeed that the latter seemingly absorbed in thoughts was not heeding his going.

The squire in his turn now passed out of the little gate. The evening was drawing in over-rapidly now, and it would be a long and dismal ride from here to Sarre.

Fortunately he had two serving-men with him, each with a lantern. They were now standing beside their master's cob, some few yards down the road, which from this point leads in a straight course down to Sarre.

Not far from the entrance to the forge, Boatfield saw petty-constable Pyot in close converse with Master Hymn-of-Praise Busy, butler to Sir Marmaduke. The man was talking with great volubility, and obvious excitement, and Pyot was apparently torn between his scorn for the narrator's garrulousness, and his fear of losing something of what the talker had to say.

At sight of Boatfield, Pyot unceremoniously left Master Busy standing, open-mouthed, in the very midst of a voluble sentence, and approached the squire, doffing his cap respectfully as he did so.

"Will your Honor sign a warrant?" he asked.

"A warrant? What warrant?" queried the worthy squire, who of a truth, was falling from puzzlement to such absolute bewilderment that he felt literally as if his head would burst with the weight of so much mystery and with the knowledge of such dire infamy.

"I think that the scoundrel is cleverer than we thought, your Honor," continued the petty constable, "we must not allow him to escape."

"I am quite bewildered," murmured the squire. "What is the warrant for?"

"For the apprehension of the man whom the folk about here called the Prince of Orléans. I can set the watches on the go this very night, nay! they shall scour the countryside to some purpose—the murderer cannot be very far, we know that he is dressed in the smith's clothes, we'll get him soon enough, but he may have friends. . ."

"Friends?"

"He may have been a real prince, your Honor," said Pyot with a laugh, which contradicted his own suggestion.

"Aye! aye! . . . Mayhap!"

"He may have powerful friends. . . or such as would resist the watches. . . resist us, mayhap. . . a warrant would be useful. . ."

"Aye! aye! you are right, constable," said Boatfield, still a little bewildered, "do you come along to Sarre with me, I'll give you a warrant this very night. Have you a horse here?"

"Nay, your Honor," rejoined the man, "an it please you, my going to Sarre would delay matters and the watches could not start their search this night."

"Then what am I to do?" exclaimed the squire, somewhat impatient of the whole thing now, longing to get away, and to forget, beside his own comfortable fireside, all the harrowing excitement of this unforgettable day.

"Young Lambert is a bookworm, your Honor," suggested Pyot, who was keen on the business, seeing that his zeal, if accompanied by success, would surely mean promotion; "there'll be ink and paper in the cottage. . . An your Honor would but write a few words and sign them, something I could show to a commanding officer, if perchance I needed the help of soldiery, or to the chief constable resident at Dover, for methinks some of us must push on that way. . . your Honor must forgive. . . we should be blamed—punished, mayhap—if we allowed such a scoundrel to remain unhung. . ."

"As you will, man, as you will," sighed the worthy squire impatiently, "but wait!" he added, as Pyot, overjoyed, had already turned towards the cottage, "wait until Sir Marmaduke de Chavasse and the ladies have gone."

He called his serving-men to him and ordered them to start on their way towards home, but to wait for him, with his cob, at the bend of the road, just in the rear of the little church.

Some instinct, for which he could not rightly have accounted, roused in him the desire to keep his return to the cottage a secret from Sir Marmaduke. Attended by Pyot, he followed his men down the road, and the angle of the cottage soon hid him from view.

De Chavasse in the meanwhile had ordered his own men to escort the ladies home. Busy and Toogood lighted their lanterns, whilst Sue and Editha, wrapping their cloaks and hoods closely round their heads and shoulders, prepared to follow them.

Anon the little procession began slowly to wind its way back towards Acol Court.

Sir Marmaduke lingered behind for a while, of set purpose: he had no wish to walk beside either Editha or Lady Sue, so he took some time in mounting his nag, which had been tethered in the rear of the forge. His intention was to keep the men with the lanterns in sight, for—though there were no dangerous footpads in Thanet—yet Sir Marmaduke's mood was not one that courted isolation on a dark and lonely road.

Therefore, just before he saw the dim lights of the lanterns disappearing down the road, which at this point makes a sharp dip before rising abruptly once more on the outskirts of the wood, Sir Marmaduke finally put his foot in the stirrup and started to follow.

The mare had scarce gone a few paces before he saw the figure of a woman detaching itself from the little group on ahead, and then turning and walking rapidly back towards the village. He could not immediately distinguish which of the two ladies it was, for the figure was totally hidden beneath the ample folds of cloak and hood, but soon as it approached, he perceived that it was Editha.

He would have stopped her by barring the way, he even thought of dismounting, thinking mayhap that she had left something behind at the cottage, and cursing his men for allowing her to return alone, but quick as a flash of lightning she ran past him, dragging her hood closer over her face as she ran.

He hesitated for a few seconds, wondering what it all meant: he even turned the mare's head round to see whither Editha was going.

She had already reached the railing and gate in front of the cottage; the next moment she had lifted the latch, and Sir Marmaduke could see her blurred outline, through the rising mist, walking quickly along the flagged path, and then he heard her peremptory knock at the cottage door.

He waited a while, musing, checking the mare, who longed to be getting home. He fully expected to see Editha return within the next minute or so, for—vaguely through the fast-gathering gloom—he had perceived that someone had opened the door from within, a thin ray of yellowish light falling on Editha's cloaked figure. Then she disappeared into the cottage.

On ahead the swaying lights of the lanterns were rapidly becoming more and more indistinguishable in the distance. Apparently Editha's departure from out the little group had not been noticed by the others. The men were ahead, and Sue, mayhap, was too deeply absorbed in thought to pay much heed as to what was going on round her.

Sir Marmaduke still hesitated. Editha was not returning, and the cottage door was once more closed. Courtesy demanded that he should wait so as to escort her home.

But the fact that she had gone back to the cottage, at risk of having to walk back all alone and along a dark and dreary road, bore a weird significance to this man's tortuous mind. Editha, troubled with a mass of vague fears and horrible conjectures, had, mayhap, desired to have them set at rest, or else to hear their final and terrible confirmation.

In either case Marmaduke de Chavasse had no wish now for a slow amble homewards in company with the one being in the world who knew him for what he was.

That thought and also the mad desire to get away at last, to cease with this fateful procrastination and to fly from this country with the golden booty, which he had gained at such awful risks, these caused him finally to turn the mare's head towards home, leaving Editha to follow as best she might, in the company of one of the serving-men whom he would send back to meet her.

The mare was ready to go. He spurred her to a sharp trot. Then having joined the little group on ahead, he sent Master Courage Toogood back with his lantern, with orders to inquire at the cottage for Mistress de Chavasse and there to await her pleasure.

He asked Lady Sue to mount behind him, but this she refused to do. So he put his nag back to foot space, and thus the much-diminished little party slowly walked back to Acol Court.

XLI

Their Name

What had prompted Editha de Chavasse to return thus alone to the Quakeress's cottage, she herself could not exactly have told.

It must have been a passionate and irresistible desire to heap certainty upon a tangle of horrible surmises.

With Adam Lambert lying dead—obviously murdered—and in the clothes affected by de Chavasse when masquerading as the French hero, there could be only one conclusion. But this to Editha—who throughout had given a helping hand in the management of the monstrous comedy—was so awful a solution of the puzzle that she could not but recoil from it, and strive to deny it while she had one sane thought left in her madly whirling brain.

But though she fought against the conclusion with all her might, she did not succeed in driving it from her thoughts: and through it all there was a vein of uncertainty, that slender thread of hope that after all she might be the prey of some awful delusion, which a word from someone who really knew would anon easily dissipate.

Someone who really knew? Nay! that someone could only be Marmaduke, and of him she dared not ask questions.

Mayhap that on the other hand the old woman and Richard Lambert knew more than they had cared to say. Sue was indeed deeply absorbed in thoughts, walking with head bent and eyes fixed on the ground like a somnambulist. Editha, moved by unreasoning instinct, determined to see the Quakeress again, also the man who now lay dead, hoping that from him mayhap she might glean the real solution of that mystery which sooner or later would undoubtedly drive her mad.

Running rapidly past horse and rider, for she would not speak to Marmaduke, she reached the cottage soon enough.

In response to her knock, Master Lambert opened the door to her.

The dim light of a couple of tallow candles flickered weirdly in the draught. Editha looked around her in amazement, astonished that—like herself—Squire Boatfield had also evidently retraced his steps and was sitting now in one of the high-backed chairs beside the hearth, whilst the old Quakeress stood not far from him, her attitude indicative of obstinacy, even of defiance, in the face of a duty with which apparently the squire had been charging her.

At sight of Mistress de Chavasse, Boatfield rose. A look of annoyance crossed his face, at thought that Editha's arrival had, mayhap, endangered the success of his present purpose. Ink and paper were on the table close to his elbow, and it was obvious that he had been questioning the old woman very closely on a subject which she apparently desired to keep secret from him.

Mistress Lambert's attitude had also changed at sight of Editha, who stood for a moment undecided on the threshold ere she ventured within. The look of obstinacy died out of the wrinkled face; the eyes took on a strange expression of sullen wrath.

"Enter, my fine lady, I pray thee, enter," said the Quakeress; "art also a party to these cross-questionings? . . . art anxious to probe the secrets which the old woman hath kept hidden within the walls of this cottage?"

She laughed, a low, chuckling laugh, mirthless and almost cruel, as she surveyed Editha's cloaked figure and then the lady's scared and anxious face.

"Nay, I crave your pardon, mistress," said Editha, feeling oddly timid before the strange personality of the Quakeress. "I would of a truth desire to ask your help in. . . in. . . I would not intrude. . . and I. . ."

"Nay! nay! prithee enter, fair mistress," rejoined Mistress Lambert dryly. "Strange, that I should hear thy words so plainly. . . Thy words seem to find echo in my brain. . . raising memories which thou hast buried long ago. . . Enter, I prithee, and sit thee down," she added, shuffling towards the chair; "shut the door, Dick lad. . . and ask this fair mistress to sit. . . The squire is asking many questions. . . mayhap that I'll answer them, now that she is here. . ."

In obedience to the quaint peremptoriness of her manner, Richard had closed the outer door, and drawn the chair forward, asking Mistress de Chavasse to sit. Squire Boatfield, who was visibly embarrassed, was still standing and tried to murmur some excuse, being obviously anxious to curtail this interview and to postpone his further questionings.

"I'll come some other time, mistress," he said with obvious nervousness. "Mistress de Chavasse desires to speak with you, and I'll return later on in the evening. . . when you are alone. . ."

"Nay! nay, man! . . ." rejoined the Quakeress, "prithee, sit again. . . the evening is young yet. . . and what I may tell thee now has something to do with this fine lady here. Wilt question me again? I would mayhap reply."

She stood close to the table, one wrinkled hand resting upon it; the guttering candles cast strange, fantastic lights on her old face, surmounted with the winged coif, and weird shadows down one side of her face. Editha, awed and subdued, gazed on her with a kind of fear, even of horror.

In a dark corner of the little room the straight outline of the long deal box could only faintly be perceived in the gloom. Richard Lambert, silent and oppressed, stood close beside it, his face in shadow, his eyes fixed with a sense of inexplicable premonition on the face of Editha de Chavasse.

"Now, wilt question me again, man?" asked the old Quakeress, turning to the squire, "the Lord hath willed that my ears be clear to-day. Wilt question me? . . . I'll hear thee. . . and I'll give answer to thy questions. . ."

"Nay, mistress," replied the squire, pointing to the ink and the paper on the table, "methought you would wish to see the murderer of your. . . your nephew. . . swing on the gallows for his crime. . . I would sign this paper here ordering the murderer of the smith of Acol to be apprehended as soon as found. . . and to be brought forthwith before the magistrate. . . there to give an account of his doings. . . I asked you then to give me the full Christian and surname of the man whom the neighborhood and I myself thought was your nephew. . . and to my surprise, you seemed to hesitate and. . ."

"And I'll hesitate no longer," she interposed firmly. "Let the lad there ask me his dead brother's name and I'll tell him. . . I'll tell him. . . if he asks. . ."

"Justice must be done against Adam's murderer, dear mistress," said Richard gently, for the old woman had paused and turned to him, evidently waiting for him to speak. "My brother's real name, his parentage, might explain the motive which led an evildoer to commit such an appalling crime. Therefore, dear mistress, do I ask thee to tell us my brother's name, and mine own."

"'Tis well done, lad. . . 'tis well done," she rejoined when Richard had ceased speaking, and silence had fallen for awhile on that tiny cottage parlor, "'tis well done," she reiterated. "The secret hath weighed heavily upon my old shoulders these past few years, since thou and Adam were no longer children. . . But I swore to thy grandmother who died in the Lord, that thou and Adam should never hear of thy mother's wantonness and shame. . . I swore it on her death-bed and I have kept my oath. . . but I am old now. . . After this trouble, mine hour will surely come. . . I am prepared but I will not take thy secret, lad, with me into my grave."

She shuffled across to the old oak dresser which occupied one wall of the little room. Two pairs of glowing eyes followed her every movement; those of Richard Lambert, who seemed to see a vision of his destiny faintly outlined—still blurred—but slowly unfolding itself in the tangled web of fate; and then those of Editha, who even as the old woman spoke had felt a tidal wave of long-forgotten memories sweeping right over her senses. The look in the Quakeress's eyes, the words she uttered—though still obscure and enigmatical—had already told her the whole truth. As in a flash she saw before her, her youth and all its follies, the gay life of thoughtlessness and pleasures, the cradles of her children, the tiny boys who to the woman of fashion were but a hindrance and a burden.

She saw her own mother, rigid and dour, the counterpart of this same old Puritan who had not hesitated to part two children from their mother for over a score of years, any more than she hesitated now to fling insult upon insult on the wretched woman who had more than paid her debt to her own careless frivolity of long ago.

"Thy brother's name was Henry Adam de Chavasse, and thine Michael Richard de Chavasse, sons of Rowland de Chavasse, and of the wanton who was his wife."

The old woman had taken a packet of papers, yellow with age and stained with many tears, from out a secret drawer of the old oak dresser.

Her voice was no longer tremulous as it was wont to be, but firm and dull, monotonous in tone like that of one who speaks whilst in a trance. Squire Boatfield had uttered an exclamation of boundless astonishment. Mechanically he took the packet of papers from the Quakeress's hand and after an instant's hesitation, and in response to an appealing look from Richard, he broke the string which held the documents together and perused them one by one.

But Editha, even as the last of the old woman's words ceased to echo in the narrow room, had risen to her feet. Her heavy cloak glided off her shoulders down upon the ground; her eyes, preternaturally large, glowing and full of awe, were now fixed upon the young man—her son.

"De Chavasse," she murmured, her brain whirling, her heart filled not only with an awful terror, but also with a great and overwhelming joy. "My sons. . . then I am. . ."

But with a peremptory gesture the Quakeress had stopped the word in her mouth.

"Nay!" she said loudly, "do not pollute that sacred name by letting it pass through thy lips. Women such as thou were not made for motherhood. . . Thy own mother knew that, when she took thy children from thee and cursed thee on her death-bed for thy sins and for thy shame! Thy sons were honest, God-fearing men, but 'tis no thanks to thee. Thou alone hast heaped shame upon their dead father's name and hast contrived to wreak ruin on the sons who knew thee not."

The Quakeress paused a moment, her pale opaque eyes lighted with an inward glow of wrath and of satisfied vengeance. She and her dead friend and all their co-religionists had hated the woman, who, in defiance of her own Puritanic upbringing, had cast aside her friends and her home in order to throw herself in that vortex of pleasure, which her mother considered evil and infamous.

Together they had all rejoiced over this woman's subsequent humiliation, her sorrow and longing for her children, the ceaseless search, the ever-recurrent disappointments. Now the Quakeress's hour had come, hers and that of the whole of the dour sect who had taken it upon itself to punish and to avenge.

Editha, shamed and miserable, not even daring now to approach her own son and to beg for affection with a look, stood quite rigid and pale, allowing the torrent of the old woman's pent-up hatred to fall upon her and to crush her with its rough cruelty.

Squire Boatfield would have interposed. He had glanced at the various documents—the proofs of what the old woman had asserted— and was satisfied that the horrible tale of what seemed to him unparalleled cruelty was indeed true, and that the narrow bigotry of a community had succeeded in performing that monstrous crime of parting this wretched woman for twenty years from her sons.

Vaguely in his mind, the kindly squire hoped that he—as magistrate— could fitly punish this crime of child-stealing, and the expression with which he now regarded the old Quakeress was certainly not one of good-will.

Mistress Lambert had, in the meanwhile, approached Editha. She now took the younger woman's hand in hers and dragged her towards the coffin.

"There lies one of thy sons," she said with the same relentless energy, "the eldest, who should have been thy pride, murdered in a dark spot by some skulking criminal. . . Curse thee! . . . curse thee, I say. . . as thy mother cursed thee on her death-bed. . . curse thee now that retribution has come at last!"

Her words died away, as some mournful echo against these whitewashed walls.

For a moment she stood wrathful and defiant, upright and stern like a justiciary between the dead son and the miserable woman, who of a truth was suffering almost unendurable agony of mind and of heart.

Then in the midst of the awesome silence that followed on that loudly spoken curse, there was the sound of a firm footstep on the rough deal floor, and the next moment Michael Richard de Chavasse was kneeling beside his mother, and covering her icy cold hand with kisses.

A heart-broken moan escaped her throat. She stooped and with trembling lips gently touched the young head bent in simple love and uninquiring reverence before her.

Then without a word, without a look cast either at her cruel enemy, or at the silent spectator of this terrible drama, she turned and ran rapidly out of the room, out into the dark and dismal night.

With a deep sigh of content, Mistress Lambert fell on her knees and thence upon the floor.

The old heart which had contained so much love and so much hatred, such stern self-sacrifice and such deadly revenge, had ceased to beat, now the worker's work was done.

BARONESS EMMUSKA ORCZY

XLII

The Return

M aster Courage Toogood had long ago given up all thought of waiting for the mistress. He had knocked repeatedly at the door of the cottage, from behind the thick panels of which he had heard loud and—he thought—angry voices, speaking words which he could not, however, quite understand.

No answer had come to his knocking and tired with the excitement of the day, fearful, too, at the thought of the lonely walk which now awaited him, he chose to believe that mayhap he had either misunderstood his master's orders, or that Sir Marmaduke himself had been mistaken when he thought the mistress back at the cottage.

These surmises were vastly to Master Courage Toogood's liking, whose name somewhat belied his timid personality. Swinging his lantern and striving to keep up his spirits by the aid of a lusty song, he resolutely turned his steps towards home.

The whole landscape seemed filled with eeriness: the events of the day had left their impress on this dark November night, causing the sighs of the gale to seem more spectral and weird than usual, and the dim outline of the trees with their branches turned away from the coastline, to seem like unhappy spirits with thin, gaunt arms stretched dejectedly out toward the unresponsive distance.

Master Toogood tried not to think of ghosts, nor of the many stories of pixies and goblins which are said to take a malicious pleasure in the timorousness of mankind, but of a truth he nearly uttered a cry of terror, and would have fallen on his knees in the mud, when a dark object quite undistinguishable in the gloom suddenly loomed before him.

Yet this was only the portly figure of Master Pyot, the petty constable, who seemed to be mounting guard just outside the cottage, and who was vastly amused at Toogood's pusillanimity. He entered into converse with the young man—no doubt he, too, had been feeling somewhat lonely in the midst of this darkness, which was peopled with unseen shadows. Master Courage was ready enough to talk. He had acquired some of Master Busy's eloquence on the subject of secret investigations, and the mystery which had gained an intensity this afternoon, through the revelations of the old Quakeress, was an all-engrossing one to all.

The attention which Pyot vouchsafed to his narration greatly enhanced Master Toogood's own delight therein, more especially as the petty constable had, as if instinctively, measured his steps with those of the younger man and was accompanying him on his way towards the Court.

Courage told his attentive listener all about Master Busy's surmises and his determination to probe the secrets of the mysterious crime, which—to be quite truthful—the worthy butler with the hard toes had scented long ere it was committed, seeing that he used to spend long hours in vast discomfort in the forked branches of the old elms which surrounded the pavilion at the boundary of the park.

Toogood had no notion if Master Busy had ever discovered anything of interest in the neighborhood of that pavilion, and he was quite, quite sure that the saintly man had never dared to venture inside that archaic building, which had the reputation of being haunted; still, he was over-gratified to perceive that the petty constable was vastly interested in his tale—in spite of these obvious defects in its completeness—and that, moreover, Master Pyot showed no signs of turning on his heel, but continued to trudge along the gloomy road in company with Sir Marmaduke's youngest serving-man.

Thus Editha, when she ran out of Mistress Lambert's cottage, her ears ringing with the fanatic's curses, her heart breaking with the joy of that reverent filial kiss imprinted upon her hands, found the road and the precincts of the cottage entirely deserted.

The night was pitch dark after the rain. Great heavy clouds still hung above, and an icy blast caught her skirts as she lifted the latch of the gate and turned into the open.

But she cared little about the inclemency of the weather. She knew her way about well enough and her mind was too full of terrible thoughts of what was real, to yield to the subtle and feeble fears engendered by imaginings of the supernatural.

Nay! she would, mayhap, have welcomed the pixies and goblins who by mischievous pranks had claimed her attention. They would, of a truth, have diverted her mind from the contemplation of that awful and monstrous deed accomplished by the man whom she would meet anon.

If he whom the villagers had called Adam Lambert was her son, Henry Adam de Chavasse, then Sir Marmaduke was the murderer of her child. All the curses which the old Quakeress had so vengefully poured upon her were as nothing compared with that awful, that terrible fact.

Her son had been murdered. . . her eldest son whom she had never known, and she—involuntarily mayhap, compulsorily certes—had in a measure helped to bring about those events which had culminated in that appalling crime.

She had known of Marmaduke's monstrous fraud on the confiding girl whom he now so callously abandoned to her fate. She had known of it and helped him towards its success by luring her other son Richard to that vile gambling den where he had all but lost his honor, or else his reason.

This knowledge and the help she had given was the real curse upon her now: a curse far more horrible and deadly than that which had driven Cain forth into the wilderness. This knowledge and the help she had given had stained her hands with the blood of her own child.

No wonder that she sighed for ghouls and for shadowy monsters, well-nigh longing for a sight of distorted faces, of ugly deformed bodies, and loathsome shapes far less hideous than that specter of an inhuman homicide which followed her along this dark road as she ran—ran on—ran towards the home where dwelt the living monster of evil, the man who had done the deed, which she had helped to accomplish.

Complete darkness reigned all around her, she could not see a yard of the road in front of her, but she went on blindly, guided by instinct, led by that unseen shadow which was driving her on. All round her the gale was moaning in the creaking branches of the trees, branches which were like arms stretched forth in appeal towards the unattainable.

Her progress was slow for she was walking in the very teeth of the hurricane, and her shoes ever and anon remained glued to the slimy mud. But the road was straight enough, she knew it well, and she felt neither fatigue nor discomfort.

Of Sue she did not think. The wrongs done to the defenseless girl were as nothing to her compared with the irreparable—the wrongs done to her sons, the living and the dead: for the one the foul dagger of an inhuman assassin, for the other shame and disgrace.

Sue was young. Sue would soon forget. The girl-wife would soon regain her freedom. . . But what of the mother who had on her soul the taint of the murder of her child?

The gate leading to the Court from the road was wide open: it had been left so for her, no doubt, when Sir Marmaduke returned. The house itself was dark, no light save one pierced the interstices of the ill-fitting shutters. Editha paused a moment at the gate, looking at the house—a great black mass, blacker than the surrounding gloom. That had been her home for many years now, ever since her youth and sprightliness had vanished, and she had had nowhere to go for shelter. It had been her home ever since Richard, her youngest boy, had entered it, too, as a dependent.

Oh! what an immeasurable fool she had been, how she had been tricked and fooled all these years by the man who two days ago had put a crown upon his own infamy. He knew where the boys were, he helped to keep them away from their mother, so as to filch from them their present, and above all, future inheritance. How she loathed him now, and loathed herself for having allowed him to drag her down. Aye! of a truth he had wronged her worse even than he had wronged his brother's sons!

She fixed her eyes steadily on the one light which alone pierced the inky blackness of the solid mass of the house. It came from the little withdrawing-room, which was on the left of this entrance to the hall; but the place itself—beyond just that one tiny light—appeared quite silent and deserted. Even from the stableyard on her right and from the serving-men's quarters not a sound came to mingle with the weird whisperings of the wind.

Editha approached and stooping to the ground, she groped in the mud until her hands encountered two or three pebbles.

She picked them up, then going close to the house, she threw these pebbles one by one against the half-closed shutter of the withdrawing-room.

The next moment, she heard the latch of the casement window being lifted from within, and anon the rickety shutter flew back with a thin creaking sound like that of an animal in pain.

The upper part of Sir Marmaduke's figure appeared in the window embrasure, like a dark and massive silhouette against the yellowish light from within. He stooped forward, seeming to peer into the darkness.

"Is that you, Editha?" he queried presently.

"Yes," she replied. "Open!"

She then waited a moment or two, whilst he closed both the shutter and the window, she standing the while on the stone step before the portico. In the stillness she could hear him open the drawing-room door, then cross the hall and finally unbolt the heavy outer door.

She pushed past him over the threshold and went into the gloomy hall, pitch dark save for the flickering light of the candle which he held. She waited until he had re-closed the door, then she stood quite still, confronting him, allowing him to look into her face, to read the expression of her eyes.

In order to do this he had raised the candle, his hand trembling perceptibly, and the feeble light quivered in his grasp, illumining her face at fitful intervals, creeping down her rigid shoulders and arms, as far as her hands, which were tightly clenched. It danced upon his face too, lighting it with weird gleams and fitful sparks, showing the wild look in his eyes, the glitter almost of madness in the dilated pupils, the dark iris sharply outlined against the glassy orbs. It licked the trembling lips and distorted mouth, the drawn nostrils and dank hair, almost alive with that nameless fear.

"You would denounce me?" he murmured, and the cry—choked and toneless—could scarce rise from the dry parched throat.

"Yes!" she said.

He uttered a violent curse.

"You devil. . . you. . ."

"You have time to go," she said calmly, "'tis a long while 'twixt now and dawn."

He understood. She only would denounce him if he stayed. She wished him no evil, only desired him out of her sight. He tried to say something flippant, something cruel and sneering, but she stopped him with a peremptory gesture.

"Go!" she said, "or I might forget everything save that you killed my son."

For a moment she thought that her life was in danger at his hands, so awful in its baffled rage was the expression of his face when he understood that indeed she knew everything. She even at that moment longed that his cruel instincts should prompt him to kill her. He could never succeed in hiding that crime and retributive justice would of a surety overtake him then, without any help from her.

No doubt he, too, thought of this as the weird flicker of the candle-light showed him her unflinching face, for the next moment, with another muttered curse, and a careless shrug of the shoulders, he turned on his heel, and slowly went upstairs, candle in hand.

Editha watched him until his massive figure was merged in the gloom of the heavy oak stairway. Then she went into the withdrawing-room and waited.

XLIII

The Sands of Epple

Five minutes later Sir Marmaduke de Chavasse, clad in thick dark doublet and breeches and wearing a heavy cloak, once more descended the stairs of Acol Court. He saw the light in the withdrawing-room and knew that Editha was there, mutely watching his departure.

But he did not care to speak to her again. His mind had been quickly made up, nay! his actions in the immediate future should of a truth have been accomplished two days ago, ere the meddlesomeness of women had well-nigh jeopardized his own safety.

All that he meant to do now was to go quickly to the pavilion, find the leather wallet then return to his own stableyard, saddle one of his nags and start forthwith for Dover. Eighteen miles would soon be covered, and though the night was dark, the road was straight and broad. De Chavasse knew it well, and had little fear of losing his way.

With plenty of money in his purse, he would have no difficulty in chartering a boat which, with a favorable tide on the morrow, should soon take him over to France.

All that he ought to have done two days ago! Of a truth, he had been a cowardly fool.

He did not cross the hall this time but went out through the dining-room by the garden entrance. Not a glimmer of light came from above, but as he descended the few stone steps he felt that a few soft flakes of snow tossed by the hurricane were beginning to fall. Of course he knew every inch of his own garden and park and had oft wandered about on the further side of the ha-ha whilst indulging in lengthy sweetly-spoken farewells with his love-sick Sue.

Absorbed in the thoughts of his immediate future plans, he nevertheless walked along cautiously, for the paths had become slippery with the snow, which froze quickly even as it fell.

He did not pause, however, for he wished to lose no time. If he was to ride to Dover this night, he would have to go at foot-pace, for the road would be like glass if this snow and ice continued. Moreover, he was burning to feel that wallet once more between his fingers and to hear the welcome sound of the crushing of crisp papers.

He had plunged resolutely into the thickness of the wood. Here he could have gone blindfolded, so oft had he trodden this path which leads under the overhanging elms straight to the pavilion, walking with Sue's little hand held tightly clasped in his own.

The spiritual presence of the young girl seemed even now to pervade the thicket, her sweet fragrance to fill the frost-laden air.

Bah! he was not the man to indulge in retrospective fancy. The girl was naught to him, and there was no sense of remorse in his soul for the terrible wrongs which he had inflicted on her. All that he thought of now was the wallet which contained the fortune. That which would forever compensate him for the agony, the madness of the past two days.

The bend behind that last group of elms should now reveal the outline of the pavilion. Sir Marmaduke advanced more cautiously, for the trees here were very close together.

The next moment he had paused, crouching suddenly like a carnivorous beast, balked of its prey. There of a truth was the pavilion, but on the steps three men were standing, talking volubly and in whispers. Two of these men carried stable lanterns, and were obviously guiding their companion up to the door of the pavilion.

The light of the lanterns illumined one face after another. De Chavasse recognized his two serving-men, Busy and Toogood; the man who was with them was petty-constable Pyot. Marmaduke with both hands clutching the ivy which clung round the gnarled stem of an old elm, watched from out the darkness what these three men were doing here, beside this pavilion, which had always been so lonely and deserted.

He could not distinguish what they said for they spoke in whispers and the creaking branches groaning beneath the wind drowned every sound which came from the direction of the pavilion and the listener on the watch, straining his every sense in order to hear, dared not creep any closer lest he be perceived.

Anon, the three men examined the door of the pavilion, and shaking the rusty bolts, found that they would not yield. But evidently they were of set purpose, for the next moment all three put their shoulder to the worm-eaten woodwork, and after the third vigorous effort the door yielded to their assault.

Men and lanterns disappeared within the pavilion. Sir Marmaduke heard an exclamation of surprise, then one of profound satisfaction.

For the space of a few seconds he remained rooted to the spot. It almost seemed to him as if with the knowledge that the wallet and the discarded clothes of the smith had been found, with the certitude that this discovery meant his own undoing probably, and in any case the final loss of the fortune for which he had plotted and planned, lied and masqueraded, killed a man and cheated a girl, that with the knowledge of all this, death descended upon him: so cold did he feel, so unable was he to make the slightest movement.

But this numbness only lasted a few seconds. Obviously the three men would return in a minute or so; equally obviously his own presence here—if discovered—would mean certain ruin to him. Even while he was making the effort to collect his scattered senses and to move from this fateful and dangerous spot, he saw the three men reappear in the doorway of the pavilion.

The breeches and rough shirt of the smith hung over the arm of Hymn-of-Praise Busy; the dark stain on the shirt was plainly visible by the light of one of the lanterns.

Petty constable Pyot had the leather wallet in his hand, and was peeping down with grave curiosity at the bundle of papers which it contained.

Then with infinite caution, Marmaduke de Chavasse worked his way between the trees towards the old wall which encircled his park. The three men obviously would be going back either to Acol Court, or mayhap, straight to the village.

Sir Marmaduke knew of a gap in the wall which it was quite easy to climb, even in the dark; a path through the thicket at that point led straight out towards the coast.

He had struck that path from the road on the night when he met the smith on the cliffs.

The snow only penetrated in sparse flakes to the thicket here. Although the branches of the trees were dead, they interlaced so closely overhead that they formed ample protection against the wet.

But the fury of the gale seemed terrific amongst these trees and the groaning of the branches seemed like weird cries proceeding from hell.

Anon, the midnight walker reached the open. Here a carpet of coarse grass peeping through the thin layer of snow gave insecure foothold. He stumbled as he pursued his way. He was walking in the teeth of the northwesterly blast now and he could scarcely breathe, for the great gusts caught his throat, causing him to choke.

Still he walked resolutely on. Icy moisture clung to his hair, and to his lips, and soon he could taste the brine in the air. The sound of the breakers some ninety feet below mingled weirdly with the groans of the wind.

He knew the path well. Had he not trodden it three nights ago, on his way to meet the smith? Already in the gloom he could distinguish the broken line of the cliffs sharply defined against the gray density of the horizon.

As he drew nearer the roar of the breakers became almost deafening. A heavy sea was rolling in on the breast of the tide.

Still he walked along, towards the brow of the cliffs. Soon he could distinguish the irregular heap of chalk against which Adam had stood, whilst he had held the lantern in one hand and gripped the knife in the other.

The hurricane nearly swept him off his feet. He had much ado to steady himself against that heap of chalk. The snow had covered his cloak and his hat, and he liked to think that he, too, now—snow-covered—must look like a monstrous chalk boulder, weird and motionless outlined against the leaden grayness of the ocean beyond.

The smith was not by his side now. There was no lantern, no paper, no double-edged dagger. Down nearly a hundred feet below the smith had lain until the turn of the tide. The man's eyes, becoming accustomed to the gloom, could distinguish the points of the great boulders springing boldly from out the sand. The surf as it broke all round and over them was tipped with a phosphorescent light.

The gale, in sheer wantonness, caught the midnight prowler's hat and with a wild sound as of the detonation of a hundred guns, tossed it to the waves below. The snow in a few moments had thrown a white pall over the watcher's head.

He could see quite clearly the tall boulder untouched by the tide, on which he had placed the black silk shade that night, also the broad-brimmed hat, so that these things should be found high and dry and be easily recognizable.

Some twenty feet further on was the smooth stretch of sand where had lain the smith, after he had been dressed up in the fantastic clothes of the mysterious French prince.

Marmaduke de Chavasse gazed upon that spot. The breakers licked it now and again, leaving behind them as they retreated a track of slimy foam, which showed white in this strange gray gloom, rendered alive and moving by the falling snow.

The surf covered that stretch of sand more and more frequently now, and retreated less and less far: the slimy foam floated now over an inky pool; soon that too disappeared. The breakers sought other boulders round which to play their titanic hide-and-seek. The tide had completely hidden the place where Adam Lambert had lain.

Then the watcher walked on—one step and then another—and then the one beyond the edge as he stepped down, down into the abyss ninety feet below.

XLIV

The Epilogue

The chronicles of the time tell us that the mysterious disappearance of Sir Marmaduke de Chavasse was but a nine days' wonder in that great world which lies beyond the boundaries of sea-girt Thanet.

What Thanet thought of it all, the little island kept secret, hiding its surmises in the thicket of her own archaic forests.

Squire Boatfield did his best to wrap the disappearance of his whilom friend in impenetrable veils of mystery. He was a humane and a kindly man and feeling that the guilty had been amply punished, he set to work to cheer and to rehabilitate the innocent.

All of us who have read the memoirs of Editha de Chavasse, written when she was a woman of nearly sixty, remember that she, too, has drawn a thick curtain over the latter days of her brother-in-law's life. It is to her pen that we owe the record of what happened subsequently.

She tells us, for instance, how Master Skyffington, after sundry interviews with my Lord Northallerton, had the honor of bringing to his lordship's notice the young student—so long known as Richard Lambert—who, of a truth, was sole heir to the earldom and to its magnificent possessions and dependencies.

From the memoirs of Editha de Chavasse we also know that Lady Sue Aldmarshe, girl-wife and widow, did, after a period of mourning, marry Michael Richard de Chavasse, sole surviving nephew and heir presumptive of his lordship the Earl of Northallerton.

But it is to the brush of Sir Peter Lely that we owe that exquisite portrait of Sue, when she was Countess of Northallerton, the friend of Queen Catherine, the acknowledged beauty at the Court of the Restoration.

It is a sweet face, whereon the half-obliterated lines of sorrow vie with that look of supreme happiness which first crept into her eyes when she realized that the dear and constant friend who had loved her so dearly, was as true to her in his joy as he had been in those dark days when a terrible crisis had well-nigh wrecked her life.

Lord and Lady Northallerton did not often stay in London. The brilliance of the Court had few attractions for them. Happiness came to them after terrible sorrows. They liked to hide it and their great love in the calm and mystery of forest-covered Thanet.

THE END

Discover more of your favorite classics with Bookfinity™.

- Track your reading with custom book lists.
- Get great book recommendations for your personalized Reader Type.
- Add reviews for your favorite books.
- AND MUCH MORE!

Visit **bookfinity.com** and take the fun Reader Type quiz to get started.

Enjoy our classic and modern companion pairings!